Praise for Susan Carroll

Twilight of a Queen

"Riveting, vibrant, and breathtaking."

—Fresh Fiction

"A super tale with strong adversaries and allies, and a terrific exhilarating story line."

—Genre Go Round Reviews

"*Twilight of a Queen* is a complex and dense story with many twists and turns."

—The Romance Reader

The other books in the Dark Queen series

"Carroll strikes a balance between froth and craftsmanship."
—*Publishers Weekly*

"Fast-paced historical fiction with a supernatural twist."
—*Booklist*

"An intoxicating brew of poignant romance, turbulent history, and mesmerizing magic."
—KAREN HARPER, author of *The Fyre Mirror*

"With a pinch of both the otherwordly and romance to spice up the deep look at the Medici era . . . Susan Carroll writes a wonderful historical thriller that will have the audience eagerly awaiting [the next] story."
—*The Midwest Book Review*

"[A] riveting tale of witchcraft, treachery, and court intrigue."
—*Library Journal,* Starred Review

"Utterly perfect—rich, compelling, and full of surprises. A fabulous, feminist fantasy from a masterful storyteller that's bound to be one of the best books of the year!"
—ELIZABETH GRAYSON, author of *Moon in the Water*

"Enthralling historical detail, dark and intense emotions and the perfect touches of the paranormal. [Carroll] leaves readers to savor every word of this superbly crafted breathtaking romance."
—*Romantic Times,* Top Pick!

"Ms. Carroll sets the stage well for intrigue and magic spells and draws the reader into her web."
—*The Historical Novels Review*

"Readers in the mood for a marriage plot spiced with magic should find that this one does the trick!"
—*Publishers Weekly*

The Lady of Secrets

ALSO BY SUSAN CARROLL

Winterbourne
The Painted Veil
The Bride Finder
The Night Drifter
Midnight Bride
The Dark Queen
The Courtesan
The Silver Rose
The Huntress
Twilight of a Queen

The Lady of Secrets

A NOVEL

SUSAN CARROLL

BALLANTINE BOOKS TRADE PAPERBACKS • NEW YORK

A Ballantine Books Trade Paperback Original

Copyright © 2012 by Susan Carroll

Published in the United States by Ballantine Books, an imprint of The Random House Publishing Group, a division of Random House, Inc., New York.

BALLANTINE and colophon are registered trademarks of Random House, Inc.

Library of Congress Cataloging-in-Publication Data
Carroll, Susan.
Lady of secrets : a novel / Susan Carroll.
p. cm.
ISBN 978-0-345-50295-7 (pbk.) — ISBN 978-0-345-53604-4 (ebook)
1. Courts and courtiers—Fiction.   2. Mystics—France—Fiction.
3 France—History—Henry II, 1547–1559—Fiction.   4. Historical fiction.
5. Love stories.   I. Title.
PS3553.A7654L33 2012
813'.54—dc23   2012032201

Printed in the United States of America

www.ballantinebooks.com

2 4 6 8 9 7 5 3 1

To my critique partners: Ella March Chase,
Leslie Langtry, and Janene Murphy,
for all your support, friendship, and encouragement.
Could never have finished this book without you ladies.

The Lady of Secrets

Prologue

*1*T WAS A FAIR DAY FOR A BURNING.

Maidred Brody had heard the guards talking just before dawn. The breeze coming off the firth was soft, a mere whisper to tickle the cheeks. Not nearly strong enough to make lighting the faggots difficult or to fan the flames away from the fodder they were meant to consume.

The fodder. They were talking about her, her own too-tender flesh and fragile bones. As the voices drifted farther away from the narrow grate that marked her only contact with the world outside her cell, Maidred shuddered. She burrowed deeper beneath the filthy straw as though she were a field mouse escaping detection.

But there was no escaping her thoughts. She rubbed her fingers over the tiny raised scar on her wrist where she had once burned herself on a hot kettle. The pain had been so intense she had wailed and carried on until her old nursemaid had given her a smack and commanded her sternly to stop raising such a fuss. If Maidred had been unable to tolerate that small burn, however would she endure being roasted alive, the greedy flames scorching and blackening her sensitive skin, peeling it away from her body?

Tears streamed down Maidred's cheeks. She shoved her fist in her mouth to stifle her sobs lest she wake her companion. But she doubted anything could disturb Tamsin.

Although old Tam was under the same sentence of death as Maidred, the crone had slept like a babe last night. Her snores resonated across the cell although the pale morning light filtered through the grate. The last morning of their lives . . .

Maidred trembled and rocked herself, trying to claw her way back to the pretty place inside her head that had sustained her through much of these last two years since her mother had died. A castle lost in the mists of a faraway island.

"I am a princess in the court of the Lady of Faire Isle, a sorceress of great power and beauty," she whispered to herself. "I live in her golden palace and wear gowns of gossamer silk. We have a hundred handsome knights to attend upon us, to protect us, to rescue—"

The creak of the heavy oak door shattered the illusion, flinging her back to the cold hard floor of her cell. They were coming for her. So soon? She scrambled up, her heart thudding as her gaoler pushed open the door.

Master Galbraith was a tall broad-shouldered man who had to duck beneath the lintel as he entered her cell. But for all his alarming size, his heavy jowls gave him the look of a sorrowful hound. He had been kind to Maidred ever since the dread sentence of death by fire had been pronounced against her. His gaze rested upon her with an expression of such pity, she felt tears start to her eyes all over again.

She glanced wildly about her cell, seeking in vain for some escape. Unbelievably, Tam slumbered on as though she had not a care in the world.

Maidred cowered back in the corner, pleading, "Please. Please don't—"

"Nae, lass," Master Galbraith interrupted her soothingly. "Dinna ye distress yourself. Not yet. I but come to bring ye a visitor."

A visitor Maidred had been dreading and expecting. The priest who would pray with her, give her the last rites. She must be as wicked as the judge had proclaimed because she could not seem to regard the advent of this holy man as any comfort, only the harbinger of death.

But it was not the dark-robed minister of the kirk who crept into the cell. It was the one person Maidred had never expected to see again. Her brother.

Maidred's breath left her in a rush at the sight of Robert Brody, a lad not much taller than herself, his hair the same golden brown. But there the resemblance ended. Although they were twins and Maidred the elder by a matter of minutes, Robbie appeared far older than their fifteen years. Grief, care, and toil had chiseled all boyish softness from his gaunt features.

Shadows pooled beneath eyes that had once sparkled with such teasing laughter, Maidred had called him her Robin Goodfellow. Back when they had played at knights, dragons, and faeries beneath the willows on the riverbank, halcyon childhood days so long ago Maidred feared she was the only one who remembered.

Master Galbraith ushered her brother farther into the cell and then stepped aside. "This could cost me my post, lad, so I cannot allow ye more than a few minutes."

Robbie nodded, passing a lean purse to the gaoler. Maidred flinched. Her brother must have bribed Master Galbraith for this visit with some of his meager supply of coin, money that he had earned with backbreaking labor in the laird's stable.

The gaoler quit the cell, closing the door behind him. Maidred stiffened as her brother drew nearer. Never had she been so glad to see anyone, but she wished he had not come. She felt so ashamed she could scarce meet his eyes, guilt-ridden for the trouble that she had heaped upon his overburdened shoulders, mortified that he should see her thus, looking like some common slattern.

How pathetic she must appear, her kirtle filthy from the effusions of her own body and the stink of the cell, a fetid mingling of urine, dung, and sweat. Her hair was matted and unkempt, her cheeks stained with her tears.

A heavy silence fell, broken only by the snuffling noises Tam made in her sleep. Then Robbie breathed.

"Good God, Maidred."

"I—I know. I must look a fright." She attempted to smile for his sake, picking bits of straw from her hair. "But it has not been so bad. I just pretend that I am a princess who has to don a disguise for now lest—"

"Stop it!"

Maidred broke off, startled by the harshness of his voice. He seized her by the shoulders, his fingers gouging her skin.

"Will you be at it, even now, spinning your ridiculous fantasies? What does it matter a damn how you look, you little fool?" He gave her a rough shake. "You are going to die today. Don't you understand that?"

"Y-yes, but it is not kind of you to remind me." She glanced up at him and saw that his angry outburst was fueled by an anguish he could barely suppress. His eyes welled with tears.

He pulled her close, hugging her so hard she thought he'd crack her ribs. She flung her arms about his neck, holding him as tight, just like they had done when they had been mere babes, frightened by a violent storm beating at the nursery windows. But this time there would be no wakening to a calmer, sunny morning.

Robbie's doublet smelled of the wide outdoors, sweet meadows and lake breezes, the kind of freedom she would never know again. Maidred whispered, "I am sorry, Robbie. So sorry."

He peeled her away from him, his eyes less angry than pained and confused. "I still don't understand, May. That day when you admitted to taking part in the witches' Sabbath, practicing evil spells against the king, I couldn't believe it. I thought they must have tortured you to make you confess."

"No, I was guilty."

"But why? Why would you do such a thing?"

Maidred spread her hands in a helpless gesture as she sought for words. Once, she and Robbie had been so close there was no need for any explanations. They had shared the same thoughts, the same feelings, and the same imaginings.

But Robbie had long ago abandoned their kingdom of dreams for the harsh wilderness of the real world. He had never been the same since their father had died four years ago.

Thomas Brody had been a wool merchant, prosperous enough to have ambitious hopes for his family, good marriages for his four daughters, a gentleman's education for his son so that Robert might even aspire to a position at court one day, despite Thomas Brody's Catholic leanings. The kirk had outlawed the old religion, but the young king James was known to be more tolerant, turning a blind eye to the religious practices of his favorites.

But a storm had destroyed Papa's small fleet and taken his life as well. That had been Maidred's first experience with how fragile a vessel dreams could be and she had shrunk from reality.

Debts had swallowed most of the Brody fortune, forcing them to leave their snug manor house. But Neve Brody had been a woman of strong and determined character, managing to turn even a humble cottage into a warm, comfortable home.

She had taken in washing and mending to enable her family to survive, but as exhausted as Mama must have been, she had never abandoned their cherished nightly custom of gathering around the fire for one of her stories. Mama had always been a gifted weaver of tales and Maidred had sat at her mother's feet, waiting as eagerly as her younger sisters.

Only Robbie had refused to listen, eschewing such faery stories as childish nonsense, too somber and too full of his own importance as the new head of the family.

To Maidred, it had felt like a betrayal. As much as she had mourned the loss of her father and their beautiful home, she had grieved even more the loss of her brother.

She had not understood Robbie at all until two years ago when the typhus had swept through their village, carrying off both her mother and her youngest sister, Elsbeth. Maidred had little time to mourn before she had been obliged to assume all the burdens Mama had carried. The washing, cleaning, mending, cooking, baking, and caring for her other two sisters, Annie and Brenna. And she was so inept at all of it. The only thing she was good at was the weaving of stories.

By nightfall she was too tired to do anything but weep into her pillow and there was no one to turn to for comfort and sympathy, certainly not her brother, who was working twice as hard as she.

She knew these thankless unending chores were a poor woman's lot in life, but she could not help wailing to herself. It wasn't fair. She had been forced to become a woman, a mother, before she had the chance to finish being a girl. To know what it was like to be wooed, to be a bride—and without a dowry, these were things she would never experience.

Her brother demanded to know why she had taken such a risk, dabbling in sorcery that cold November midnight. Maidred remembered that it had been a particularly trying day. She had burned the porridge, ripped an irreparable hole in her only decent frock, discovered their supply of potatoes had turned black and would not last the winter. Annie and Brenna had whined more than usual, Annie especially fretful because she was coming down with the ague. She had thrown up all over Maidred's shoes.

By the time Maidred had collapsed upon her cot, she had been pure exhausted. But she had still found the strength to steal from her bed hours later when the night was at its darkest, the moon hiding its face behind a veil of clouds. She had tiptoed past her sleeping siblings, crept out of the cottage, and raced to join in the forbidden revels being held inside the kirk. And why? For the most selfish and ignoble reason.

She had just wanted a small taste of excitement in her life, a wee bit of magic. But there was no way she could make Robbie understand that and she was too ashamed to try.

Moistening her lips, she said, "First off, you must know I would never have gone that night if I had known what was really going to happen, what wicked purpose—"

"What did you think would happen? A coven of witches gathering in a church after midnight!"

"I didn't know they were witches. I thought they were wise women like in those stories Mama used to tell us about the beautiful Lady of Faire Isle."

"Stories, Maidred! There is no magical Lady of Faire Isle, no gifted wise women. Only witches or at least spiteful old crones who delude themselves they possess some dark powers."

"Not all of them. There truly are genuine cunning women and there is much to learn from them. All about healing and useful white magic and even how to conjure the dead. Just think of it, Robbie. If we could contact Mama, see her, speak to her again." Maidred regarded her brother wistfully. "Wouldn't you want that too?"

"No!"

The vehemence of her brother's reply took Maidred aback. "Why not?"

"Because it would be unnatural, against the will of God." Rob shuddered and crossed himself. "Even if it could be done, do you think I could ever face our mother after the way I broke my promise?"

"What promise?"

"I swore to Mama on her deathbed that I would look after my sisters always, keep you safe."

"Oh, Robbie. So you have done. You've worked yourself

nigh to death keeping food on our table. And the time that angry dog came after us in the lane, you flung yourself in its way and you were the one who got bit. So brave, just like the noblest of knights."

Maidred cupped his cheek in a comforting gesture as her mother would have done. "That I have come to such a pass is not your fault, my dear Robin Goodfellow. It is all my own stupidity."

She could see from the iron set of his jaw, the pain in his eyes, that her words had no effect upon him. Her brother would carry the guilt of her death inside him until the end of his days. For that sin alone, Maidred feared she deserved to be burned.

He curled his fingers around her wrist, holding on so tight, as though he would never be able to let her go. "I tried so hard to find a way to save you, May. I went begging to everyone I could think of, some of Father's old friends from the guild, the bishop, the provost. I tried to explain that you had been led astray, that you meant no harm."

Robbie shook his head in despair. "They all said the same thing. There was naught to be done but pray for your soul and Master Galbraith said that all I could do was give you . . . this."

He released her and withdrew something from inside his doublet. Maidred expected that it might be a rosary or some holy relic. Just like Papa, Robbie adhered to the tenets of the Catholic faith.

Whatever the gift was, Robbie seemed loath to hand it over. He thrust a small pouch into her hand and cupped her fingers around it. "Here take this. Hide it beneath your shift."

Maidred stared at the pouch, squeezing it gingerly. It seemed to be filled with some grainy substance.

"What is it?"

"Something that will make sure you do not suffer over-much. It—it will take your pain away."

"Oh!" Maidred breathed. She feared the terrible agony of the flames more than she did death itself. "What am I supposed to do? Do I swallow some—"

"No. Just tie the pouch around your neck and keep it close to your heart."

"Is it an amulet of some sort? Is it magic?"

Robbie was unable to meet her eyes. "Yes," he said hoarsely. "It's magic."

His words were greeted with a high-pitched laugh that startled them both. Maidred spun around to discover that Tamsin had awakened, or perhaps she had been alert for some time. Knowing the wily old woman as she now did, it would not have surprised Maidred if Tam had been feigning sleep while listening in on their conversation.

Tam leaned against the wall, her thin arms dangling over her bent knees, her eyes agleam with amusement.

"Aye, powerful magic," she cackled. "The kind that will scatter your soul clear up to the heavens."

Robbie rounded on the old woman. "Shut up, you old hag. You are the one who has been the ruin of my sister. This is all your doing."

"Truly?" Tam raised her thick gray brows in mock astonishment. "I thought you just said you were to blame. Anyone but dear little May."

"You were the one who filled her head with nonsense about sorcery, lured her to the church that night."

"Is the fisher to be blamed if the foolish wee fishy has a taste for its bait? There are worse things your sister could have done. She could have been stealing out to spread her legs for some lusty lad."

"Damn you!" Robbie clenched his fists and took a step toward Tamsin.

Maidred seized hold of his arm. "Robbie, please. Just ignore her."

As I should have done.

"You have no idea how much pleasure I will take in watching you burn, you loathsome crone. If you were not already bound for hell this day, I vow I'd snap your neck myself."

He meant it. Robbie's arm felt like steel beneath Maidred's grasp. The bitterness and anger in his face alarmed her. She would have never imagined her gentle brother capable of such hatred.

"Robbie," she pleaded, trying to draw him away from Tam.

The old woman appeared unmoved by his fury or his threats. Tam got to her feet, shaking out her tangled mass of gray-white hair. She yawned, stretching her arms and arching her back like a scrawny cat.

She smiled at Robbie. "Regretful as I am to disappoint you, laddie, I won't be going anywhere. The devil will have to wait for me a bit longer. Nor will heaven be getting itself another angel in the form of your bonny sister. No one is going to die today."

"If you believe that, then your brain is as rotted as your soul. You have broken the sacred law against practicing witchcraft—"

"Sacred law!" Tam cut him off with a contemptuous sniff. "That law has been writ down in the books since my grandmother's time and how many witches have been burned? None, I'll warrant you. Oh, I have been hauled up before the magistrate and condemned for sorcery before. I've been imprisoned, chained in the pillory. Once I was even flogged. But that is all that ever came of it."

She shrugged. "We are not like those barbaric English, hanging poor folk for a little magic. The Scots have a healthy respect for their cunning women."

"This time is different," Robbie said. "The king himself is coming here today to witness the sentence being carried out."

"Aye, and that will be our salvation. King James will pardon us."

"Will he?" Maidred asked. Tam looked so confident, Maidred felt a flicker of hope, like glimpsing a far-off light in a night of unending darkness.

Robbie pressed her hand. His face was still taut with anger, but his eyes gentled. "No, May, he won't. This witch and her friends made a waxen image of the king to bring about his destruction. That is not just witchcraft. That is treason.

"The king believes that when he sailed to Denmark to fetch home his new bride, the coven brewed up storms to prevent his ever returning to Scotland. Why would he pardon those he deems responsible?"

"Because the king was present in the court the day I was examined." Tam smiled slyly. "I whispered a few private words in his ear, showed him exactly how powerful a cunning woman I am."

"Then you sealed your own doom, you old fool."

"Nae, our king is a soft man, afeard of his own shadow. How many times have the great lairds of this land plotted and rebelled against the king? And how many of them have been put to death by the king's command? Very few. The king is always quick to forgive, eager for reconciliation.

"That's because our good king Jamey has no stomach for violence." Tam grinned at Maidred. "So don't you fret, lass. Just watch me and do as I do. When the king arrives, drop to your knees, fake a few tears and a little repentance. Cry out to His Majesty for his mercy and we'll both come out of this all right. You'll see."

Maidred trembled. Weep, beg, and appear contrite? She would have no difficulty with that because her tears would be genuine, her remorse sincere. But could the king be so easily moved?

Maidred wanted to believe Tam, but she had placed too much faith in the old woman's assurances before to be comforted.

She looked instead at her brother and it was Robbie's expression that heartened her. His face had gone still, but his eyes blazed with the same hunger that threatened to consume her.

The hunger of hope.

ROBERT BRODY SHOVED HIS WAY THROUGH THE CROWD MILLing in the streets. Jostled and pushed from all sides, Robert thrust back, jabbing his elbow sharply into the paunch of a burly merchant.

"Oof! Easy there, lad," the man said. "No need to be so impatient. There should be space for all of us to get a good look. These two witches are only the first to die. There will be many more trials, many more burnings to come." He chortled. "So if you don't manage to squeeze to the front of the crowd today, you can come earlier and gain a better position for viewing next time."

Rob gritted his teeth, fighting the urge to drive his fist into the man's jovial countenance. But if he ever started punching, he feared he'd never stop. This sea of smiling faces and merry voices infuriated him, sickened him.

A holiday mood prevailed, as though they had all come to attend some harvest-day fair instead of watch an innocent girl burn alive. Many of these fools had even brought their children to witness this horror.

Rob shook with the effort to contain himself. He had been perishing to lash out at someone ever since the sentence of death had been passed upon Maidred. But he couldn't afford to do anything rash that might get him injured or arrested.

He still had two other sisters waiting at home, dependent upon him. Taking deep breaths, he conjured up an image of Brenna and Annie until he was able to check his anger.

He loved his two younger sisters, but they were not the same as Maidred. She was his twin. Born in the same hour, fashioned of the same blood and bone, she was the light to his shadow, the keeper of the dreams he had long ago abandoned. How could he endure to lose her?

But maybe he wouldn't have to. He had tried to pay no heed to anything Tamsin had said, but maybe the old crone really was a witch. Her words seemed to take possession of his mind.

No one is going to die today. The king will pardon us.

He was afraid to believe her. He had steeled himself to accept Maidred's death and now that miserable old woman threatened to breach his armor, giving him hope. A hope so sharp, it was painful, pressing like a dagger tip against his heart, threatening to draw blood.

He sought refuge in his reason. Was there any rational basis for thinking that the king might pardon Maidred? Rob tried to recall all that he had ever heard about James Stuart, sixth king of Scotland.

A cradle king, they called him, elevated to the throne when a mere babe after his mother had been deposed by her rebellious Protestant lords, who had risen up against the Catholic queen.

Mary had fled to her cousin, Elizabeth Tudor, for refuge, only to find herself the captive of the English for the next eighteen years. She had finally been charged with treason and beheaded by the English four years ago. The same Scots who had once reviled Mary as a Jezebel and a Papist whore cried out at her death and elevated her to martyrdom. The entire country had gone into mourning.

Lost in grief for his own father around the same time, Rob had barely noticed. Now he wondered about the king, what effect losing his mother in such a fashion had had upon James. Perhaps knowing what it was like to have a member of his family executed so unjustly would render James more compassionate.

Surely Rob had heard from someone other than Tamsin that James was reputed to be a merciful man, and who could fail to take pity on Maidred? She was so young, so innocent, and a comely lass.

James would have to have a heart of stone not to be moved by Rob's sweet sister. And yet Rob had heard darker whispers about the king, that James's heart was far more apt to be touched by the sight of a handsome lad than that of a maid.

Naught but a scurrilous rumor, surely. Had not James recently married a lovely Danish princess? He had been such

an eager bridegroom, he had done something unheard of for
a king. He had not waited for his beloved Anne to come to
him, but had risked leaving the safety of his kingdom to sail
to Denmark to secure his princess.

And almost died. Violent storms had battered the king's
fleet, nearly sending the king and his bride to a watery grave.
Storms that were attributed to the witches' coven gathering
at the kirk, weaving their foul spells. What man would not
want vengeance against those who had threatened the life of
his young wife?

But the king was said to be a scholar, a man of vast intelligence and knowledge. He was likened to the great King
Solomon. No matter what old Tam claimed she had whispered in the king's ear, could any man so wise truly believe in
her nonsense? Could the king look upon Rob's childlike sister
and imagine Maidred possessed of an evil power to brew
storms and sink ships?

Rob's head swam as he weighed the possibilities, balancing reason against his own desperate wishes. The scales of
his mind teetered, leaving him torn between hope and despair.

Lost in his thoughts, he was taken unaware when the
crowd fell back, nearly knocking him off his feet. Righting
himself, he saw the cause of the commotion. A horse and cart
had emerged from the castle, two women tied in the back.

"Witch! Witch! Devil's strumpet!" The cries went up.

As the wagon lumbered past, the prisoners were pelted
with clumps of mud and rotting cabbages. Rob tried to put a
stop to it, but there were far too many in the crowd hurling
abuse.

Rob's only comfort was that most of it was aimed at Tamsin, although he was astonished to see that there was some-one who cared about the crone's fate as well.

Two slatternly-looking wenches with red hair trotted alongside the cart and stretched out their hands to the old woman. "Granddam! Granddam!" they wailed.

Rob supposed he should have felt some pity for the two girls when the guards drove them back. But his jaw hardened. Tamsin had had no compunction about luring his innocent sister into danger, but obviously the wily old woman had taken care that none of her own kin should be put at risk. Those two strumpets had not been among those arrested at the church, but surely they must be as steeped in witchcraft as their grandmother. If there were any justice, they should have been bound with Tamsin in the cart instead of Rob's sweet sister.

Like Tamsin, Maidred had been stripped down to her shift, and her hair . . . those wayward silky curls that Rob had oft tugged at and teased his sister for being so vain. That golden brown mane had been shaved to a stubble, leaving Maidred looking like a shorn lamb. So young, so scared and lost.

Thrusting himself forward, Rob waved his arm so that she might see him, know he was there. Her lips curved into such a brave little smile, it nigh broke his heart. She touched the front of her shift where the pouch he had given her was concealed. Despite the hope Tamsin offered, he had insisted Maidred wear it and his sister had not resisted, believing it to be magic.

Rob felt sick. What kind of man did a thing like that? Fastened a lethal dose of gunpowder around his unsuspecting sister's neck. No man at all, only a boy too weak and ineffectual to do anything but help his sister to a less agonizing death. He should have tried harder, found some way to rescue her even if it cost him his life.

The king was Maidred's only hope. As the cart trundled onward, Rob kept pace, trying to keep in her view, a difficult feat with so many people milling about him.

Caught up in the crowd, Rob followed the cart through the city gates, toward an open stretch of field. He could see the stakes mounted on the rising ground, the faggots heaped and waiting, all a safe distance away, where no stray spark could bring disaster upon the buildings of Edinburgh.

As the cart was reined to a halt, Rob craned his neck, looking desperately about him. Where was the king? Surely James should have arrived by now. Perhaps he wasn't even coming.

Had not Rob also heard that the king had an abhorrence of crowds? Perhaps James had changed his mind about attending. Perhaps the rumors were untrue and there had never been any possibility the king would come.

Rob watched as his weeping sister was dragged from the back of the cart. He bowed his head, feeling overwhelmed by despair. He should never have listened to Tamsin, should never have for a moment allowed himself to believe . . .

"The king. The king!"

The excited shouts brought his head whipping back up. His heart thudded as he saw the approaching contingent of horsemen, the royal pennant flying. The knife of hope returned, piercing him more painfully than ever.

The crowd drew back respectfully as the horsemen rode into their midst and drew rein, some half dozen in all. Rob scanned the faces of the mounted figures, trying to pick out James Stuart.

"Which one is the king?" He didn't realize that he had spoken the question aloud, until someone answered.

The genial merchant Rob had jostled against earlier pointed a thick finger. "There. The wee man in the center."

Rob would never have described the king as a wee man, but James Stuart appeared dwarfed in the midst of the strapping, rugged lords who attended him. A slender young man with a trim beard, his dark clothing was unremarkable, bearing none of the regal trappings one might expect of a king.

His gloved hand fidgeted with the clasp of his cloak. He was clearly loath to be here, not eager to witness the grim spectacle to come. The thought increased Rob's hope.

Tamsin wriggled free of her captors. She flung herself to her knees before the king, crying, "Mercy, great king. Take pity on a poor old woman who repents the error of her ways and would serve you forever as a grateful and loyal subject."

Maidred followed suit, sinking down beside Tamsin. His sister was unable to speak for her sobs. She held up her bound hands in a pleading gesture that to Rob was more eloquent than any words.

The king stared down at his reins, patting the neck of his chestnut mount. He refused to look at the two women and Rob's heart sank.

Knocking several people aside, Rob fought his way forward and knelt beside his sister. Of the two of them, Maidred had always been the bright weaver of words, Rob more awkward in expressing himself. But with Maidred's throat clogged with tears, it was up to him to find the words to move the heart of a king.

"Please, Your Grace," he stammered. "Have mercy. My sister is but fifteen. She was misled. I beg you. Just look at her and you will see her innocence and goodness. She is no witch.

She would never seek to harm anyone, especially not you, our gracious king.

"I have already lost both my parents. Maidred is everything to me. If I am to lose her too—I cannot bear it."

Rob's voice cracked. It was difficult for him to beg, to bare his raw emotions to the impassive young man who towered above him.

But his plea induced James Stuart to look at him, the king's dark eyes roving over Rob with an expression of interest and compassion.

The king's gaze flicked from Rob to Maidred and then back again. Rob sensed the king's hesitation and held his breath.

It seemed to him the gathered throng did as well. The only thing that broke the silence was a loud snort. Not from one of the horses, but one of the king's retainers.

One of the lords who attended upon the king leaned forward to pass a remark to the rough-hewn knight mounted next to him. Both men smirked.

Rob could not hear what had been said, but it obviously had been audible to the king. James flushed a bright red. His face hardened and he lowered his hand.

"Proceed," he commanded.

"No!" Rob's throat burned with the force of his protest. But the single syllable was lost beneath Tamsin's cries of outrage and her granddaughters' howls of fury. Maidred sobbed as she and Tamsin were seized by the guards and wrenched to their feet.

The iron hold that Rob had sought to keep on his emotions snapped like a rusted dagger. He leapt up, fighting to wrest Maidred from her captors. He succeeded for a moment, straining his weeping sister close to his heart before she was wrenched out of his arms.

"Robbie!" She wailed as she was dragged away to be bound to the stake.

All reason forgotten, Rob lashed out in a blind haze of fury in an effort to get to his sister. Punching, kicking, gouging, he hardly felt the blows being dealt him from all sides until a hard club to his temple caused him to reel.

Strong hands forced him to his knees and a gruff voice rasped in his ear.

"Stop, lad. You'll do neither her nor yourself any good by this. You canna save her."

Blinking away the blood that trickled in his eye, Rob made out the heavy features of Master Galbraith, the turnkey. The old man and another young guard had Rob firmly pinned, but he struggled, his desperation fueled by the first whiff of smoke, the crackle of flames.

Above the murmurs of the crowd, he could hear old Tamsin's howls of rage.

"Damn ye to hell, James of Scotland. May ye one day also perish in fire. My curse upon the House of Stuart!"

The old woman's shrill invective dissolved into shrieks of agony as the flames leapt higher. But it was Maidred's screams that tore at Rob. Even as his strength ebbed, he made another frantic effort to free himself.

Then the explosion rang out and he went still. The loud retort sent a wave of panic through the crowd. Rob was dimly aware of frightened outcries, the shrill whinny of horses, the stamping of feet. But the chaos all seemed muted, like a scene muffled by a heavy fog or something out of a dream.

Maidred's cries had ceased, and to Rob, it was as though

the entire world had gone silent. His captors had released him, but he made no move to rise. Hot tears flowed down to mingle with the blood staining his cheeks. Master Galbraith gave his shoulder a rough pat. The gruff gaoler pressed something into Rob's hand before walking away.

As the crowd began to disperse, Rob summoned the strength to rise to his feet. He had not the courage to look in the direction of the pyre that consumed what remained of his sister. Instead his gaze came to rest upon the king.

James fought to get his nervous mount under control. For a moment his eyes locked with Rob's. The king was the first to look away. Bringing his horse about, he rode off in the direction he had come, closely followed by his retainers.

Rob stared after him, the acrid smell of smoke and the reek of burned flesh thick in his nostrils. He could hear the continued crackle and hiss of the fire. He knew he would carry that sound and that scent with him until the day he died.

It felt like those flames were inside of him, burning in the hollow of his heart left by Maidred. Rob's gaze followed the king until James vanished beyond the city gates.

One small wave of James Stuart's hand was all it would have taken to spare Maidred. Rob had felt certain the king had been close to doing so. So what had stayed him? Some sniggering remark from one of his great lords? The fear of their sneers, their ridicule of his weakness if he dared show any compassion?

The king was weak and as much of a coward as he was reputed to be. The fire in Rob's heart blazed hotter, burning him with hatred unlike anything he had ever felt. He uncurled his fingers, finally taking note of what Master Galbraith had given him.

A small lock of his sister's golden brown hair. Rob's eyes threatened to fill with tears again, but he blinked them back fiercely.

Damn ye to hell, James of Scotland. May ye one day also perish in fire.

Tamsin's curse echoed through Rob's mind, the empty venom of an old hag dying in agony, futile words unless someone was man enough to make the curse come true.

"And that I will, May," Rob whispered, clenching the lock of hair tight in his fist. "Even if it takes me the rest of my life."

Chapter One

THERE WAS LITTLE HOPE OF RETURNING TO THE ISLAND THAT night. Ominous dark clouds dimmed the sun, robbing the day of precious hours and a more gentle passage into evening. The wind picked up, rendering the waters of the channel whitecapped and choppy.

The Lady of Faire Isle struggled to keep the hood of her cloak from being tugged back, exposing her countenance to the rough salt tang of the breeze. Soft brown hair framed a face that was pale, her unblemished complexion and short stature making her seem younger than her thirty-one years. But her green eyes, always too solemn, too watchful, made her appear far older.

Picking her way carefully along the rocky shore, she peered across the channel for a last glimpse of her home, but the distant outline of Faire Isle was obscured by the shadows cast by the clouds. Margaret Wolfe hitched her breath, feeling that peculiar pressure in her chest she often had when she left the security of her island, a sense that disaster loomed just over the next horizon.

That was because the newly appointed Lady of Faire Isle had the sight, folks on the island and the mainland would whisper in awed tones. To a certain degree she did, but Margaret Wolfe attributed her tension more to her uncertain childhood. Anyone who was the daughter of a mad witch like Cassandra Lascelles was bound to face life with a high degree of apprehension. As her old nurse, Mistress Waters, had oft told Meg, *"You are a wary old soul, my pet. I do declare you were born anxious."*

Meg's present anxiety was heightened by the behavior of her traveling companion. Seraphine Beaufoy, la Comtesse de Castelnau, was a golden blond goddess of a woman, as tall as Meg was short.

The comtesse barked out orders in clipped tones, commanding the oarsmen who had rowed her and Meg from the island to drag the dinghy farther up the beach and conceal it beneath a pile of driftwood and seaweed. The wind snapped at Seraphine's cloak, revealing the masculine garb she had donned, a disguise that would have fooled no one, for her short doublet and breeches only accented her lush curves.

But Seraphine was more concerned with practicality than deception. One could not wield a sword trussed up in a corset and petticoats. And Seraphine was armed with both a pistol and a rapier strapped to her waist. Clearly she had a presentiment of possible danger, but there was one marked difference between them, Meg thought. If trouble came, Seraphine would relish it.

Seraphine strode back to Meg, looking satisfied with her disposal of the dinghy. "There. At least the boat will remain secure and we shall not be cut off from our only route of escape. I have ordered Jacques and Louis to stand guard."

"Surely you are being a little dramatic. I have come across to the mainland many times to treat ailments and never had a need to escape."

"There is a huge difference between delivering some peasant's babe and trying to cure a girl who claims to be possessed of demons and well you know it, Margaret Wolfe."

"Not the way I have heard some poor women shriek and curse when in the midst of their labor pains."

Meg's mild attempt at humor did little to ease the scowl on Seraphine's face. "I will tell you again, I don't think you should be interfering in this matter." Her tone softened as she added, "You are not obliged to atone for all the evil your mother did while she was alive. You don't have to ride to the rescue anytime someone breathes the word *witch*."

"That is not what I am doing," Meg started, but was stopped by a look from Seraphine, the shrewd assessment of one who had been her friend for too many years and knew her far too well.

"Well, not entirely," Meg amended. "As the new Lady of Faire Isle, is it not my duty to be a protector of women, especially other daughters of the earth?"

"I don't think Ariane would have wanted you meddling in the superstitious affairs of folk on the mainland. My aunt would have counseled you to be prudent."

"Since Ariane is no longer here, we cannot ask her." It was a source of great sorrow to Meg and she was unable to keep the quiver from her voice.

Ariane Deauville, the former Lady of Faire Isle, had been all things to Meg these last fifteen years. Friend, mother, and teacher, she had instructed Meg in all the lore of the daughters of the earth, wise women gifted in the arts of healing and white magic.

None was more gifted than the one acclaimed as the Lady of Faire Isle, a time-honored title bestowed upon the woman best suited to be the leader among the daughters of the earth in each generation. Meg had been humbled and honored beyond measure when Ariane had chosen her to be her successor.

It had been a role Meg had not expected to assume for a good many years, as the title only passed upon the death of the previous Lady. But when her health had begun to fail, Ariane Deauville had broken with tradition and abdicated in Meg's favor.

"Call me selfish, my dear," Ariane had told her. *"But I want to spend whatever time I may have left with my husband and son, traveling to places I have only read of in books, learning the secrets of healing and lore of other countries."*

Meg would never have dreamed of calling her friend selfish. No Lady had ever served Faire Isle and the daughters of the earth more devotedly than Ariane. If she could find a measure of peace and a cure for the illness that slowly devoured her, Meg could only wish her Godspeed.

Yet that day last spring when Meg had stood upon the dock, smiling and waving until the ship had disappeared from view, she had blinked back tears. She had been overcome with grief and a panicked feeling of being left to don a pair of shoes her feet would never grow large enough to fill.

She had striven hard to do so, grateful for the encouragement and support of Seraphine. But now when her friend wielded Ariane's presumed wishes as a weapon, she could not help telling Seraphine.

"Are you not the one who has been telling me that when any situation arises, I must stop trying to guess what Ariane would have done? I must learn to employ my own judgment."

"Not when you are wrong."

"You mean when I don't agree with you."

"Isn't that the same thing?" Seraphine demanded, then laughed. "Very well. Let us go find this foolish chit who claims to be beset with demons, so you can unbewitch her. With any luck, we may yet manage to avoid the storm and return to Faire Isle before dark. Although it would have been helpful if that idiot boy who came to beg your aid had waited to show the way."

"Poor Denys was far too anxious to return. It matters naught. Pernod is a small village and the girl's family owns the local hostelry, the Laughing Dolphin. Mademoiselle Tillet will not be hard to find."

"Lead on, then."

Pernod, like many of the villages on the Breton coast, was inhabited largely by fishermen. Over the years, a rough track had been worn up the rocky beach. Seraphine's boots were far better suited to the terrain than the clumsy pattens Meg had donned to protect her shoes.

The comtesse had acquired a reputation at the French court as a woman of grace, charmingly seductive and full of a playful indolence. Seraphine, when she was on a mission, was an entirely different creature. Meg's shorter legs were hard-pressed to keep pace with Seraphine's lengthy strides.

By the time they reached the point where the track widened into the lane through the village, Meg was panting a little. As she had told Seraphine, Pernod was a small place, boasting little more than a score of dwellings, a tiny church, and a hostelry. At least the stout stone walls of the cottages provided a break from the wind, allowing Meg to ease her grip on her hood.

The dusty lane was deserted, the village eerily quiet, but for the occasional banging of a shutter and the rustle of the trees. The silence rendered Meg uneasy. Given the hour, she would have expected to see fishermen returning with the day's catch, young boys wending homeward from their toil in the common field, or distracted mothers shooing stray children inside to their supper.

"What is this, some sort of ghost village? Where is everyone?" Seraphine demanded. "Mayhap the Tillet girl's demon has carried everyone else off as well."

"Don't say that! Not even in jest. It is more likely that everyone has retreated indoors for fear of the approaching storm."

Meg sought to reassure herself as much as Seraphine, but a part of her could not believe it. These Breton coastal people were hardy folk, accustomed to dealing with rough weather. They would not be driven to bolt their doors against the mere prospect of a little rain, thunder, and blustering wind.

Meg could think of only one thing that might have sent such a redoubtable breed of people into cowering inside their cottages: the fear that a witch walked among them.

Meg prayed it was not so. She had hoped to deal quietly with the Tillet girl's claims of bewitchment, resolve the matter before the rumors and panic had time to spread. The kind of panic that could result in innocent women being accused of witchcraft, tortured, and hung.

As she and Seraphine rounded a bend in the lane, Meg

spotted the inn sign creaking in the wind. The Laughing Dolphin was a modest hostelry that seldom saw much custom
beyond local travelers. But on this somber dark afternoon, a
stranger lingered in the doorway.

The man looked as out of place in this rugged fishing village as a satin doublet would have appeared strung on a wash
line of coarse homespun shirts. Despite the dust that clung to
his boots and the short cape that hung off one shoulder, there
was a quality about his garments that marked him as a gentleman.

He was of no more than medium height, his figure far
from imposing, but something in his self-assured manner
gave him the appearance of being taller. A fine-looking man,
Meg could not help noting. Some might even have said a
beautiful one, with his lean chiseled features and smooth-
shaven complexion, rather pale for one traveling during the
summer months. The breeze stirred the feathers of his toque
set upon waves of golden brown hair. His head tipped up as
he studied the darkening sky.

Seraphine let out a low whistle between her teeth. "So
who is this fine young buck?"

"I would have no idea," Meg murmured, uneasily. "It is
rather unusual for such a visitor to pass through a remote village like Pernod."

"You are afraid he might be the devil you have been summoned to exorcise? He looks far too pretty for that."

Meg glared up at her friend, but stopped as a sudden
thought struck her. "Good lord, 'Phine. You don't think your
husband might have sent him?"

Seraphine looked taken aback by the notion before giving
a derisive laugh. "What! Monsieur le Comte engage someone
to find his errant wife and drag her back to Castelnau by the

hair of her head? Gerard would not have the spine. And I doubt my dear husband wants me back any more than I desire to return to him."

Meg could not agree with that, but she knew it would be of little use to argue the point. She had tried ever since Seraphine had arrived on Faire Isle five months ago.

"Moreover, that man isn't even French," Seraphine continued. "Very likely he is English."

"How can you possibly know that?"

"Only look at the square cut of his doublet. No self-respecting French gallant would venture abroad wearing a garment so lacking in style."

She and Meg had been speaking in low tones as they neared the inn, but the stranger's attention riveted upon them. He straightened from the doorway and he stared. Meg felt the full weight of his gaze, hard, assessing, and far too intimate.

Meg shrank deeper inside her hood, her cheeks burning. "What business would an English gentleman have here in Pernod? And why does he stare so?"

"I don't know. Perhaps I should ask him and give him a lesson in manners."

To Meg's dismay, Seraphine halted, staring back at the stranger. With a challenging lift of her chin, she drew back her cloak, resting her hand upon the hilt of the rapier strapped to her side.

"Seraphine! Stop it," Meg hissed. "I hate it when you do this."

"Do what? Honor my father by wearing the sword he gave me?"

"I don't object to you wearing it, so much as you itching to stick it in somebody."

Meg held her breath as she awaited the man's reaction to Seraphine's aggressive gesture. The moment stretched out before he lowered his gaze. He bent in a grave bow and disappeared into the inn. Meg's relief was so keen, a tremor coursed through her. But Seraphine—damn the woman—actually looked disappointed.

She eased her cloak back over her sword. "That's that. Both of us are a little too much on edge, getting into a fret over nothing. Just some fool Englishman who has doubtless lost his way and seeks shelter from the incoming storm. He likely hoped to pass his time with some local wench." Seraphine's eyes danced with mischief as she added, "Just a hint, my dear. Next time you venture off your island, you really should try not to attract so much attention."

Meg choked between a laugh and a vexed oath. "Wretch! If men are of a mind to stare, it is always at you."

"But *you* are the one they never forget. I daresay it is those fey green eyes of yours. One look into them and a man is lost forever." Seraphine teased, but there was a wistful note to her voice as well.

Meg shook her head, dismissing Seraphine's words as nonsense or wanting to because she had striven most of her life to be forgettable, to be invisible, hidden by the mists of Faire Isle.

Perhaps she had overreacted to the stranger, her irrational fear just another part of the bleak legacy left her by her mother. For most of her childhood and youth, she had every cause to fear, to know what it was to be hunted. Every stray glance, every stare that lingered too long, every stranger who crossed her path could herald danger.

But surely those days were long behind her now. Her great enemy, the Dark Queen, Catherine de Medici, was dead these fifteen years and more. Meg's witch of a mother, Cassandra Lascelles, was gone longer still, swallowed up by the waters of the Seine. Likewise Cassandra's coven of fanatic devotees had all been destroyed, slain by witch-hunters or imprisoned, tried, and put to death.

There was no one left to menace Meg's peace anymore, no one to come after her. So why should the encounter with this stranger cause the back of her neck to prickle? Some voice inside her whispered that his coming here, his interest in her was no mere chance.

When she was younger, she would have heeded that voice. As she grew older, she became less attuned to the fey side of her nature, more inclined to question her instincts, to dismiss her extraordinary senses as folly.

Her pulse tripped nervously as she and Seraphine crossed the yard and approached the archway where the stranger had vanished. Meg wished that Bridget Tillet was a fisherman's daughter, dwelling in some remote cottage far up the beach. More than anything, she wished herself back on her island.

When Seraphine shoved open the inn door, they were beset by a cacophony of noise and overpowering scents, the odor of strong spirits and cooked meats mingling with the stench of unwashed bodies.

At least the mystery of the absent villagers was solved. Meg's heart sank as she entered the crowded taproom. Most of Pernod appeared crammed inside, every vacant stool and bench filled. Others leaned upon the bar counter, gesturing and arguing, the sound like the buzzing of a wasp's nest that had been disturbed. Meg could make out little of what was being said, but the tone was unmistakable, angry and frightened.

The traveler she had encountered outside sat a little removed from the locals. Of all the people present, he was the only one still and silent. Perhaps that was the very quality that drew her eye, that aura of isolation that clung to him, made him seem alone even in the midst of this crowd.

As Seraphine closed the door behind them, all heads turned in their direction and the entire room fell silent.

"Merde," Seraphine muttered.

Although Meg would not have expressed herself so crudely, she agreed with the sentiment. The air crackled with tension like green logs tossed upon a roaring fire. Meg caught a few whispered words. *"The Lady. Faire Isle. Sorceress."*

Meg was subjected to a score of stares, some curious, some hostile. She was known to many of the villagers, although folk from the mainland sought Meg's healing skills with more wariness than they had the previous Lady of Faire Isle.

As she drew back her hood, a few of the villagers crossed themselves as though seeking protection from the evil eye. Meg flinched, wondering if they had ever done so with Ariane, or did these simple folk perceive something more sinister in Meg's countenance? A trace of Cassandra Lascelles's darkness trapped in her daughter's eyes, despite all of Meg's efforts to bury her past.

But it was not the stares of the villagers that unnerved her. She was aware of the stranger studying her, his eyes quiet and watchful. Meg averted her gaze.

"Clear the way," Seraphine growled, preparing to shoulder a path for Meg through the crowd. It was unnecessary. They fell back, whether out of fear or respect Meg could not tell, perhaps a mixture of both, for while they eyed Meg uneasily, they gaped at Seraphine. Whether she was clad in leather breeches or dripping with satin and jewels, Seraphine was very much Madame la Comtesse. Her haughty expression defied anyone to cry shame upon her or even remark upon her unwomanly apparel.

Someone in the room found his tongue to ask, "So is it true then? Is the Tillet girl bewitched?"

Other voices piped up.

"Do you know who cursed her?"

"Can you save her, milady?"

"Is your own magic strong enough to remove the curse?"

Before Meg could frame a reply, Seraphine said, "There is no bewitchment. The Lady is here to heal the girl who likely suffers from *mal de bêtise.*"

"*Mal de bêtise?* What is that?" A boy quavered.

"A disorder that attacks your wits, rendering you incredibly stupid. I hear that it is highly contagious."

"Seraphine," Meg remonstrated, observing the confused scowls that her friend's sarcasm produced.

"The best thing for you all to do is return to your homes," Seraphine added. "In case you haven't noticed, there is a storm coming."

No one budged. To Meg's relief, she spied young Denys Brunel near the door leading to the kitchen. He stood conferring with two lanky ginger-haired men. The younger of the two had his arm wrapped about the shoulders of an elderly woman who wept into her apron.

Denys's face lit up at Meg's approach. At least someone looked glad to see her, she reflected. The boy hastened to perform introductions.

"Milady, this is Master Raimond Tillet and his son, Osbert. And this is Madame Sidonie Tillet, the grandmother of my poor Bridget—" Denys paused, reddening before amending, "I mean Mademoiselle Bridget Tillet, the girl that I told you about who is so sorely afflicted."

The two men nodded curtly, but the old woman staggered toward Meg. Squinting at Meg through her tears, she clutched Meg's hand. Sidonie Tillet's grip was strong, her skin rough and work worn.

"Oh, milady, bless all the saints that you have come to remove this curse from my poor granddaughter."

"Well, I—" Meg began, only to be cut off by a stern voice that she recognized.

"This is no work for women. This is a matter for the holy church." Meg started as Father Jerome, a spare man in his late forties, descended the wooden stairs that led to the chambers above.

Meg had crossed paths with the priest on previous visits to Pernod. Unlike some of the lower clergy, he was a fairly educated man and tolerant of women like Meg as long as she confined her craft to midwifery or healing the sick. But his stern look warned her that he regarded her appearance in this matter as an incursion into his realm.

Ignoring Meg, he addressed Raimond Tillet. "I have examined your daughter. In my opinion, she is indeed possessed of demons and an exorcism must be performed. I must ride north to consult with my bishop before—"

"And while you are doing that, Bridget could die," Osbert Tillet snapped. "There is only one thing that can help my sister and that is to hunt down the witch that cursed her and destroy her."

Meg's heart missed a beat as there was a chorus of assent from the rest of the room. She felt Seraphine tense beside her and noticed the movement beneath Seraphine's cloak as her friend clutched at the hilt of her sword.

"And just who would that be?" Seraphine demanded.

"Who else could it be but la Mère Poulet?" Osbert asked.

"What!" Meg exclaimed. "You cannot mean that poor old beggar woman who keeps a chicken on a leash for her pet?"

"It is her familiar," Osbert said. "I hear her talk to it all the time. Once when I laughed at her for doing so, she put a curse on me and the very next week, I sprained my ankle."

"What nonsense," Seraphine began hotly, but Meg gave her arm a cautioning squeeze.

"Please allow me to see Mademoiselle Bridget," Meg said, appealing to the girl's grandmother. Despite her tears, Sidonie seemed by far the calmest, most reasonable person in the room. "You sent for me for my healing skills. I am sure I can find some natural cause for Bridget's ailment and the right herbs to cure her."

"That is already being tried. The doctor is attending to Bridget even now," Raimond said before the old woman could reply. "I am sorry that my mother summoned you all this way for nothing, mademoiselle." The innkeeper puffed out his chest with an air of great importance as he announced loud enough for the entire room to hear. "But *my* daughter is being treated by a genuine healer, a most learned physician."

"This wretched little village boasts of a doctor?" Seraphine asked.

The innkeeper bristled at Seraphine's scornful tone, but he replied courteously enough. "*Non,* madame. This physician, Dr. Blackwood, is traveling in the company of the English lord who is stopping at the inn tonight. Most fortuitous for my poor daughter."

Meg's gaze was drawn back toward the stranger seated near the hearth. She thought that he observed them all with the cool detachment of a spectator at a play, waiting to see how the drama would unfold.

"If Mademoiselle Tillet is being tended to by this Dr. Blackwood, then you have no need of the Lady." Seraphine's fingers closed over Meg's arm. "Come on. If we hurry, we can still cross the channel before the storm breaks."

Both Denys and Madame Tillet cried out in protest.

"Please, do not go, milady," the old lady begged. "You are the only one who can save my granddaughter. I have no faith in this English doctor."

"How unfortunate, but that is not our concern," Seraphine said.

"Yes, it is." Meg said. When Seraphine tried to hustle her away, Meg dug in her heels. "'Phine, you know how ignorant these medical men can be, more versed in Latin than any useful healing arts. God knows what vile draughts and emetics he will pour down that poor girl's throat."

"I daresay she will survive. Many do."

"And many don't."

Bending closer, Seraphine muttered in Meg's ear. "I am more concerned with your survival than hers. You were already taking enough of a risk interfering in this matter, but now with the village priest and some damn fool doctor involved—"

"All the more reason that poor girl needs me. I cannot walk away now."

"Yes, you can. Just put one foot in front of the other and head in that direction."

Seraphine thrust her toward the door, but at that moment, a scream echoed from the regions abovestairs. Loud and shrill, it was as unsettling as the cry of a banshee. Sidonie whimpered in alarm and the men looked frightened. Even Seraphine paled, muttering, "Holy Mother of God!"

Meg wrenched free of Seraphine and bolted toward the stairs. The innkeeper tried to stop her, but he was blocked by his son.

"*Non,* Papa. Let the Lady go to her," Osbert said. "The only one who can break the curse of a witch is another witch."

"The Lady of Faire Isle is no witch!" Seraphine snarled.

The taproom instantly turned into a hubbub of arguing voices, punctuated by the screams from above. Ignoring them all, Meg raced up the stairs. She only stopped when she realized Seraphine was hard on her heels.

"No," she said, turning back to her friend and speaking in a low urgent voice. "If I cannot help this girl, I am not sure how this will end."

"I am. They will take up that old beggar woman for witchcraft and you as well."

"That is why you must go find la Mère Poulet and hide her."

"Be damned to her. Old Mother Chicken must shift for herself. I am not leaving you."

"Seraphine—"

"No!"

Meg studied the adamant set of Seraphine's jaw and sighed. "Stay, then, but try to reason with these men and keep any of them from going in search of the old woman."

"Now, that I can do." She started to unsheathe her sword, but Meg's hand shot out to stay her.

"No, this is not a task for an Amazon warrior, but for Madame la Comtesse and her considerable charms of persuasion."

"Why can I never make you understand that it is far more effective to knock men's heads together rather than try to beguile them?" Seraphine said, but she relented, easing her rapier back into its scabbard. "Oh, all right. Circe it shall be, not Hippolyte."

"Thank you." Meg grimaced as another shriek sounded from above.

Seraphine glanced upward uneasily. "I doubt this doctor will appreciate your interference any more than the village priest. You be careful, Meggie."

"I will. I have dealt with such ignorant fools before. I am sure this is nothing I cannot handle, just a young girl indulging a bout of hysterics."

Despite her brave assertion, Meg felt a shiver go through her as she headed back up the stairs. She had confidence in her abilities as a healer. She had been taught by that wisest of women, Ariane Deauville, and Meg had learned well.

Yet it wasn't Ariane's gentle image that filled Meg's mind as she climbed the stairs, but that of Cassandra Lascelles with her ebony hair, ice-white skin, and unseeing dark eyes.

Of a sudden, Meg was a child again, creeping up to the forbidden tower room where Maman lit the black candles and bent over the steaming copper basin. Muttering her incantations, Cassandra would call forth spirits from the water, make the chamber echo with deep sepulchral voices.

As a rational daughter of the earth, Meg wished she could deny that such black magic existed, but she had seen it for herself. She feared it could only be a matter of *when*, not if, she ever encountered such evil again.

Perhaps even now it lay in wait for her at the top of the stairs in this humble inn. Meg trembled and then steeled herself. She was no longer Cassandra Lascelles's daughter, but the Lady of Faire Isle, the bringer of light and reason.

The horrible cries originated from behind the first door to the left. Meg started to knock, and stopped, the distraught sounds from beyond making all formality seem foolish.

She pushed open the door, entered the bedchamber, and caught her breath, feeling as though she had just stepped into hell. An inferno of a fire blazed on the hearth, rendering the room hot and airless. The flames sent shadows on the wall, the glow making the faded bed curtains appear as red as blood.

Candles had been lit, in the wall sconces, upon the mantel, and on a small table, as though someone believed that with enough light, the devil could be kept at bay.

It hadn't worked, Meg thought with a small shiver. He hovered over the bed, in the guise of a tall dark man.

She closed the door quietly, her arrival unnoticed by the trio on the opposite side of the room. The doctor fought to subdue the girl writhing beneath the bedcovers. An older girl looked on, wringing her hands, her face as pale as her linen coif.

"Mademoiselle Bridget! You must be still," the doctor said, his voice thick with an odd accent. He snapped at the older girl. "Don't just stand there like a block of wood. Help me to restrain your sister."

Bridget flailed, her fist striking the doctor in the eye. He jerked back and swore, while Bridget shrieked to her sister, "Charlotte! Help me."

"Please, Bridget," Charlotte quavered. "You must try to fight this evil spell."

"I can't. Oh, how she tortures me."

"Who, dearest?"

"La Mère Poulet. Can you not see her?"

"No. Where is she?"

"There."

Meg froze, fearing that the girl meant to point a trembling finger in her direction, but Bridget gestured toward the ceiling.

"She is there! Hovering above my bed. Oh! Cannot you hear her horrible laugh? Do you not see her?"

Charlotte looked wildly about the bedchamber and actually ducked as though she expected some vengeful spirit to fly down upon her, claws bared. "No, Bridget," she quavered. "I confess I do not see anything."

"That is because there is nothing to see," Blackwood said. Nursing his injured eye, he groped for something on the table while ordering Charlotte to gain command of herself. "Stop behaving like a fool and help—"

But Charlotte had had all she could endure. With a frightened sob, she fled from the room, nearly knocking Meg over in the process.

Dr. Blackwood noticed Meg and whipped upright. He towered over her when he straightened to his full height. His brawny shoulders, combined with his shabby manner of dress, gave him more the look of a field hand than a doctor. His disheveled brown hair and beard were badly in want of a trim, his eyes appearing bloodshot and shadowed from want of sleep.

"Who the devil are you?" he growled. His glare felt forceful enough to hurl her back through the door. But Meg stood her ground.

"I am the Lady—" Meg checked, always feeling preten-

tious announcing her title. She finished simply, "I am Margaret Wolfe."

The doctor's lips curled in contempt. "The cunning
woman from the island? That's all I need. Although you might
prove some help if you weren't such a scrawny thing."

"I beg your pardon!"

His gaze raked over her. "Do you think you are strong
enough to help me hold that chit down?"

"Hold her down for what?"

"The wench needs to be bled." Blackwood raised his arm
and Meg noticed the sharp gleam of the lancet he clutched in
his right hand.

Her gasp was lost in the howl that erupted from Bridget.
The girl burrowed beneath the covers until not even the tip of
her head was visible.

"It would not matter how strong I was," Meg said. "I
would not aid you in such a barbarous practice."

"Then you are of no use whatever. Get out."

He turned back toward the bed, but Meg darted round
him.

"You are the one who should go." She reeled back in dis-
taste as she breathed in the odor of strong spirits. She suddenly understood the odd accent of his speech.

"By God, monsieur! You are drunk."

A red stain spread across Blackwood's cheekbones. "I
may have consumed a little burgundy, but I am sober enough
to know what needs to be done."

"Bloodletting? Is that the only remedy you doctors know?
Slicing open someone's veins?"

"The girl's womb is full of noxious humors that are making her hysterical. Bleeding is the only remedy."

"What would you know of a woman's womb or any other part of her anatomy?"

"Oh, I assure you I have made a most thorough study of the female body." The suggestive slur in his voice only increased Meg's anger.

"And what do you know of a woman's mind or soul?"

"Do you have one? I believe there is some debate on that point."

"Then go and debate it with your friend downstairs. And attempt to sober up while you are about it. The only thing worse than an ignorant doctor is an inebriated one."

She turned her back on him and stepped toward the bed. But he grabbed her arm and spun her about. "And leave you here to give credence to this girl's nonsense? I think not. There is something far more dangerous than a drunken doctor and that is a witch claiming to possess supernatural powers of healing."

"I claim nothing of the kind. Let me go."

"I will when you are on your way out the door."

His grip tightened painfully, but Meg refused to flinch. Their gazes locked in a silent battle of will. Meg stared deep into his eyes and it felt like falling into the depths of a well. She had never encountered an expression so dark, so cold, and so empty. Not since the last time she had looked into her mother's eyes.

Meg's anger dissolved into fear. Her gaze flicked from Blackwood's stony gaze to the sharp lancet he gripped in his hand.

When the door swung open, she glanced around in relief. For once she would have welcomed the sight of Seraphine charging in with sword drawn. But rescue came from a quarter she would have never expected.

The strange Englishman stood in the doorway, frowning as he took in the scene before him.

"Armagil, what is going on? Let her go."

The man's command was so soft-spoken, Meg feared the doctor would pay no heed. But Blackwood blinked and glanced down at the lancet as though becoming aware of his menacing posture.

He released Meg, growling to his friend. "Take her out of here."

Meg rubbed her sore arm, bracing herself for a fresh assault, but the other man only shook his head. "No, Gil. I think you are the one who must come away."

Blackwood glowered at his friend. "The devil I will."

The two men spoke in English in low voices as if they thought she could not understand. Or perhaps as though she had become a thing of no importance, not even present. The conflict of will was between them now, Blackwood's gaze dark and ferocious, his friend's calm and steady.

"The girl's sister is down there raising an uproar, Gil. She claims you are doing nothing to ease her sister's suffering."

"Perhaps I could if I was allowed to proceed. I was close to resolving this matter until *she* intruded." Blackwood gestured angrily toward Meg. "Why did you let her come up?"

"Because she was expected. Except for the landlord and the village priest, it is clear that all these people place a great deal of faith in her skills."

Blackwood snorted.

"Whereas I was worried all along that you are in no condition to deal with this."

"I am fine."

"Are you, Gil? Look at your hand."

Blackwood gazed down at his trembling fingers, grimaced, and clenched them into a fist. His friend stepped forward, placing his hand on Blackwood's shoulder with the kind of gentling gesture he might have used on a restive steed.

"Come away. There is nothing you can accomplish here. Let us see what the lady can do."

"You expect me to walk away, just so you can satisfy your curiosity about this witch? Damn it, Graham, you know what could happen—"

"I know, but there may be better ways of dealing with it. Come, Gil, before the girl's brother or some of those other hot-tempered louts belowstairs take a notion to come storming up here. We cannot afford to find ourselves at the center of anything that might draw down upon us the attention of local authorities."

Blackwood regarded his friend belligerently and swore. He shrugged off his hand and then stormed out of the bedchamber without looking back.

Meg had all but held her breath during the entire exchange. "Thank you," she said.

The Englishman stared after Blackwood, but Meg's quiet words drew his attention back to her. He bowed stiffly and addressed her in French. "My apologies for my friend, mademoiselle. Blackwood can be rather abrupt and difficult, but he is a good doctor except for when . . ."

"When he has been imbibing too much wine?"

"In his defense, he did not expect to attend to any patients this evening."

Meg appreciated the man's loyalty to his friend, but she could not allow this excuse. "Is it not the mark of a good doctor to always be prepared to minister aid when needed?"

He fell silent as though unable to argue the point. Meg studied his eyes. She thought if sorrow were a color, then this man's eyes would be tinted with it. Instead they were blue, a startlingly vivid blue.

"We have had a long journey to arrive at this place," he said at last. "Dr. Blackwood is very wearied. We both are. But I assure you he will trouble you no further, Mademoiselle Wolfe."

His easy use of her name jolted Meg. As the man prepared to leave, she said, "You appear to know who I am, but I still have no idea of who you are, monsieur."

"My name is . . . Graham." He hesitated before adding, "Sir Patrick Graham, at your service, milady."

He surprised her by taking her hand and lifting it lightly to his lips. And then he was gone.

Chapter Two

AS THE DOOR CLOSED BEHIND SIR PATRICK GRAHAM, MEG watched him go with a bemused frown. Under different circumstances, she would have been favorably impressed by the knight, calm, serious, gentle in his manners, traits that she admired in a man and such a contrast to his rough brute of a friend.

But the Englishman's presence in Pernod had alarmed Meg from the start and the conversation she had overheard between Graham and Blackwood did nothing to allay her anxiety.

She did not have the leisure to fret over it now. A groan from behind her reminded Meg of that. She hastened over to the bed to find Bridget quivering beneath the coverlet.

"It is all right, Mademoiselle Tillet," Meg said. "Dr. Blackwood is gone. No one will hurt you now."

The only response was another moan. When Meg tried to ease back the covers, Bridget clutched them tighter.

"I am Margaret Wolfe, the healer from the island. Your grandmother sent for me to help you, Bridget. Please allow me to look at you."

The girl's frame shook beneath the blankets as though she were stricken with an ague. Meg managed to wrest the blanket back far enough to expose Bridget's face.

She touched her hand to the girl's brow. For one who was supposed to be fevered, Bridget's skin was cool, although damp, her blond hair matted. She reeked of the sour odor of sweat, but that was not surprising between the crackling fire and all of these candles. The bedchamber was stuffy and overwarm. Meg felt beads of perspiration gather on her own brow.

The door opened and Sidonie Tillet crept into the room. Bridget's grandmother approached the bedstead anxiously.

"How fares the poor child? Can you help her, milady?"

"I hope so."

Bridget panted, her eyes clenched shut. She tried to strike Meg's hands away, but Meg captured one of the girl's flailing arms. She groped for Bridget's wrist and managed to take her pulse. A little hectic, but surprisingly normal for one claiming to be possessed.

"Tell me. What other symptoms has your granddaughter exhibited?" Meg asked.

"Vomiting, fever, and strange swelling. Fierce pains and terrible bouts of trembling as though something seizes hold of her and shakes her like a cloth poppet. She cannot even rise from the bed. She says demons are pinning her down."

"And when did all of this begin?"

"I first noticed signs of the sickness coming upon her three days ago. Bridget would be distressingly ill upon arising. I caught her vomiting behind the cowshed and I—" The old woman flushed. "I am ashamed to tell you what I suspected and accused my poor girl of, but then Bridget fell down into a terrible fit."

"Did she indeed?"

"It soon became clear this was no natural woman's ailment but the workings of some terrible witchcraft."

Bridget bucked and shrieked as though to confirm her grandmother's words. She tossed her head from side to side.

Meg clasped the girl's head to stop the wild movements. "Bridget. Bridget Tillet. Open your eyes and look at me."

The girl writhed beneath Meg's restraining grasp. When Meg repeated her command in a firmer voice, Bridget's eyelids fluttered open. Meg stared deep into the blue depths, capturing Bridget's gaze and holding it.

The girl's eyes were remarkably clear, unclouded by anything other than fear and defiance. From the time she had been a child, Meg had been adept at the ancient wise woman's art of reading the eyes. She felt she had lost some of her skill as she had grown older, but Bridget Tillet was a simple country girl. She possessed neither the cunning of madness nor the guile to keep Meg from discerning her thoughts.

Discomfited by Meg's probing, Bridget twisted her head to one side, letting out a howl of protest when Meg peeled back the blanket further to examine her.

Bridget's chemise was soaked with sweat, outlining her thin frame. There did appear to be a slight protrusion in the region of her abdomen. Meg ran her hands gently, but firmly over the swelling. Bridget jerked beneath her touch, scrabbling for possession of the coverlet.

"Grandmère! Help me. Make her stop."

Sidonie clutched her granddaughter's hand. "I am here, my child. What ails you, dearest? Tell me where it hurts."

"Everywhere. I ache, I burn! Old Mère Poulet torments me so. She swears not even the Lady of Faire Isle shall save me. Oh, cannot you hear her horrible cackling laugh, Grandmère?"

"No. Oh my poor angel!"

Poor devil would have been a more apt description of Bridget Tillet, Meg thought. She swallowed the caustic remark, realizing it would do little good. The girl was faking this possession and doing it badly. Meg had encountered far more clever deceivers. But Bridget's performance was quite good enough to terrify the credulous villagers of Pernod and cause a harmless old woman to be hanged for witchcraft.

She longed to seize Bridget by the shoulders and shake a confession from the foolish girl, but that would prove no remedy. If she confronted Bridget and called her a liar, the girl might well turn on Meg, naming her as a witch in league with la Mère Poulet to torment her. Meg realized if she was to have the truth out of Bridget Tillet, it would require more subtle means and she would have a better chance of that if she was alone with the girl.

Meg drew the coverlet back over the girl. "Alas," she said. "It is all too apparent this poor child is cursed. Fortunately, I do know how to break this witch's hold over her. There is a powerful spell I can use, but I will need help."

"Anything," Sidonie said. "Anything to save my granddaughter."

"I need you to go below and brew up a kettle of water. And you—you must, er, fetch some garlic. Chop up a large quantity of it."

"Garlic?"

"Yes," Meg replied solemnly. "For my spell."

The old woman looked mystified by her request, but hastened below to obey. As Sidonie left the room, Meg caught a glimpse of Denys Brunel pacing on the landing. He darted an anguished look in the direction of the room.

It struck Meg that the young man took far too tender an interest in these events for one who claimed to be merely a good friend of the Tillet family. An idea formed in her mind, one not without its risks, but she hoped it would succeed.

She stepped out into the hall, offered the boy a reassuring smile, but refused to answer any of his anxious questions. She sent him down to fetch Seraphine, and when her friend approached, Meg asked, "How fare matters below?"

"Well enough, I suppose." Seraphine said in a disgruntled tone. "No one has left to go after old Mère Poulet, but that is due less to my charms than that blasted English doctor. He has been lavish with his coin, buying wine for everyone."

And no doubt would soon have the entire village befuddled with drink and all the more dangerous for it. Passions always flamed higher when fueled by spirits. Damn the wretched man, Meg thought. She needed to resolve this situation and do it quickly.

In a few terse words, she told Seraphine what she required. Seraphine frowned in bewilderment and then shrugged, hastening to fulfill her request.

Meg proceeded to extinguish most of the candles until only one remained. Bridget had gone quieter without her grandmother to witness her performance. She had dragged the coverlet up to her nose, watching Meg's every move.

"What are you going to do?" she asked.

"Cast a spell to cure you, I trust."

"Will it hurt?" It was a frightened child's question. Meg gazed into Bridget's wide wary eyes and her urge to throttle the girl abated a little.

"No, my spell is a very powerful one, but it will ease your suffering and clarify your mind."

Seraphine returned to the room and passed the object she had been sent to retrieve to Meg, slipping it into her hand. Seraphine was bursting with curiosity, longing to stay to see what Meg was about. But Meg shooed her friend back down-stairs.

"Are you ready?" she asked.

"I guess so," the girl whispered. "But what about the hot water and the garlic? Should we not wait for Grandmère to fetch them?"

"Er—ah, no," Meg said. "I won't need the garlic until later. Far better that we begin at once, don't you think?"

Bridget nodded in reluctant agreement even though she was clearly dreading the prospect.

Meg positioned herself before the remaining lit candle, fully aware of the eerie glow it would cast over her face. She wracked her mind for the memory she seldom visited, that of Cassandra Lascelles standing over her steaming copper bowl.

Meg had gleaned little by way of love, wisdom, or guid-ance from her late mother. But there was one thing Cassandra had taught her: how to perform the part of a witch.

Meg spread wide her arms and intoned an incantation in the ancient language of the daughters of the earth, long lost to the present world. She sang out the words at random, nothing but a jumble.

Bridget lowered the coverlet to her chin, her eyes saucers

of blue as she watched Meg. Meg held one fist high above the candle, slowly uncurling her fingers. She switched to French, addressing Bridget.

"I have here a lock of hair taken from the head of thine enemy. If this be the hair of the true witch that torments thee, when this lock is burned in the flame of the consecrated candle, then shall ye be free."

Bridget sat up straighter, scarce breathing as Meg held the lock of hair to the candle flame. Meg muttered a few more nonsense words, trying not to wrinkle her nose at the stench of burning hair.

She held the wisp of hair until the flame came close to scorching her fingers. Snatching back her hand, she declared, "There, it is done. The spell is broken."

Bridget released her breath. "I believe I do feel better."

"Truly? Because if I made a mistake, if the hair I burned was not that of the true witch—"

"Oh, yes. It had to have been. Look. I can even sit up now." Bridget wriggled upward, bracing her back with the pillow. "I am so grateful to you, milady. I hope I shall be well now, but what is to prevent la Mère Poulet from cursing me all over again?"

"La Mère Poulet?" Meg feigned a blank look. "She was not the witch tormenting you. It was not her hair that I burned."

"Then . . . then who?"

"The hair belonged to Denys Brunel."

"Denys?" Bridget gasped and shook her head. "No, it cannot have been. It was la Mère Poulet. I saw her, hovering above me on the ceiling."

"A mere illusion, conjured up by Master Brunel. It appears he is a most skilled young warlock, but he did not fool me. I have long suspected him. Now I must go tell the others and see that the boy is arrested for witchcraft."

Meg started toward the stairs.

"No!" Bridget flung off the covers. The girl who had claimed she was too weak to stand leapt off the mattress. She ran after Meg, clutching her arm.

"No, you can't accuse Denys. No one will believe you."

"Of course they will. The entire inn will have witnessed my friend, Madame la Comtesse, snip a lock of Denys's hair and fetch it to me."

The girl's fingers dug into Meg's arm. "That stupid test proves nothing. Nothing at all."

"Certainly Denys will have to be examined more thoroughly. When he is in custody, they will strip him naked, search him for witch marks. Any moles or freckles they find, they will have to pierce with pins."

"Stop it!" Bridget cried. "Denys would never hurt me. He is no warlock."

"I am sure he will be reluctant to admit that he is, so they will have to torture a confession out of him."

"What? No, they c-can't." Bridget pressed her hand to her mouth, looking as though she would be ill.

"Oh, yes they can. I have heard the boot is most effective. It is an iron clamp they fasten to the leg and then tighten the screws until bones are crushed. Denys will never be able to walk again, but that is of little concern since he will be hung as soon as he confesses, which he will do. No one can endure the agony of the boot."

"No! They can't do such a horrible thing to him. Not to Denys."

"Why not?" Meg leveled a hard look at her. "Is not that what you wished done to old Mère Poulet?"

Bridget's eyes filled with tears. "She is a nasty, spying old hag. She saw me and Denys—" She jammed her fist in her mouth.

"Yes?" Meg prompted. "She perhaps saw you and your young swain making love and you feared she would tell. Was that a good enough reason to want a poor old woman dead? Especially when your secret is bound to be known soon enough."

Meg trained her gaze on the girl's midriff. Bridget clutched her arms over her womb. Her tears spilled over, cascading down her cheeks.

"I didn't want her dead, just gone. I never thought they would kill her, just drive her out of the village before she could tell. Grandmère caught me being ill and she started to suspect. She and Papa would be so angry. I had to come up with some kind of tale, something to keep them from finding out. I never meant it all to go so far. I just needed more time to figure out what to do." Her voice thickened, choking with tears.

Bridget sank down to the floor, drawing her knees up to her chin. She buried her face against them, her shoulders shaking with the force of her sobs.

Meg tried to harden her heart against the girl, tried to remember how much misery and suffering Bridget could have caused with her deception. But she looked so young, lost, and frightened.

Meg hunkered down beside Bridget. She placed her arm around the girl, a little awkward at first. Meg had learned nothing of mothering from Cassandra Lascelles, but Ariane Deauville had taught her a great deal.

Meg gathered the girl closer, rocking her in her arms.

"I—I didn't mean to cause so much trouble," the girl snuffled against her shoulder. "I—I was just so scared."

"I know."

"I never intended for it to go so far. But once I had begun, I didn't know how to stop."

"Fortunately all still may be remedied if you but have the courage."

"But—but I don't know what to do," the girl wept. "What am I to do?"

"The bravest thing that you can," Meg said gently. "Tell the truth."

Chapter Three

THUNDER BOOMED AND THE SKY CRACKED OPEN, DISLODGING a hail of rain. The water cascaded over the inn, obscuring all view of the lane leading through the village. Sir Patrick Graham lingered by the window watching as a flare of lightning lit up the darkness. He far preferred the sounds of the storm raging outside to the din of coarse voices that had filled the taproom up until an hour ago.

The chamber was mercifully empty now. When the truth of the Tillet girl's bewitchment had been exposed, the villagers had staggered homeward, as baffled and deflated as an army that had assembled for a battle that never came.

Graham had been astonished by the outcome himself. When Margaret Wolfe had helped the trembling Bridget down the stairs to make an announcement, Graham had expected the worst, that a witch hunt was about to be launched and there would be nothing he dared do to interfere. Worse still, he feared he would be unable to prevent Armagil from trying to do so. His friend had been even deeper in drink by that point.

Graham had held his breath along with everyone when Bridget Tillet began to speak in a halting, timid voice. One had to strain to hear the girl's confession of her own guilt. The claim of bewitchment had been a hoax, a lie to hide the fact the girl was with child.

Graham could not begin to imagine the courage it must have taken Bridget to face the entire village and admit such a thing. He might have admired the girl for it, except that he would have wagered his last shilling the chit was neither a particularly brave or honest girl. He was sure that the girl's extraordinary confession was somehow due to the quiet woman who had stood behind Bridget, her hand resting on the girl's shoulder.

How on earth had Margaret Wolfe brought this about? It was almost as if she had placed some kind of spell upon the girl.

After Bridget's confession, there had been cries of outrage and anger, mostly from the girl's family. The rest of the villagers had slunk away. Many of them would be nursing a sore head tomorrow, thanks to Blackwood's liberally supplying everyone with wine.

Armagil had done much to lighten the mood even before the Tillet girl had emerged to make her announcement. Refilling glasses, clapping a shoulder here, trading a jest there. These dour, suspicious villagers had soon been in a fair way to forgetting that the doctor was both a stranger and an Englishman to boot.

That didn't surprise Graham. When Armagil chose to exert himself, he possessed a bonhomie that Graham lacked.

Sir Patrick could not even remember at what point he had lost all taste for the pleasures that others enjoyed, when life had become merely a question of survival.

He crossed the taproom to where Armagil occupied the table farthest from the hearth, as was the doctor's habit. Blackwood had finally succumbed to the effects of the wine he had imbibed. He slumped forward, his head pillowed on his arm.

If his friend had one failing, Graham thought, it was a tendency to overindulge in strong spirits. But Graham could not condemn Blackwood for it. He supposed each man must find his own way of dulling the sharp sword of memory, of coping with burdens imposed by the past.

"My poor Gil," Sir Patrick murmured. "Time to get you to your bed, old fellow."

He hesitated before touching Blackwood. Armagil could be dangerous if roused too suddenly, especially if Gil was in the throes of one of his nightmares. But the doctor emitted soft snores, his expression one of such rare peace, Sir Patrick envied him. If he could have ever achieved such a state of insensibility in the bottom of a bottle, Graham might have been tempted to try it.

Another clap of thunder sounded just as the inn door cracked open. A short, coarse-featured young man burst inside and slammed the door closed behind him. He brushed back his hood. Despite the protection of his woolen cloak, he was soaked through, his coppery hair plastered to his brow.

Alexander McMahon stole a wistful glance toward the crackling fire, but the serving man knew his duty well. He strode straight to his master and made Sir Patrick a low bow.

"Mooshieur."

Patrick winced. Alexander's mangling of the French language was painful to the ear and the information the man brought him too vital to risk any incomprehension. The innkeeper and his family had withdrawn to the region of the kitchens. Patrick still stole a cautious look about him. The need to get Armagil up to his bed forgotten for the moment, Graham pulled his servant closer and addressed the man in his native Scots dialect.

"What have you learned?" he demanded.

Alexander paused to slick wet hair back from his brow. "I did as you bade me, Sir Patrick. I followed the lady and her companion when they left the inn."

"And?"

"They haven't gone far. There is some sort of shed behind the inn. The landlord told them they might bed down there for the night, rather grudgingly I thought. I fear the sorceress makes him uneasy. She seems to have that effect on most of the folk hereabout. On me as well." Alexander shuddered. "They do say this lady has the sight. Her eyes can pierce a man's soul and strip all his secrets bare."

If that were so, Patrick thought, it was a most dangerous gift for a woman to possess. Especially for a man like himself who had so much to conceal.

When he had first realized he would be forced to seek out this Lady of Faire Isle, he had no idea what he would find. Perhaps that the famed lady was no more than a myth, or if she did exist, she would prove to be some malicious old crone or a mad hermit, or even a Circe, seductive and sinister.

The tall shameless beauty who flaunted herself so brazenly in masculine garb had seemed far more likely to prove a legendary sorceress than Margaret Wolfe with her short stature and solemn, unassuming manner.

And yet there had been a moment upstairs in the bedchamber when he had experienced a small taste of her power. When her gaze had locked with his, he had experienced a jolt. An odd presentiment had come over him, as though in that instant, some connection had been forged between them, the thread of their lives destined to intertwine for good or ill.

Sir Patrick moved his hand from his brow to his chest, making the sign of the cross. That was one blessing of this long hard journey through France. In England, he had to spend every waking hour concealing who and what he was. But at least here he was not obliged to hide his faith.

"What now, sir?" Alexander asked, prodding Patrick from his thoughts. The younger man wrung some water from the dripping end of his cloak. "It is a lucky chance that brought this sorceress here, is it not? Now we do not have to go to her cursed island in search of her."

Alexander was a superstitious man. He had heard too many eerie tales of the Faire Isle as an enchanted place, a haven for witches. He had been dreading the journey, wasting far too much of his coin upon protective amulets. Sir Patrick wished he could tell the young man that they could forget about the Lady.

Margaret Wolfe made him uneasy. He wished he could let her sail back to the obscurity of her island, but whether he liked it or not, she had become necessary to his plans.

"What do you wish to do, Sir Patrick?" Alexander asked again. "Will you approach the Lady tonight?"

Patrick studied the rain beating against the windowpanes and considered. It was obvious that Margaret Wolfe was settled in for the night. No one, not even one acclaimed as a powerful sorceress, would risk the channel crossing in such a storm. It was equally obvious from what he had witnessed that she was no fool, this Lady of Faire Isle. He would have to approach her more carefully than he had ever imagined.

"No," he said, clapping his servant upon the shoulder. "Come help me get Dr. Blackwood to bed, then go dry yourself off and retire. The morning will be soon enough to seek out the Lady."

Sir Patrick was a patient man. He had bided his time, waiting years to see the cause of justice served.

He could afford to wait one more night.

Chapter Four

THE THUNDER FADED AWAY AND THE WIND DIED, LEAVING only the steady patter of the rain. Meg stood in the doorway of the Tillets' cowshed, resting her head against the wooden frame. She hadn't realized how tensely she had been carrying herself ever since leaving Faire Isle. Not until now when she was able to relax, lulled by the soothing monotone of the rain, did she feel the ache of her muscles.

She was suddenly exhausted, although she ought to bestir herself to help Seraphine arrange the bundles of straw and the blankets Sidonie had provided to bed them down for the night.

But Seraphine had already tended to that and now she was making the acquaintance of the shed's other occupant, a spotted milk cow with large brown eyes. The comtesse, who could be so haughty and so fierce, stroked the cow's muzzle and crooned softly to it, displaying a tenderness Seraphine rarely revealed to any creature that walked on two legs.

When she saw that Meg observed her, she stopped at once, looking sheepish. She joined Meg in the doorway.

"It appears that the storm has passed us, just a deal of noise and bluster when all is said and done."

Meg realized that Seraphine was referring to far more than the weather. "Yes, but it could have proved very different."

"It is only owing to you that it didn't." Seraphine leaned up against the opposite doorframe. "Master Tillet might have shown you some gratitude for persuading his daughter to tell the truth. At least he could have offered you more comfortable accommodation for the night."

"I exposed Bridget's frailties. People seldom thank one for that. They often prefer the comfort of a lie. And I don't mind the cowshed. It is warm and dry."

And farther away from the inn chamber that would house the English travelers. Meg rubbed her hand over her bruised forearm, sore from Blackwood's iron grip. But she wasn't terribly disturbed by the memory of the doctor's coarse behavior. For some inexplicable reason, it was the other one, Sir Patrick with his sad eyes, who left her more unsettled.

"You were very forbearing and kind to that foolish Tillet chit," Seraphine said. "I just wanted to slap her."

"She had her grandmother for that. The only thing that saved Bridget from a severe beating is the fact she is with child."

"I doubt her swain will be as fortunate."

Meg sighed in wearied agreement. The last she had seen of Denys Brunel had been the young man tearing out of the inn, Bridget's brother in heated pursuit.

"Denys appeared very fleet of foot," she said. "And hopefully the onslaught of the rain will cool Osbert's temper. I believe the worst is over, but in the morning, I would still like to find la Mère Poulet. You know how it is once a woman has been libeled as a witch. She could still be in danger. We must convince her to leave with us, come to the safety of Faire Isle."

"That should be amusing. Trying to persuade some half-witted old woman to abandon the village she considers home. She will probably try to scratch our eyes out or set her chicken upon us."

"Nonetheless . . ."

"Nonetheless, you are right." Seraphine swept her a graceful bow. "As always I defer to your wisdom, my Lady of Faire Isle, and seek to do your bidding."

Meg laughed. "Ridiculous woman."

Seraphine straightened, her grin fading. "You took a terrible risk coming here, Meg. No matter how well it all turned out this time, you know how these things can go."

"I do," Meg murmured. It usually started so simply, just as it had done here in Pernod. A child late for supper, a young girl detected in some transgression, or a boy caught neglecting his chores, hoping to avoid punishment, seeking any excuse. Or in other instances, someone fell mysteriously ill, well beyond the ignorant local doctor's ability to cure.

"It was not my fault I am late, Maman. I was bewitched."

"The cabbages did not wilt because I forgot to water them. They were cursed by a witch."

"Your wife did not die because of the potion I gave her. I am a skilled physician. But no one can fight the power of a witch."

The tale would spread, the rumors begin to fly, and someone would be sought to take the blame. Usually some poor old beggar woman like la Mère Poulet, often not right in her wits. Under the pain of torture, she would spin tales of her own, accusing others of witchcraft.

What began as a small lie would fan into a frenzy like a hot coal dropped into a pile of dried straw. Meg had heard tales of villages nearly depopulated of their women until reason prevailed, bringing an end to the torture, the trials, and the hangings.

Seraphine continued to complain of Bridget Tillet. "Stupid girl. What could she possibly have been thinking?"

"She didn't think. She was too frightened. Not that I am making excuses for her, but you can imagine what it must be like for an unwed girl to find herself with child, the disgrace of it. Her family, her entire village could turn against her, drive her out. How vulnerable, helpless, and terrified such a young woman would be. Exactly the sort of girl my mother used to . . ."

Meg trailed off. She seldom spoke of Cassandra Lascelles, not to anyone, not even her good friend Seraphine. Seraphine said nothing, merely watched her, waiting.

Meg swallowed and continued, "My mother was wont to prey upon desperate girls like Bridget, using their plight to persuade them to join the coven of the Silver Rose. She offered them protection, freedom from shame and want, even promised eventual wealth and power.

"All she required in return was a blood oath of loyalty. They could even bring their new babe as long as it was a girl. My mother, you see, had no use for a male of any age, so if any of the girls bore a son, he had to die. The poor little boy was left abandoned on a hillside, exposed to the elements, to perish of starvation."

Meg's eyes stung. "I often wondered how many of them died, wailing out for the comfort of a mother who never came, crying until their voices grew too weak."

Seraphine wrapped her arm about Meg, who rested her head upon her taller friend's shoulder, the rain pouring down outside, a blur before her tears.

"Do you know the worst of it, 'Phine?" she asked when she was able to continue. "My mother wrought these horrors in my name. Megaera, her Silver Rose as she insisted upon calling me, the daughter who was expected to become a powerful sorceress one day and conquer the world."

"A madwoman's dreams," Seraphine gave her a bracing hug. "You were a child, as innocent as any of those girls Cassandra lured in with her lies. You were not responsible for anything she did and you are no longer her Silver Rose. You are now the Lady of Faire Isle.

"The past is as dead as your mother, Meg. Let it go."

Meg mopped away her tears with the back of her hand, wishing it could be that simple. "At least things will end better for Bridget Tillet than it did for those girls who fell prey to my mother's lies.

"Monsieur Tillet is angry with his daughter at the moment, but he will forgive Bridget. Denys Brunel may not be the sort of husband he would have desired for his daughter, a poor fisher lad with not even a cottage to call his own, but I am confident he will consent to the match rather than see his daughter further disgraced. The banns will be cried and they will be happily wed."

"Or at least forced to be so."

"No, truly. I think Denys and Bridget do care for one another. Bridget, I am sure, loves him deeply."

"She loves the illusion of her young swain, the person that she believes him to be. Perhaps it would not be wise to inquire how she feels in ten years' time."

The exact amount of time Seraphine had been wed. Meg caught the bitter edge in her friend's voice. When she peered up at her, Seraphine moved away, locking her arms over her bosom.

"Tomorrow morning, I shall return to Faire Isle," Meg said. "What will you do?"

"Why, I shall go with you. What else did you think I would do?"

"I think you should return to your husband."

Seraphine's only reply was a hard laugh. She tried to retreat deeper into the shadows of the barn, but Meg caught hold of her arm.

"Gerard loves you as much as you do him."

Seraphine shook her off. "Don't be a romantic fool, Meg. Marriage has nothing to do with love, especially among noble families. It is a purely mercenary arrangement, a matter of trade. The man barters his title and estates for a woman's dowry and the use of her womb."

"That was not the way of it for you, 'Phine, and you know it."

"So I was a starry-eyed little fool when I first met Gerard. I'll thank you not to remind me."

"Someone needs to," Meg began, but Seraphine interrupted her harshly.

"Stop, Meg. Just . . . stop. Even if I admit I once felt something for Gerard, that is ended. He took my son, sent my little François to be a page in the household of his good friend, the marquis. And now my boy is dead."

"It was an outbreak of the pox, which can strike any-where. Gerard could not have anticipated such a thing. He was as torn with grief as you."

Seraphine shook her head in angry denial. "François would still be alive if I had been able to keep him at home with me as I wished."

"But is it not the custom among noble families to send sons away to be fostered?"

"Oh, yes." Seraphine's mouth curved bitterly. "To give the boy a proper education, prepare him to take his place in the world, make important and valuable connections. When did Gerard ever care about anything like that?

"If the man had ever had any ambitions, he could have gone to Paris and found a place at court. My husband is a clever man and he is of the right religion to curry favor with the king, unlike my own poor father."

It was another source of great bitterness to Seraphine. Her father, Captain Nicolas Remy, had served the king for years, long before His Majesty had become Henry IV of France. Captain Remy had fought for Henry when he had been merely the king of the small principality of Navarre, the stronghold of the new religion, the Huguenot faith.

But when Henry had been offered the chance to ascend the throne of France, he had seized it, even if it meant aban-doning the faith of his loyal Huguenot subjects. "Paris is worth a mass," the king had declared after his witty fashion.

"The king betrayed my father by abandoning our reli-gion," Seraphine said. "And I betrayed Papa as well when I wed a Catholic."

"I do not believe your father ever felt that way," Meg re-plied. From what she had seen of Captain Remy, the man was honorable to his core, true to his country and the faith he espoused, but he was in many ways like his king, a moderate man, no religious zealot.

In her youth, Seraphine had been far more fierce in her defense of the new religion. It had been a testament to her great love for Gerard that she had surrendered her beliefs to become a Catholic. Seraphine seldom ceded anything to anyone.

"Your father has always admired and respected Gerard. As did you," Meg reminded Seraphine.

"That was when I thought we shared the same dreams and ambitions. As a woman, I knew I could never achieve anything of significance. But I could have helped Gerard become important and powerful, the kind of man who could make his mark on the world.

"But Monsieur le Comte has never cared for anything but living quietly in the country, tending to his estate, work that a reliable steward could have done. Gerard might as well have been some peasant farmer for all he cares of what goes on in France beyond his own acres.

"I saw something different in my son. As young as he was, there was a spark of greatness in François. But now he is gone and I am even more to blame than Gerard. If I had ever troubled to learn as much of the healing arts as I did swordplay—" Seraphine bit down on her lip, her eyes filling with tears.

But she refused to shed a single one. Meg wondered if Seraphine had ever allowed herself to truly weep for the loss of her son. Knowing Seraphine, she doubted it.

Meg touched her friend's hand. "François's death was not your fault any more than it was Gerard's. Sometimes all the healing skill nor all the care in the world is enough to protect a child—"

"So you would be like that priest and tell me what? That

my son's death was the will of God? A matter of fate? What would you know of it anyway? You have never had a child, Meg. Nor are you ever likely to."

Meg flinched as though she had been struck, drawing her hand away. Seraphine was instantly contrite.

"Oh, God, I am sorry, Meggie. I didn't mean that. You know what I am like when I am hurting, like a wounded she-wolf snarling and snapping at everyone." She clasped Meg's hand, squeezing it. "Forgive me."

"There is nothing to forgive. I only wish I possessed some sort of potion or balm that could heal your pain."

"I fear there is no magical cure for grief. Only the passage of time, or so I am told." Seraphine released Meg, her expression darkening again. "Gerard had another solution. He felt that we should attempt to have another son. As though I have not tried to give him other heirs. I have the graves of three stillborn babes to prove it. That François lived beyond his infancy seemed a miracle. I don't think a woman as weak and wicked as I will ever be granted another such blessing."

"You are neither wicked nor weak. You have the most fiercely loving heart and you are the strongest woman I have ever met."

"You think so, Meg, but in truth I am a miserable coward. I cannot face the prospect of ever burying another child. I told Gerard he should set me aside, find himself a younger, more fertile bride. If he bribed enough church officials, I am sure a dissolution of our marriage could be brought about. I could retire somewhere to a convent and live a life of quiet contemplation and scholarship."

Meg nearly choked at the image of Seraphine as a nun. It would be like shutting up a lioness in a pen full of lambs. Seraphine herself was aware of the ridiculousness of the notion. Her lips quivered, and as soon as her eyes met Meg's, she laughed. Meg could not help joining her. The mirth was a healing thing and it gave Seraphine an excuse to wipe a stray tear from her eye.

"Perhaps I am not suited for the convent," she conceded. "But the sad truth is I don't think I was ever suited to be a wife and mother either. I have no idea what I am fit for."

"You have so many wonderful gifts. You are so bold, spirited, and intelligent."

"Ah, but we both know I would have been better off if I wasn't. A quick wit is always more of a curse than a blessing. Intelligence is never valued in a woman."

"It is on Faire Isle. I oft think about the night of the choosing, when Ariane named me as her successor. But you were her niece. If I had never come to Faire Isle, she would surely have selected you and you might be so much happier."

"Don't be absurd, Meg. Ariane was far too wise to have ever chosen me. My aunt loved me, but she recognized my flaws far better than you do. I am an impulsive, quick-tempered creature, and I have none of your gifts for healing. It was you who were meant to be the Lady of Faire Isle. A true daughter of the earth, content with your quiet life, spending your days growing your herbs, poring over your books, and teaching the old lore to others. The peace and security of that island is all that you have ever wanted.

"As for me . . ." Seraphine shrugged. "I think I would have been better off if I had been born a man. I would have been free to travel, to soldier, or hold an important post in the government. Perhaps I could have accomplished something of value before I die. Or maybe I am just destined to be one of those miserable people who are always restless, never content with their lot."

"Oh, 'Phine," Meg began, but Seraphine cut her off with a quick smile. "No, I am sorry, Meggie. I never meant to burden or worry you. You should realize by now that I always rant and spout a deal of nonsense, especially when I am tired. It is time we both got some sleep."

Seraphine turned away, signaling that she considered the conversation at an end. Meg watched with a mingling of love and frustration, feeling that there was much more to be said, but she had no idea what it was.

Surely she ought to be able to do something or conjure up some sort of wisdom to soothe her friend's troubled spirit. Meg wracked her brain as she often did, trying to recall what Ariane might have said or done.

But all she could call to mind was something Ariane had told her one afternoon when Ariane had been teaching her how to brew a potion to fight off the infection in wounds.

Ariane had glanced up from the powder she was grinding with her pestle. *"I can teach you a good many things, my dear. How to mend bones, how to curb fevers, stitch cuts, ease a woman through the pangs of childbirth. But when you are the Lady of Faire Isle, people will come to you for advice as well on troubles of the heart.*

"Too often you will have no solution to give them. All you will be able to do is listen with kindness and sympathy. You cannot take on their sorrow as your own, even the pain of those whom you love deeply. There will be times when you must stand back and let others find their own healing."

"But how will I know?" Meg had asked anxiously. *"How will I know when I should try to help and when I should not interfere?"*

Ariane had smiled ruefully. *"Ah, my dear, that is some-*

thing I cannot teach you. You will have to learn that for your-self."

Meg sighed as she settled down on her bed of straw beside Seraphine. The silence stretched out and she realized Seraphine was already fast asleep. It was something Meg had always envied her friend, Seraphine's ability to close her mind to turmoil and painful thoughts. She could drop off to sleep as soon as her head touched the pillow, just like snuffing out a candle.

Even the cow had gone quiet, no longer shifting about in her stall. Meg alone was left wakeful, staring up at the rafters, her mind churning over her conversation with Seraphine, the feeling that she had somehow failed her friend.

When Seraphine had first turned up on her island, Meg had welcomed her with open arms. She had been dismayed to learn that Seraphine had fled from her husband, but believed that all Seraphine needed was some quiet time to reflect and to heal.

But that had been over five months ago and Seraphine showed no signs of dealing with her grief. The woman simply wouldn't be still long enough to reflect upon anything.

If she were braver or firmer, Meg thought, she should risk Seraphine's wrath and send for the comte. Despite all Seraphine's fierce assertions, Meg was convinced that her friend still loved her husband.

And why would she not? Gerard Beaufoy was a gentle man, kind and compassionate. He had gifted Seraphine with far more than a title and wealth. He had brought to their marriage a steadiness that Seraphine needed to balance her wild, impulsive nature.

Gerard possessed exactly the attributes that Meg would

have wanted in a husband herself. That is, if she had ever dared to think of marriage at all. But she had learned at a very young age the dangers of opening her heart to anyone.

She had been not much more than a child when she had experienced her first infatuation with the young man that her father had hired to be her music tutor. But Alexander Naismuth had proved as treacherous as he was handsome. He had known of the dark legacy Meg had inherited from her mother and his only interest had been in acquiring all those dangerous secrets.

Meg's infatuation had nearly cost her own life and that of her father and stepmother as well. It had taken years for Meg to ever trust another man again. Not until . . . *Felipe.*

His mere name conjured bad memories, but enough time had passed that the image of his face, the recollection of how it had felt to be locked in his embrace, had become a blur and that was just as well. The pain was gone, but the scar remained, forming a tough seal over her heart.

Meg shifted to her side, Seraphine's words echoing through her mind.

"You were meant to be the Lady of Faire Isle . . . content with your quiet. The peace and security of that island is all that you have ever wanted."

Seraphine was right and yet there were times when Meg felt as though she paid a high price for her safety, the costly coin of loneliness. How long had it been since she had known the touch of a man? It had been years since she had even been kissed . . . until tonight.

Her mind painted a clear image of the way Sir Patrick Graham had looked as he had carried her hand to his lips. The strong chiseled lines of his cheeks and jaw, the crisp wave of his hair, the vivid blue of his eyes, the gentle curve of his lips.

He was a beautiful man and she would have had to have been as insensible as a stone not to feel some flutter of attraction. She held up her hand, trying to inspect it in the darkness as though some trace of Graham's kiss might linger on her fingertips. But all she was aware of was the bruises that Dr. Blackwood's rough grip had left on her arm.

She had had little leisure to reflect upon the strange conversation she had overheard between the two men. Now fragments of it played over and over in her mind, rendering it even more difficult for her to fall asleep.

"Come, Gil," Sir Patrick had said. *"We cannot afford to find ourselves at the center of anything that might draw down upon us the attention of local authorities."*

What did that mean? That Graham and Blackwood were involved in some sort of clandestine activity, traveling without the proper papers? Perhaps they were English spies or guilty of some crime or perhaps she was merely letting her imagination run mad.

It was natural that two Englishmen traveling on foreign soil should be loath to run afoul of French justice. There was no need to read anything sinister into Graham's remark. She found the recollection of something that Blackwood had said far more disturbing.

"You expect me to walk away, just so you can satisfy your curiosity about this witch?"

Curiosity about the witch . . . there could not have been any words more likely to rouse Meg's alarm. She had worked far too hard to bury her past to risk rousing the interest of any passing stranger. Unfortunately, she had done just that by getting involved with the Tillet girl.

Whether Graham's arrival in Pernod was a matter of pure chance or owing to some secret design, it didn't matter. By this time tomorrow, she would be back safe on her island and not likely to see either man again.

She closed her eyes, willing both Graham and his friend from her mind. Breathing deeply, she drifted into a troubled sleep.

Chapter Five

FIRE.

The red-gold flames lit up the night, the scent of the smoke acrid in Meg's nostrils, filling her with a sense of urgency. She had to locate the source of the blaze, extinguish it before it was too late. She stumbled through the narrow streets clutching the water pail in her hand. The glow seemed brighter, hotter, just ahead of her.

The tall buildings that hemmed her in suddenly vanished, leaving her surrounded by a mob of people. Their hell-lit faces were twisted into ugly sneers as they raised their fists and chanted, "Burn, witch. Burn!"

Meg recoiled in horror. Piles of burning faggots had been heaped about the feet of two women chained to stakes. One of them was a young girl, not much more than a child. She screamed in pain and fear. Even through the haze of smoke, her beseeching eyes found Meg.

"Help me, great Lady of Faire Isle. I beg you."

Meg tried, but the bucket of water weighed her down and the crowd blocked her way. She fought her way forward, water sloshing over the side of the pail as she pushed and shoved.

The flames leapt higher around the terrified girl. Meg broke free of the crowd, raised her bucket to hurl the water and then . . . nothing.

The pail was empty.

Meg sobbed as the flames engulfed the girl. The world seemed to explode around her, hurling Meg to the ground.

She flung her arms over her head to protect herself against the deafening roar. When she finally dared lower her arms, the night had gone quiet. No trace remained of the pyre or the girl, save a few glowing embers. The mob also had disappeared, leaving Meg alone with a faceless figure shrouded in black.

He loomed over her, pointing an accusing finger at Meg. "You did this. You are to blame for the execution of my sister."

"You are wrong," Meg said. "I tried to save her."

"Your legend lured her to her death and he signed the warrant. Both of you must pay for your cruelty."

"I don't know what you mean. Who are you? Who is this 'he' you are talking about?"

The phantom did not answer. Instead he brandished a flaming torch. "Burn, witch. Burn!"

Meg shrank back, but too late. The flame caught the sleeve of her gown, setting the fabric ablaze . . .

"No!" Meg bolted upright, slapping at her clothing. It took her a moment to realize that she was not on fire. She was menaced by nothing but stray bits of straw that clung to her skin, causing it to prickle. Meg brushed the wisps aside.

She exhaled a deep breath and dragged her hands over her face to force herself more fully awake and shake off the last vestige of her nightmare.

She wondered if she had cried out. Surely her thrashing about should have been enough to rouse Seraphine, but the woman slept on, undisturbed. The sight pricked Meg with a rare sense of irritation.

She longed to shake Seraphine awake and— And do what, tell her friend she had had a nightmare? Seraphine would merely roll over and growl at Meg to forget about it and go back to sleep. It was only a bad dream.

Yet there had been a time when Seraphine would have been obliged to take Meg's dreams more seriously. When she had been younger, Meg had been tormented by nightmares of a more prophetic nature. But it had been years since she had been afflicted with such vivid dreams and those at least had made a rough kind of sense.

Her visions had always involved people she knew, like her good friend, Jane Danvers, or her great enemy, Queen Catherine, not dreams about a girl Meg had never seen before. And yet there was something familiar about the girl, something about her eyes and the cast of her countenance that reminded Meg of someone she had met.

But who? Meg wracked her memory, but the recollection was as elusive as grasping at wisps of smoke. She flopped back down on the blanket with a wearied sigh. Closing her eyes, she drifted in and out of a fitful sleep.

When the first light of morning crept into the cowshed, Meg hailed it as a relief. The sun seemed like a peacemaker, declaring a truce in her battle with a restless night.

Rubbing bleary eyes, she struggled to her feet and winced at the stiffness in her back. She stretched and yawned, gazing down at Seraphine, curled up on her mound of straw as though she were nestled in the downiest of feather beds.

Meg was in no hurry to rouse her. As swiftly as she was able to fall asleep, Seraphine had a tendency to bolt awake. Not for her the languor with which most noblewomen faced their mornings. Seraphine would leap out of bed like a knight in full charge, ready to tilt with the new day.

Meg needed a slower, gentler beginning. She liked the quiet of those first moments of morning, to reflect, to gather her strength to face whatever the day might hold. She tiptoed past her sleeping friend and stepped outside.

The sky was overcast, heavy with the threat of more rain. The breeze that stirred Meg's hair carried with it the smell of wet grass and an earth washed and renewed. Meg breathed deeply, savoring the rich aroma, willing it to clear her mind of bad dreams, disturbing strangers, and all the distressing events of yesternight.

No one else was stirring except for an ostler heading toward the stables, perhaps to ready the mounts for the Englishmen. It behooved travelers to get an early start and she hoped Sir Patrick Graham would be eager to do so. She would be glad when the two men resumed their journey. But she doubted Sir Patrick would have much success rousing Blackwood before noon. The last Meg had seen of the doctor, he had been slumped over a table in the taproom, in a fair way to being dead drunk.

But that was the unfortunate Sir Patrick's problem. Meg had one of her own. The sight of a scraggly rooster, strutting through the stable yard, reminded her of her resolve to find la

Mère Poulet and coax her to the safety of Faire Isle. Even though Bridget's accusations had been proved false, there would be those who would regard the old woman with increased hostility.

Meg knew little of her other than those few times she had seen la Mère Poulet begging outside the inn or one of the cottages. Whenever Meg had tried to approach her, the old woman had shied away, disappearing into the field beyond the village. La Mère Poulet was wary of strangers, a caution that Meg understood and respected.

Meg always had left her offering of food upon a tree stump and retreated. After the events of yesterday, winning the woman's trust had become a matter of greater urgency.

But first Meg had to find her. Surely in a village the size of Pernod, that should not prove too difficult. Meg fortified herself with another lungful of bracing morning air and returned to the shed to wake the sleeping countess.

〰〰

THE MORNING WANED SWIFTLY ALONG WITH MEG'S OPTIMISM. By the time she made her third circuit of the village without encountering la Mère Poulet, Meg seethed with a mingling of frustration and anxiety.

Over Seraphine's protests, she and Meg had parted company to search in opposite directions. Meg only hoped that Seraphine was having better luck than she was. La Mère Poulet lived as a vagrant, but the poor old soul must have sought refuge from the storm somewhere last night.

Surely someone in Pernod might have been compassionate enough to give the old woman shelter. But Meg had seen little of kindness in any of the faces she had encountered this morning. No one was inclined to offer her so much as a good morrow, let alone answer her inquiries after la Mère Poulet.

Meg overheard enough mutterings to guess at the rumors being spread, that Meg had employed some dark magic to induce Bridget Tillet to confess. If she had possessed such power, Meg thought she would have used it to melt some of these stony hearts and to grow herself a new pair of feet, ones less sore and aching.

She trudged back down the lane, feeling the full effects of her restless night. She had not taken the time to breakfast or even wash her face this morning. Tired, bedraggled, and hungry, she recollected a barrel left to gather rainwater near the inn. At least, she might take a brief pause to refresh herself.

Meg headed in that direction, shoving up her sleeves in anticipation of a reviving splash of water. Unfortunately someone else had the same idea. Meg drew up in dismay to discover Blackwood there before her.

The doctor bent and thrust his entire head inside the barrel. He came up dripping, water streaming from his hair and beard. Meg would not have been surprised to see him shake it off like a mongrel dog. But considering the amount of wine he had imbibed last night, it would have been an action most ill-advised.

Blackwood had enough wit to realize that. Using both hands, he slicked his hair back from his eyes. He straightened as his bloodshot gaze came to rest upon her. Every instinct she possessed urged Meg to beat a swift retreat, but something inside her revolted at allowing herself to be intimidated by this man.

She didn't understand what imp took possession of her,

perhaps one born of her own frustration and exhaustion or her intense dislike and contempt for Blackwood. In an action far more worthy of Seraphine, Meg stepped closer and announced in a loud bright voice, "Good morrow!"

She was gratified to see Blackwood wince.

"There is nothing good about it, so kindly refrain from shouting at me."

"Did you have a difficult night, Doctor? You look most unwell. I daresay you are suffering from a surfeit of black humors coursing through your veins. Perhaps it would help if you were bled."

He regarded her dourly. "I don't think anything would help my head except for decapitation. What the devil do these Bretons put in that vile brew you call wine? Even the chunk of amethyst I keep in my purse was of no avail."

"Amethyst? Of what use would that be?"

"You have never heard that an amethyst has the power to ward off the effects of too much drink? What manner of cunning woman are you?"

"You seriously believe in such nonsense? What manner of doctor are you? Instead of putting the rock in your purse, shove it in your mouth next time."

"My mouth?"

"Yes, then it would serve a twofold purpose. Keep you from drinking and exposing your ignorance. Good day to you, monsieur."

Meg turned to make a haughty exit, but Blackwood caught hold of her wrist. His grip was not as painful as the last time, but firm enough to prevent her twisting free.

"Unhand me at once!"

Blackwood ignored her, inspecting the bruises on her forearm. "Did . . . did I do that?"

"Since I cannot recall wrestling with anyone else last night, you must be to blame. Now let me go before you snap my wrist as well."

He frowned, releasing her. Meg rolled down her sleeves, covering the bruises.

Blackwood had a naturally ruddy complexion but a deeper stain of red washed his cheeks. "Sorry. I didn't mean— I was just—"

"Drunk? Men frequently use that to explain away loutish behavior. A poor excuse in my opinion."

"Mine too. That is why I never use it."

"Then what excuse do you offer?"

"That I am an ass."

"I entirely agree with you, but I am astonished you so freely admit it."

"Why not? It is not as though it is a condition I can easily conceal. I would like to blame it on the wine or assure you it doesn't happen that often. But drunk or sober I must warn you I am an ass most of the time."

Meg studied him, trying to decide if he was in jest or earnest. His expression was solemn, but a hint of wry humor touched his lips. She had to bite back an unexpected urge to smile.

"Thank you for the warning, monsieur. I shall do my best to avoid you."

"You should," he agreed affably. "But not just yet, because I happen to be the ass who has found what you are looking for."

"How do you know I have been searching for anything?"

"My dear woman, you have been rushing up and down the lanes all morning. The entire village knows you have been hunting for that old woman they call la Mère Poulet and are unable to find her."

"And you claim that *you* have been able to do so?"

"Oh, yes." Blackwood grimaced, displaying the angry red scratches on the back of his hands. "And I have the battle scars to prove it."

᛭᛭᛭

MEG FOLLOWED BLACKWOOD DOWN THE BEACH, HER HEART full of misgivings. She had little reason to trust the man. His claim of where he had found la Mère Poulet made little sense.

This stretch of shore was far too open and exposed, the rocks offering little by way of concealment or shelter. A rough wind blew off the channel and Meg was obliged to constantly brush tangles of hair from her eyes.

She cast a nervous glance over her shoulder, aware of how far they had strayed from the confines of the village. If Blackwood had lured her down here for some sinister purpose of his own, there would be no one to see, no one to hear Meg's cries but the gulls that wheeled overhead.

But Blackwood did not appear to care whether she accompanied him or not. When she lagged behind, he did not even look back to make sure she was still there.

Meg quickened her steps to draw apace with him. If nothing else, his large frame provided a break from the wind. Blackwood had lapsed into silence since leaving the village, which suited Meg.

It made it easier to study him. She hardly knew what to think of the man. She would have expected him to be still abed at this hour, nursing a throbbing head, or if he was able to rise, then eager to saddle his mount and be off. Blackwood didn't strike her as the sort of man to bestir himself for his closest friends, let alone take the trouble to search for a half-mad old woman he had never even met. She could only question what the doctor's motives might be.

The doctor . . . that was another thing that unsettled her. Blackwood was unlike any other physician she had ever met, most of them pompous graybeards in their long black robes, more eager to show off their Latin and Greek than display any useful healing skills. Blackwood appeared as arrogant and ignorant as any of the breed, but he lacked the pedantic manner. With his broad shoulders, strapping height, sun-burned complexion, and rough beard, he more resembled a mariner or a soldier, the kind of rogue who would loll about in alehouses between battles, drinking away his coin or losing it at dice.

It was difficult to guess his age. Lines creased his eyes, but those were likely the wages of hard living and dissipated habits. His upright bearing and the vitality of his movements suggested a man in his prime, perhaps not much more than thirty.

Blackwood angled a sidewise glance at her and scowled. "Don't stare. It's rude."

"I am sorry," Meg said, although she thought that Black-wood was hardly the one to lecture her on good manners. "But you puzzle me exceedingly. Why did you bother seeking out la Mère Poulet?"

"I imagine for the same reason that you are. To keep an innocent old crone from ending up with her neck stretched. That is the only reason I staggered upstairs last night to try to deal with that lying little strumpet."

"Then you realized that Bridget was faking her illness?"

"Any fool could tell . . . well, except the ones that live in this village. I scarcely had to examine the chit before I wanted to wring her skinny neck."

"Because you despise liars?"

Blackwood laughed. "Lord no, I am an accomplished liar myself. I rather admire the art except when it is fueled by malice or intended to cause pain and ruin."

His expression darkened. "No, it is injustice that I hate and I have seen too damn much of that. I'd do battle with the devil himself before I'd ever see another innocent harmed."

"Bridget behaved very badly, but she is hardly the devil." Meg cast him a troubled look. "You knew she was faking and yet you were going to take your knife to her."

"I only brandished my lancet to alarm her, to get her to admit the truth."

"I doubt your crude method would have worked. You came closer to frightening her into hysterics."

"So what brilliant means did you employ? The entire village suspects you of mesmerizing or enchanting the girl. I confess that I, too, am curious to know your secret."

Meg hesitated, but decided there could be no harm in telling him. As she explained her ruse with the burned lock of hair, Blackwood looked grudgingly impressed.

"Very clever, milady. I will have to remember your little trick if I am ever confronted with a similar situation."

"I doubt that you could pull it off. After all, you are not . . . what was it you called me last night? *A witch with pretensions to supernatural powers.*"

Of all Blackwood's insults, Meg was surprised that she still remembered that one so well or that it had had the power to sting.

He came to an abrupt halt. "Did I say that to you? Then I must have been drunker than I realized."

The wind ruffled his hair, making him appear wilder and rougher than ever, but something gentled in his face. "Forgive me. I am truly sorry."

He meant it. There was none of his usual offhand manner or mockery in his tone. His apology astonished her, left her more confused about the man than ever.

Meg stared up at him, desperately trying to read Blackwood's eyes. They were not as dark as they had appeared by the dim light of the candles last night, but rather a deep blue-gray, the same hue as the overcast sky.

She remembered being alarmed by his gaze, finding it as chillingly empty as her blind mother's had been, but she was wrong. If anything, there was too much going on behind Blackwood's eyes, the man more of a cauldron than an abyss; too many simmering emotions, thoughts, and memories for her to gain an accurate read on him.

Her earnest probing appeared to make Blackwood uncomfortable. He resumed walking, his features settling into his usual indolent expression.

"Ah, here we are at last," he said. "Chez la Mère Poulet."

He indicated a distant structure that looked at first like nothing more than the wreckage of a boat that had been washed ashore. Perhaps at one time, that was what it had been.

But as they drew nearer, Meg saw that the broken hull had been cobbled together with other stray boards to form a shelter of sorts. The hut had been constructed far up from the shore's edge, nestled among some jutting rocks to protect it from the wind. One strong gust would surely have been enough to bring the entire ramshackle thing crashing down.

Meg marveled that last night's storm had not been enough to do so.

Blackwood clambered upward in a series of long strides. Plucking up the hem of her skirts, Meg proceeded more slowly. Even so, she nearly lost her footing and stumbled.

Blackwood turned and offered his hand to steady her and Meg accepted after only a brief hesitation. His palm was warm and not calloused, as she would have expected considering the rest of his rough exterior. His hand was surprisingly well formed, strong with long fingers, his nails clean and neatly trimmed.

He pulled her beside him on the ledge near the hut. On closer inspection, it bore the appearance of a low wooden cave with a flap of canvas nailed over the opening.

"Hortense," Blackwood called out. "It is me. I have returned as promised."

"Hortense?" Meg asked as she withdrew her hand from his grasp.

"Hortense Matisse. That is the real name of the woman you all call la Mère Poulet."

"How do you know that?"

"I asked her."

Which was more than anyone else had ever thought to do, including her, Meg reflected with a twinge of shame.

The canvas flap stirred, and Hortense peered out, twitching her sharp nose like an inquisitive ferret. The old woman brightened at the sight of Blackwood, her lips parting in a near-toothless grin. The beaming smile vanished when she noticed Meg.

"Who's that with you?" Hortense demanded.

"This is the famous Lady of Faire Isle. She has been looking for you, too."

"Why?"

Meg hunkered down so that she would be at eye level with the old woman. "Because I have long wanted to make your acquaintance, la Mère Poul—I mean Hortense."

"That would be Madame Matisse to you, mistress sauce box."

"I do beg your pardon. I did not mean to offend you. I have come to extend you an invitation to visit my island."

"That vile place? No, thank you."

"I fear you must have heard too many alarming stories from the villagers about how Faire Isle is the haven of witches."

"Witches, bah! I am not afraid of witches. I enjoy pretending to be one myself from time to time." The old woman laughed before puckering into a frown. "It is the other tales of your island I don't like, the fact that the place is full of women."

"Faire Isle is mostly the home of many women, the wives and daughters of captains and sailors who are long absent at sea."

"I don't much like the company of women." Hortense leered up at Blackwood. "I prefer men."

"We do have some men. There is a small harbor on Faire Isle where trading vessels dock from the mainland. There is an inn called the Passing Stranger where seamen and merchants gather."

"Would he be there?" Hortense interrupted, pointing at Blackwood.

"Well, no—"

"Then I am not interested."

The old woman ducked into her cave, the canvas falling back into place. Meg looked up at Blackwood. His expression was grave, but she could tell he was trying not to laugh. She had a strong suspicion that the doctor had anticipated her difficulty with Hortense, but had kept silent, relishing the prospect.

She straightened up, saying tartly, "You might have warned me how she was going to react."

His eyes widened in feigned innocence. "How the devil was I supposed to know?"

"The two of you appear to have become fast friends. She seems quite smitten with you."

"I frequently have that effect on women, especially the nearsighted ones."

Meg glared at him and then expelled a frustrated sigh. She wracked her brain for another way to approach the old woman, a more persuasive argument, but she could not come up with anything. She was tired, she was hungry. She just wanted to go home. But she had to try again.

She moved toward the hut, reaching out to twitch the canvas flap out of the way to peek inside. But Blackwood stopped her.

"I wouldn't do that if I were you. Hortense doesn't care for uninvited guests, but Marcela is even worse."

"Marcela? Who is Marcela?"

"Hortense's chicken." Blackwood displayed the back of his scratched hand. "Marcela hates visitors or perhaps just me. I cannot blame her after the way I mauled her about, trying to mend her broken wing."

"You tried to heal an injured *chicken*?"

"I admit I am far more accustomed to ripping the wings off of a capon, especially after it has been broiled to a nice golden brown and accompanied by a generous helping of roasted turnips.

"I made an effort to help Marcela, but with little success. Have *you* ever tried to put a splint on a chicken?"

"No, I—" Meg began, when she was struck by the ridiculousness of this entire situation. An image filled her mind of Blackwood struggling with a squawking hen, pecking and scratching at him, its feathers puffed up with fury. Meg couldn't help it. She laughed.

Blackwood tipped his head to one side to peer down at her. "Ah, so you do know how to laugh. I was beginning to wonder. You are such a serious little thing."

Meg tried to resume her gravity, but her lips quivered. Blackwood crooked his fingers beneath her chin. He tipped her head up, inspecting her countenance.

"You ought to laugh more often. It improves your face. You look almost pretty."

It was the sort of compliment she would have expected from Blackwood, blunt almost to the point of being offensive. Yet Meg preferred it to the kind of flattery she'd had from other men who had told her she was beautiful, which she knew she wasn't. At least Blackwood's words, the warmth of approval in his eyes, seemed genuine enough to bring a faint blush to her cheeks.

Annoyed with herself, Meg pushed his hand away. Between the hostile chicken, the eccentric old woman, and Blackwood, who seemed a bit mad himself, this was beginning to feel like being caught up in a dream stranger than the one she had had last night.

A dream that was destined to wax stranger still, Meg thought as she noticed the two figures traveling in tandem down the beach, heading rapidly in their direction. The pairing of Sir Patrick Graham and Seraphine struck Meg as being as incongruous as herself and Blackwood.

Sir Patrick looked as somber as he had last night. Even the wind tugging at his short cloak and feathered cap did little to ruffle his aura of calm. Seraphine on the other hand resembled a wrathful goddess, her blond hair cascading over her shoulders in a wild tangle, one hand twitching on the hilt of her sword.

Blackwood stiffened beside her. He also had caught sight of the pair. He swore under his breath, not the sort of reaction that Seraphine usually engendered in men.

But as Meg and Blackwood descended the rocky slope to meet the pair, Meg realized that Blackwood did not even appear to notice Seraphine. His unwelcoming scowl and his stony regard were directed at his friend.

Sir Patrick bowed to Meg, but before he could speak, he was cut off by Seraphine. "Damnation, Margaret Wolfe, you frightened me half to death. What did you think you were doing, disappearing this way?"

"I was searching for la Mère Poulet. You do recall that was why we split paths and took separate directions."

"Which I never thought was a good idea. But I thought you would at least have the good sense to confine your search to the village, not go wandering off to some remote spot with this—this—" Seraphine gestured toward Blackwood.

"This doctor," Meg filled in before Seraphine could come up with a more insulting epithet. "I am sorry if I worried you, but all is well. We have found la Mère Poulet, or rather we must thank Dr. Blackwood for that."

Seraphine appeared more inclined to run the man through than thank him. She glowered at him as though she had caught him attempting to ravish Meg. But the doctor was oblivious to Seraphine's murderous look, his attention focused on Sir Patrick.

"Graham, you should have waited back at the inn. There was no need to come in search of me. I told you I could handle this matter."

"I was sure that you could, at least with regard to the old woman. I did not come here in search of you." Graham's tone was as mild as Blackwood's was curt. The knight shifted to address Meg.

"It was you whom I needed to find this morning. I was hoping that I could speak to—"

"So there she is. Speak," Seraphine said.

"I would speak to you alone," Sir Patrick continued as though he had not been interrupted. "Would you honor me with a few moments of private conversation?"

"No!" Seraphine and Blackwood snapped in unison.

"This is a waste of your time, Graham," Blackwood added. "She will not be interested."

Seraphine scowled. "And there is nothing you could have to say to her that I cannot hear."

"*She* is standing right here," Meg said tartly. "So will you kindly allow *her* to reply?"

Seraphine grabbed Meg's arm and dragged her aside. "Meg, you should not go anywhere alone with that man. You were foolhardy enough to wander off with that drunken doctor."

"I thought you had decided Dr. Blackwood and Sir Patrick were naught but a pair of idle travelers. You even teased me for being so nervous about them."

"I have changed my mind. There is something amiss with both of them, especially Graham. He has been asking far too many questions about you at the inn, among the villagers. He even had the impertinence to press me for details about how long you had been the Lady of Faire Isle, where you hailed from before that. I get the impression the man wants something from you. I have no idea what that might be, but I don't like it."

"Neither do I. But would it not be better to speak with Sir Patrick and find out?"

Seraphine pursed her lips. "I suppose. My father taught me it is always best to know as much of one's enemy as possible. But only go a few yards down the beach with that man. You stay within my sight."

Meg nodded in agreement and then stepped toward Graham, who patiently awaited her decision.

"I cannot imagine what you have to say to me, Sir Patrick, but I am willing to listen."

Blackwood muttered something and Meg half expected him to protest again. But when she looked at him, he merely shrugged as though the matter was no longer of any consequence to him.

"Five minutes," Seraphine warned Graham. "That is all the time the Lady can spare. The two men—the two very large, muscular young men—who rowed us over from Faire Isle are preparing our boat to launch. Jacques and Louis fear we are due for another rainstorm, so we must gather up the old lady and go."

Meg looked up at the hut. The canvas stirred and she saw Hortense observing them. When she realized she had been spotted, Hortense ducked back out of sight.

"Er, Seraphine, that may prove a little difficult. I don't think la Mère Poulet wants to be *gathered.*"

"Where is she? Hiding up there beneath that pile of wood? I'll fetch her out fast enough."

Seraphine started up the hill only to have her way barred by Blackwood.

"I'll fetch her. I can persuade her far more readily than you."

"How?" Seraphine sneered. "By trying to get her drunk? Regaling her with bottles of wine as you did the entire tap-room last night?"

"No, by tossing you into the channel. I am sure Hortense would find that far more entertaining."

"I should like to see you try it!"

Blackwood strode toward the hut with Seraphine hard on his heels, the two snarling at each other the entire way. Meg watched them go uneasily.

"You need have no fear for your friend, my lady," Sir Patrick said. "Blackwood might roar and bluster, but he would never harm a woman."

Meg turned toward him. "Actually it was not my *friend* I was worried about."

"Yes, I have observed that Madame La Comtesse can be a trifle . . . forceful, but Blackwood is equally hardheaded. I fear that yon slope might be about to witness a battle to rival anything between the gods upon Mount Olympus. Perhaps we might retreat to a quieter distance." He offered her a rueful smile and his arm.

Meg hesitated. Seraphine had referred to Graham as the enemy, but Meg was having difficulty thinking of him that way. Not just because he was a handsome man, which he was. He had the sort of Adonis countenance capable of melting most women's defenses.

Unlike the unkempt Blackwood, every article of Graham's clothing was neat and clean. The only thing at all out of place was a single gold-tipped curl that persisted in straying across the man's forehead, but only added to his charm.

Yet it wasn't his physical appearance that Meg found attractive, but his courteous manner, his gravity, the melancholy in his gaze that tugged at something in her own heart. When he smiled, it didn't reach his eyes, but not in the chilling manner she had observed in cold, calculating men.

It was more as if Sir Patrick had long since forgotten how to smile and had to struggle to remember. Meg could understand that all too well, weighed down as she often was with memories of her mother, the fear of the past she had buried rising up to haunt her again.

So what was Sir Patrick's great burden? Meg wondered as she rested her hand upon the crook of his arm and they strolled along the shoreline.

"I hope that my request for this talk did not alarm you," he said.

"That will depend on what it is about and who you are."

"I told you. I am Sir Patrick Graham and—"

"I know your name." Or at least she believed she did. He could well be traveling under an assumed identity, although she had no reason to think so.

"A name tells one nothing," Meg went on. "It gives me no idea of who you are."

"I am no one of any particular importance, the oldest son of a modest but respected family from Middlesex. After being educated at Oxford, I journeyed to London to make my fortune, as so many young men do.

"I have achieved neither great success nor great failure. At present I am engaged as clerk for the king's privy council."

"That sounds quite important to me."

"There are many such clerks, overworked and poorly paid. Still I do not complain. It is a mark of good fortune to acquire any post at court, no matter how minor."

"Then I congratulate you, but I am more confused than

ever. What brings a clerk of the English privy council to such a remote place as Pernod?"

"Pernod was not my final destination." He stopped and stared down at her. "You were. I was coming to Faire Isle in search of you."

"I see," she said, forcing a light note to her voice. "Should I be alarmed or flattered?"

"I do not think you are the sort of woman who cares to be flattered. But you should know that the legend of the Lady of Faire Isle is known and spoken of, even in London."

Meg could endure that, as long as it was the legend of the Lady under discussion. Not Margaret Wolfe or, worse still, Megaera.

"So what did you hear about the Lady of Faire Isle that induced you to come in search of her?" Meg asked.

"That she—I mean you were a sorceress of incredible beauty and power, well versed in all the arts of magic and healing. I confess I did not believe it. I thought it must all be a myth."

"Now that you have met me, you can see that it is."

"On the contrary, after what I witnessed at the inn last night, I realized that the stories about you are all true. The way that you resolved the matter of Mistress Tillet's bewitchment—"

"The girl was not bewitched! I did nothing but expose her trickery. That was all."

"All? You saw through her lies when no one else did. You knew she was faking."

"Apparently so did your friend, Blackwood."

"But you were the one who brought an end to it. I am told you have much experience in these matters of feigned bewitchment."

"From time to time, I have been called upon to deal with someone behaving as if they were possessed, claims that always prove to be false."

"Always? Then you do not think that there is such a thing as bewitchment, that someone really could be cursed by a sorceress?" Graham searched her face intently. "You do not believe in the existence of evil?"

Meg thought of her mother and suppressed a shiver. "I do not dismiss the possibility of such black magic, but I pray it would be rare."

"If someone was damned by a witch, could you help them? Could you remove the curse?"

"I don't know." Meg frowned up at him. "Whom do you believe has been cursed, Sir Patrick? You?"

"No, I thank God."

"Then some friend of yours?"

"I cannot presume to call him that."

Graham's hedging started to irritate Meg. "Then what can you presume to call him? What is this man's name?"

Graham paused and finally said. "James Stuart."

"James Stuart?" Meg stared at him, incredulous. "You cannot possibly mean—"

"Yes, I do," Sir Patrick replied gravely.

"James Charles Stuart, the king of England."

Chapter Six

MEG REGARDED SIR PATRICK IN STUNNED SILENCE, WONDER-
ing if she had lost all ability to judge a man's character. She
had believed Graham to be sober and sensible, but it would
seem as though he was as mad as his friend.

"I am sure I did not understand you," Meg said. "You are
telling me that you believe the king of England is possessed?"

"Not possessed, *cursed*. His Majesty labors under the
weight of a terrible curse that was laid upon him."

If Blackwood had told her such a thing, Meg would have
been tempted to dismiss the remark as more of the man's odd
humor. Graham looked so earnest, she did not know what to
think.

"I fear I am explaining all this very badly," he said. "Perhaps I should start over again at the very beginning when all
these tragic events were first set into motion."

"Yes, perhaps you should."

They walked for a moment in silence as Sir Patrick strove to marshal his thoughts.

"It all began nearly fifteen years ago in Edinburgh. James Stuart had not yet succeeded to the English throne. He was but the king of Scots, a young man and in need of a bride. His choice settled upon Princess Anne of Denmark and James made an extraordinary gesture for a sovereign king. Rather than having his bride fetched to him as is the custom, James sailed across the waters to wed the princess in her own land.

"It was a romantic decision rather than a wise one. Our country has never been a tame—"

"*Our* country?" Meg echoed. "But I thought you said that you hailed from Middlesex?"

Sir Patrick looked discomfited by her interruption. "My mother was from Scotland, so as a lad I spent many summers on my uncle's manor and felt quite at home there. But to continue what I was saying, *Scotland* is a rough land with a long history of rebellion, powerful lairds rivaling each other for power, constantly ready to challenge the king, especially one who displayed any sign of weakness.

"James had one subject who was particularly troublesome, the Earl of Bothwell. He was the nephew of that same Bothwell who had abducted the king's late mother, Mary Stuart. I fear the lairds of Bothwell have always been unruly, troublesome subjects.

"The present earl took full advantage of the king's absence to lay a plot against His Majesty of a most dark and unexpected nature. When King James tried to sail home to Scotland with his new bride, the royal fleet was beset with storms."

Meg stiffened beside Sir Patrick, aware of the direction his tale would take.

"It was a miracle the king was able to come to safe harbor. It did not take long after that for it to be discovered—"

"That a coven of witches was responsible," Meg said. "You need not continue, Sir Patrick. I am sorry to say I am quite familiar with what happened next."

"How could you be? You could have been no more than a child when this all occurred."

"I was old enough and we have a collective memory for sorrow on Faire Isle, particularly where it concerns the fate of wise women. When word of the Scottish witch trials reached our island, we all went into mourning. All of those poor lost souls, hundreds of innocent women and men as well, accused of conjuring against the king, being arrested and tortured. So many put to death, burned at the stake."

Meg closed her eyes briefly, willing away the terrible image. "It is the secret dread of every woman who dares to practice the arts of healing and keep the ancient knowledge alive. You cannot possibly imagine—"

"Yes, I can and I share your horror of such a death." Something caught in Sir Patrick's throat and he coughed to clear it. "But not everyone who was arrested was innocent. There was a coven of witches who gathered at midnight in a church. They profaned that holy place with their satanic rituals, burning wax figures of the king, chanting evil spells to brew up storms to destroy his fleet."

"Evil and profane, certainly, but still nonsense. I have never known anyone with the power to conjure storms or cause harm by playing with wax poppets. Your king should have directed his anger at whoever instigated this treasonous plot against him."

"That was thought to be the Earl of Bothwell. He was also accused of witchcraft, but the charges were eventually dismissed. No one could link him to the witches and many believed the charges were false, an effort to discredit the earl. Bothwell had many powerful enemies at the king's court and then there was the strange matter of the woman known as Old Tam."

"Old Tam?"

"That was what most people called her, but at her trial she was listed as Tamsin Rivers. Out of all those tried and condemned, she appears to have been a genuine witch."

"What makes you say that?"

"His Majesty claims that she knew things about him, intimate details that no stranger should have known. It was Old Tam who cursed the king. She did so with her very last breath as she was being consumed by the flames."

"If I was being burned alive, I am sure I would have hurled curses at him, too."

"No, you would not have. Not from what I have witnessed of your courage, kindness, and forbearance."

Meg was flattered by the warmth of his praise, although she did not deserve it. Sir Patrick did not know her, what she had almost done. Few people did.

She thought of the blackest moment of her life when she had hovered by the bedside of her enemy, Catherine de Medici, the witch blade laced with poison hidden in the folds of Meg's skirt. More than the queen's life had teetered in the balance that day. Meg's soul had as well. She had come so close to surrendering to the darkness that day, only saved by a breath of hesitation, a whisper of sanity. The memory would always remind her of what she was capable. If she did not remain vigilant, it would be far too easy to become her mother's daughter.

"It was a most terrible curse that old woman laid upon

the king," Sir Patrick continued. *"Damn ye to hell, James of Scotland. May ye one day also perish in fire. My curse upon the House of Stuart!"*

Meg started at the change in his voice, thick with a Scottish accent. Meg's father could easily have pulled off such a performance. Martin Wolfe was a gifted actor, but Meg would have thought such skill of mimicry beyond the quiet Sir Patrick. Was the accent some holdover of memory from his boyhood summers in Scotland?

She regarded him curiously. "How well you remember all of this, Sir Patrick. Were you present at the old woman's execution?"

"No, I but repeat the curse as I was told by the king. These words have preyed upon His Majesty's mind ever since that day."

"And therein lies the power of a curse, the mental torment that it can inflict upon its victim. Obviously the curse has not come true. Many years have passed and the king remains unharmed."

"Thus far. But of late, the king has been much tormented. He claims to have received notes that appear to be written in blood, notes that threaten him. *The curse is upon you, James Stuart. Soon you will burn.* Even more disturbing, His Majesty has seen *her.*"

"Who?"

"Tamsin Rivers."

"The woman he executed? Impossible!" Meg exclaimed. "Surely the king was mistaken."

"His Majesty swears he will never forget that old witch's evil countenance. He has seen her on a number of occasions, clamoring for alms in the company of a blind beggar woman at the crossroads, spying upon him from a copse of trees when he was hunting. Once he even saw her lurking outside the palace walls at Whitehall."

"And did anyone else ever see her?"

"Well, no. The king did send his yeoman guards after her, but she had vanished into thin air.

"Like a ghost," Sir Patrick added uncomfortably. When Meg made an impatient sound, he asked, "You do not believe the dead can rise from their graves?"

Meg longed to declare that she didn't, but she was haunted by the memory of Cassandra Lascelles waving her gaunt white hands over her steaming copper basin, conjuring forth the vision of some terrifying spirit.

"I do not discount the possibility of a ghost," Meg said. "But I think it far more likely your king suffers from delusions of the mind. Perhaps he is finally having an attack of conscience over all of those women he burned."

"Or an attack brought on by a witch's curse."

"Either way, I am not sure why you are telling me all of this."

Sir Patrick halted and turned to face her. "Because I was hoping you would return with me to London and use your extraordinary powers to help His Majesty."

Meg stared at him, incredulous. "If you were hoping that, sir, I fear you are infected with the same madness as your king."

"It is not madness. Indeed, there is precedence for such a thing. When the late Queen Elizabeth was threatened by an enemy trying to hex her, she consulted a magus, Dr. John Dee."

"That was entirely different. Dr. Dee was Elizabeth's astrologer and tutor and yet there came a time when he had to flee England to escape charges of sorcery. If such a thing could befall a man who was the queen's trusted confidant for years, how do you think I would fare with a king who is notorious for burning witches? Since James Stuart came to the English throne, I hear that your laws against witchcraft are more stringent than ever."

"Nay, I assure you the king is much wiser than he was in his youth, much more careful about leveling accusations of sorcery. The harsher laws against witches are due to parliament rather than the king."

"Oh, that makes me feel so much better," Meg said tartly. "I would only risk running afoul of the entire English government."

"The king would answer for your safety. I will admit His Majesty does not often seek advice from any woman, but these recent disturbing events have made him desperate."

"Then he should rely upon his own ministers and officials to investigate." Meg resumed walking, wanting to put an end to this disturbing proposal, but Sir Patrick kept pace beside her, his voice low and persuasive.

"None of them possess your skill or your knowledge of the supernatural."

"What if this has nothing to do with the supernatural? It seems to me far more likely that someone is playing some malicious jest upon His Majesty with the design of tormenting him or seeking revenge. Did this Tamsin Rivers have any family?"

"She may have had some granddaughters. There were two young women rumored to have attended her execution, but if so, they fled Edinburgh shortly thereafter."

"Very prudent of them. It is never healthy to have a witch for a grandmother." Or a mother, Meg thought bleakly.

"Of course, there was also the other woman Tam spoke of at her trial. She heaped scorn upon the notion that she was in the service of the Earl of Bothwell or even the devil. *'I serve no man,'* she boasted. *'I serve no one but my mistress, the greatest sorceress who ever lived, Megaera.'"*

Meg steeled her countenance not to react, but she could not help flinching at the sound of her former name.

"You have heard of this witch?"

"No, I—I—" If Sir Patrick had not given her such a shock, Meg might have been able to make a plausible denial. Instead she stammered, "Well, yes, there—there have always been these stories about a sorceress called the Silver Rose. Nothing but ridiculous myths, I am sure."

"The Silver Rose. But that could explain a great deal."

"Explain what?" Meg asked sharply.

"The report given by one of the guards the king sent out to seize Tamsin Rivers when she appeared in the courtyard. He could locate no trace of her, but on the ground, he found a curious scattering of petals, but like none he had ever seen. The rose petals glittered as though they were coated with silver."

Meg felt the color drain from her face.

"You have gone so pale." Sir Patrick peered down at her. "Are you unwell?"

Meg moistened her lips, which had suddenly gone dry. "I—I am fine. It is only I—I must have forgotten my cloak back at the inn and I was struck with a sudden chill."

"Here. Allow me."

Before Meg could protest, he swept off his cape and draped it about her shoulders. The fabric was warm from his body heat and redolent of sandalwood. He did up the silver clasp at her neck and touched his hand to her cheek.

"Better?" he asked with a smile.

"Yes. I thank you." She was aware that her heartbeat had quickened and she tried to draw away, feeling embarrassed. But he caught both of her hands in the warmth of his grasp.

"If you would consent to return with me to England, you would travel under my protection. I would spare no effort to see to your safety and comfort. You cannot imagine how much I need—how much the king needs you. Will you come?"

Their gazes locked and Meg felt dangerously drawn by the plea in his deep blue eyes.

"I don't know. I need time to think."

"I wish I could allow all the time you require, but as you must understand, this is a matter of some urgency. I can afford to linger here but one more day. If you could give me your answer by this evening?"

Meg nodded, turning away from him. She realized she had broken her promise to Seraphine and wandered well out of view of la Mère Poulet's makeshift hut.

Quickening her pace, she outstripped Sir Patrick on the walk back or perhaps he lingered behind on purpose to allow her time to mull over all that she had heard. Meg huddled beneath the cape, grateful for its enveloping warmth. She was still chilled by the revelation of Old Tam's boast.

"I serve no one but my mistress, the greatest sorceress who ever lived, Megaera."

Meg struggled to recall all those times her mother had forced her to appear before the Silver Rose devotees, Meg sweltering in heavy robes and wearing a crown as though she had been a queen. Seated upon a throne so high her feet had not even touched the floor, Meg had been obliged to extend her small hand while the members of the coven had knelt to her and pledged their homage.

Try as she might, Meg could not recollect anyone who had been named Tamsin Rivers. But that was hardly surprising. There had been far too many of those deluded women her mother had recruited to the banner of the Silver Rose.

After the drowning of Cassandra Lascelles, the coven had scattered, fleeing from both witch-hunters and the Dark Queen's soldiers. Was it possible that one of them had managed to escape as far away as Scotland?

It shouldn't matter because Old Tam was dead. Meg could not believe her spirit had risen to torment the king and carry out her curse. But someone was doing so, someone very much alive and possessing knowledge of the coven, someone with the ability to coat roses with a silver sheen.

Who? Meg shivered, too afraid to consider a certain possibility. Lost in the turmoil of her thoughts, she did not notice Armagil Blackwood until he loomed in her path. Unable to check her steps, she collided with him. It was like walking into a granite wall and she stumbled back. He seized her shoulders to steady her.

"Whoa! Watch where you are—" He broke off as he caught sight of her face. "What the devil's the matter with you, woman? You look like you have seen a ghost."

He had no idea. Meg had to suppress a hysterical urge to laugh. She stammered some excuse about having walked too far and being tired, but Blackwood didn't appear to listen.

His gaze riveted on Sir Patrick's cape draped about her shoulders and one of his brows lifted. Meg was annoyed when her cheeks heated. She shrugged away from Blackwood and self-consciously smoothed the folds of the fabric.

Before he could make some irritating remark, Meg asked, "How is Hortense?"

"I have persuaded her to go to Faire Isle and Madame la

Comtesse is helping the old lady gather up her things. That should not take long, but you had better make haste before Hortense changes her mind. Both of you need to head for that island of yours. *And stay there!*"

There was no mistaking the edge behind Blackwood's last three words or the sharp look he gave her.

"I imagine you are aware of what Sir Patrick has asked me to do," she said.

"I am and he did so against my counsel."

"But he said the king—"

"The king be damned. Go back to Faire Isle and forget all of this. Don't meddle in what is none of your concern." Blackwood spoke so harshly and looked so angry, Meg retreated a step.

"Is that your advice or a warning?"

"Take it how you will. I make no claims to any nobility or chivalry. But occasionally, I am prompted by the better angel of my nature, although I rarely heed her whisper anymore." Despite his anger, something bleak dulled his eyes. "But you would be wise to do so."

He strode away before Meg could question him, heading back up to Hortense's hut. He brushed past Seraphine, who had arrived in time to hear his last remark.

She regarded Meg suspiciously. "Wise to do what? What is going on, Meg? What did Graham want with you?"

Meg longed for more time for quiet reflection, but she saw no way of avoiding Seraphine's questions. She related the conversation between her and Sir Patrick as succinctly as possible, while bracing herself for the inevitable explosion.

She had barely reached the end of her tale before Seraphine shrieked at her. "Have you taken complete leave of your senses? What do you mean, you need time to consider your answer? There can be only one reply to such a mad request. Hell and damnation, no!"

"It is not that simple."

"Yes, it is." Seraphine paced up and down, flinging out her arms in a wild gesture as though mere words were not enough to express the depth of her outrage. "Risk your neck by traveling all the way to England to save James Stuart from his own demons? Why? You know what that man is. Among other things, he is the author of a treatise on how to detect and examine witches. His *Daemonology* might as well be a witch-hunter's bible."

"I know. I read it upon Ariane's advice. She believed it wise to make a study of the superstitions and misunderstanding regarding witchcraft."

"She told me to read it, too. I got as far as the first chapter before I tore it to bits and threw what was left into the fire."

"James Stuart was a young man when he wrote the book. Sir Patrick believes the king has grown wiser."

"Wiser how?" Seraphine scoffed. "Has he honed his talents for tormenting and burning innocent women? He seems to me skilled enough. He is already responsible for the death of too many."

"Nonetheless—"

"There is no 'nonetheless' this time, Meg. I know you feel obliged to investigate any rumor involving your mother's old coven, but—"

"I fear it is more than a rumor this time. The king has most likely imagined seeing Tamsin Rivers, but those silver petals the king's guard found were very real.

"That guard was fortunate it was only the petals and not the rose itself with its poisonous thorn. A most deadly toxin, it produced a terribly painful, lingering death. Even among the coven, there were few Maman trusted to brew it. It was a difficult potion to get right and I hoped . . . I believed everyone who knew how to do so was dead."

Meg bit down upon her lip. "Sir Patrick mentioned something else that alarmed me, although he could not know the significance of it. He said the king believed he saw Tamsin Rivers in the company of a beggar woman, a *blind* beggar woman."

Seraphine halted her pacing to stare at her. "Oh, Meg! You cannot be imagining that your mother might be behind all of this? That Cassandra Lascelles is still alive? You saw her drown."

"No, I saw her vanish beneath the waters of the Seine, but her body was never found. I presumed she was dead, but a part of me has always wondered and feared."

"But if somehow she had survived, she would have surely tried to come after you. You were her only daughter, her only hope of making her mad dreams come true."

"You forget my father hid me away in England for a time and then I came to live under Ariane's protection on Faire Isle. And Maman was so disgusted with me. She had come to think me unworthy of being the Silver Rose. What if she gave up on me, but not her dream of a sorceress ruling the world in place of kings? What if she has been alive and plotting all this while?"

"Ah, don't do this, Meggie." Seraphine caught Meg by the shoulders. Her grip was firm, but her voice was unusually gentle. "Do not torment yourself with these wild imaginings. Do not let Sir Patrick and his tales of his stupid mad king make you afraid again."

"I have never stopped being afraid of my past, 'Phine. I have only managed to suppress it. If I went to England, it would not be for the sake of Sir Patrick or his king. It would be for me, to lay my own ghosts to rest."

"*If?* You sound as if you have already made up your mind."

Meg realized that she had, but she said nothing, her silence speaking for her.

"All right, then. I have just one more question," Seraphine said.

Meg braced herself for more of her friend's fierce arguments, but Seraphine just emitted a defeated sigh.

"When do we leave?"

Chapter Seven

THE *ORION* CUT A PATH THROUGH THE MUDDY WATERS OF THE
Thames, the tide and the rhythm of the galley oarsmen pulling the vessel steadily upriver. Meg was able to make her way
to the port-side rail without the deck pitching beneath her
feet as it had done during the rough crossing of the English
Channel and around the coast through the North Sea.

The sun had barely arisen, the distant banks still wreathed
in mist. The only other people stirring above deck were members of the crew and the other passenger who was not of Sir
Patrick's traveling party.

John Johnston had come aboard at St. Malo. He introduced himself as an agent for a wool merchant in London
whose master had sent him to the Low Countries in hopes of
establishing new markets. A tall man with thick reddish-
brown hair and a bushy beard, he preferred to keep to him-

self, which suited Meg. Johnston's rigid manner and cold eyes rendered her uncomfortable.

The rough passage had not affected Meg as adversely as Seraphine, but she was grateful to find herself in calmer waters. The air this morning was brisk with the hint of an early autumn. Meg had forgotten her cloak, but she was reluctant to return to the cabin she shared with Seraphine to fetch the garment.

If they could have made the journey entirely by horseback, Seraphine would have been an intrepid traveler and an agreeable companion. Seraphine mewed up in a ship for so long was an entirely different creature, but Sir Patrick had been anxious to return to London as soon as possible. He had insisted that considering the state of the roads in England, traveling upriver was the swiftest route. Seraphine had reluctantly agreed, but she had been miserably ill from the moment they had weighed anchor.

Meg had done her best to alleviate her friend's suffering, but when Seraphine had commanded Meg to go and leave her to die in peace, Meg had been relieved to comply.

She clung to the deck rail and lifted her face to the fresh breeze. She was no fonder of traveling by ship than Seraphine, but her unease stemmed less from any physical discomfort than the pressing weight of memories.

For years Meg had harbored a secret dread of water, an anxiety that she had finally conquered by doing her best to suppress her recollection of her mother's drowning. But as she peered over the side of the ship into the brackish waters of the Thames, her thoughts eddied as well, dragging her back to the last day she seen her mother alive.

Meg had thwarted Cassandra Lascelles's scheme to release a poisonous miasma over the gardens of the Louvre, destroying the dowager French queen Catherine de Medici and anyone unfortunate enough to be near her.

Her plot discovered, Cassandra had been forced to flee, dragging Meg along with her. Maman had been furious and Meg had trembled in fear of the punishment that she knew would come. Cassandra Lascelles was skilled in the art of inflicting pain, especially upon her own daughter.

But Papa had arrived in time to snatch Meg away from her mother. When the palace guard had overtaken them, Cassandra had fled, stumbling into the river. The current had been so swift, the water soaking Maman's gown, the weight of the fabric dragging her down. No one had been able to save her.

But you should have tried, a voice inside her insisted.

I was only a child. A small, frightened little girl, the rational part of Meg responded. Yet a trace of guilt always lingered. No matter what else she had been, Cassandra had been her mother. Even while Meg had dreaded the prospect that Cassandra might be found alive, a small part of her heart had hoped for it as well.

That Cassandra would return, be the mother Meg had always wanted, hold her tenderly and tell her she loved her. The fantasy of a child, Meg reflected sadly. She knew full well, if Cassandra had survived, she would only have sought to involve Meg in more of her mad schemes.

If Maman had indeed survived . . . The prospect sent a chill through Meg and she wrapped her arms about herself.

She heard the sound of a footfall behind her. Sir Patrick, she thought, an involuntary smile touching her lips. Without being obtrusive, he tended to keep a watchful eye out for her, seeing to her every comfort on the journey, just as he had promised.

Meg turned from the rail to greet him, but her smile froze. She tensed to see Blackwood bearing down upon her, wearing his customary scowl, a woolen cloak slung over his arm.

"For a woman who is acclaimed to be so wise, you lack much in common sense. Here, take this before you catch your death of a chill." Blackwood did not drape the garment about her as tenderly as Graham would have done. He flung the cloak about her shoulders the way he would have tossed a blanket over the back of his horse.

"Thank you," Meg murmured in surprise. Blackwood had avoided her ever since the day he had delivered his warning. He had made it clear he didn't want her coming to England and was angry at her for doing so, scarce speaking a word to her during the entire voyage. To Meg's discomfort, she had often caught his gaze trained upon her whenever she had strolled along the deck with Sir Patrick. Blackwood had the most unsettling stare.

As Meg did up the clasp, she frowned, realizing the cloak was her own. "You entered my cabin to fetch this?"

"I thought I'd look in on your friend and see how she was faring. I *am* a doctor, you know," he added somewhat defensively.

"And how did Madame la Comtesse respond to your inquiry after her health?"

"She threatened to throw the chamber pot at my head, so I snatched up your cloak and beat a swift retreat."

"Very prudent of you. Seraphine has excellent aim."

"Mayhap she does, but since I seem to inspire an urge in women to throw things at me, I have grown very good at ducking."

Meg laughed in spite of herself and he smiled, the first time he had smiled at her in days. She found herself unexpectedly warmed by it.

He joined her at the rail. Sir Patrick always maintained a courteous distance, but Blackwood stood so close, he brushed against her. He had an overwhelming presence, as though he was taking in her share of the air and leaving her slightly breathless.

Meg edged away from him. She was never one to chatter, but she felt galvanized into nervous speech. "Sir Patrick says we will reach the port at Gravesend soon. From there we must change to a barge that will take us the rest of the way. Sir Patrick believes there is a chance we may make London by nightfall."

"Graham is likely right."

"Seraphine will be glad of it. She thinks being aboard this ship is like being clapped up in gaol."

"If she thinks that, obviously Madame la Comtesse has never been in prison."

"And you have?"

"Yes."

Meg should have been used to his bluntness by now, but she knew of few men who would so casually admit such a thing. Blackwood must have caught her startled look, for he laughed.

"Don't be alarmed. I spent a year enjoying the hospitality of Newgate, but not for anything like murdering my patients. I have killed off a few, but purely by accident. I was in prison because I was up to my ears in debt."

"An entire year for that?" Meg said indignantly. "I have always found the concept of punishing debtors in such a fashion absurd. How is one to pay off one's obligations when locked away from any gainful employment? I suppose you had a friend to come to your rescue?"

"Not exactly. When King James came to the throne, he issued a general pardon to all thieves, bawds, and ne'er-do-wells like me, a release order for everyone in prison; well, except for murderers and Catholics. So I was set at liberty." Blackwood withdrew a leather flask from beneath his cloak and uncapped it.

"God save the king." There was an edge of mockery to his toast. He took a swallow and offered the flask to her. When she declined with a shake of her head, he insisted. "It is Aqua Vitae. It will help you get warm."

"It is far more likely to give me a raging headache and destroy my stomach. You should not drink such vile stuff. If you must indulge in strong spirits, you should try usquebaugh. My mother, Catriona O'Hanlon, swore by it."

"You had an Irish mother?"

"*Stepmother,*" Meg amended, although she had never thought of Cat that way, more like a wise and loving older sister. "My father wed her the year I turned ten."

"And what of your own mother?"

The question caused Meg to tense, her gaze drawn to the dark ripples of the river. An image flashed through her mind of Cassandra's white hand breaking the surface of the water one last time before she vanished.

"She drowned when I was nine."

"An accident?"

"What makes you ask that?" Meg asked sharply.

"I don't know. Just something about your expression." His gaze probed hers. His eyes, which could appear almost blue at times, tended toward gray this morning, reflecting the darkness of the sky and river. "Your mother would not have been the first to seek such a desperate solution to overwhelming despair. The tidewaters of the Thames wash up many such poor souls every year."

"My mother didn't kill herself," Meg said, but her mind returned to those last few minutes of her mother's life when everything had unraveled for Cassandra Lascelles. Her plots, her dreams, even her possession of Meg. When she had realized she was unable to prevent Martin Wolfe from taking her daughter away, Cassandra had fallen to her knees, tears streaming to her cheeks.

"No! What have you done to me? You can't take my Silver Rose! She's all that I have."

Maman had been so proud, so fierce, she never displayed any weakness, never ever cried. Was it possible she had thrown herself into the river? Meg could not be sure, but she insisted, "It was an accident. My mother was blind. She stumbled too close to the water's edge."

Blackwood covered her hand on the deck rail with his. "Either way, it was not your fault."

Wasn't it? Meg had never been entirely sure about that either. Once again she was startled by Blackwood's perception. It was almost as if the man could read eyes, which would have been quite unfair because she could not read him at all. She only knew that he was being unexpectedly gentle and kind.

His fingers entwined with hers and he ran his thumb lightly over the back of her hand. An idle gesture on his part, she was sure, but it was having the most unaccountable effect on her, causing her skin to tingle.

She drew away from him. Tucking her hands beneath her cloak, she sought to change the subject.

"It would appear you are no longer angry with me."

"For what?"

"Ignoring your warning to return to Faire Isle."

"My *advice*," Blackwood amended. "Yes, perhaps I was vexed you did not have the good sense to go back to the island with Hortense."

"I am still astonished that she did. You never told me how you persuaded her."

"It wasn't difficult. I merely told her if she was a good girl and went to the island, I'd return to bed her one day."

"*You what!* You would really do such a thing?"

"Perhaps . . . if I was drunk enough." Blackwood paused, appearing to enjoy her shock for a moment before saying, "No, of course I wouldn't."

"So you made that poor old woman a promise you had no intention of keeping. You ought to be ashamed of yourself."

"I would have told Hortense anything to persuade her to go where she would be safe. I would have made you the same promise if I thought it would have worked." His gaze slid over her with frank appraisal. "Although in your case, it is a promise I would have been tempted to keep."

"Such a promise would have held no inducement for me."

"No? That is only because you have never been to bed with me."

"Nor will I ever!"

"Likely you won't," Blackwood agreed with a mock sigh. "Because you have already fallen under the spell of Graham's melancholy blue eyes."

Meg felt her cheeks flame. "I have done no such thing."

"No need to be so mortified, my dear. You are not the first poor lass to have done so, but it will avail you nothing. Graham is rather single-minded when it comes to his pursuits and those don't include chasing after women."

"That is because Sir Patrick is a most chivalrous and courteous gentleman. So much so that I wonder that you and he are friends. You seem a most unlikely pair."

"As do you and Madame la Comtesse."

Meg averted her face, staring across the waters toward the mist-shrouded embankments. She was irritated with Blackwood for flustering her, even more annoyed with herself that she did not flounce away from him. But she was unable to resist the opportunity to learn more about Sir Patrick.

"You and Sir Patrick have been friends for a long time?" she asked.

"Since we were students together at Oxford. We were among the humble beings that had to work for our tuition, so we were snubbed by the sons of wealth and privilege. Not that Graham much noticed or cared. He was always so deep in his books. I suppose I should have been similarly absorbed with my studies, but I found it more entertaining to lure Graham from the path of virtue."

"You hoped to become a doctor. What was Sir Patrick's aim?"

"Martyrdom," Blackwood muttered.

"I beg your pardon?"

A grim look had settled over Blackwood's features, but he forced a smile to his lips. "I mean that the man was a martyr to his study of Greek and Latin."

"I don't think you meant anything of the kind. I know a little bit about Oxford College. I have heard that many of the deans have a reputation for secretly encouraging the preservation of the Catholic religion. Sir Patrick's faith."

Blackwood made a dismissive gesture with his hand, but Meg continued, "I have seen him make the sign of the cross and once I even observed him praying over his rosary beads."

"The man needs to get rid of that blasted thing before we make port. If Graham is caught with the beads, it could cost him his freedom, maybe even his life. At the very least, he would lose his position at court and have to pay a hefty fine."

"Then the English government is no more lenient toward those of the Catholic faith than it was during Elizabeth's reign?"

"Lenient!" Blackwood snorted. "If anything, the council is more intolerant since James took the throne. When he was angling to become the king of England, James Stuart had smiles and promises for everyone. Catholics rejoiced, feeling they had cause for hope, but it swiftly became apparent we have a king who would rather hunt than govern. He seems content to leave the question of religion to parliament, especially now that James has discovered how lucrative the persecution of recusants can be. Confiscated estates and heavy fines can furnish a monarch with many fine horses and hunting dogs."

Meg blinked in surprise at his impassioned speech. From what she had observed of his behavior aboard ship, Blackwood treated everyone with a genial indifference. She had never seen him display such emotion.

"You do not seem to have much love for your king," Meg said. "I would have thought you might feel some gratitude toward him."

"What, for his munificence in pardoning a wretch like me? He would have done far better to exercise his mercy upon someone who truly deserved it."

"Is this the real reason you were so angry at me for coming to England to deal with the curse? You despise James Stuart so much you do not wish me to help him."

"I don't give a damn whether you help him or not. I much

doubt that you can. No one can save James Stuart from his own folly." Blackwood forced a laugh and relaxed his taut features into a sardonic expression. "But I shouldn't judge him so harshly when I am as great a fool. I have now placed my life squarely in your hands. When you have your audience with the king, all you have to do is report my treasonous utterances and it will be the devil to pay for me."

"I would never do such a thing."

"No, you would not, would you?" Blackwood tipped her face up to his and studied her. "You are such a solemn and prim little thing, but those eyes of yours. So mysterious, so full of hidden fire. I think you could pierce a man's soul with them, mesmerize him into spilling all his secrets into your hands."

"Do you have so very many secrets then, Dr. Blackwood? I confess I can find no window into your mind at all."

"I am right glad of that, milady. Because if you read the thoughts chasing through my head, you'd likely have the countess run me through."

Blackwood bent forward and kissed her. He grinned and strode away, leaving Meg a little breathless and annoyed, at herself as much as him.

She had experienced far more tender and coaxing embraces, but none that had made her heart pound like this. Blackwood's kiss had been hard, quick, and startling, like brushing up against a red-hot iron. Meg had to resist the urge to fan herself with her hand.

If Blackwood chanced to look back, he would only be amused. But he appeared to have found a new quarry to torment. Mr. Johnston's expression was far from welcoming as Blackwood approached.

Another man would have taken the hint, but Meg doubted

that anything short of a clout to the ear would have rebuffed Blackwood.

He greeted Johnston with a hearty clap on the shoulder and a hail-fellow-well-met grin. Even from across the deck, Meg observed Johnston grit his teeth. Johnston made it quite clear he preferred to be left alone and Blackwood persisted in approaching the man at every opportunity.

Meg suspected the doctor did so just to annoy the dour Mr. Johnston. Blackwood seemed to possess a mischevious streak, treating even the most serious matters as a jest.

His heated speech regarding the injustices dealt to England's Catholics had astonished and confused her. She wondered if Blackwood, like his friend, was also a recusant. Yet she had difficulty imagining Blackwood that devout.

Still, he and Sir Patrick had been close friends at Oxford, poor struggling students. That was another remark Blackwood had made that surprised her. Sir Patrick claimed he came from gentry, a landed family from Middlesex. They certainly should have been able to afford a good education for their only son.

But like many recusant families, they may have been impoverished by the crown. If that were the case, Sir Patrick displayed no bitterness. Unlike Blackwood, Graham was completely devoted to King James. Or he seemed to be. For all of his kindness and courtesy, Meg was not sure that she understood Sir Patrick any better than she did Blackwood.

Meg was distracted from her thoughts by the unexpected sight of Seraphine stumbling toward her. Deep shadows pocketed her eyes and her lustrous hair tumbled in tangled waves about her shoulders, but a faint hint of color crept back into her pale cheeks.

"So you did not die after all," Meg greeted her.

Seraphine's steps were cautious as though she still expected the deck to heave, or her stomach. "I have decided to live, at least until we get to shore. I am damned if I will die on this floating coffin."

"We are drawing near Gravesend."

"Yes, I am," Seraphine said with a dramatic sigh.

"I mean *Gravesend,* the port where we will disembark . . ." Seraphine brightened.

". . . and catch the barge to London."

Seraphine groaned and joined Meg at the deck rail, taking great care to keep her gaze averted from the river. The mist had burned away and Meg spied a trio of children playing upon the distant embankment. They waved at the passing ship and Meg lifted her hand in acknowledgment.

"So where is your devoted swain this morning?" Seraphine asked.

"If you mean Sir Patrick, I have no idea. I daresay he may still be below, asleep in his hammock."

"While I was dying in that wretched hole of a cabin, it gave me much time to think about you."

"Heaven help me," Meg said, but Seraphine ignored her and went on. "I have always believed you too preoccupied with the past and your mother. But I think I know what your true problem is, Margaret Wolfe."

"Pray enlighten me." She might as well invite Seraphine to do so, because her friend would speak her mind anyway.

"You live far too quietly on that island of yours. You are thirty-one years old, unwed, and still a virgin. If you had more experience of the world, you would not be so spellbound by Sir Patrick, too ready to trust the first handsome man to cross your path."

Meg glared at her. First Blackwood and now Seraphine

accused her of being smitten with Sir Patrick; this was beyond irritating.

"I am not entranced by Sir Patrick. Nor am I a virgin."

Seraphine had her eyes half-closed as the breeze played across her face. But they flew open wide. "What! You don't mean because of that Naismuth boy who kidnapped you and held you to ransom? That villainous music tutor ravished you?"

"No! Sander was reprehensible, but not evil enough to despoil a ten-year-old girl."

"So who then?"

Meg regretted her outburst, but realized that Seraphine would give her no peace until Meg confessed. "I took a lover, a Spanish sea captain who made berth on Faire Isle.

"As daughters of the earth, we are taught to believe that the union between a man and woman is a most natural thing and I confess I have always been curious. The experience did not disappoint. It was warm, comforting, and very pleasant. There was nothing shameful about it."

"Of course, there wasn't. The only shameful thing is that you never confided about this man to *me*. But I know you too well, Meg. Natural or not, you would have never given yourself so intimately to any man if you had not given your heart as well."

"I did believe I loved Felipe. I even thought of marrying him."

"So what happened?"

"I felt obliged to tell him about my past . . . all of it."

Seraphine groaned. "Why must you always be so infernally honest?"

"Should one not be with the person one loves?"

"No! Certain small deceits are often necessary to keep love alive."

"Withholding the truth of my past was far too large a deceit."

"And how did this Captain Felipe receive your honesty?"

"Just as you might expect. When I told him about the coven of the Silver Rose and about Maman and all her witchcraft, he was horrified and shrank away from me. But only until he had time to think about it. Then he was intrigued, wondering what I had learned from Maman and the *Book of Shadows,* what power I might be able to wield with my knowledge, what riches I could acquire. Just like Sander Naismuth, the dear and trusted friend of my childhood."

Meg fetched a wearied and bitter sigh. "With deep regrets, I was obliged to send Felipe away from Faire Isle and ask him never to return."

"Oh, Meggie! I am so sorry." Seraphine enveloped her in a hard, compassionate hug, only to draw back with a frown. "But you have a rejected lover out there who knows all your secrets."

"Felipe would never betray me. He swore upon his medallion of the Blessed Virgin to keep my secret and he would never break such an oath. He had that much honor in him and in any case he is now on the far side of the world. He sailed to make his fortune in la Florida and found it. From what I heard, he was appointed governor of one of the new Spanish colonies there."

"Good. That saves me the trouble of going to find the wretch and cut off his—er—heart."

Meg smiled. "You need not harbor such vengeful thoughts on my account. I have long ago recovered from any hurt Felipe dealt me."

"Except for the urge to burrow deeper into your island and never trust again." Seraphine eyed her shrewdly. "How long ago was your liaison with Captain Felipe?"

"Three . . . no, perhaps closer to four years ago."

"Far too long. When one is tossed by a mean-tempered steed, it is well to get quickly back into the saddle again."

Meg tried to protest that Felipe was not a horse, but Seraphine was not listening.

"You need to take another lover," she mused. "But this time keep your heart and your secrets to yourself. And choose someone whose lovemaking does not inspire such adjectives as *warm, comfortable,* and *very pleasant.* Your gentle Sir Patrick will never do, despite his handsome face." Seraphine's gaze traveled across the deck to where the doctor was harassing the very annoyed Mr. Johnston.

"Blackwood should be your man."

"Blackwood?" Meg laughed. "You don't even like him."

"I don't need to. I am not the one who should bed him."

"Neither am I."

"You should at least consider it. Blackwood is a rogue, the kind of scoundrel who would make a good lover, but leave your heart unscathed. I know enough of men that I would wager he would bring a deal of fire and passion to your bed."

"Is that what Gerard did for you?"

"No, I was the one who brought the fire to our marriage." Seraphine looked a trifle wistful. "But I must admit, Monsieur le Comte kindled marvelous well."

This was the opening Meg had been seeking, to once more urge the possibility of Seraphine reconciling with her husband. But she was prevented by Sir Patrick joining them.

With Seraphine and Blackwood both insisting that she

was enamored of Sir Patrick, it was all Meg could do to meet the man with any degree of composure. But she refused to allow their nonsensical accusations to turn her into some foolish blushing chit. Forcing herself to look him in the eye, she greeted him cheerfully.

"Good morrow, Sir Patrick."

"Good morrow, milady." He took her hand and bowed over it, his lips curving into his shy half smile that touched Meg in some way she could not explain.

She was not infatuated with Sir Patrick. Meg was sure of that and yet she could not deny she was drawn to him, something in his sad blue eyes calling to her like the haunting rhythms of the sea.

He retained her hand, his gaze meeting hers for a long moment until Seraphine gave an exaggerated cough. He released Meg and turned his attention to Seraphine.

He bowed. "Madame la Comtesse. I hope you are feeling better?"

"Somewhat. I will not feel entirely well until you get me off this ship."

"Your ordeal will be over soon, I promise you. I hope to have both of you comfortably installed in my own house by tonight and then arrange Mistress Wolfe's meeting with the king for tomorrow or the next day at latest."

Seraphine's brows rose with haughty surprise. "You are entirely too hasty, monsieur. You have already denied us enough time to prepare for this journey. Neither of us has brought any attire appropriate for an audience at court. We will require at the very least a fortnight to visit the shops, acquire a skilled dressmaker, and I may have to send back to Paris for some of my jewels."

"None of that will be necessary." Sir Patrick smiled at

Meg. "I promise you your meeting with the king will be very informal and of a most private nature."

Meg, who had listened to Seraphine's plans with dismay, was relieved by Sir Patrick's assurance, but Seraphine scowled.

"You propose to sneak the Lady of Faire Isle up the back stairs of the palace as though she was some lowly spy or a hired doxy? I think not!"

"I intend no insult to the Lady. But you must appreciate the delicacy of this situation. The utmost discretion is required. His Majesty would not wish the story of his curse to become a matter of court gossip."

Seraphine gave a derisive laugh. "It likely already is if his court is anything like the one in Paris."

"But I agree with Sir Patrick," Meg said. "I would prefer my meeting with the king to take place as quietly as possible."

Seraphine opened her mouth to argue, but she was forestalled by the sound of a louder altercation taking place. Angry voices carried across the deck, drawing Sir Patrick's attention away. Meg followed his gaze to where Mr. Johnston clearly had had enough of Blackwood's company.

The doctor had retreated a step, flinging up his hands, but the gesture was more mocking than placating. "If I am mistaken, I beg your pardon, Guido."

The agent's weathered face stained a darker red. "I told you, the name is *Johnston*. John Johnston. You would do well to remember that, you drunken fool."

He jabbed his finger against Blackwood's chest. Blackwood continued to smile, but Meg saw his hands curl into fists. Sir Patrick had clearly noticed as well.

"Excuse me," he muttered and sprinted across the deck. Crew members had paused in their work, faces avid in the expectation of a brawl. But Sir Patrick insinuated himself in between Blackwood and Johnston. Meg could not hear what was being said, Sir Patrick's voice low and intense.

The doctor relaxed, but Johnston remained rigid, as tightly coiled as a snake that could easily be provoked to strike.

"There is something dangerous about that man," Meg murmured to Seraphine.

"Which man? Sir Patrick or Blackwood?"

"Mr. Johnston." Meg frowned. Something about him had rendered her uneasy from the moment he had come aboard, and she struggled to articulate the feeling. "He neither behaves nor dresses like other merchants I have seen. He carries himself like a soldier, erect, vigilant, looking over his shoulder as though in anticipation of an attack. I do not think Mr. Johnston is at all what he claims to be."

"You could easily say the same for Dr. Blackwood or Sir Patrick Graham. This Johnston joined us in St. Malo?"

"Yes, when you were first confined to your cabin."

"And he was quite unknown to anyone before?"

"Mr. Johnston behaved as though he was unacquainted with Sir Patrick or Dr. Blackwood."

Seraphine's gaze narrowed as she studied the three men still engaged in low conversation. "They do not act as if they are strangers."

Meg was receiving the same disquieting impression. Seraphine turned to her, her face earnest. "There is still time to turn back, Meg. When we reach Gravesend, we could slip away and find a ship to carry us back to Faire Isle."

"I would like nothing better, but I can't, 'Phine. At least not until I have met with the king and judged the truth of this troubling matter for myself."

"Then insist upon His Majesty receiving you properly at

court. You are not some Gypsy girl. You are the Lady of Faire Isle."

"You would enjoy such a public reception, but you know I shudder at such a thing. I always prefer to attract as little notice as possible."

"There is a great danger in that, Meg. Fade into the wood-work and no one will notice if you disappear."

"You would."

"But perhaps not in time to save you."

"Sir Patrick has said—"

"Damn Sir Patrick. You place far too much blind faith in that man's assurances."

"Not a blind faith, but I do trust his honor enough to see me safely through one meeting with the king. And one meeting is all I require. If I am to uncover the truth of this curse and the connection with Maman and the Silver Rose coven, I do not believe I will find my answer at Whitehall, which is just as well. Could you imagine me trying to make my way among a palace full of ambitious, gossiping courtiers, up to my ears in intrigue?"

"My dear friend," the countess replied somberly. "I fear that you already are."

Chapter Eight

FIREWORKS SPLINTERED THE SKY WITH ICICLES OF LIGHT THAT shimmered to earth, vanishing into the dark waters of the Thames. Decks of the vessels riding at anchor and the rooftops of houses on the banks were all crammed with spectators. Cries of delight were punctuated by outbursts of raucous laughter and cheers.

The stretch of the Thames that flowed past London was always a challenge to navigate, wherries and tilt boats darting like fireflies among the stately barges and three-masted ships. The celebration made it even more difficult for the passenger barge from Gravesend to maneuver to the landing steps.

Armagil Blackwood, Sir Patrick Graham, and his servant Alexander were among the first to alight, but Blackwood soon lost sight of the other two men. As he wove his way through the revelers that crowded the docks, he trod on the toes of a dockworker. But the lanky fellow was either too good-humored or too numb from the amount of sack he had consumed to object.

"Sorry," Blackwood shouted to make himself heard. "What the devil is all this?" He gestured toward the eruption of another spray of fireworks. It appeared to emanate from the direction of Whitehall.

"Celebration," the dockworker yelled back.

"Of what?"

"The king's deliverance from conspiracy."

Blackwood felt his heart miss a beat. His gaze darted in search of Graham, but he was nowhere to be seen. Fighting to contain his alarm, he asked, "What conspiracy was this?"

"Don't know. Some plot against the king's life that was foiled years ago in Scotland. King James likes to mark the anniversary of it."

"Oh, *that.* I had forgotten," Blackwood said. For one terrible moment, he had feared . . . He exhaled, able to breathe again. When the dockworker's attention strayed back to the sky, Blackwood slipped away and found a quiet spot behind some stacked crates and barrels.

The laughter, the revelry, and the endless drunken toasts to His Majesty's health were mercifully muted. Blackwood drew forth his own flask, his lip curling with contempt. Two years ago, after Queen Elizabeth had died and James of Scotland had been named as her successor, bonfires had been lit and the wine had flowed. The aged virgin queen was at long last dead, the crown passed to a man in the prime of life who had already proved his ability to sire heirs. A new era would surely dawn for England, one of prosperity, stability, and opportunity. Optimism had prevailed until James Stuart descended upon London with hordes of Scottish fortune-seekers in his wake. The king himself regarded England's coffers as a bottomless treasure trove.

It had not taken long for the country to become disillusioned with its new king, although one could not discern that from the buoyant mood of the crowd on the docks tonight. Londoners were eager to embrace any celebration, no matter the cause.

Blackwood drank a toast to the folly of his fellow men. And then another to his own. As the fiery liquid burned a path down his throat, he amused himself by watching a group gathered near the landing steps. A doxy moved among them plying her wares, the torchlight just enough for Blackwood to make out the red glint of her hair and a white expanse of bosom spilling above her low-cut gown. While the minx distracted the gentlemen, no doubt she had a confederate nearby picking pockets and cutting purses.

The thought was enough for Blackwood to make sure his own purse was still fastened to his belt. The city streets could be hazardous enough by day, let alone after dark. He wondered what had become of Graham.

Sir Patrick and Alexander had set out to arrange for the cart and horse to convey the ladies and their belongings back to his house. Perhaps they were having some difficulty, owing to the unusual amount of activity in the streets, but Blackwood had no doubt Sir Patrick would achieve his end.

From the time that Blackwood had first known him, Graham had always been good at arranging things, efficient, with a close eye to detail. If there had still been monasteries in England, Blackwood could imagine Graham as the abbot, carefully regulating the life of the order.

Unfortunately he could just as easily imagine Graham organizing a rebellion or quietly planning an assassination. A sobering thought; Blackwood took another swallow. He wasn't drunk, but feeling woolly-headed and tired enough to long for his bed.

He was about to go in search of Graham when he spotted him returning to the landing with a pair of linkboys, holding lit torches, trailing in his wake. Blackwood hailed his friend, managing to gain his attention above the rest of the din.

When Graham joined him, he frowned at the flask in Blackwood's hand, but made no remark upon it.

"Alexander is waiting with the cart," he said. "But I judged it best to wait until the fireworks are over and the crowd disperses before escorting Mistress Wolfe and the Countess. I had entirely forgotten this celebration was planned."

"As did I." Blackwood took another swallow. The flask was nearly empty. "For a moment, I wondered if James had died in our absence and we had acquired a new king. It would certainly save you a deal of trouble."

"For the love of God, Gil!" Sir Patrick cast a glance about him and drew Blackwood deeper into the shadows. "We are back in London. Please show a little discretion and mind your tongue."

"I will if you mind the use of your trinkets."

"If you are referring to my rosary, I have already hidden it in the lining of my doublet."

"And what about this?" Blackwood brushed aside the fold of Graham's cloak and drew forth the silver chain fastened about Sir Patrick's neck. The small locket containing the sacred strands of hair dangled between Blackwood's fingers.

Graham snatched the locket away from him. He reverently brought the locket to his lips. "No one but you would even understand its significance to me."

"What, not even your good friend Johnston?"

Graham scowled as he tucked the chain back out of sight. "That is another thing I must admonish you about. Whatever possessed you to bedevil Johnston that way? You know what an uncertain temper the man has. From now on, I must ask you to leave him alone."

"That would prove no hardship to me. I don't like Guido Fawkes. He's a singularly humorless man, but if he means to pass himself off under a false name, he could have chosen something better than *John Johnston.*"

"Unfortunately, when it comes to constructing lies, the man is not as creative as you."

Nor you, Blackwood was tempted to retort, but he didn't want to quarrel with his friend. "I don't know what you are plotting, Graham. I could hazard a guess, but I don't want to. But I think you and your friends would be wise to disassociate yourself from Fawkes. He is far too volatile."

"Fawkes—I mean Johnston—is a soldier, an expert in the use of ordnance and firearms."

"So are you."

"Only when aiming at wooden targets or hunting waterfowl. I have never leveled a weapon at the heart of a man before."

"Neither have I."

"Do you think that you could?"

Blackwood considered for a moment before answering, "Oh, yes. I think I could be far better at taking life than saving it, if I allowed myself to be."

"I am not sure that I could, no matter how just my cause."

Graham looked shamed by the admission. "That is why my association with Mr. Johnston is necessary."

"But you don't need *her*."

Graham did not feign confusion or demand to know who Blackwood meant. Blackwood sensed that the Lady of Faire Isle was weighing as heavily upon Graham's mind as his.

"Margaret Wolfe has become necessary to my plans whether I wish her to be or not," he said.

"Why? You have never believed in witchery or the powers of these so-called cunning women. And yet you dragged me the length of France to find this one."

"I did not drag you anywhere. You insisted upon accompanying me. And Mistress Wolfe is no ordinary ignorant cunning woman. She is well read, a lady of great learning. I have enjoyed much interesting conversation with her during the course of our voyage, despite the fact that she is pagan in her beliefs."

"If she is a pagan, will that help to quiet your conscience if any harm should come to her?"

"If I have placed her in danger by fetching her to London, I had no choice," Graham replied irritably. "It is not *my* fault that the king insists upon seeing her."

"What if the Lady does manage to cure His Majesty of his belief that he is cursed? I wager that would not suit your aims. Did you not wish to see him driven mad?"

"All I want to see is James Stuart held accountable for his sins and I would think you would desire the same."

Blackwood could not make out Graham's face well in the darkness, but he noted the hardening of Graham's jaw. It was an expression that Blackwood was uncomfortably familiar with, stony, unfeeling, only Graham's eyes alive with a blaze so hot, they chilled.

He had known Graham for so long and loved him as much as Blackwood was capable of loving anyone, like the brother he had never had. But he preferred Patrick Graham, the gentle scholar, the compassionate friend who kept all of Blackwood's secrets, helped him to bed when he drank too much, listened to accounts of all his sins, and passed no judgment. Graham the fanatic disturbed and repulsed him.

Graham drew closer in an effort to peer sharply at his face. "Why are you suddenly showing such concern for the Lady of Faire Isle? Do you mean to appoint yourself her protector?"

"Lord, no. Knight errantry is your forte, not mine."

"But you do fancy her."

When Blackwood shook his head in denial, Graham insisted, "I saw you kiss her."

"I kiss every pretty woman I meet. It is a careless habit of mine." Blackwood hoped the darkness was enough to conceal the rush of blood to his face. Kissing Margaret Wolfe had been a mistake. He had only done it to tease her, bring a halt to her questions that probed too deep. He had never expected to find her mouth warm, sweet, and yielding enough to stir his lust.

The line of Graham's jaw softened, but his voice was grave as he said, "Armagil, I beg you, nay I must insist, you have nothing to do with Margaret Wolfe. My affairs are complicated enough without you seducing the Lady of Faire Isle."

"I have no intention of doing so. I like my wenches coarse and earthy, with big bosoms and plump arses. I have no taste for ethereal females like Mistress Wolfe. She is the sort of woman calculated to make a man think and feel too much and those are two activities I strenuously avoid."

His words coaxed a laugh from Graham. "Good. Then you will avoid Margaret Wolfe as well."

He glanced up toward the sky, which had gone silent, surrendering its darkness to the usual scattering of stars and the solemn light of a three-quarter moon.

"It appears the festivities are at an end and the crowd dispersing. I should go fetch the ladies, but I am glad we have reached this understanding." Graham smiled at Blackwood and headed toward the barge tethered near the landing stairs.

"I am right glad that you are so glad," Blackwood muttered as his friend moved off into the darkness. "But I still don't understand a blasted thing."

He realized now that Graham had deftly avoided answering any of Blackwood's questions regarding Margaret and how she figured in Graham's plans, whatever they were.

At the top of the landing stairs, Graham was accosted by the red-haired doxy. She sashayed closer, reaching out to touch him, but he sprang back. Although his revulsion was evident, he engaged the woman in a few moments of conversation before bowing and moving on. No doubt Graham had abjured the woman to forsake her sinful way of life. Advice that had fallen on deaf ears. The woman merely shrugged and pranced off to accost someone else.

Blackwood smiled. At times, Graham could be so naively earnest and at others . . . Blackwood's smile faded. At other times, Graham worried the devil out of him.

Although they had much in common, he and Graham were very different men. Neither of them had experienced a halcyon youth, both plagued by memories that were the stuff of nightmares. But Blackwood chose to bury his past deep beneath the rubble of chaos that was his present life. Graham nurtured his grievances like live coals on a hearth, fanning them to a white-hot pitch. Blackwood had always feared that one day those embers would flame out of control, consuming Graham and anyone unfortunate enough to be close to him.

That day might be approaching at a perilous rate, but how could he help Graham when he couldn't even conquer his own demons? The harsh truth was that he'd never been any good at saving anyone. He was a complete failure as a doctor and a miserable excuse of a friend. The best he could do was honor Graham's request and keep his distance, especially from Margaret Wolfe. That should prove no hardship.

But he was beset by a vivid image of moonlight spilling through the loft of his lodgings, bathing the Lady of Faire Isle as she sprawled on his bed, her body lithe, warm, and naked. Modesty and primness forgotten, her face would be flushed with passion, her lips cherry ripe. Her green eyes all come-hither, she would welcome him to bury himself deep in the tight delta of—

"Christ's blood," Blackwood swore, pinching the bridge of his nose to dispel the vision before it had its inevitable effect on his body. Too late, he could already feel himself get hard.

Was it possible to feel this degree of arousal from one stolen kiss? Maybe there was something of the witch about Margaret Wolfe or maybe it was his own perversity. Tell him something was forbidden and he immediately yearned after it.

He tipped up his flask for a drink. Empty. He gave a hollow sigh. What he really needed was a night of oblivion, dicing at some low tavern, getting drunk on sack, and going upstairs with some willing doxy.

As though he had conjured her up with the thought, the red-haired wench he had observed with Graham accosted him.

"All alone, sir? Perhaps in need of a little companionship?" She ran her hands over the curve of her bosom with a giggle. Despite her efforts to play the coy girl, the days of her youth were far behind her. The rouge smeared on her cheeks only accented the lines that creased her eyes and the cloying scent of her perfume repulsed him.

"Off with you, woman. I have no interest in your wares."

"That is because you have no idea what I am selling. I have many skills."

"Such as?"

"I am a fortune-teller, especially adept at the art of hydromancy. I could read the waters of the river and tell you your future."

"I would be far better able to predict yours. Death by the French pox or the hangman's noose if you don't find yourself a different line of trade." He tried to brush past her, but she seized hold of his hand.

"Your future doesn't interest you, Dr. Blackwood?"

He started at her use of his name, squinting at her in the semidarkness. Something about her stirred his memory, that red fall of hair, the feline smile. "Have we met before? Do I know you?"

"I know *you* very well, Doctor." She upended his hand and lifted it close to her face. "Your palm tells me everything. If you won't let me predict your future, perhaps you would like me to recite your past."

She grinned. Her tongue darting out catlike, she licked his palm. Blackwood swore and jerked his hand away.

"My past is none of your concern. You'd do well to remember that."

If she perceived the menace in his tone, she was unimpressed by it. She gave a throaty laugh and pranced on her way. Grimacing with disgust, Blackwood wiped his palm on his doublet.

"Stupid wench," he muttered, trying to dismiss the encounter. She had greeted him by name. That in itself was not remarkable. Many of his patients came from the alehouses and gaming pits. He was well known in the less respectable quarters of London.

Far more disturbing was her hint that she knew something of his history. Blackwood rubbed his temple, wishing his head was clearer. Then he might recollect where he had met the girl before. Had he been with Graham at the time? That seemed highly unlikely, unless it had been upon one of those occasions when Graham had made another bootless attempt to save Blackwood from himself, venturing to the alehouse to drag Blackwood home.

Blackwood turned around for another look at the girl, but she had already melted into the night.

❈❈❈

AMELIA SKIPPED ALONG THE ALLEY, HUMMING A SOFT TUNE, even though she knew she was being reckless. Despite the keenness of her vision, it would be all too easy to trip over a stray paving stone or step into a rut and turn her ankle.

Even greater was the danger of calling too much attention to herself in an area of London infamous for the predators that lurked in the shadows. But Amy was in far too good a humor for her usual caution, and besides, she accounted herself as one of those denizens of the night, the dirk she kept concealed beneath her cloak always ready to hand. Many a man who had mistaken her for a plump partridge realized too late he had seized hold of a falcon when her talons struck deep, drawing blood.

But the crowds at the celebration tonight must have offered better sport for the footpads and pickpockets. Amy passed down the alley unmolested. It was not until she reached the wooden stair that led to her lodging above the alehouse that something stirred in the darkness. Amy came to a halt, but too late.

The cloaked figure sprang, shoving Amy against the alehouse wall. Amy's heart leapt with fright, but she reacted quickly, unsheathing her knife.

She was poised to strike when her attacker screamed, "Boo!" and broke into familiar laughter.

Amy lowered her knife, releasing a shuddering breath. Fear was swiftly replaced by anger, and she cursed, calling her older sister Beatrice every vile name she could think of.

Bea only laughed harder. She shoved back the hood of her cloak, a sliver of moonlight playing over her grinning face. Amy might well have been gazing at her mirror image, the same auburn hair, high forehead, and long nose. Except that her sister's eyes were a shade cooler, her face much leaner than Amy's rosy-cheeked softness. Amy was the spring to Bea's winter, or so their grandmother had always said.

Amy sheathed her knife. "Damn you, Bea. You scared the devil out of me."

"Oh, I doubt that," Bea mocked. "Anyway, it serves you right for tripping along like some careless little fool *and* for being out so late. What took you so long? Did you find out anything?"

Miffed by her sister's trick, Amy ignored her questions. She stomped up the stairs, close followed by Bea, who was

still snickering. Her sister's mirth only added to Amy's sense
of injury.

Inside their lodging, she refused to look at Bea or speak
to her. Amy whipped off her cloak and tossed it upon the bed,
knowing that would annoy her sister. Bea liked things tidy.

She was gratified to hear Bea's vexed oath as Amy moved
closer to the hearth. She and Bea shared a small, mean room,
not worth the five shillings a week the rapacious alehouse
owner, Mistress Keating, charged them. The furnishings consisted of little more than a straw pallet, a small pine table, a
pair of stools, and a storage chest.

But Bea had kindled a crackling fire and Amy held her
hands to the blaze. Until that moment she had not realized
how chilled she was. The autumn nights were getting raw and
Amy did so hate to be cold.

The warmth of the fire did much to restore her good
humor, that and the sound of Bea huffing about the chamber.
Without glancing around, Amy knew that Bea was hanging
up Amy's cloak and grumbling as she did so. Amy's lips twitched
into a smug smile.

Bea no longer appeared quite so jovial when she joined
Amy by the hearth. "All right, I am sorry for frightening you,"
she said, although Amy did not think her sister sounded quite
sorry enough.

Amy started to tell her so when she was distracted by a
strange plaintive sound. "What was that?"

"Nothing."

The noise came again. *Meow.*

"That sounds like a cat," Amy accused. Bea's eyes sparkled with malicious mischief, darting toward the far corner of
the room.

Amy shoved past her, tracking the mews to their source.

A wooden cage was tucked behind the wardrobe chest. A small ginger-haired cat cowered behind the bars.

Amy drew back in disgust. She loathed cats; nasty, sly, slinking things. They made her skin crawl and her nose itch. Whipping around with her hands on her hips, she confronted Bea. "What is *that* doing here?"

Bea sauntered over to join her. " 'Tis my new friend."

"That looks more like Mistress Keating's friend, Grimalkin, to me."

Bea hunkered down by the cage, poking her fingers through the bars. The creature's fur stood on end, its frightened meows louder. Bea grinned. She liked being feared. It gave her a sense of power. She was very like their late grandmother in that regard.

When Bea unlatched the cage door, Amy skittered back. "Oh, pray, don't take that thing out of there."

Bea ignored her. The creature hissed when Bea reached for it, but she only laughed, even when the beast scratched her. She hauled it out of the cage by the scruff of its neck. The cat yowled and struggled, but Bea locked it in a tight grip beneath her arm, holding it fast so it could neither bite nor scratch.

Amy peered at the creature from a safe distance, noting the blaze of white fur on its brow above its wide frightened eyes.

"That is Grimalkin. What are you doing with him?"

"I borrowed him, without Mistress Keating's consent of course. You should have seen her searching for him all afternoon, calling here, kitty, kitty, setting out saucers of milk. It was heart-wrenching." Bea gloated. "Mistress Keating dotes on this miserable puss as much as evil King James does on his hunting dogs."

Amy's nose itched and she suppressed the urge to sneeze. Backing off further, she scolded her sister. "Mistress Keating is a right old bitch, but you are not wise to plague her, Bea. We have not the time or the funds to seek out other lodgings."

"She has no idea that I am the one who stole her precious Grimalkin and the bitch deserves to be plagued. She called me a slut and a whore."

Bea often laughingly described herself in those terms, but she did not stomach such insults from anyone else. Nor was she one to ever forgive and forget any injury, so Amy realized there was little point in trying to reason with her sister.

"Just keep that thing away from me," she said.

Bea made a playful motion as though she would hurl the cat at Amy. She laughed when Amy leaped back and then settled herself upon a stool, the cat locked in a death grip upon her lap. Oblivious to its pitiful cries, Bea stroked it behind the ears.

"Enough about the cat. Tell me where you have been tonight and what you have seen."

Amy sneezed and her eyes watered, neither of which made her feel much inclined to answer her sister. But she replied sulkily, "I was down to the docks and I saw Dr. Blackwood alight from a barge from Gravesend."

"Damn Blackwood! Who cares a fig for him? The drunken fool is of no use to—" Bea began irritably, only to stop as the realization struck her. "Wait! If the doctor has returned to London, then that must mean Sir Patrick Graham has returned as well."

Bea was being so annoying this evening, between the mean trick she had played earlier and fetching home that horrid cat. Amy would have liked to punish her by clamming up, and telling her not another word. But the good tidings Amy had acquired bubbled up inside of her and could not be suppressed.

"Oh, Bea! Sir Patrick has kept his pledge. He has fetched the Lady to England."

Amy waited for Bea to squeal with delight and share Amy's excitement. She should have known better. Bea seldom got excited nor did she ever squeal. Leaning back against the wall, she continued to pet that accursed cat.

"How can you be so sure it was the Lady?" she asked

"Because I hid myself near the landing stairs and watched as Sir Patrick helped the Lady of Faire Isle from the barge. I caught a glimpse of her."

"You caught a *glimpse*?"

Her sister's sneering tone nettled Amy. "I saw enough of her to tell that Margaret Wolfe is exactly as the old woman described her, small, delicate, but possessed of a mystical aura. Or dare I call her by her true name, Megaera, our revered Silver Rose?"

"I would not just yet, if I were you."

"But I tell you it has to be Megaera. Sir Patrick found her just as he promised."

"It was not a promise he gave willingly, only because we obliged him to."

"No matter. He has kept his side of the bargain."

"Or is ready to trick us into believing he did. He could have fetched any woman here and called her the Lady of Faire Isle."

"Sir Patrick would not do such a thing. He is a man of honor, a holy man."

Bea pursed her lips together and made a rude noise.
"Those are the worst kind of men, capable of any sort of
treachery or lies to further their cause, then scurrying off to
wipe the slate clean by confessing and doing penance. You
are such a fool, Amy. I think you are half in love with your
pretty Sir Patrick."

"Am not," she retorted. But she took an agitated turn
about the room to conceal the rush of heat to her cheeks.
When she was drifting off at night on her rough pallet, she
had indulged in some agreeable fantasies about being wed to
the beautiful Sir Patrick, living in his fine house, sleeping in
his feather bed, dining upon rich cream and strawberries
whenever she desired. *My Lady Graham.*

Such a foolish daydream and so wrong. Being a devotee
of the Silver Rose meant vowing never to marry, never to
love. Men should be nothing more than diversions and idle
playthings on the road to power, the quest to become a sorceress, well-versed in all the dark knowledge. Amy's late
grandmother would be so ashamed of her granddaughter for
indulging in such ridiculous dreams of Sir Patrick. Granddam
would likely turn over in her grave. That is if a woman who
had been reduced to a pile of charred bone and ash could
even be said to have a proper grave.

Regaining command of herself, Amy spun back to face
her sister. "I am not besotted with Sir Patrick, although he is
so handsome. He would make a far more agreeable pet than
that mangy cat. I would like to lock *him* up in a cage."

"Perhaps one day you shall, but in the meantime, Amy,
show a little caution and good sense. This woman Sir Patrick
brought to London may well turn out to be the Silver Rose,
but we must make test of her."

"Oh, yes. If she is Megeara, she will know much of the

dark arts. I so want her to teach me everything she learned from the *Book of Shadows* and how to fashion witch blades."

"Even if this woman is Megaera, she might be loath to share her knowledge. Remember, she turned her back on the coven, abandoned her title of Silver Rose."

"Only because she was a silly little girl and her father spirited her away. She is a grown woman now."

"A woman who has shown no inclination to revive the coven."

"She must be forced to do so. We will never be able to perform the ritual without her. She must be obliged to remember who she truly is, to recall her great destiny."

"And if she refuses to be reminded?"

"Then she will pay the price for her treachery, just as evil King James will be forced to pay for what he did to our grandmother." Amy stamped her foot in sheer frustration, her previous elation quashed beneath Bea's doubts and irritating questions. But it was ever thus with Bea, on the sunniest day, conjuring up dark clouds to darken Amy's horizon.

Amy glared at her sister, but Bea was too absorbed by that damned cat to notice. Bea's stroking was having its effect. Grimalkin had ceased to meow and struggle to escape. The cat had relaxed, beginning to trust Bea. Stupid creature.

"So what do you suggest we do?" Amy asked sullenly.

"Keep watch over Sir Patrick and this lady he has brought back from France, but make no attempt to approach her until we find positive proof of her identity."

"Of course, I had already thought of that myself," Amy replied loftily. "And I will consult my water oracle, see what I can learn of what the future holds."

The thought lifted Amy's spirits and she bustled over to

the chest to fetch her copper bowl and candles, even though it did bring her in closer proximity to the cat, which caused a fit of sneezing.

Bea cuddled the creature close to her. "You and your hydromancy. If you want to predict the future, everyone knows that reading entrails works much better."

"Ugh. But it is so bloody and messy."

"Yes, but unlike you, my dear sister, I always clean up after myself." Bea smiled and stroked the little cat's throat.

"Be a love, Amy, and lend me your knife."

Chapter Nine

MEG TOSSED AND TURNED, KICKING THE COVERLET ASIDE. Even though the four-poster bed had two thick mattresses supported on a lattice of tied leather strips, even though her pillow was stuffed with down, she could find no ease from her dream.

Meg raced through the narrow streets, the landscape of her nightmare hauntingly familiar this time. She knew why she was here.

The fire had not yet been lit. The two figures were just being dragged to the stakes. She could see the old woman, her withered features suffused with hatred as she spewed out her rage against the king.

"Damn ye to hell, James of Scotland. May ye one day also perish in fire. My curse upon the House of Stuart!"

The wails of the young girl could scarce be heard above the old woman's fury. As the pair was shackled to the stakes,

Meg struggled to reach the girl, but her feet felt weighted down as though she was the one in chains.

Someone else also fought to save the girl. A lanky boy battled with the guards that surrounded the pyre. It took two full-grown men to wrestle him to ground.

"Robbie!" the girl cried as another guard lit the pile of faggots heaped around her feet. Meg staggered forward, realizing in despair that she was again too late.

The girl was lost in a haze of smoke and crackling flames. Meg could hear harsh racking sobs, but the sounds did not emanate from the girl.

It was the boy . . .

Meg jerked awake, her cheeks wet. For a moment she thought she was soaked in sweat, a consequence of her harrowing nightmare. But as she brought her hands to her face, she realized the moisture came from her eyes. She had been crying in her sleep and small wonder. Even awake, she could still hear that boy's harrowing cries.

Meg rubbed her hands down her face to wipe away her tears and the last vestiges of the dream, the same one she had been having ever since she had arrived in London three nights ago. The stakes, the fire, the venomous old woman, the terrified young girl, and the boy who fought to save her.

"Robbie," Meg murmured as she sat up, leaning back against the pillows. Just saying his name filled her with an inexplicable sorrow and confusion.

During her youth, she had experienced vivid dreams about people she knew, dreams that seemed to warn her of future events, some she had been able to prevent. But why should she keep having these nightmares about complete strangers, a past that she had never witnessed and was powerless to change? It made no sense.

"But dreams often don't." Meg recalled the echoes of her own voice as she had comforted an old soldier who had ventured to Faire Isle seeking relief from the sleeplessness and nightmares that plagued him.

"Dreams are usually the result of an unquiet mind or some great stress. Find peace during your waking hours and the dreams will fade," Meg had told the old man, giving him a draught that would aid with his sleep.

Meg frowned at the recollection of her simple advice, so easy to give, so difficult to apply to oneself. She doubted she could brew a potion strong enough to make her nightmare vanish, nor did she expect to find peace anytime soon, certainly not today.

Sir Patrick had finally been able to arrange for her meeting with the king. The mere thought of it was enough to tie a knot in Meg's stomach. She tried to put it out of her mind as she rose from the bed, noting the empty pillow beside her.

Although it was barely light outside, her bedfellow was already absent, but Meg had ceased to be surprised by that. Sir Patrick Graham's house was a comfortable, but modest one. She and Seraphine had been obliged to share a bedchamber.

It did not matter, because each morning, Seraphine had arisen early and been off upon her own errands. Meg often forgot that her good friend was also the comtesse. As such, she had once traveled to London as part of the French ambassador's train with her reluctant husband, Gerard, in tow. Seraphine was not without acquaintances among the English nobility and she intended to use those connections to find another residence.

Madame la Comtesse did not like being lodged under Sir Patrick's roof. She did not trust the man and she was determined that she and Meg move to someplace where they could be more comfortable and at ease.

Meg would not find any comfort until she could return to Faire Isle, but she did nothing to discourage Seraphine. Meg did not care to be so beholden to Sir Patrick either. Although the man continued to show her every kindness and courtesy, she had seen little of him these past three days.

Claimed by his duties at Whitehall and his efforts to arrange her meeting with the king, Sir Patrick had been absent as much as Seraphine, both of them leaving Meg on her own far too much, to worry about the possible resurrection of the Silver Rose coven, to fear that it might somehow be connected to her mother.

She would have welcomed any diversion, even Blackwood's company, despite how provoking and teasing he could be. But she had not seen him since the evening they had arrived in London. He had disembarked from the barge, melted into the crowd upon the landing, and just disappeared. He had not even bothered to say good-bye, although she had no idea why that should trouble her.

She had little expectation of ever seeing Blackwood again now that he had returned to London. She was sure he must be preoccupied with dicing, drinking, attending cockfights, however such a man passed his time. She could not imagine him devoting himself to the care of the sick, and given what she knew of his medical abilities, that was likely just as well.

She would not have given Blackwood another thought except for the tension and tedium of these past days. She was not accustomed to such idleness, to being so restricted. Both Seraphine and Sir Patrick felt it wiser and safer for her to remain quietly at his house, awaiting her audience with the king. Meg had agreed—for the present. If she hoped to uncover the source of this mysterious threat against His Majesty, she needed to begin by speaking with James Stuart. But after that Meg also had connections in London . . .

She donned her dressing gown and drifted over to the window that afforded a pleasant vista of Sir Patrick's garden, the tidy beds arranged in an orderly and controlled fashion. But it was a foggy morning and the view was obscured by the mist.

Meg saw someone stirring near the apple tree and thought it must be Hubert Chalmers, Sir Patrick's gardener. A pleasant man of middle age whose paunch had begun to make kneeling difficult, he had welcomed Meg's help with the pruning and weeding, aid that Meg had been eager to offer. She had never been fond of needlework and was far too distracted to focus on a book. But working in the garden, burying her fingers deep in the rich soil, was an activity both familiar and comforting to her. It had helped ease this time of anxious waiting and she was grateful to Mr. Chalmers for affording her the opportunity.

She lifted her hand to rap on the glass to gain his attention and wave a greeting. But she froze, her knuckles poised in midair.

It was not Chalmers, but a woman, her slender form concealed beneath a long gray cloak, her hood pulled forward to conceal her features. It could not be Seraphine because the woman was far too short. One of Sir Patrick's serving maids perhaps?

No, none of them required the use of a cane and this woman relied heavily on hers, employing it to ease her way to the edge of the garden path.

Meg thought she saw the woman drop something, but perhaps she was mistaken. Instead of bending to retrieve anything, the woman paused and tipped up her head to peer toward the house. Meg's hand dropped back to her side, her heartbeat quickening. She could make out nothing of the stranger's features and yet she had a sense that the woman was staring straight up at her.

Meg fought against the urge to shrink away from the window. The hairs at the nape of her neck prickled and she felt a chill course through her unlike anything she had known. Not since the last time she had stood trembling before Cassandra Lascelles.

"Maman?" Meg whispered.

She jumped and spun away from the window when her bedchamber door opened and Seraphine sailed in, brisk and full of purpose.

"You are awake. Good. Because there is much to be done and little time—" Seraphine broke off, studying Meg's face. Meg could only imagine how pale she must appear.

"What is it? What's wrong?"

"I—I—" Meg turned back to the window to gesture toward the woman in the garden. But there was no one there. She had simply vanished if she had even been there at all. Perhaps James Stuart was not the only one seeing ghosts from his past.

"I thought—"

What? That she had seen her mother return from the dead?

"Nothing," Meg mumbled, feeling foolish over the way she had allowed her imagination to leap out of control.

Ordinarily Seraphine would not have been satisfied by such a vague answer. She would have pressed Meg until she had the truth, but Seraphine seemed distracted herself. She had a retinue of maidservants trailing in her wake.

Three young women labored under a pile of parcels, steaming water buckets, and a tray of food. They were followed by a footman toting a hip bath.

"What is all this?" Meg asked.

"Your armor. You are not meeting the king unprepared." Like a general supervising her troops, Seraphine ordered the setting up of the bath and then dismissed the footman. While two of the maids filled the tub with hot water, the other one piled the parcels upon the bed. Meg watched all these preparations with mounting trepidation even though she attempted to jest.

"Armor? Do you mean you have purchased me a padded vest to wear beneath my gown? Don't you think I will look rather foolish, all puffed up like pigeon?"

"My dear Meg, by the time I have finished with you, you will not look like any sort of feathered creature unless it be a bird of paradise." Seraphine stripped the wrapping away from the largest parcel, triumphantly displaying a blue gown of richest velvet.

"Oh, 'Phine, what have you done? I thought we agreed any finery was unnecessary."

"You may have agreed. I never did. Sir Patrick may smuggle you up the back stairs, but when you stand before the king, you will be resplendent, commanding the respect owed to the Lady of Faire Isle. Proud, your head held high like the grandest queen in Christendom."

"It will take more than a fine gown to effect such a transformation." Meg fingered the soft folds of the gown. It had been many years since she had owned anything so fine, not since those long-ago days when she had lived with her father in London. After Martin Wolfe had rescued Meg from the horrors of her mother's coven, he had done his best to erase

Meg's past. He had installed her in an elegant home, bought her all the fripperies, pretty gowns, and jewels any normal girl could desire. Poor Papa had been so determined to transform his plain little witch into a dazzling princess. It had not worked then and Meg doubted it would now.

But gainsaying Seraphine was like trying to steer a straight course in the face of a hurricane gale and Meg could not summon up the energy to fight her friend on this. Meg simply did not care what she wore, but since it was a matter of importance to Seraphine, Meg submitted.

She could have actually enjoyed soaking in the hip bath if she had been allowed to close her eyes and drift off into the quiet place in her mind. But that was quite impossible with one maid buffing her nails, another vigorously scrubbing her back, while Seraphine stuffed her with bread and honey.

Meg had no appetite, but Seraphine insisted that Meg could not face her meeting with the king on an empty stomach and Meg conceded that she was right.

After she was toweled dry, Meg stood meekly while they commenced dressing her, although she felt like a cloth doll being pulled this way and that by four eager girls. She had heard of what knights endured to be readied for battle, how long it took to be encased in a full suit of armor. Meg thought it could hardly be worse than this as garters were fastened to hold up her stockings, her waist was cinched by a corset, followed by a farthingale and layers of petticoats. She wondered how she would even move without tripping, especially in the white kid shoes that pinched her feet, the wooden heels far higher than she was accustomed to wear.

After the velvet gown was draped over Meg's head, Seraphine dismissed the maids, much to Meg's relief.

"I will finish attending to milady myself," Seraphine said,

shooing the young women out the door. As Seraphine fetched the sleeves, Meg smoothed her hands down over the gown, marveling at the snugness of the fit.

"How were you able to acquire a gown exactly to my measurements?" Meg asked.

"Easily. I took that old brown frock of yours and allowed the seamstress to pick it apart for a pattern."

"Seraphine!" Meg shifted to scowl up at her friend. "That frock was my favorite."

"It was hideous."

"It was also excessively comfortable and practical, which this gown most definitely is not," Meg complained.

Oblivious to Meg's grumbling, Seraphine merely ordered her to hold still. Meg subsided, feeling slightly ashamed as she realized how peevish she sounded.

"I am sorry," she said. "I don't mean to seem ungrateful. The gown is lovely and I do thank you for it. How did you manage to have it readied in only three days?"

"I told you," Seraphine replied, frowning as she concentrated on the hooks that fastened the demi-cannon sleeves to the bodice of the gown. "I am not without acquaintance in London. When I explained my urgent need, the Countess of Shrewsbury was kind enough to lend me the use of her seamstresses, and by court standards, this is not a very elaborate dress."

It seemed quite elaborate to Meg and costly. She asked uneasily, "And did the countess lend you money as well?"

Seraphine laughed. "Bess Throckmorton? Hardly. That woman did not amass a fortune by doling it out to others." She sobered as she moved on to the other sleeve. "I am not without funds of my own, Meg. Even though I am separated from Monsieur le Comte, I may draw upon his agents as I please."

"Another man might have tightened the purse strings in order to bring his wife to heel," Meg could not help pointing out.

"Gerard would never do that. He has never been mean in that regard. He has always tried to give me anything I wanted. Unfortunately, he cannot give me what I desire the most."

"And that is?"

"My little boy. I want my son back." Seraphine's eyes filled and Meg hoped her friend would at last give vent to the grief she had dammed up for so long. But Seraphine blinked hard. She strode to the bed to fetch the starched cuffs and ruff, and when she returned, she changed the subject.

"This gown would never do at our court in France. The neckline is far too high, but Bess warned me that King James is something of a prude."

"Did the countess tell you anything else that might be of use?"

"She said that like most monarchs, James likes lavish compliments. Do you have any idea how you should address the king?"

"I assume it would be incorrect to call him 'Most high and royal witch burner.'"

Ordinarily Seraphine would have returned a witty rejoinder, but she frowned instead. "This is no matter for jests, Meg. Royalty, even the most liberal minded of them, are extremely jealous of their position. One must handle a king with care."

As Seraphine proceeded to educate her in the intricacies of court etiquette, Meg was tempted to remind her this would not be the first time she had been given a private audience with royalty.

But she supposed she could not count when she had been

the prisoner of Catherine de Medici and Meg had been steeling herself to kill the Dark Queen. There could be no question of protocol when one was plotting regicide.

There had also been the time during her childhood days in London when Meg had run away to fling herself, trembling, before Queen Elizabeth. She had idolized the English queen with a youthful adoration, blind to all the woman's faults, so that meeting had gone well enough. Meg had secured the boon she had desired, the release of her older friend, Lady Jane Danvers, from the Tower.

Elizabeth had been intrigued by Meg's power to use a gazing globe to peer into the future . . . intrigued and disconcerted. When she had restored Meg to her father, Elizabeth had commanded Martin Wolfe:

"We would strongly advise you to convey her to this Faire Isle as soon as possible. Besides being a remarkable girl, Margaret is also one of the most unnerving we have ever met. Therefore we think our English climate might not prove at all suitable for such a rare French rose."

It was as well Seraphine knew nothing of that meeting. If Seraphine had any idea that Meg had been banished from England, her friend would have never allowed Meg to return to London.

But that was over twenty years ago. Queen Elizabeth was dead, most of the ministers who had served her deceased as well or retired from their high offices. Meg doubted that anyone would recollect the encounter between the late queen and an insignificant little girl, but that was a chance that Meg had to take.

Dragging her thoughts back from the past, Meg strove to absorb Seraphine's instructions.

". . . and the king loves flattery. So you should address

him in such terms as 'O wisest of kings since the great Solomon' or 'most royal all-beloved king of hearts.'"

"I could never say such a thing and keep my countenance and surely the king would laugh or be disgusted."

"No, His Majesty will lap it up like honey."

"Even if I sounded so false?"

"He'd never notice. A royal court is no place for sincerity."

As Seraphine fixed a golden girdle about Meg's waist, she went on. "The king fancies himself a scholar, so you might compliment him on his learning. He is fluent in Latin and Greek and very fond of debate."

"In that at least, I might accommodate him. My own Latin and Greek are—"

"Skills you'd best forget. The king has a very poor opinion of the intellect of women and I doubt he'd welcome being challenged by one."

"If he thinks so poorly of women, then why would he have taken such pains to have me fetched to him?"

"That is exactly what worries me. That and why it has taken three days for a king desperate to be cured of a curse to grant you an audience."

"That question has troubled me as well," Meg admitted.

"No matter how cautious Sir Patrick has been in his arrangements, if he thinks he can keep this all quiet, then the man is a fool. Bess tells me there are already whispers about this strange curse afflicting the king. After this meeting, I fear there will be rumors about you as well, speculation about the cunning woman who journeyed so far to cure the king."

"I hope not. All I want is to meet quietly with His Majesty and find out what he can tell me of this supposed witch who cursed him."

"If your aim is to wangle information out of the king, then you'd best learn to flatter him and employ your feminine wiles."

"You would be far better at that."

"I know. But thanks to the way Sir Patrick has arranged all of this, I cannot even be there to watch over you. So I must arm you as best I can."

As Seraphine marched over to the bed to undo the last parcel, Meg said, "If you have bought me a dirk, I hardly think it wise for me to attempt to smuggle a weapon into the king's presence."

"It wouldn't be, especially since I cannot imagine you using it. But to please me, fasten this to your girdle."

Meg blinked when she saw what it was, an elegant fan with ivory handles. "What do you expect me to do with that, flirt with the king?"

"No, I expect you to use it to keep an eye on your back since I will not be there to do it for you."

Seraphine unfurled the fan to display a tiny mirror attached to the center. Meg was tempted to laugh, but she checked herself. This seemed a trifle melodramatic, but Seraphine was deadly earnest as she demonstrated how to hold the fan and use the mirror to observe what was happening in the background.

"Take this and practice until you can use it subtly. Now off with you while I summon Louise and Estelle and get ready myself."

"But 'Phine. You know you cannot accompany me."

"I am all too aware of that. I intend to find us an ally should this meeting of yours with the king go wrong. Bess has promised to present me to Queen Anne."

"Does the queen have that much influence with her husband?"

"I don't know. The king is said to be very fond of his wife. He vulgarly refers to her as 'our Annie' even before the entire court. Gerard had his pet name for me, but he reserved it for those times we were alone, *intimate.*" Seraphine's voice lingered over the last word and her eyes softened with remembrance. Then she hustled Meg out the door.

MEG PACED THE UPPER HALL, PRACTICING, BUT NOT WITH THE fan as Seraphine had commanded. Meg was far more concerned with her ability to walk in the high-heeled shoes without tripping and making a complete fool of herself. She wobbled along the landing, trying to keep her farthingale from swaying in awkward fashion, and resisting the urge to tug at the stiff ruff that scratched her neck.

Rigging herself out in this finery was a mistake, just as she had feared it would be. The gown, the shoes, the fan, all of Seraphine's warnings and instructions did little to bolster Meg's confidence; quite the opposite.

She took another turn about the hall only to draw up short when the door to Sir Patrick's bedchamber opened and his manservant Alexander emerged.

Meg started to greet him, inquire after his master's whereabouts, but before she could even get out the words "Good morrow," Alexander ducked past her, his golden hair falling like a shield over his eyes.

Meg was not surprised or affronted. The Scotsman avoided speaking to her whenever he could. Meg was fully aware that

Alexander regarded her with a mixture of fear and loathing, a natural reaction since the Scot had made it clear from the first he considered her a witch.

It saddened Meg, since in all other respects Alexander seemed a worthy man and slavishly devoted to Sir Patrick.

Gripping the rail, she descended the stairs to the lower hall, which she found deserted. Meg hesitated for a moment before directing her course toward the door that led out to the garden, although she did not know what she expected to find. The cloaked woman, if there indeed had been one, would be long gone. Perhaps Meg might find some trace of her, to prove that Meg had not been imagining things.

As she entered the garden, Meg strove to recollect exactly where she had seen the woman appear to drop something. Over there, beneath the apple tree, she thought. Meg started in that direction when she heard masculine voices. Two men strolled into view from behind the shrubbery. One was the gardener Chalmers, the other Armagil Blackwood.

Meg froze, her heart doing a curious kick against her ribs. She had a strong inclination to retreat. She felt awkward enough in her unaccustomed finery without displaying herself before Blackwood's cynical gaze.

But it was too late. Both men had already seen her, Chalmers dipping into a bow that caused his belly to double over his belt. Blackwood merely stared, taking in her altered appearance with a lift of his brows that could have betokened anything from surprise to amusement.

Meg held her head high and approached with more grace than she had ever imagined possible. Just as she was congratulating herself, she stumbled, but Blackwood caught her arm to break her fall.

"Steady," he said. There was no longer any mistaking his expression. His eyes danced with amusement.

Her cheeks firing, Meg tugged free of his grasp, striving to regain her dignity. She was aided by Chalmers's warm greeting and beaming smile.

"So, milady, you are all ready for your visit to Whitehall. If I may be permitted to say so, you look very handsome."

"You may, thank you."

"I have just been speaking of you to Dr. Blackwood. He was good enough to bring me a remedy for my stones, but I was informing him it was no longer necessary. Mistress Wolfe fixed me up a potion that has set me quite to rights."

"Has she indeed?" Blackwood said, looking none too pleased about it.

Meg lifted her chin in a challenging manner. "There is a certain herbal medication that I have learned to brew that works quite well in the treatment of stones."

"Most certain it does. This morning, I was able to piss without screeching—" Chalmer's plump face reddened. "Er—begging milady's pardon for my vulgarity."

"Oh, that's quite all right, Chalmers," Blackwood drawled. "Any woman who plays at being a doctor can hardly be troubled by feelings of delicacy."

Before Meg could think of a retort, Chalmers was hailed by one of the maidservants beckoning him toward the kitchen door. With an uneasy glance at Meg and Blackwood, the gardener excused himself.

After Chalmers's retreat, an awkward silence ensued. No doubt that Blackwood felt that by treating Chalmers, she had encroached upon his territory. But she was not about to apologize for it, especially when she caught sight of the vial clutched in Blackwood's hand. The small clear glass bottle held a white beadlike substance that actually appeared to be *moving*.

"What is that, Dr. Blackwood?"

Blackwood held the bottle up for her closer inspection. "Lice."

"No wonder Mr. Chalmers was so grateful for my medicine. You expected the poor man to swallow those?"

"No, the lice are meant to be inserted in the tip of a man's cock."

When Meg shuddered, Blackwood snapped, "It may seem repulsive, but it has been known to work."

"I cannot imagine how. I have never heard of anything so ridiculous."

"No more ridiculous than some woman who putters with herbs claiming to know better than a doctor trained at Oxford."

"Perhaps we should ask Mr. Chalmers who knows best. Good day to you, sir." With a nod of icy dignity, Meg turned to stalk away as best as she was able.

She had not gone far down the garden path, when Blackwood called after her, "Mistress Wolfe. Wait."

Meg ignored him and kept on going, but he came after her and seized hold of her arm. Meg stiffened, "Let go of me. You are wreaking havoc with my sleeve and trampling Sir Patrick's asters."

Blackwood spared a glance down at his boots. "Oh, blast Graham and his tidy little garden. Every time I am here, I want to snatch up a trowel and dig up the borders, let the flowers run wild as nature intended, like heather on a hill."

Meg started to nod, but checked herself, unwilling to concede that she could possibly agree with Blackwood on anything. She glared until he released her.

"I did not intend to sound so curt just now," he said. "I spoke out of concern for you as much anything else. It is not wise for a woman to go about dispensing medicine."

"Surely many women in England do so. Is it not considered part of a woman's duty to know how to tend the ailments of her household?"

"Yes, her own family and servants, but she would hardly saunter about the country, attending to strangers. Here in London, even midwives must obtain a license from the bishop before aiding women in their confinements.

"If your potions should ever fail, you could so easily be charged with witchcraft."

"Do you not think I know that? It is a risk I have run all my life," Meg said, unable to keep the bitterness from her voice. "The same danger any wise woman faces. Let but one patient die, and whether it is our fault or not, we could find ourselves facing the hangman's noose whereas you doctors could destroy an entire village with impunity."

"Not an entire village, just a small household or two. Kill off more than that and one's practice would likely decline."

Meg's lips twitched, but she refused to allow him to provoke her into smiling.

"Forgive me," he coaxed, his eyes softening. "You know I can never remain serious about anything for long. It is a fatal flaw in my character. If I have offended you, I am sorry."

His unexpected apology took Meg aback, defusing her anger.

"I am sorry as well," she said. "I did not mean to insult you either."

"Good. Then pray, allow me to fix your sleeve."

Meg noticed that her right sleeve had come partially unhooked. Before she could object, Blackwood stepped closer to refasten it. He worked the hooks every bit as deftly as Seraphine had done. The man appeared far too familiar with the intricacies of feminine dress.

It was not an opportune moment to recall Seraphine's opinion of what a good lover Blackwood would make. Meg caught herself staring at his hands, large, strong, with long fingers. It would not be difficult to imagine those hands caressing . . .

Meg squirmed, cutting off the thought and averting her gaze. To ease her embarrassment, Meg jested. "You are quite good at that, Dr. Blackwood. If your medical practice fails, you might find employment as a lady's maid."

"I doubt that. I am more adroit at undressing a woman, a skill most ladies' husbands find objectionable."

He did up the last hook and stepped back, his gaze raking over her. "There. You look . . . beautiful."

Meg gave a wry laugh.

"That is not the sort of reaction a man hopes for when he pays a lady a compliment."

"I could not help it. You sounded so surprised and I remember you telling me you did not think me handsome. Although you did allow that I was *almost pretty* when I smiled."

"Ah, but mistress, you are smiling."

Meg realized that she was. She schooled her features into a more sober expression. "You are merely dazzled by the gown, which is quite lovely."

Blackwood paced around her in a slow circle, studying her from every angle. "No, I don't think I like the gown. It is an unfortunate color for you. Blue would look better on Madame la Comtesse."

"Whereas a woman as plain as myself should wear nothing but brown or gray."

"You should wear green, a deep forest shade to match your eyes, or a deep gold brocade that would draw attention to your hair, those hints of auburn that catch the sunlight."

"Oh." Meg was accustomed to Blackwood's blunt honesty and teasing remarks. She would never have expected a compliment that sounded genuine. He was looking at her the way most men stared at Seraphine. The realization left her feeling flustered.

"Is that what you would prefer?" she asked.

"What I would prefer is to see you garbed in a great deal less."

When Meg gasped, his eyes widened in an expression of feigned innocence. "I only meant you should get rid of that farthingale. I cannot imagine who invented such an infernal device, some sour-faced virgin or dour puritan no doubt. All that cursed whalebone cage does is keep a man at a distance."

Despite Blackwood's complaint, he still managed to stand quite close, tracing one knuckle along her cheek.

"I do approve of the way the comtesse has arranged your hair, pulling it back from your face."

"You consider that an improvement."

"Aye, it makes it so much easier to kiss you."

Heat simmered in his eyes, his intention writ clear upon his face as Blackwood leaned closer. Seraphine's words echoed through Meg's mind.

"Choose someone whose lovemaking does not inspire such adjectives as warm, comfortable, and very pleasant. Blackwood should be your man."

Meg did not want or need a man. Yet she could not summon the will to move. Her heart beat faster as she awaited his kiss.

He paused, his mouth a breath from hers. Blackwood sighed and drew back, gathering up her hands.

An expression of rare seriousness settled over his features. "You will be careful today, Margaret."

It was the first time he had ever used her name, and the way he pronounced it was unexpectedly grave and sweet.

"Y-yes," she stammered, confused and surprised that he had not kissed her, even more surprised by her disappointment. "I am always prudent."

"No, you aren't or you would have stayed on Faire Isle. King James may strike you as being crude and even a bit of a fool, but he is very shrewd. He is a weak man, but that only makes him dangerous. There is no one more treacherous than a coward. You should also be wary of the king's little beagle. He has been known to bite."

Blackwood squeezed her hands. "And you should be careful with Graham as well."

"Sir Patrick?" Meg asked in astonishment. Was Blackwood warning her against his good friend?

Blackwood hesitated as though struggling with himself before he went on, choosing his words with great care. "Graham is a good man except when he is blinded by his zeal. He suffered a tragedy in his youth that affected him deeply, shaped the man he has become. He—"

But whatever else Blackwood intended to say was checked by the arrival of Sir Patrick himself. Graham entered the garden, pulling up short at the sight of them.

Blackwood dropped her hands and stepped away from her, but not, Meg feared, before Sir Patrick had seen, though she hardly knew why that should matter. Blackwood looked self-conscious, although he made a swift recovery.

"Graham." He greeted his friend after his usual offhand fashion.

"Blackwood," Sir Patrick returned curtly. He bowed to Meg with none of his usual courtesy, his gaze taking in her new gown. Although he made no remark upon her altered appearance, Graham seemed far from pleased. As he turned back to his friend, she detected a spark of anger in Graham's eyes.

"What brings you here at such an early hour?" he demanded. "I thought you never bestirred yourself much before noon."

"Occasionally I manage. I came to bring Chalmers a remedy for his stones, but since he prefers Mistress Wolfe's potion to my lice, I have packed my little friends away and was on the verge of returning home."

"One moment if you please." Sir Patrick turned toward Meg, forcing a stiff smile to his lips. "Mistress Wolfe, if you will excuse us, I need to have a private word with Dr. Blackwood."

The tension between the two men was so palpable, Meg felt reluctant to leave. But other than defying Sir Patrick's request, she had little choice. She curtsied to both men, but it was Blackwood's gaze that she met. His eyes seemed to reach out to her before he looked away.

As Meg walked toward the house, Blackwood tried to not stare after her and failed. She was learning to manage those higher-heeled shoes, her retreat graceful and dignified.

A half-smile touched his lips. Strange, but when Meg wore her simple dresses and serviceable boots, she exuded a quiet confidence. Trussed up in that fancy gown, she appeared uncertain, vulnerable, and somehow younger, arousing in him a fierce protectiveness.

He didn't want to feel such tenderness any more than he wanted this confrontation with Graham. But there seemed to be no way of avoiding either.

As soon as Meg was out of sight, Graham rounded on him. "What are you doing here, Blackwood? And don't give me any nonsense about an urgent need to fetch lice to Chalmers. You could have sent the remedy with that boy you usually engage to run your errands."

"Tom was nowhere to be found this morning. Besides, do I require an excuse to call upon you now?"

"You did not come to call upon me. You came to see *her* and after you promised to stay away."

"I don't recall that I exactly *promised.*"

"You agreed it would be for the best."

"Mayhap I did, but if I do feel a certain interest in Mistress Wolfe, I don't know why it concerns you to such a degree. You might deplore my amorous pursuits, but you have never sought to interfere."

"Mistress Wolfe is far different from one of your doxies. She is a guest in my household, under my protection."

"And do you mean to protect her?"

To Blackwood's unease, Graham avoided the question. Instead he fired back one of his own. "Have you been enchanted by her?"

The question was so ridiculous Blackwood laughed. But Graham was obviously quite serious.

"I am glad you find the idea amusing because I don't," he said. "I have never seen you regard any woman as tenderly as you do her. I fear you are in danger of being bewitched by her."

"You're daft."

"I hope so. Margaret Wolfe may call herself a healer, but

she admits to knowledge of white magic and she is a confessed pagan. To become enamored of such a woman would imperil your immortal soul."

"My soul?" Blackwood could not help but laugh again. "We both know I am well on the road to hell." He sobered as he added, "But I never wanted you marching alongside me. Graham, whatever you are conspiring, I beg you to stop."

A haunted look shadowed Graham's face. "I can't."

"You mean you won't, even if you endanger Margaret Wolfe and destroy yourself in the process."

"Sacrifices are often necessary when one acts in the name of God and justice."

"Justice! I hate it when you turn sanctimonious. At least be honest with yourself and acknowledge your plot for what it is."

"What would that be?"

"Revenge."

A muscle worked in Graham's cheek, his only response to the accusation. "I must collect Mistress Wolfe and be off to Whitehall. It would not do to keep the king waiting. Your servant, Blackwood."

Graham accorded him a curt bow before striding toward the house. Blackwood suppressed the urge to charge after him and try to thrash some sense into the man. It would do no good. That steely glint had sparked in Graham's eyes, that fanatical expression Blackwood so hated.

Blackwood strode off in the opposite direction, angry at Graham for being so obdurate, at Meg for not having the sense to stay on Faire Isle, and at the king for . . . far too many reasons.

Most of all Blackwood was angry at himself because all he wanted to do was return home and drown in strong drink. When had he turned into such a worthless piece of dung?

As he stalked past the apple tree, he caught sight of something glittering on the ground. He drew up short for a closer look.

"What the devil?" He bent down and retrieved the strange object, a white rose frosted with something so silvery, it sparkled in the sunlight. Blackwood had never seen the like.

He studied it as he let himself out the garden gate. The flower pricked his thumb and he swore. The rose's thorns were as sharp as the tip of a knife.

Blackwood fumbled in his purse and produced a handkerchief in which he carefully enfolded the flower. His thumb was bleeding and he sucked at the tip of it, to stop the flow.

He had never seen a flower as perfectly formed as the silver rose. It was beautiful, but so unnatural, it filled him with unease. Who could have created such a thing? Not Chalmers, that was certain. He was a good gardener, but hardly a clever man and not given to any sort of grafting or experimentation.

Chalmers had said that Meg had been helping him in the garden. Far more likely the rose was something of her fashioning, but for what purpose? Did it have some extraordinary healing properties? Then why would she have been so careless as to drop it? All good questions that Blackwood needed to ask her. It would give him a marvelous excuse to see her again.

The woman has you bewitched. Graham's accusation resounded through his mind.

Nonsense, Blackwood wanted to sneer. But he could not help reflecting that perhaps Graham was not the only one being less than honest with himself.

"God's blood," he muttered. "I need a drink."

As he strode away, he never noticed the old woman observing him from a safe distance.

As the woman watched Blackwood making off with the precious silver rose, she quivered with anger, banging the tip of her cane on the ground.

"Damn, damn, *damn*!"

She whirled and headed in the opposite direction, her youthful steps belying any need for a cane. Her white wig itched something dreadful, and the first thing Amy did when she joined her sister was snatch the hairpiece from her head.

"Well, how did it go?" Bea asked.

"The test failed," Amy cried.

Bea rolled her eyes. "I might have known you would bungle it. I should have gone myself."

"You couldn't have done any better! It was all going well enough. The lady spied me in the garden and I am sure she must have seen me drop the rose.

"I thought she would come rushing out at once, so I hid myself to watch and see how she reacted to the silver rose, because then we would know for certain if she is Megaera."

Amy waved the cane in agitation. "I waited and waited and she never came, only Dr. Blackwood and that gardener, so I was obliged to slip out of the garden before I was caught. I didn't know what to do so I lingered outside, hoping I could steal back after Blackwood left, which he finally did. With the rose!"

She concluded her breathless recital with a vexed sigh.

"You allowed Blackwood to take the rose?" Bea chided. "Oh, Amy, you little fool."

"I could not prevent it, I tell you." Amy was so angry and distressed, tears started to her eyes.

"Now we will have to fashion another rose and we shall have to try the test again."

"It is not my fault. It was Blackwood's. What was he even doing there? He pricked his thumb on the rose and it serves him right. The spineless, useless sot! Ohh, I would like to put a curse upon him."

"If he got pricked by the thorn, cursing him would be a wasted effort." Bea shrugged. "The man is as good as dead."

Chapter Ten

WHITEHALL SPRAWLED OVER TWENTY-THREE ACRES, A MAZE of courtyards, passages, offices, and apartments. The towering brick walls of the palace spanned King Street, the wings connected by the arched bridge that formed the upper stories of the gatehouse.

Escorted by Sir Patrick, Meg made her way along the congested street, peering upward at the palace skyline, a dizzying array of towers and chimney stacks. She was assailed by a rush of memories, of the time she had made this journey alone as a child, frightened but determined to see Queen Elizabeth.

Meg could only marvel at the courage of her former self. Had she been so much braver then or only more naïve about the risk she took? So much ill could have befallen a girl venturing alone through London to cast herself before the queen known as Gloriana. Vacillating in her moods, Elizabeth could be cruel when her formidable temper was aroused, or kind, warm, and generous as she had shown herself to Meg.

Meg prayed she would fare as well with James Stuart, a man she knew only as the notorious destroyer of witches. As they neared the main gate, Meg's stomach knotted with apprehension and Sir Patrick's demeanor did nothing to reassure her.

Sir Patrick evinced none of the courtesy she had come to expect from him. He had scarce spoken to her during the journey to Whitehall. As the carriage creaked slowly through the crowded streets of London, he had stared out the window. But Meg would have wagered that he had seen none of the half-timbered houses or bustling shops. His gaze had appeared focused on some vision apparent only to himself.

Whatever it was, it had afforded him no pleasure. The set of his mouth was tense, the expression in his eyes alternating between sorrow and something harder, determined. Did his grim mood have something to do with the upcoming meeting with the king or Armagil Blackwood? When she had reluctantly left the two men alone in the garden, Meg had been certain they were on the verge of a quarrel.

When Meg had mentioned her fear to Seraphine, her friend had teased her, congratulating Meg on her conquests and setting the two men at odds over her. Meg had rolled her eyes at Seraphine's nonsense. But it was obvious from Sir Patrick's dark mood, he and Blackwood had fallen out over something. Meg would have given much to know what had passed between the two men, but Sir Patrick's shuttered expression invited no questions.

Sir Patrick did recall his manners enough to offer her his arm, and although it felt stiff and unyielding beneath her touch, Meg was grateful for the support. The traffic was at its worst outside the court gate, where courtiers sought access to the palace under the watchful eyes of the warden. Servants, forbidden entry, lolled about as they awaited the return of their masters. Adding to the throng was a cluster of high-spirited young gallants who lingered to ogle arriving ladies, hoping to catch a glimpse of ankle as the bejeweled and satin-clad beauties alighted from carriages.

Observing the overwhelming press of people, Meg could only shake her head as she mused. "My memories of the last time I was here are so blurred. I wonder now how I ever managed to slip inside to see the queen."

Sir Patrick halted, staring down at her, his eyes hard with suspicion. "You have been to Whitehall before? You never mentioned that."

Meg already regretted her impulsive comment. "That is because there was little to mention. I believe I did tell you I lived in England briefly with my father and I was fascinated by tales of Queen Elizabeth, so one day I ran away from Papa and somehow stole into the palace to catch a glimpse of her for myself."

"I doubt it would have been that difficult for you. The late queen was much more accessible to the common people than King James. His Majesty abhors crowds."

He lapsed into silence again as he steered her away from the court gate. They crossed a plaza that led past the tiltyard, the royal lists that had been the site of many famous jousts during the reigns of Elizabeth and her father, the formidable Henry the Eighth.

Meg was distracted for a moment, imagining the pageantry of the tournaments, the pennants snapping in the breeze, the sunlight glinting off the armor of the knights and their richly caparisoned horses, the shouts of encouragement from excited spectators.

The tiltyard bore an aura of emptiness and neglect on this quiet autumn afternoon. When Meg remarked upon that, Sir Patrick unbent enough to reply, "King James has little taste for public spectacles."

"Not even a tournament?"

"No, he dislikes any sort of military display. He actually shudders at the sight of naked steel."

"He is a man of peace, then?" Meg asked dubiously.

"Yes, at any price."

The remark was so curt, Meg wondered if it indicated Sir Patrick's disapproval of his king's policy. She doubted that because Sir Patrick was such a gentle man himself. If he disapproved of anyone, Meg had the strong feeling it was *her*.

He guided her toward the corner of the tiltyard where a flight of wooden stairs led up to another gallery of the palace. Unable to endure any more of Sir Patrick's frosty behavior, Meg dug in her heels.

"Sir Patrick, have I done something to offend you?"

He appeared disconcerted by her blunt question. He started to frame some polite denial when Meg cut him off.

"Is it my new gown?" She self-consciously smoothed out the velvet folds. "I know you advised against any finery but—"

"No, the gown is fine. It makes you appear quite respectable."

"Very respectable, and not in any way as elaborate as the gowns of those other ladies I saw arriving, nothing to draw the sort of notice you wish to avoid."

"And yet you certainly attracted enough notice from Dr. Blackwood."

There was an edge to his words that caused Meg to wonder. Could Seraphine possibly be right about Sir Patrick being jealous of Blackwood? No, surely that was ridiculous.

"I gather that you have quarreled with Dr. Blackwood and I am sorry for it." Meg added uncomfortably, "And I should be sorrier still if I am somehow the cause of it."

She waited for him to deny it. Her dismay deepened when he failed to do so, lapsing into silence and staring fixedly at the ground.

When he finally looked up at her, his face had softened and he ventured to take her by the hand.

"Mistress Wolfe, you must understand. I brought you to England and thus that makes me responsible for anything that should occur. My friend Blackwood's conduct toward women—" Sir Patrick sighed. "Well, let us just say that his behavior is not always as moral as it should be. It is a weakness in his character, and you would be wise to keep your distance from him."

"I assure you, sir, that while Dr. Blackwood has a tendency to flirt, it is merely idle play. Nothing of an unseemly nature has happened between us."

"No, no, I did not mean to imply that it had. Blackwood is in essence a good man, but there is a great spiritual emptiness in his heart that leaves him vulnerable to temptation. His loneliness is responsible for most of his sins. Sometimes I think that I am his only true friend."

"Has he no family?" Meg asked.

"I believe none that he acknowledges or cares for, but it is difficult to tell. You may have noticed that Blackwood is rarely ever serious about anything. Between his jests and his lack of tact, the man holds people at a distance. He is often enough to provoke a saint, which I am not.

"We have disagreed before, but our quarrels are soon mended. If I have been out of sorts and rude to you in consequence, I do beg your pardon."

Sir Patrick smiled and carried her hand to his lips. Meg acknowledged his apology, but her mind whirled in confusion. Patrick Graham and Armagil Blackwood claimed to be such good friends, but in the span of a few hours, each of them had warned her against the other. So which man was to be believed?

And what did Sir Patrick mean, that Blackwood had no family he acknowledged? Blackwood was one of those men whose quick wit, wry humor, and blunt honesty could leave one deceived into a feeling of false intimacy, that one knew more of him than one did.

But she knew even less about Blackwood than she did of Sir Patrick, his personal history, his family background, where he hailed from. She would have liked to ask Sir Patrick a great many more questions about his friend. But he forestalled her with another smile as he urged her up the stairs.

"We must not keep the king waiting."

Sir Patrick clearly meant to tell her no more about his friend and perhaps regretted having said so much. But what did it matter? Meg had not come to England to make a study of Armagil Blackwood, she reminded herself.

Her sole purpose was to sort out the truth about the possible reemergence of the Silver Rose coven and the fate of her mother. To do that she first needed to confront James Stuart, the witch burner. As she trudged up the steps, her heart thudded like a prisoner mounting the gallows.

Sir Patrick seemed to sense her tension. Behaving more like his amiable self, he attempted to reassure her, "This way leads directly into the most private part of the palace. It is reserved for only the most privileged of the king's courtiers and guests."

His smile should have made her feel better, but it didn't. If she was being treated like an honored guest, she realized how much was expected of her, that she would either cure the king of his curse or convince James that she had.

Meg well knew the way of these things. Succeed and she would be hailed as a wise woman. Fail and she could be called a witch, and it was well known what James Stuart did to witches.

Sir Patrick exchanged a few words with the yeoman of the guard and they were permitted to pass through the gate above the arched roadway. They followed the passage through to the bewildering range of chambers that composed the heart of the palace.

Sir Patrick pointed out the rooms as they passed. "There is the chamber where the privy council meets. That way leads to the Chamber of Ordinary Audience, where nobles hoping to the see the king are obliged to wait. Beyond that door is the king's own cabinet. That passage connects to the king's withdrawing room and bedchamber."

He spoke rapidly, as though his own tension had increased. The way ahead of them was barred by a cluster of courtiers, all men. Gathered in a tight knot, they were discussing a matter that must have been of some importance, from their grave expressions. Meg could not understand what was being said, their voices low and many of them thick with Scottish accents.

Sir Patrick leaned down to murmur in her ear, "The king's inner circle of private attendants, his closest friends and advisors."

If that was who these men were, it appeared as though the king had chosen to surround himself with many of his fellow Scots. Meg could only speculate as to how much resentment that must have caused among his English subjects.

As she and Sir Patrick approached, one of the men broke away from the group and strode forward to meet them. Sir Patrick introduced him as Thomas Percy, one of the king's gentleman pensioners, his private bodyguard. Percy was tall with an imposing frame. His face was that of a man not much older than forty, but his hair had turned prematurely white.

"This is Mistress Margaret Wolfe," Sir Patrick said.

As Meg dipped into a curtsy, Percy's gaze swept cursorily over her. "Ah, the cunning woman you have brought to cure the king."

"I will do what I can, but . . ." Meg's words trailed off as she realized Percy was not even listening.

He turned to Sir Patrick, speaking in low tones. "There has been another incident today. I am sure you shall hear of it from the king. He is much disturbed, so distressed he speaks of retreating to his palace at Nonesuch and again canceling the opening of parliament. You *know* how vital it is that he should not do that."

"That won't happen," Sir Patrick said. "There will be no further delay, I promise you."

"I pray you are right. There is far too much at stake. You were supposed to have dealt with this." Percy was considerably agitated, his voice tending to rise. Sir Patrick placed a cautioning hand on his arm, drawing him farther away from Meg.

While the two men engaged in conversation, Meg feigned interest in one of the tapestries adorning the wall. Sir Patrick's words were unintelligible. Most of the snippets she gleaned came from Percy.

"... *must meet soon* ... *Johnston* ... *edgy. Too much delay* ... *risk discovery.*"

Johnston? Meg supposed it was a common enough name and yet she could not help thinking of the mysterious man who had accompanied them on the voyage from France. Who was it who risked discovery? This Johnston? Thomas Percy? Sir Patrick? And discovery of what?

Meg strained to hear more, but Sir Patrick brought the conversation to an abrupt end. Drawing in a deep breath, he rejoined Meg.

"Percy informs me that His Majesty is awaiting us in the long gallery."

Meg wondered what else Percy had said that etched a deep line between Sir Patrick's brows. He made a visible effort to relax his face as he escorted Meg through the crowd of courtiers.

The gentlemen fell back to allow them passage, some acknowledging Sir Patrick with brief nods and murmured greetings. Meg steeled herself not to blush as she was inspected by a myriad of masculine gazes, some curious, some scornful, and some inscrutable. She felt a little like a mouse being eyed by dozens of hungry hawks.

All of Seraphine's warnings of the dangers to be found at court, all the intrigue, the plotting, rushed back to Meg. Suddenly her friend's gift of the fan imbedded with its tiny mirror no longer seemed so ridiculous. She fingered the ivory handle as they entered the long gallery, expecting to have to run another gauntlet of royal attendants. She was surprised to find the vast chamber empty save for the king and one of his hunting dogs.

At least Meg assumed this was the king. He was dressed modestly compared to the opulence of the men she had encountered in the outer hall. He wore a silver-gray doublet, a cloak of black tabinet slung over one shoulder, his only adornment a diamond brooch affixed to his hat.

He wrestled with the black hound in a spirit of seemingly carefree playfulness. But the sunlight pouring through the tall windows illuminated James Stuart's haggard expression. The dog leaped up, bracing its paws on the king's chest, licking at the ends of his beard. Rather than rebuking the animal, James appeared to welcome its boisterous affection.

Meg had heard so many tales of this king, James Stuart, the witch burner, the author of the infamous *Daemonology*. His reputation was so black among the wise women on Faire Isle, Meg would not have been surprised to find a misshapen monster, his cruelty etched upon his face. She would never have expected a man who looked so ordinary, almost vulnerable as he took comfort in his dog.

It was the hound who alerted James to their arrival, the dog getting between them and issuing warning barks.

"Eh, quiet, Jowler. Sit!" the king said. The melancholy cast of his face brightened as his gaze fell upon Sir Patrick. "There you are, my good lad. I was begun to think you had forgotten all about your poor king."

"Never, Your Grace." Sir Patrick left Meg to sink to one knee before the king, but James would have none of it, lifting the younger man to embrace him.

The king's dog ambled over to inspect Meg. She tensed, remembering Blackwood's advice to be wary of the king's little beagle, but this was a large hound and the dog appeared friendly enough. Meg extended her hand to be sniffed.

"Good dog, Jowler," she said, venturing to stroke one of his ears.

The king had finally released Sir Patrick from his hearty

embrace, but he kept one arm slung about his shoulders. Sir Patrick looked slightly discomfited by James's display of affection. He had described himself to Meg as only an insignificant clerk at court, but it was clear the king had a high regard for him.

His voice thick with the accent of his native Scotland, James spoke so rapidly Meg had difficulty understanding him. But as her ear grew more accustomed, she realized that the king had launched into a complaint about his eldest son, Prince Henry.

"What ails the lad he must defy me in this manner? This morrow he engaged in swordplay beneath my very windows. He knows right well I have forbidden any such dueling within the palace grounds."

"I am sure the prince meant no disrespect, sire," Sir Patrick said. "It is but the high spirits of youth. Prince Henry is a most athletic boy with much energy to expend."

"Then let him expend it in some proper activity such as coursing game or snaring birds. But the lad has no liking for such good sport. I'll be damned afore I ever make a hunter of the boy."

The king heaved a deep sigh. "And I don't know how much longer I'll have to make a proper king of him either. If anything were to happen to me—"

"Nothing will, sire."

"You think not, laddie? I feel as if this great evil that has been stalking me draws nearer. While you were gone, I have had such fearsome dreams of that witch and her curse . . . of burning."

"I have brought someone to you who I hope will help with that." Sir Patrick eased from beneath the weight of the king's arm. "The wise woman that I told you of, the Lady of Faire Isle."

James Stuart's gaze at last turned in Meg's direction. She had bent down to scratch the hound's muzzle, the dog bathing her hand with his tongue.

"Jowler!" The king patted his thigh with an imperious gesture. "Come!"

The dog scrambled back to his master's side. Meg slowly straightened, uncertain what she should do, loath to be summoned like an obedient hound herself.

The king solved that problem for her. Commanding the dog to stay, James approached her. He had an awkward gait. Although he was not a large man, his legs appeared almost too spindly to support his body.

He came directly up to Meg and then retreated one step, the action of a man wary of strangers. It showed in the king's eyes, narrowed and suspicious.

As Meg made her curtsy, Sir Patrick stepped forward to murmur, "Mistress Margaret Wolfe, Your Grace."

The king inspected her thoroughly before bidding her rise. "So mistress, you claim to be a *wise* woman." James shrugged and quoted in Latin, *"Un idea perplexi na."*

"The idea of a wise woman would be strange to many men," Sir Patrick said. "But I assure you Mistress Wolfe is possessed of surpassing intelligence, although of course her wit is not as profound as that of Your Grace."

"Humph." The king's expression conveyed a mingling of doubt and contempt that irritated Meg. She had traveled too far and risked too much to be met with such ridicule.

She fired back without thinking, *"Quid quid latine dictum sit altum videtur."*

Sir Patrick looked appalled, shooting her a reproving glance. The king arched his brows in surprise and then frowned.

"Very true, mistress. Anything spoken in Latin can make one sound wiser than one is."

"It can also make one sound impertinent," Meg said, recalling Seraphine's cautions about challenging the king's vanity. "Forgive me, Your Grace. In my foolish effort to impress you, I misspoke. My command of Latin is nowhere near as great as yours, most . . . most gracious learned prince."

The flattery stuck in her throat, ringing false to Meg's ears. But the king's mouth curved with the hint of a smile.

"Your apology is accepted, mistress. You need not try so hard to impress. Your Latin is passable, but I would not expect a woman to tax her brain with such learning. The queen never does. Our Annie confines herself to her music, her stitchery, and arranging masques and other pretty divertissements for our court's entertainment."

"I possess no such skills, Your Grace."

"No, your skills lie elsewhere, do they not? You are reputed to be a great sorceress, familiar with all practices of curses and dark magic."

Meg caught the hint of accusation in his voice. She unfurled her fan and fluttered it before her face to conceal her alarm. "I make no such claims. Any gifts I possess are devoted to healing, the study of herbs and their curative powers. I have naught to do with the dark arts, and in all honesty, I have never believed in curses."

"You would if one had been placed on you," James retorted. "The venom that witch hurled at me has long preyed upon my mind and it has grown worse of late. I do not dare look out at my own garden for dread of that evil creature rising up before me."

James darted a nervous glance toward one of the long windows. Either because he could not resist the compulsion or he felt the need to test his courage, he strode over to peer out. Meg and Sir Patrick quietly followed.

The garden below would have been a lovely place in the full flowering of summer. It looked rather bleak this late in the autumn, all growth withered beneath the breath of an early frost, the pathways littered with dried leaves.

"The ghost of that witch struck again early this morning," James said.

"What? You mean here at Whitehall, within the very walls?" Sir Patrick exclaimed.

"No, outside. She nailed a dead cat to the posterior gate and left a message splashed in blood. *Davy's son. Burn in hell.*"

"Who is Davy's son?" Meg asked.

An awkward silence followed her question. Sir Patrick cast an uneasy look at the king, whose lips had compressed in a thin angry line.

At last James replied, "The name refers to me, a slur upon my birth. There have always been scurrilous rumors that I was the bastard son of David Rizzio, the court musician."

"No loyal subject would believe such a thing," Sir Patrick said.

"And what about the disloyal ones?" The king's voice quivered with anger. "It is an infamous slander against me and my mother. To even suggest that she could have behaved so wickedly— My mother was a deeply religious woman, a saint and a martyr. All of Scotland mourned her murder."

That same Scotland had once reviled the Catholic queen, the ministers of the kirk calling her a Jezebel and a Papist whore, her rebellious subjects forcing her into exile. Meg suspected that much of this mourning had to do with outrage in Scotland against the English who had dared to execute Mary of Scots.

James's eyes actually filled with tears. Meg sought to make some polite soothing reply, but what little she knew of Mary Stuart did not accord with sainthood.

The late queen of Scots had been very much a woman of flesh and blood, romantic, passionate, and imprudent. She had lived a life steeped in scandal, suspected of conspiring to murder her husband and eloping with the infamous Earl of Bothwell. Driven from the Scottish throne, Mary had taken refuge across the border, only to become a prisoner of the English for the next eighteen years. In her absence, her son James had been crowned as king of Scotland.

Engaged in a plot to assassinate Elizabeth and take over the English throne, Mary had finally been convicted and beheaded. James now spoke so heatedly in his mother's defense, but it was well known that when she had been on trial for her life, he had made little effort to save her.

The tears in his eyes spoke as much of guilt as grief. Mary Stuart's schemes had posed a danger to a young king seeking alliance with Elizabeth, hoping to be named as the childless English queen's successor. His mother's death had infused James with as much relief as sorrow, a conflict of emotions Meg understood too well. She had felt much the same when Cassandra Lascelles had drowned.

But what if she didn't? What will I do if I discover she is still alive and behind all of this?

The thought suffused Meg with a sensation akin to panic.

She quashed the fear, forcing herself to concentrate upon what the king was saying.

". . . if that witch can draw so near to Whitehall, I am not safe here. Her fearsome curse was not pronounced just against me, but upon the entire house of Stuart. I should go into retreat, find some refuge for my family outside of the city."

Sir Patrick frowned. "But Your Grace, the opening of parliament—"

"Must perforce be delayed."

"No, I cannot allow that!"

When the king stared at him in surprise, Sir Patrick flushed and amended, "I mean that Your Grace must not allow some witch to bring a halt to the affairs of government or intimidate you. This curse must be ended and I am sure the Lady of Faire Isle can perform some spell to do so."

Meg cast Sir Patrick an indignant look. She thought she had made it more than clear to the man that she claimed no such power, nor would she lower herself to perform some nonsense ceremony.

She turned to the king. "Your Grace, there is no such spell because there is no curse. You are a rational man. Surely you must see that those angry words were but the ranting of an old woman dying in agony."

"An old woman?" The king glared at her. "Do you think I am incapable of telling the difference between a mere woman and a witch?"

Yes.

Meg suppressed her instinctive response and hedged. "I have read Your Majesty's treatise on witchcraft and realize you are considered an expert on the subject."

"I do not boast of my own achievements, but aye, I am

acknowledged as such. So much so that on my last visit to Oxford, the learned doctors had a woman brought before me who claimed she could transform into a succubus and drain the life from her neighbor's cattle. I examined her most thoroughly."

"And what became of the poor—I mean the woman?"

"I realized the unfortunate soul was but mad and advised that she be kept close confined by her family and treated with the proper medicines to calm her brain."

Meg stared at him.

"You look surprised, Mistress Wolfe. Did you suppose me one of those irrational fanatics who see witches everywhere, ready to torch every addled old fool, every wench spitefully accused by jealous neighbors?

"No! I made a purge of witches years ago in Scotland, but they were all implicated in a treasonous plot against me. My judgment never erred . . . except perhaps the once."

James faltered, his expression deeply troubled. As though sensing his master's distress, Jowler whined and sidled closer. The king petted him absently.

"There was a young woman condemned to die alongside the witch who cursed me. A mere girl really, but she had been caught in the church performing the satanic ritual along with all the other witches.

"The girl claimed she had been misled, did not know what she was doing. She wept and begged to be spared. I might have pardoned her if not for—"

James swallowed. "There have been far too many plots against me since I was a mere babe. I have always been too lenient with my enemies. This time I could not afford to be, but the memory has long burdened me."

"Of this girl?" Meg asked.

"No, for all her seeming innocence, she was as guilty as the others. It was the boy who haunted me, the lass's brother. He knelt before me and pleaded so movingly for his sister's life. It pained me to inflict such sorrow upon him.

"Robin . . . Robbie, I believe was his name. His sister cried out to him as she was chained to the stake. He fought like a wild thing to save her. And after, when all was done, he looked up at me, his eyes filled with such raw grief, such anger, such hatred." James shuddered.

"And what became of him?"

"I do not know for sure, but I heard some tale after of him taking his own life in the wildness of his grief. May God forgive him, if that be true. I hoped the report was false. He was such a beautiful lad. I can never forget him."

The parallels between James's story and the strange dreams she had been having were far too great for coincidence, Meg thought, fluttering her fan. As she did so, she caught a glimpse of Sir Patrick's face reflected behind her. A strange look crossed his features, but when Meg spun around to look at him, she decided it must have been some distortion of the mirror.

He wore his usual expression of grave concern as he said, "A sad story indeed, Your Grace. But I am sure it is not this boy who has risen from the dead to torment you."

"No, it is that damned witch who cursed me, Tamsin Rivers."

Meg feared she had already been far too blunt, questioning the king's wisdom. She tried to proceed more delicately.

"Forgive me, Your Grace. But what was it about this Tamsin that convinced you that she was a witch of such power?"

"Mistress Rivers admitted as much. She even boasted about worshipping some devil woman, some evil sorceress she called Megaera."

"But it is still possible that Tamsin Rivers was just a madwoman."

"Nae, she was a witch I tell you. The things that she said to me at her trial, what she whispered privately in my ear." Even after all these years, James looked shaken by the recollection. "She repeated to me intimate words I had spoken to my bride on my wedding night. How could she know of such things?"

"She must have read your eyes."

When James regarded her questioningly, Meg was forced to explain. "It is a skill that is acquired by many daughters of the earth."

"Daughters of the earth?"

"That is what we prefer to call ourselves, the women who have struggled to preserve the ancient knowledge of the arts of healing and white magic. Among those gifts is the ability to read eyes, the windows to the heart. Those capable of doing it well can often perceive actual thoughts, sometimes even memories."

"Do you possess this gift?"

The prudent thing would have been for Meg to deny it. Seraphine had rebuked her more than once for being too honest. But she said, "Yes, Your Grace, but only a little."

"Show me."

Meg was taken aback and tried to demur, but the king stepped closer, repeating his command. Meg had little choice but to raise her eyes to meet his.

When she had been younger, she had been far too skilled

in the art of reading eyes. It was not always a comfortable thing to be able to read another's thoughts. Meg had left her ability unused for so long, it had grown as rusty as a neglected sword.

But it was all too easy to read James Stuart. For all his shrewdness, there was something vulnerable about the man. Her gaze locked with his and she peered deeper into his mind. It was like walking into a castle whose drawbridge had been left carelessly open.

She did not have to probe far before she stumbled across the fear that had governed much of his life, the dread of being betrayed, of being murdered like the father he had never known, like so many others James had loved.

She realized the king was not as thick of chest as he appeared. He wore a padded garment beneath his doublet to protect himself from an assassin's dagger, afraid that it would not prove enough. As she went deeper and deeper into the fortress of his mind, she was assailed by a dizzying array of visions, rebellions, conspiracies, battles, James being abducted, held captive, barely escaping the sword held to his throat. And finally, behind the last door, a small boy crouched in the corner, shivering in terror, the sleeve of his doublet smeared with blood.

"Sweet heaven," Meg murmured. "You were only five years old when you watched your grandfather bleed to death from an assassin's bullet. And you thought it was your fault it had happened, that you were being punished by God because—because—"

Meg pushed a little deeper. "Because of the little bird you had inadvertently crushed, the wren you had wrestled away from your friend, Jocky . . . Jocky O'Scliattis."

James had been staring at her as if mesmerized, but he jumped back at her words, his face drained of color. Sir Patrick likewise paled, so far forgetting himself as to make the sign of the cross.

Luckily James was too focused on her to notice. He started to speak, but no words came, yet the unspoken accusation seemed to hover in the air. *Witch.*

Meg fidgeted with the handle of her fan. "Forgive me, Your Grace. I did not mean to alarm or offend you. This is why wise women who possess this gift use it sparingly. It is wrong to invade someone's most private thoughts or pain without a compelling reason. Only those daughters of the earth who have turned to the darkness employ it with malicious intent."

"Like this Tamsin Rivers did with me." Some of the king's color had returned, but he maintained a wary distance from her. "Then you admit she was a witch."

"Yes, I—I fear she must have been."

"Therefore her curse was also real." James exhaled a deep breath. "Very well. Cure me of it."

"Your Majesty?"

"Use your powers or your white magic or whatever you call it and break this curse."

"B-but—"

"Is that not why Sir Patrick brought you to me?"

"Yes, but—" Meg faltered in dismay, looking to Sir Patrick for help. He said nothing, steadfastly avoiding her gaze almost as if he had become afraid of her. Meg could not blame him after her foolish demonstration with the king. She had spent most of the voyage from France assuring Sir Patrick that she was no sorceress, that she possessed no extraordinary powers.

"Well?" the king barked. As though sensing the tension in his master's voice, Jowler got to his feet. Even the dog seemed to scowl at Meg, as the king regarded her with impatience.

"What do you intend to do to rid me of this curse?"

Chapter Eleven

"AN EXCELLENT QUESTION, YOUR MAJESTY," MEG THOUGHT, but it was someone else who gave voice to the remark.

Meg whipped around to see who had dared enter the king's presence, uninvited and unannounced. A man, soberly attired, he could not have stood much above five feet, although perhaps the fact that he was hunchbacked made him appear shorter than he was. His complexion was pale as though he seldom saw the sun, his face deep-lined, his mouth small and pinched.

"Salisbury." The king greeted him, sounding a trifle displeased at the man's intrusion. Undeterred, the man advanced.

Sir Patrick murmured in Meg's ear. "Robert Cecil, the Earl of Salisbury, the king's secretary of state."

Meg could not decide if Sir Patrick was passing information or issuing a warning. She tensed even though no man could have appeared more unassuming or harmless than Lord Salisbury as he made his bow to the king.

"Forgive the intrusion, Your Grace. I heard that this meeting with the cunning woman was taking place and I ventured to join you."

"Ha! You mean you would have liked to prevent it." The king directed a wry smile at Meg. "My lord Salisbury does not approve of witches."

"Neither do I," she said.

"Indeed, mistress?" Salisbury accorded her a polite nod of acknowledgment. His tone was mild, but his eyes were shrewd as they assessed her. Meg had a disquieting notion that she knew his lordship from somewhere, but that was impossible. Yet something about the man's steady gaze rendered her uneasy.

"His Majesty has been most troubled of late regarding past matters of witchcraft. I do not see how consulting another woman familiar with such arts can add to his peace of mind."

When Meg opened her mouth to protest, Lord Salisbury cut her off. "No matter how benign you claim your magic is, surely all such dabbling in the supernatural is against the will of God."

The earl cast Sir Patrick a stern look. "And that is why I strongly advised Sir Patrick against arranging his meeting."

"I did so at the king's behest," Sir Patrick protested.

"Aye, I insisted upon meeting the lady of Faire Isle. I was very curious about her skills."

Salisbury raised one brow. "What skills would those be, Your Majesty?"

"I was on the verge of finding out when you interrupted," James replied irritably. "Mistress Wolfe was about to lift the curse."

"I crave your pardon, liege." Salisbury bowed again. "It would seem the lady had best proceed."

All three men turned to stare at Meg, the king expectant, Sir Patrick grave as usual, and Salisbury skeptical.

This was the moment Meg had dreaded, when she would be called upon to perform some miracle. She should have better prepared, considered more carefully how she would respond.

She thought about asking for candles, a basin filled with holy water to perform some mock ceremony as she had done to trick Bridget Tillet. All she needed to do was make James believe the curse had been lifted.

But the king was no ignorant village girl to be so easily fooled by some mysterious incantations. Might not her best course be honesty?

A royal court is no place for sincerity, Seraphine insisted. But that is exactly why it might work because it would be so unexpected. Perhaps Meg was being naïve, but amidst all the lies, the intrigue, the honeyed flattery, could not a simple act of truth be like a cleansing wind?

Bracing herself, Meg said, "There is no magic that can defeat a curse."

Lord Salisbury's mouth twisted wryly as if to say he knew as much. Sir Patrick stole an uneasy look at the king, who scowled at her.

"Then you are saying there is nothing you can do?"

"No, there is one thing." Meg fastened her fan back to her belt, willing her fingers not to tremble. "After all, what is a curse? Merely an evil wish, so what would its countermeasure be?"

When none of the three men vouchsafed a reply, Meg said, "A prayer. That is the only thing that can answer a curse."

She approached James Stuart with her hands outstretched. His first instinct was to shy away, but the king was so astonished by the gesture, he allowed her to touch him.

His hands were like James himself, a strange contrast. His fingertips were those of a scholar, stained with ink, but his palms were toughened by frequent contact with leather reins, the mark of a horseman, an avid hunter.

Meg clasped James's hands and intoned, "I pray to—" She hesitated, realizing now would not be a good time to invoke any goddess or the mother earth.

"I pray to God, to our great Father in heaven, to protect this king from all harm, all evil."

James had been avoiding meeting her eyes, but his gaze was drawn to hers. Meg peered deep into his eyes, willing him to believe in the power of her words.

"May God and all His angels hear my prayer, that James Stuart be blessed with a long and peaceful reign, that he serve his kingdom wisely and well. That this same blessing be conferred upon his heirs, the entire house of Stuart."

A heavy silence fell and then she heard Lord Salisbury say, "Amen."

The king drew his hands away, breaking the contact that had bound them together however briefly.

"That is it, then?" James asked dubiously. "The curse is ended?"

"Does not Your Majesty believe in the power of prayer?"

"Well, yes, but—"

"Then the rest is entirely up to you, the strength of your own mind. Your Majesty is reputed to be a second Solomon." Meg decided that at this juncture, a little flattery would not hurt. "I am sure you are far too wise to truly believe that these recent events were caused by any specter from your past."

"So did I only imagine seeing a woman I believed to be dead? Am I going mad?"

Meg thought of her fear she had seen her mother in the garden. If the king was going mad, then so was she.

"No, Your Grace. I am sure you did see someone, but not a ghost. These messages written in blood, the trail of silver petals your guard found, these were all quite real, but the signs of an enemy of flesh and bone who conspires to torment you."

"My view of the matter entirely," Salisbury said.

"Humph! Then the lady's accord should please you, Salisbury."

The king fell into a frowning silence, scratching the ends of his beard. "Well, I would far rather there was no sorcery involved. Like any God-fearing man, I am alarmed by the supernatural. But as for the machinations of ordinary men—" James gave a wearied shrug. "I have survived too many such plots in my lifetime."

"I doubt Your Grace would have to search far to find the source of this one," Salisbury said. "Treasonous subjects, those who still cling to the Roman faith, are the ones most likely to wish Your Majesty harm."

"God's blood, Salisbury, you believe there are Papists hiding under every bed, sharpening their daggers."

"Perhaps not under every bed, but there are still far too many of them, willing to do whatever is necessary to see a Catholic monarch on the throne."

Did Meg imagine it or did Lord Salisbury dart a glance in Sir Patrick's direction? It was difficult to be sure as the secretary's expression was so bland.

Meg spoke up quickly. "I don't think this plot is inspired by any religious fervor. It strikes me more as revenge, someone familiar with the witch trials in Scotland, nursing a grudge, perhaps a relative of someone who was condemned."

"Another follower of this Megaera perhaps?" the king suggested.

"P-perhaps," Meg agreed.

"You know something of this sorceress then, Mistress Wolfe?" Salisbury asked.

Meg folded her hands to suppress the tremor that coursed through her. "Only a very little. Of course one hears wild stories from other daughters of the earth. You know how— how women love to gossip."

The king gave Meg an indulgent smile, which eased some of her tension. "Very true, that is why any serious investigation of treason is hardly a matter for a woman. From here on, I will trust this matter all to your capable hands, Salisbury. Whenever there is any plot a-brewing, I can trust to my little beagle to ferret it out."

Little beagle? The remark confused Meg until she realized with a jolt that the king beamed at Lord Salisbury. This was clearly the king's pet name for his first minister. Meg did not think the secretary relished the form of address, but he forced a smile and accorded James a stiff bow.

"I thank Your Grace for your confidence in me. I shall always do whatever is necessary to keep Your Majesty from harm."

It sounded like the sort of flattering reply any courtier might make. Meg wondered if she was the only one who detected the edge of warning in it, a warning that felt aimed at her. She edged a step backward, casting a longing glance toward the door.

"Your Majesty must have much to discuss with Lord Salisbury. I should not take any more of your time when there is so little I can do except to offer a humble healer's advice. In times of great stress of the mind, one must take particular care of the body. I would recommend fresh air, sunshine, and diversion to improve your spirits."

James beamed at the suggestion. "Why, you are indeed right wise for a woman, Mistress Wolfe. There is nothing like a good ride to the hounds."

Salisbury cleared his throat delicately. "There is much to occupy Your Grace, pressing matters of business, petitions, writs to sign—"

"Pah! That is your idea of diversion, my lord. Not mine. Nae, I think I need must repair to my hunting lodge."

When the secretary appeared about to protest further, James silenced him with a solemn look. "It is for the sake of your king's health."

Salisbury could not repress an audible sigh. "So Your Grace always tells me."

"But what of the opening of parliament, Your Grace?" Sir Patrick asked. He had stood by so quietly all this time, Meg wondered if the king even realized he was still present.

But now James smiled fondly and smoothed his hand down Sir Patrick's sleeve. "Oh, I shall return in plenty of time for that. But for now, I shall hunt and you shall join me."

"I fear Sir Patrick has other duties—" Salisbury began.

"Which can wait. You will come, laddie. You may even bring that friend of yours, Androcles."

"Who, Your Grace?" Sir Patrick asked.

"The man who removed the thorn from Jowler's paw last spring and applied that goodly salve that healed him fit to hunt the very next day."

"You mean Armagil Blackwood."

"Aye, him. A most amusing man and very good with dogs." James gave Sir Patrick's cheek a playful pinch.

The king's spirits appeared much restored. He whistled for his dog. Barely acknowledging their obeisance, James left the gallery with Jowler hard on his heels.

Meg straightened from her curtsy, releasing a soft breath. This ordeal was over and she had survived, although she was not sure how much she had gained from this audience. Precious little, she feared. She longed for escape and she sensed that Sir Patrick felt the same.

But Lord Salisbury barred their path. "Your pardon, Mistress Wolfe, but I wonder if I might have a word with you *alone.*"

"Well I—I—" Meg stammered, looking to Sir Patrick for rescue, but none was coming.

He bowed to Salisbury. Even though he gave her an apologetic glance, she still felt abandoned as the door closed behind Sir Patrick, leaving her alone with the secretary of state.

"Beware of the king's little beagle. He has been known to bite."

How like Armagil Blackwood to couch what should have been a serious warning in such jocular and cryptic fashion. Meg would have a thing or two to say to the man when she saw him again. *If* she ever saw him again . . .

Lord Salisbury studied her in silence, a technique Meg was certain was calculated to make her ill at ease and thus off her guard.

It was working, but she determined not to show it. She

met his gaze levelly, although she kept her hands tucked in the folds of her skirts as though she did expect to have her fingers snapped off at any moment.

"When I heard the king was granting you an audience," he said at last, "I made some inquiries. I have heard many strange and fantastic tales of the Lady of Faire Isle."

"Your lordship does not strike me as the sort of man to listen to idle reports."

"Oh, I listen to everything, mistress. I was especially fascinated by the tales of your midnight revels held high atop the cliffs among the druid stones."

"Council meetings such as you might hold yourself with the other privy secretaries. Only ours were a gathering of wise women coming together to share our knowledge of the healing arts."

"Cunning women from all over France, Spain, Italy, and Ireland."

"Yes," Meg conceded, wondering where this was heading.

"And England. You must know the names of many of them, some here in London, perhaps."

Meg saw the trap and struggled to evade it. "No, I fear that I do not. It has been a long time since such councils were held on Faire Isle and they were but poorly attended in recent years. I no longer know where to find any of the English daughters of the earth, and even if I did—" Meg regarded him defiantly. "I did not come here to help you launch a witch hunt."

"Exactly why did you come, mistress?"

"I came at Sir Patrick's behest."

"Sir Patrick," Salisbury said thoughtfully, mulling over the name in a way that disquieted Meg.

"He begged me to come and ease the king's mind of his curse."

"I see. I suppose there is a precedent for such a thing. My late mistress, the good Queen Elizabeth, was wont to consult her necromancer Dr. Dee on such matters."

"You served Elizabeth?"

"For many years, although not always in so high a post as the one I hold now. I began as a mere clerk to my father, Lord Burghley, when he was the secretary of state. So I was often at court, enough that I remember a curious incident when the queen consulted another sorceress, a little girl, if you can imagine."

Meg could, all too well. She felt the color drain from her cheeks as she realized why Salisbury seemed familiar to her. The day she had slipped into the palace to approach Elizabeth, she had been overwhelmed, the entire court a vast sea of faces. But Salisbury was such an unusual-looking man with his dwarflike stature, hunched back, and pale face. Somewhere in the back of her mind, she must have noted him. But how much did his lordship remember? Could he possibly discern in her traces of the frightened child she had been?

Salisbury said, "This little girl flung herself at the queen's feet and claimed that she was the Silver Rose, this infamous Megaera. What think you of that, mistress?"

Meg's mouth was so dry, she had difficulty replying. "I think the child must have been fed a surfeit of fairy stories and possessed too much imagination. There is no Megaera."

"So you say," Salisbury returned politely, but his eyes seemed to pierce her clean through. Several tense moments passed that felt like a lifetime to Meg before the man bowed and stepped aside.

"You intrigue me, Mistress Wolfe. We must speak again, I think. Very soon."

MEG DID NOT FEEL ABLE TO BREATHE UNTIL SHE WAS OUTSIDE the palace walls. As she and Sir Patrick crossed the tilt-yard, it was all she could do not to run. Even hampered by her heels, she outstripped Sir Patrick. She wanted to find Seraphine and flee back to Faire Isle as swiftly as they could manage.

Lord Salisbury *knew.* He knew of her past, that she had once been Megaera. Even as that panicked thought raced through her head, the more rational part of her mind struggled to reassert itself.

Salisbury might suspect, but he was not sure or she would have been arrested before she had ever left the palace. And how could she leave England when this mystery of who was tormenting the king was no closer to being solved?

Sir Patrick caught up with her. He had said nothing in Whitehall where there was a danger of being overheard. But he seized her by the arm to slow her progress, his voice full of concern.

"What happened back there, Mistress Wolfe? What did Lord Salisbury want of you? You appear most distressed."

"Distressed?" Meg wrenched her arm free and rounded on him. "Yes, I suppose that I am. What his lordship wanted was to interrogate me, which you might well have guessed. Why did you leave me alone with him?"

"Because no matter how politely Lord Salisbury couched his words, it was not a request. He is a powerful man, per-haps even more so than the king. I have known great nobles wait as much as four days for the honor of a private audience with his lordship."

"I did not feel honored. I felt threatened. I fear he suspects me of being a witch, perhaps even the one behind this plot against the king. And I think he suspects you as well."

"Suspects me? Of what?"

"Of being a Catholic."

Meg expected Sir Patrick to stammer out a denial. He looked oddly relieved.

"Perhaps Lord Salisbury does suspect, but it hardly signifies. The king knows I am a Catholic."

When Meg stared at him, astonished by his cool admission, Sir Patrick shrugged.

"His Majesty does nothing to prevent his ministers from persecuting Catholics, but he makes allowances for his favorites. His Grace once had a groom who was even a priest in hiding. James knew of it and did nothing. After all, the man was good with horses. Of course when Father Benedict was caught holding a secret mass, James felt obliged to let him be arrested. But the king is more than willing to turn a blind eye to your faith as long as you don't inconvenience him by practicing it."

There was bitter edge to Sir Patrick's voice that Meg had never heard before when he was speaking of his king.

"You sound as though you do not appreciate the king's tolerance. I thought you were completely devoted to him."

"My feelings regarding the king are of no import. I am more curious about yours."

"I fully expected to hate him," Meg said and then admitted reluctantly, "but I could not. I pitied him more than I could have ever imagined."

"You *pitied* him?"

"Yes. You would, too, if you had read his eyes as I did. He lived his entire childhood, indeed most of his life, in dread of being betrayed, murdered, of losing everyone he loves." The same terror that Meg had experienced at her mother's hands. "If you have never lived with such fear, you cannot imagine what it is like."

"I believe that I could."

"I am not excusing some of the horrible things James has done, but he is not some ruthless tyrant without conscience. He seemed full of genuine remorse when he spoke of the brother of that girl burned for witchcraft, the boy whose grief he could never forget."

"Robert Brody?" Sir Patrick's harsh laugh startled Meg. "You place far too much faith in the king's conscience or his memory. James Stuart would not remember that boy, even if he tripped over him."

Meg frowned. How did Sir Patrick know the boy's full name? She was certain the king had never mentioned it. She started to ask Sir Patrick, but he had already turned away, striding ahead of her.

Not, however, before she caught a glimpse of his expression, the same one she had fancied she'd seen in her little mirror back at the palace. Only now she recognized it for what it was, a hatred that ran so deep, it was almost savage in its intensity.

Dear God, Meg thought. *Robbie.*

※※※

MEG FASTENED THE BUTTONS OF HER PLAIN FROCK, GRATEFUL to be shed of the finery she had worn to Whitehall. Seraphine had not yet returned, so Meg had had to summon one of the maids to help free her from the cage of the close-fitting velvet gown, layers of petticoats, corset, and farthingale.

As soon as she was released, Meg had dismissed the girl, needing to be alone with her thoughts. As she had shrugged into her own simple dress, she had hoped to feel more herself, her sense of equilibrium restored. But her mind was in turmoil over her recent meeting with the king, Lord Salisbury's veiled threats, and most of all, her suspicions regarding Sir Patrick.

Or should she say Robert Brody?

No, surely she was mad to entertain such a notion. Sir Patrick Graham was the scion of an old, established household. Even descending from more modest gentry, his family had to be well known.

That a boy from Scotland bent on revenge could assume the identity of an English knight, gain a position at court, even obtain the favor of the king . . . it was impossible.

She had nothing to base her suspicion upon except for a few unguarded moments when Sir Patrick had allowed his mask to slip, when he had revealed he knew Robbie's name and when he had made that acid remark.

"James Stuart would not remember that boy, even if he tripped over him."

Little enough to sustain such a wild supposition, and yet somehow in her heart, Meg was convinced. Robert Brody and Sir Patrick were the same person.

She had tried to study Sir Patrick more closely on the journey back from Whitehall. But he had retreated behind his familiar courteous façade. It struck Meg that he took great pains not to meet her eyes for too long, understandably wary after her performance with the king.

But Meg doubted that she could have read Sir Patrick's

eyes, no matter how hard she tried. She had never met any man better at guarding his thoughts and emotions. If he was Robert Brody, he would have had years of practice.

The question was how long could a man who had suppressed such a bile of rage and hatred endure before he erupted with all the violence of a volcano? When they had returned to the house, Sir Patrick had excused himself, declaring he had an important meeting to attend.

But a meeting with whom? Thomas Percy, the gentleman pensioner who had accosted Sir Patrick at Whitehall? The mysterious Mr. Johnston? Or even, heaven forbid, the witches who were haunting the king?

The more that Meg tried to sort out this intrigue, the deeper she stumbled into a fog where even the landscape of what she thought she knew became unfamiliar.

Only one thing was clear to her. If Sir Patrick Graham was indeed Robert Brody, then James Stuart was in grave danger and very likely Meg was as well. Because if Sir Patrick hated the king and had no wish to save him, why had he taken such great pains to fetch Meg to London? What did he really want of her?

Meg wished that Seraphine would return soon so that she might ask her opinion. Could Sir Patrick in truth be Robert Brody, or was Meg losing all reason?

She could well imagine Seraphine raising one eyebrow in skeptical fashion and drawling, *"Yes, my dear friend, I think your suspicions are correct. You are officially mad."*

Meg paced the bedchamber, wracking her brain for some way to confirm the matter one way or another. She might try questioning Sir Patrick's servants, but she doubted that would avail her much. They were all of them as guarded as their master, which was exactly what one might expect in a household where the Catholic faith was still espoused in defiance of the law. And perhaps even Sir Patrick's most trusted servants were not privy to all his secrets.

Of course there was one person more than any other likely to know the truth regarding Sir Patrick. Armagil Blackwood insisted that he knew Patrick Graham from the days of their youth when they had been students at Oxford together.

But Blackwood also cheerfully admitted to being a notorious liar. He and Graham were such close friends. If Sir Patrick was plotting something against the king, it would be reasonable to assume Blackwood was part of the conspiracy.

But Blackwood had advised her to be wary of Sir Patrick. And Sir Patrick had done likewise, warning her to be careful of the doctor. It was enough to drive any woman mad.

Meg pressed her fingers to her temples, a headache starting to throb. She winced when a rap sounded at the bedchamber door, but she called out permission to enter. A breathless maid darted in to bob a curtsy.

"Oh, mistress, you must come down at once. There is a messenger arrived to see you and he declares the matter is urgent, one of life and death."

"Who is the message from? My friend, the countess?"

"No, mistress. The messenger is young Tom, the lad who runs errands for Dr. Blackwood."

Blackwood? Mystified and uneasy, Meg followed the maid to the hall below where a dark-haired boy awaited, pacing up and down and beating his fists against his thighs as though in an agony of apprehension.

He was red-faced and sweating as though he had run a marathon. But when he espied Meg, he rushed up the stairs, intercepting her midway.

"Mistress Wolfe?" he panted. Not waiting for her to confirm her identity, he clutched at her sleeve.

"My master, Dr. Blackwood, bade me to fetch you to him."

"What is wrong?"

"He is sick, taken real bad. You have to come afore it is too late." The boy tugged on her arm, but Meg resisted, eyeing the boy warily.

"Your master seemed quite hale when I parted from him this morning." After a moment's thought, Meg asked gently, "Has Dr. Blackwood been drinking?"

"No!" The boy's face worked and then he burst into tears.

"Master has been poisoned."

Chapter Twelve

MEG FOLLOWED TOM DOWN THE NARROW THOROUGHFARE, feeling as though the breath was being squeezed from her lungs. Panting from her efforts to keep pace with the boy, Meg felt suffocated by the buildings that towered over her. Crossing London Bridge was like making one's way through a tight dark tunnel.

During her childhood days in the city, Meg had never liked the bridge with its close-packed houses and shops, the roar of the waterwheels below the arches, the clatter of carts and horses, the constant shouts of wherrymen, dockworkers, and hawkers. How like Armagil Blackwood to choose to dwell in the middle of such noise and chaos. It was no place Meg would have ever wanted to live . . . or die.

A drover urging a small herd of cows to market added to the crush of traffic. Meg managed to snag hold of the sleeve of Tom's jerkin to keep them from being separated in the crowd. To keep from being trampled, they flattened themselves back against the stone wall of one of the bridge supports.

"How—how much farther?" Meg panted.

"Not much. Just the last house but one on the Southwark side of the bridge. But we must hurry."

Tom clutched his side, the boy appearing on the verge of collapse, looking as frantic as when he had first come to fetch Meg.

Although her heart raced, Meg struggled to subdue her own panic enough to ask the questions she should have before blindly following this boy across half of London.

"Why are you so sure Dr. Blackwood was poisoned?"

"Because master said so."

"And how did he appear?"

"Horribly pale, groaning like he was in mortal agony."

"Was it something he ate? Something he drank?"

"I don't know, mistress."

"But why did he send for me? Why not another doctor?"

"I don't know. Master just insisted you were the only one who could help him."

"Why would he do that? He has little respect for my healing abilities."

"I don't know," Tom wailed. "Please, mistress, we must make haste."

As the last of the cattle surged past, an opening appeared in the crowd and Tom shot through it, leaving Meg to follow as best she could, clutching the handle of the bag that contained her herbal remedies and surgical implements.

She had long thought of herself as a cautious, reasonable woman. She had every reason to be wary of Armagil Blackwood. Yet all she had needed to hear was that he was ill, perhaps even dying, and she was ready to rush to his side without a second's thought. Yet now was hardly the time to question her own sanity or wonder that a man she barely knew could have such an effect on her.

She was relieved when they arrived at their destination, a cookshop wedged between a warehouse and an alehouse. Above the shop, four stories of lodgings jutted out at irregular angles and Blackwood needs must live at the very top.

By the time she had climbed flight after flight of stairs, Meg had a stitch in her side and was gasping for breath. Without pausing to knock, Tom flung open Blackwood's door and rushed inside. Meg hobbled after him.

It was like entering a tomb, cold and dark. No fire crackled on the hearth despite the chill of late October and the shutters on the narrow windows were fastened closed. As Meg's vision adjusted to the gloom, she saw that the lodging consisted of one large room, sparsely furnished. The most prominent object in the room was the tester bed. Meg could make out the figure of a man huddled beneath the bedclothes.

Tom rushed to the bedside. "Oh, master, how fare you? I have brought the lady, just as you bade me."

"Where is she?" Blackwood rasped.

"Here." Meg hastened forward, dropping her medical bag. She wrestled open one of the shutters, allowing the late afternoon sun to fall across the bed. She flinched when she saw Blackwood's face, ghost-white beneath the fringe of his beard.

His hair was matted with sweat, his eyes hollowed with pain. "Margaret, you came apace." Despite his obvious suffering, he crooked one corner of his mouth. "That eager to arrive at my bed?"

"This is no time for any of your foolish jests." Snatching

up his hand, she felt for his pulse. It was alarmingly fast. "Tom said you think you have been poisoned. What happened? What did this to you?"

"You did." Blackwood shifted his head on the pillow and grimaced, even that slight movement seeming to cause him pain. "Damn it, why couldn't you cultivate marigolds and daisies like a normal woman?"

Meg frowned at him, wondering if he was waxing delirious. "What are you talking about?"

Blackwood pulled free of her grasp, gesturing toward a small table near the bedside. "That little memento of your gardening."

Meg inspected the objects on the table, a half-melted candle and something that glinted silver, wrapped in the folds of a handkerchief. Meg's breath caught in her throat. She knew what it was even before she drew back the linen cloth to reveal the rose in all its lethal beauty.

"Cor!" Tom exclaimed, drawing closer. "What's that?"

"Don't touch it," Meg and Blackwood both cried.

Tom shrank back, alarmed.

"Where did you get that?" Meg demanded of Blackwood.

"Found it . . . in the garden where you dropped it."

"I didn't. That flower is none of my fashioning. So you pricked yourself on its thorn? Where?"

Blackwood held up his right hand. It was swollen, the tiny wound on his thumb starting to fester.

"Oh, why did you have to touch it? Why couldn't you have left the rose alone?"

Blackwood gave a weak laugh. "You know me. Never can keep my hands off pretty things." He regarded her intently. "You didn't fashion the rose, but you obviously know what it is."

"Yes."

"So . . . am I dying?"

Meg looked away, but he must have seen the fear in her eyes. She knew the deadly power of the poison that coated the rose's thorn all too well. She had been forced by her mother to translate the recipe for it from the *Book of Shadows*. Never mind that she had been but a child, bullied and terrorized by Cassandra Lascelles. Meg still felt guilty for all the lives Cassandra had claimed with the poisonous roses. And now she would be responsible for one more. Tears brimmed in Meg's eyes.

Blackwood pressed her hand. "It is of no consequence if I am dying, my dear. I was just curious, that is all."

"It is of consequence to *me*," she said. Stripping off her cloak, she went to open her bag, making a rapid assessment of what vials of dried herbs she had and what she would need.

Tom trailed after her, asking in a low voice, "What can I do, mistress? How can I help?"

"It's far too cold in here. You can start by building a fire on the hearth, a good roaring one."

"Master wouldn't like that. He never has a fire lit unless he has to, deep in the winter when the water in the washbasin is apt to freeze."

Glancing around at the paucity of Blackwood's surroundings, Meg could guess the reason for that. Blackwood lived in straitened circumstances, likely one step away from being sent back to debtor's prison.

"Your master is not in charge today. I am." Meg fished some coin out of her purse and pressed it into the boy's hand. "Go buy some firewood, as much as you can carry, and get back here as fast as you can."

Tom stole one more anxious look at Blackwood, then nodded and darted out of the room. Meg unpacked her herbs and found a cauldron, but until she had a fire there was little more she could do.

She paced back to the bed. Blackwood had closed his eyes, his jaw clenched. That was the cruelty of this particular poison. It did not act swiftly. A strong man like Blackwood might last for several days, suffering agonies more painful than being stretched and broken on a rack.

But Blackwood might not endure that long. Meg pressed her hand to his brow. The fever was already setting in. His eyes fluttered open and he smiled wanly up at her. "So what sorcery are you plotting to use on me, milady?"

"No magic, but I believe I can brew an antidote."

"Will it cure me?"

Most certainly she longed to assure him, because she wanted to believe that herself. But she could not lie to him. "I hope that I can, but in case the worst should befall, is there anyone you would wish me to send for?"

"For some maudlin deathbed parting? I think not."

"Not even Sir Patrick?"

"Hellfire, no! He'd plague me to death with his paternosters, praying for my soul. And besides, he'd not approve of you being here with me."

"I realize Sir Patrick considers himself my protector, but he is no kin to me, and under the circumstances, he can hardly think you are out to seduce me."

"It would be the other way around, my dear. Graham thinks that you have been bewitching me."

"What nonsense. He can't possibly—" Meg broke off, realizing that Graham could and very likely did believe that. It would explain the tension she had sensed in him, the disapproval of her even though he had denied it. If he truly was Robert Brody, he would have every reason to mistrust any woman he suspected of being implicated in the darker arts, like the witch who had ensnared his sister. He might well despise Meg as much as he did King James. But then why would Sir Patrick have sought her out, fetched her back to London to cure the king?

Meg had so many questions about Sir Patrick and she was sure Blackwood could answer many of them, but now was hardly the time.

She stroked Blackwood's forehead. "Is there no one else who should be told how gravely ill you are? No member of your family?"

Her question appeared to give Blackwood pause. But he shook his head. "No, it is far too late for any tender reunions. If I am dying, there is only one thing you can do for me, Margaret."

"Anything. You have but to name it."

"Kiss me."

"Dear God, Blackwood, can you not be serious, even at a time like this?"

"I am being serious. What! Would you deny a dying man his last request?"

He secured her hand and tugged her down to sit upon the bed beside him. He attempted to smile, but his voice was infused with a wearied resignation. Blackwood believed he was dying, but he didn't much care. The thought saddened and angered Meg.

Impulsively, she leaned down and pressed her lips to his far harder than she intended. She sensed his surprise and then he slipped his hand beneath her hair, cupping the nape of her neck.

He returned her embrace with a ferocity that should have been beyond his strength. Holding her captive, he kissed her with all the desperation of a drowning man who had been thrown a rope.

Or perhaps the desperation was hers. Her lips parted as she tasted of his heat and a passion the like of which she had never known. She kissed him greedily until the healer in her reasserted itself, reminding her that the fire on his lips was not merely the product of desire.

She yanked back, gasping out an apology. "I—I am sorry. I shouldn't have—" She pressed her hand to his brow again. "Your fever grows worse. You are burning up."

"I certainly am." He gave a shaky laugh. His gaze met and held hers with an intensity as deep as their kiss.

"I fear Graham was right. You have bewitched me. You almost make me want to—"

"To what?"

He swallowed. "To live."

"Then do it. I am not in the habit of losing the people that I care for so easily."

"You mean the people *in* your care."

"Yes, of course that is what I meant," she said, although she was not so sure herself. Confused by her own emotions, she leaped off the bed and paced to the window.

Where was Tom with the firewood? What was keeping the wretched boy? She glanced at Blackwood, who had closed his eyes. Despite his bravado and feigned nonchalance, she saw the way he ground his teeth against a spasm of pain. It was only going to get worse as the poison ran its course, until every muscle in his body would feel as though it was spiked with hooks ripping sinew away from bone.

When she heard Tom's footfall on the stairs, Meg flew

partway down to meet him, helping the boy haul the bundle of wood to the hearth. As they began to prepare the fire, Blackwood scowled at them. But other than muttering something about "damned waste of wood," he made no further protest.

Once the fire blazed on the hearth, Meg worked as though possessed of a fever herself, grinding herbs, measuring and tossing them into the boiling kettle. The poison had started its course through Blackwood's veins this morning and Meg felt like a frantic hunter racing to overtake her prey, all the while knowing there was nothing more dangerous than a cornered beast.

She stirred the pot, wishing she could allow the infusion to steep longer, but she cast a glance toward Blackwood. Complaining of the heat, he shoved the coverlet down, exposing the bare contours of his chest, his skin glistening with sweat. She was running out of time and she knew she would have to take an action that was so drastic and strange that Tom would never understand.

She would only alarm the boy, so Meg dispatched him in quest of more wood. As soon as he was gone, Meg delved deep into her bag and drew forth the implement that she seldom used and was most careful to keep hidden. Folding back the soft piece of leather, she uncovered a thin stiletto with a needle-sharp tip. The hilt could be twisted so the knife could be filled with liquid that would be injected beneath the skin.

A *witch blade*. That was what her mother had called it, and the implement had been but one more means for the followers of Cassandra Lascelles to dispense her poison. The hilts had all been adorned with a silver rose, but the one Meg had created for her own use was plain. As a child, Meg had loathed and dreaded the witch blades, but as an adult, she had realized that an object that had been designed for evil could be employed for good.

Carefully she filled the hollow of the blade with the anti-dote she had brewed. When she approached the bed, she saw that Blackwood had drifted into a troubled sleep. She wished he could remain that way. It would make what she was about to do so much easier.

But he wakened as soon as she bent over him and touched his arm. His eyes were clouded with confusion for a moment and then widened when he noticed what she had clutched in her hand.

"What the devil is that?"

"It—it's—um—something I learned about from an ancient text that I read. It was difficult to translate the word for it, but I believe it was called a *syringe.*"

Blackwood drew his arm protectively back to his chest. "Never mind what it is called. What does it do?"

"Well, the blade is hollow, filled with the medicine that I brewed. By inserting the needle into your arm, I can send the antidote through you more swiftly than having you swallow it."

When he frowned, she added, "It is no worse a proceeding than the way you are always bleeding people and much more effective, I assure you."

"I expect you had best get on with it then."

"I can show you exactly how it works. If you look closely at the hilt—"

"Never mind the explanations. Just do it." He allowed his arm to flop back to the bed, exposing his wrist. Meg propped the blade upon the table while she prepared him, thoroughly scrubbing his skin. She tied a length of cord around his upper arm, and then felt for a vein, finding a large strong one.

Blackwood watched her proceedings with a cool detachment, the kind she was usually able to summon when working to heal someone. But to her dismay, her fingers trembled.

She had employed the witch blade before to dispense other potions, to save other lives, but she had never attempted to combat her mother's poison before. Cassandra Lascelles would have never allowed her to do so, although Meg had always believed that she could defeat her mother's venom if she ever had the chance.

Her moment had finally come and she was terrified. She could be about to save Blackwood's life or she could be on the verge of killing him herself.

She felt paralyzed until Blackwood startled her by reaching for her hand and carrying it to his lips.

"I trust you, Margaret, but if this doesn't work—"

"It will work," she cried. "It has to."

"Then make haste, love, because my fingers are getting numb."

Meg took a deep breath. Steadying herself, she reached for the blade. She found his vein again and poised the tip over it.

"This is going to hurt. It will feel like I am setting your veins afire."

"You already do that just by touching—" He gasped as Meg plunged the blade tip into him and depressed the hilt.

"God's blood!" He bucked upward so violently Meg cut him deeper than she intended. She made haste to pull the blade out and apply a bandage to the wound, a task made more difficult by the way he was thrashing.

Somehow she managed to secure the bandage and wrench away the cord that bound his upper arm. Blackwood had flushed a dark red and his lips were clamped in an effort to halt his flood of obscenities.

Meg caught his face between her hands, terrified he was on the verge of a seizure. "Blackwood! Armagil, please tell me what you are feeling."

"Like a ruined castle assaulted by an army of torch-wielding peasants." He groaned. "And I think the peasants are winning."

"Then let them. Let them burn the poison away."

"Easy for you to recommend. You aren't the one being sacked and pillaged."

He clutched at her wrists, his entire body rigid. Meg watched him, feeling more helpless than she ever had in her life. The moments seemed to grind on with agonizing slowness.

Blackwood panted for breath, but little by little Meg could feel his body relax, his grip on her wrists easing.

"Are you feeling any better?" she asked.

"Better than what? Having a hot spike shoved up my arse?"

She felt relieved when he was able to force a laugh.

"Aye, it seems a trifle better," he said, letting go of her. The dark red ebbed from his cheeks, leaving him appearing drained.

"So now what happens?" he asked.

"Now comes the hard part." Meg massaged her sore wrists. "We wait."

※※※

THE AFTERNOON FADED INTO EVENING, THE DARKNESS OF THE oncoming night staking its claim upon Blackwood's chamber. Meg lit what candles she could find, taking care to keep the candelabrum well away from the bedstead lest she disturb Blackwood.

But he had fallen so deep asleep, it would take more than the soft flicker of a few candles to rouse him. Meg told herself she should be relieved. She had feared he would be more restless, more wracked with pain, even delirious with his fever.

She knew how virulent her mother's poison was. Even injecting her antidote directly into his veins, Meg had never expected it would work so quickly, that Blackwood would be able to lie so still, that he could sleep like—

Like the dead.

The thought chilled Meg and she swept it from her mind. She paced to the bedside and groped for his hand, taking his pulse for about the hundredth time. He didn't even stir at her touch, his hand heavy and limp in her grasp.

But his skin was cool and his pulse steady enough. She only wished that it beat a little more strongly. Behind her, Tom added more logs to the fire. He had been silent for so long, Meg had half forgotten he was still there. He used the poker to stir the embers until the flames licked around the new logs. Rising to his feet, he dusted his hands off on the back of his breeches.

"I am going to have to go now, Mistress Wolfe," he said in a loud whisper. "I am already late to supper and my mother does not like me abroad after dark."

"Very wise of her."

The boy shuffled his feet and stared at the floor. Earlier he had badgered Meg with so many questions regarding Blackwood's condition, she had been unable to endure it and had silenced the boy with a gentle reproof.

She sensed now what Tom was bursting to ask her and

that he was afraid to do so. Coming away from the bedside, she said, "I believe your master is doing better. I hope in the morning when he wakes, he will be more himself."

If he wakes. Meg looked quickly away so the boy could not see her fear.

Tom heaved a deep sigh of relief. "Thank you, mistress. There will be many more than me right pleased to hear it. I know master wouldn't have wanted me telling anyone how sick he is, but I couldn't help it. I was so worried and there are many folks hereabouts that care much about the doctor. They sent him a few things to help him recover." The boy gestured toward a basket he'd set atop the oak wardrobe chest.

Meg had been so caught up in tending to Blackwood, she had not even noticed. She went to inspect the basket of simple gifts, a small loaf of brown bread, a few apples, a wedge of cheese, a pot of honey.

"I thought—that is, I was led to believe that Dr. Blackwood's only friend was Sir Patrick Graham."

"Er—well, these others are not as noble or respectable. Mostly they are the street people, the vendors, the tinkers, and the doxies that ply their trade down by—" Tom broke off, looking sheepish. "Not that I know anything about such women."

"No, of course not," Meg soothed, anxious to keep him talking and to learn something more about Armagil Blackwood. "So these tinkers and—and doxies are Dr. Blackwood's friends?"

"No-ooo, more like people he has tended to, stitching up cuts, setting broken bones, even delivering a babe or two, things most physicians would scorn to do. Most poor people could never afford a doctor anyway, especially not one trained at Oxford. Master practices his healing in places most doctors would be too proud or afeard to go, the poorest tenements and taverns in the city, and folks are right grateful to him for it."

"I imagine they would be. He must not receive much else by way of compensation."

"Wouldn't do the doctor any good if he did. He empties his purse for any beggar with his hand out. My mother says it's not prudent for a man to be that softhearted. I told Dr. Blackwood that, but he just laughed and said, 'Do you know what would happen to me, Tom, if I amassed too much coin? I'd have to fight off droves of wenches determined to end my bachelor days and wed me for my fortune.'"

Meg smiled. That sounded exactly like something Blackwood would say. She could almost hear him. The thought brought a curious lump to her throat as she gazed at the unconscious man on the bed. She had to resist the urge to check his pulse again or try to rouse him. Surely he was but lost in a deep healing sleep. He would awaken come morning. She had to believe that.

Turning back to the boy, she said, "Dr. Blackwood appears to confide in you a great deal, Tom."

"Oh yes, especially when he—" The boy flushed.

"When he drinks too much," Meg filled in gently.

The boy bristled, squaring his thin shoulders. "Most men enjoy their ale, mistress, and—and the master is never a mean drunk like some. He mostly takes a drop too much those days when he loses someone in his care."

He added so quietly Meg had to bend closer to hear him. "Master was drunk for three days after my sister died."

"Dr. Blackwood sought to cure your sister? And he failed?"

"It wasn't his fault. It was the cursed pox. Our whole

lodging was under quarantine. No other doctor or apothecary or even a cunning woman would have come." Tom's eyes flashed an angry challenge at her. "But Dr. Blackwood did and he brought me and my mother through it. But not my grandfather and not Bess."

Meg studied the boy and noticed the few pits the pox had left on his face. Tom had to have been one of the more fortunate ones, surviving a disease that either killed or left its victims horribly scarred. The pox was a most virulent affliction, and even with all the knowledge she had culled from the ancient texts, everything she had learned from Ariane Deauville, Meg had lost more than one person to its ravages.

"I am so sorry, Tom."

The boy's anger faded, his eyes welling with tears. But when Meg attempted to press his hand, he pulled away from her and shrugged.

"You don't have to be. My grandfather and Bess are in heaven with my father. That is what my mother says and she *knows* such things. She tried to tell that to Dr. Blackwood when he got so bitter, blaming himself, especially for Bessie dying. Sh-she was only twelve.

"But my mother said that when the Lord calls, you have to answer and it was Bessie's time. All any of us could do was light a candle and pray for her. But Dr. Blackwood—" Tom shook his head sadly. "He doesn't put any faith in God. He said, 'I won't be praying to any deity that would cut down such an innocent girl and leave a useless wretch like me still breathing.' So my mother and I, we pray for Bessie every Sunday and we pray for Dr. Blackwood too."

Tom gave a loud sniff and wiped his sleeve across his eyes. Meg's heart ached for the boy and even more for Blackwood. She knew how it felt to strive so hard to save someone and have that life ebb from your grasp. She had never sought to drown that sense of failure in a bout of strong drink, but there were times when she had wished she could.

She glanced toward Blackwood, fighting a ridiculous urge to rush to his side and comfort him. A comfort he would be quick to laugh off or reject even if he could feel it.

Tom must have misinterpreted the nature of her glance because he snapped, "Don't you be looking at master that way. He did his best to save my sister. He's a good doctor, no matter if you don't think so."

"I never said—"

"Yes, you did. He told me you consider him a charlatan."

"He told you that? I did not think my opinion would be of any consequence to him."

"Well, it is, although he hates that it matters. But he said he has never met any other woman like you and he—" Tom cast a guilty look in Blackwood's direction. "Oh, lord, he wouldn't have wanted me telling you that. Master says I chatter worse than a gossiping fishwife. He is always threatening to sew my lips closed. I daresay he'll do it now."

"No, I promise you I won't breathe a word of anything you have told me."

"Thank you." Bidding her a gruff good night, Tom turned to go.

Meg hesitated a moment before darting after him. The boy was already out the door and halfway down the first flight of stairs when she called out to him.

"Tom."

The boy paused midstep to look back at her. "Aye, mistress?"

"I don't suppose in all his confidences, Dr. Blackwood has ever spoken of his family?"

Tom pursed his lips and Meg could clearly read what the boy was thinking, that he had already spilled far too many of his master's secrets.

"Please, Tom. I have every hope your master will recover, but with him this ill, it would be better if someone of his kin were informed."

"Perhaps so, mistress. But the doctor never talks of his family, even when he's been drinking."

"Oh." Meg nodded in disappointment. She bade Tom good night and started to close the door when the boy charged back up the stairs.

He appeared to wrestle with his conscience a moment before blurting out, "There has always been talk that the master is old Armagil Black's son."

"Armagil *Black*?"

"Well it stands to reason, doesn't it, mistress, the names being so similar? How many men do you know who have been christened Armagil?"

"Only one."

"I've heard tell of two and they are said to be much alike in their stubbornness. According to all the gossip in the street, Dr. Blackwood and his father had a terrible falling-out and have not spoken to each other in years, the doctor even going so far as to alter his last name."

"But if Mr. Black knew how ill his son was, this quarrel could be mended. If you could take word to him in the morning, surely he would come."

"I doubt it, mistress. Tomorrow is a hanging day at Tyburn. Father Gregoire, a Jesuit priest, is going to be drawn and quartered."

"What sort of man is this Mr. Black?" Meg exclaimed.

"His son comes this close to death and he would be unwilling to forgo his pleasure in watching a man being eviscerated?"

"You don't understand. There'd be no hanging or quartering if he did." Tom fetched a deep sigh.

"Old Gilly Black is the executioner, mistress."

Chapter Thirteen

NIGHT FELL OVER LONDON BRIDGE, THE ONLY LIGHTS VISI-
ble the lanterns burning in front of the houses.

"Nine of the clock, look well to your locks, your fire, and
your light," the watchman's voice echoed. Somewhere in the
distance, a dog howled, but otherwise the vast bridge was
silent.

Meg fastened the shutters closed, no longer as concerned
with muting the street noise as she was with stemming the
chill of night seeping through the windows.

It was the only thing she could think of to do to help
Blackwood, who had finally roused from his deep sleep. She
had stoked the fire as hot as she could, piled as many blankets
on him as she could find, but he shivered uncontrollably.

Meg returned to the bedside, attempting to pack the cov-
erlets tightly around him.

"C-cold. So cold," he said.

"I know. Do you feel strong enough to stand? Perhaps I could make you a pallet and help you to lie closer to the fire."

"No!"

"I should have had Tom fetch more wood before he left. I may have to go out in search—"

"No," he rasped again. He rolled over to look up at her. "D-don't leave me. Climb into bed and w-warm me."

His eyes were dull and heavy, but he managed a semblance of a smile. "Not t-trying to seduce you. Just don't want to be alone when—"

"You are not going to die," she cried, but she hastened to comply with his request, removing her shoes, stockings, frock, and petticoat with fingers that had turned wooden and clumsy.

She stripped down to her shift and then scrambled beneath the covers to take him in her arms. He was trembling all over and his skin felt like ice. Meg pressed herself hard against him, wishing she was a larger woman, her curves more warm and generous, like Seraphine.

She was too slight, too thin to offer him the kind of heat that he needed. She was all but crushed in his embrace, his body shaking hard enough to shatter them both.

As she rubbed her hands vigorously over his back, Blackwood tried to speak. "M-meg. Must tell you s-something—"

"No, save your strength. Whatever it is, it will keep until morning."

"D-don't think s-so." But his teeth chattered too hard, rendering further speech impossible.

Meg clutched him tighter, trying to infuse him with her heat and strength. She held him until her arms throbbed with pain, until she was spent to the point of weeping from exhaustion.

The chills wracking his frame finally stopped, allowing her to draw a ragged breath of relief. She felt his tension ease, his arms going limp and falling away from her.

"Blackwood?" Meg struggled upright to peer down at him.

His head fell back on the pillow, his eyes closed, his complexion as white at the sheets.

"Armagil!" She felt for the pulse in his neck, but her fingers trembled and she couldn't find it. She pressed her ear to his naked chest, listening for the beat of his heart. It was there, but faint, his breathing quick and shallow.

A sob welled in Meg's throat and she fought to suppress it. Raining hot tears on his chest would do the man no good. She had to think of something else to do. Except there wasn't anything else. The antidote had been her only hope of defeating the poison.

Meg caressed her hand over Blackwood's jaw, the roughness of his beard abrading her palm. She had known him for such a short span of time and for much of that time she had believed she despised him. And now she could not bear the thought of losing him.

She studied his face in the flickering candlelight. She had seen him drunk, angry, mocking, teasing, or lustful. Never had he looked so vulnerable, so gentle for a man who was a hangman's son.

Could Dr. Blackwood have chosen a profession more opposed to that of Gilly Black? Was that what had caused the rift between the two men? Meg knew that the grim trade of executioner was like many other occupations in one respect. The skills of the father were expected to be passed down to the son. What horrors Blackwood must have witnessed in his youth to cause him to defy his father.

Meg respected Blackwood for that defiance because she knew all too well what it would have cost him. The deepest longing of any child was to revere a parent, to seek their love and approval. But when one perceived one's father or mother as being wrong, even a monster, the pain and guilt were immense.

"I am sorry," she whispered. "Sorry that I did not understand, sorry if I hurt you by accusing you of being a bad doctor, but you are not an easy man to comprehend. You rarely speak seriously and you behave as though you care about nothing."

Except that she had seen for herself that that was not true in the way he had tried to expose Bridget Tillet's lies about la Mère Poulet, how he had gone out of his way to make sure the old woman was safe.

Far more than that, he had been the only one who had troubled to find out Hortense's real name, treating her as though she was a woman who mattered and not just some mad old crone.

Considering all that, Meg should not have been surprised by Tom's revelations about how Blackwood ventured into the poorest quarters of the city, taking on the most desperate cases even at the risk of his own life.

She might deplore some of his methods, the bleedings, the use of lice, but he could hardly be blamed for that. Trained in the ignorant practices that most doctors followed, Blackwood had not had the benefit of Ariane Deauville's teaching.

Any man wanting to be a good doctor could have learned much from the former Lady of Faire Isle. But the kind of physicians Meg had encountered would have been too arrogant to avail themselves of Ariane's ancient knowledge, dismissing her as naught but a simple cunning woman.

Meg had even heard of some doctors who never saw their patients, merely had their symptoms described in a letter and wrote back their cures. Brewing medicine and dealing with broken bones were beneath them. The distribution of potions was the province of apothecaries, the setting of bones and stitching of cuts was left to barbers. And no physician of any standing wasted his university education upon the lower strata of society.

That he tried to use his medical knowledge to treat the poor made Blackwood a remarkable doctor, even when he failed. As for not caring, the man cared too much to the point of drinking himself to oblivion whenever he lost a patient.

She had discovered a great deal about Armagil Blackwood tonight, but there was so much more she needed to learn.

Meg stroked his brow. "I wish we could begin anew. I want to know you better, but for that to happen, you have to fight this poison and stay with me, Armagil, do you hear?"

She pressed her lips to his.

"Please stay."

"TWELVE O' CLOCK AND ALL IS WELL."

The watchman's voice rang out as he made his round through the environs of Westminster.

Midnight. The witching hour. Sir Patrick tried to suppress the thought as he avoided the watch. But as he stole away from the stairs that led up from the river landing, the hairs on the back of his neck prickled. He had to resist the urge to keep looking over his shoulder.

Ever since he had had the misfortune to become entangled with those loathsome Rivers women and their mad plot to torment the king, he lived in constant dread of being followed by those witches. He remembered all too well his shock the first time they had accosted him. It had been on a foggy evening when he had been hastening home from one of his secret meetings. The two women has risen up before him like wraiths conjured up from a sorcerer's cauldron.

How horrified he had been to discover that they knew all about him and the conspiracy to slay the king. One of Thomas Percy's servants had lain with Beatrice Rivers. While deep in his cups, the lackey had revealed far too much.

"Be not alarmed, Sir Patrick," Amy Rivers had cooed. *"My sister and I would never betray your secrets. We also have our reasons for hating King James and wish to help you destroy him."*

At first they had pretended to come from a family persecuted and ruined because of their adherence to the Catholic faith, thus forcing Amelia and Beatrice into a life of degradation in order to survive. But it had not taken long for the women to reveal their true nature.

He did not know which of them he found to be the worst, Beatrice with her mocking eyes and cruel smile or Amelia with her syrupy voice and ridiculous efforts to be all coy and girlish.

But he reminded himself he would soon be rid of them forever. It would all be over in less than a fortnight, everything . . .

He quickened his pace, hurrying through the area the locals referred to as the Cotton Garden. Westminster Palace loomed ahead of him, the ancient walls softened by moonlight, shadows concealing the havoc time had wrought upon the red sandstone. It had been a long time since Westminster was an official royal residence, not since the days of Edward the Confessor. Much of the original structure had been destroyed by fire. What remained had become a curious jumble of parliamentary chambers and law courts rubbing shoulders with private lodgings, wine shops, taverns, and brothels.

Patrick tipped back his head, peering up at the upper story of the palace's left wing. Known as the Queen's Chamber, it was where James Stuart would address the House of Lords in ten days' time. Patrick tried to picture it as a blackened shell, stone rubble and fallen beams. Tried and failed. Such destructive imaginings held no reality. Those centuries-old walls appeared too strong, too smugly serene beneath the pale October moon.

He lowered his gaze and made his way toward a door on the ground floor of the palace, directly beneath the Queen's Chamber. He rapped out the prearranged signal and waited, casting a nervous look about him.

The door creaked open a crack. He could just make out the face of Mr. Johnston, the man's eyes a mere glint above his thick mustache and bushy beard. When he recognized Patrick, he opened the door wide enough to allow him to enter and then closed it quickly behind him.

"Sir Patrick," Johnston growled by way of greeting.

"Johnston," Patrick began, but considering the hour and the place, such pretense seemed unnecessary.

"Mr. Fawkes," he amended.

Fawkes carried a lantern, but it cast a feeble glow to illuminate the vast cavelike chamber that yawned before Patrick. Thick with dust and cobwebs clinging to the wooden beams, the room appeared empty except for piles of fallen masonry and the enormous stack of firewood.

Patrick had heard about the cellar that had been leased

when the arrangements had first been made. But he had never yet seen it for himself. It was not at all the small, underground hole that he had imagined.

"What was this place?" he asked Fawkes.

"I believe it once served as the kitchens for the old palace."

It was not Fawkes who answered, but another voice that echoed off the chamber's cavernous walls. Patrick started, glancing to his right where two men emerged from the shadows.

One was Thomas Percy, his shock of white hair and pale face visible against the backdrop of the walls and his own dark clothing. He gave Patrick a terse nod, but the man who had spoken, Robert Catesby, stepped forward and wrung Patrick's hand with as much warmth and ease as though they greeted each other in one of the antechambers at Whitehall.

Catesby was a handsome man, tall and athletic. He possessed a quality that Patrick envied and was hard-pressed to define. Catesby had a kind of radiance that drew other men to him. He easily gained their trust.

Catesby made a graceful gesture that encompassed the entire chamber. "This place has served no purpose for years, except to be leased out as a storeroom, which makes it ideal for our purposes, located as it is, directly below the old Queen's Chamber."

Patrick glanced up at the wooden beams of the ceiling. It presented but a weak barrier between this chamber and where parliament would convene. But the very openness of this vast room disturbed him.

Catesby was indisputably the leader of their group, having worked on this plot for the last two years. As a latecomer recruited only the past summer, Patrick still felt like an outsider. He had never questioned any of Catesby's arrangements or decisions before, but now he could not help but demur.

"I had imagined a cellar, some small room all but forgotten. Is there not a danger in employing this large storeroom so readily accessible? What if someone inspects this place and notices all of that?" He pointed at the mountain of wood.

"Unlikely. No one ever comes down here," Catesby said.

Fawkes added, "You can see that most of the tracks through the dirt were made by my boots. But if by chance someone did become curious to have a look at the old kitchens, what would they see? Just the firewood I have amassed to get me through the winter. My lodging is close by."

"It would seem a great deal of firewood for one person," Patrick said.

Fawkes gave a thin smile. "I am a very cold man."

Catesby strode over to the woodpile. He reached for one of the logs, easing it aside. Patrick moved closer to watch, but he maintained a cautious distance as did Thomas Percy, a fact that did not escape Fawkes's notice.

The man laughed. "You need not be so nervous, gentlemen. You'll come to no harm as long as Catesby doesn't conduct his inspection while holding a lighted torch."

Catesby eased away several of the logs, exposing the end of one crate. "So how many of these are there now?"

"Thirty-six," Fawkes said.

When Catesby started to pry off the lid, Fawkes protested, "There is no need for that. I have kept careful watch over the powder, tested it frequently to make sure it does not become decayed."

"Decayed?" Patrick asked.

"Aye, when gunpowder sits for too long, it breaks down

into its various parts of ammonium and sulfate. It becomes utterly worthless. That is what happened to the first supply we laid in over a year ago. Replacing it was a costly and risky business. That is why we cannot afford another delay, so I hope you have done your part, Sir Patrick."

Before Sir Patrick could answer, Thomas Percy spoke up for him. "He has. The king's fears have been allayed by that cunning woman Sir Patrick fetched from France. She convinced the king the curse has been lifted, although I cannot fathom how. We all know what a poor opinion of women the king has and Mistress Wolfe did not look like anything out of the ordinary."

Didn't she? From the moment Patrick had first seen Meg, he had sensed something different about her, something fey that had disconcerted him. He marveled at Percy's inability to see it.

Fawkes regarded him curiously. "So how did she convince the king? What magic did she employ?"

"None." But Patrick shifted uneasily as he recalled the way Meg had stared into the king's eyes as though she not only had the ability to read James's mind, but could influence his thoughts as well. Patrick would have been ashamed to admit it to a hardened soldier like Fawkes, but he had become afraid of Meg, so terrified of her strange power, he was leery of returning to his own home.

"She appeared to simply hold the king's hands and pray over him."

"She *prayed* over him?" Percy marveled. "Odd sort of behavior for a witch."

"It little matters how she did it," Catesby said. "The important thing is that the king will not delay the opening of parliament again."

Fawkes looked skeptical. "Aye, unless those witches do something further to torment him."

"They won't. They want to see James punished as much as we do, but they will cease their mischief. I shall see to it," Sir Patrick said.

Catesby appeared satisfied. He turned back to his inspection of the crates. "You are sure we have accrued enough powder?" he asked Fawkes.

"Enough to blast away the chamber above us and every man in it."

"Every man, woman, and child," Sir Patrick murmured.

"We all knew that Queen Anne and Prince Henry would attend the opening ceremony with the king. Is that now a problem for you, Sir Patrick?" Catesby asked.

"No, but the king might bring his youngest son as well. Prince Charles is only four years old."

"He's always been a sickly lad. So weak he just learned to walk this year. He'd be likely to die soon anyway," Fawkes said.

"Is that what we must tell ourselves to justify the slaughter of an innocent?"

Fawkes glared at him. "This is a holy war, Sir Patrick, and in any conflict, there are always innocent casualties."

Patrick knew that better than anyone, but he could not dispel the image of little Charles taking those first wobbly steps, James kneeling down and holding his arms wide until the boy tottered into them. Then with a laugh of triumph, he hugs his son and lifts him up, James's face beaming with fatherly pride and joy.

Patrick closed his eyes against the memory, forcing another image of James Stuart to the forefront of his mind, the cowardly king, just like any other monarch, callous and indifferent to the suffering he caused.

Patrick groped beneath his jerkin, his fingers closing over the locket that held the precious strands of *her* hair and for a moment, his grief was as savage as if it were only yesterday that—

"Sir Patrick?" Fawkes's voice dragged him back to the present. Patrick opened his eyes to find the mercenary soldier all but in his face as Fawkes demanded, "Am I the only one who remembers that a good and holy man is slated to die today? In the eyes of God, Father Gregoire is worth a thousandfold more than that sickly Stuart whelp. Yet our priest is to be executed in the most brutal fashion possible, hanged, cut down while he still lives, his bowels torn out before his own eyes."

"I am well aware of that, Mr. Fawkes." Patrick took a step back and crossed himself. "None of us has forgotten and we will all pray for Father Gregoire."

"We are past the point of praying," Fawkes snapped. "Unless we want to see our brethren continue to be slaughtered, we must act and with none of these womanish qualms."

"Aye, but what of our brethren in parliament?" Thomas Percy protested. "There will be men in that chamber who are as committed to the true faith as we—young Lord Monteagle, Lord Montrose, and my own kinsman, the Earl of Northumberland. If we could but find some means to warn them to stay away from the parliament—"

"We have already discussed this, Thomas," Catesby said, a thread of impatience in his voice. "I deplore the loss of those good men as much as you, but any attempt to alert anyone can only serve to arouse suspicion. Far too many know of our plans already. If anyone breathes a word in the wrong quarter, we all risk exposure."

Patrick had wrestled with his own conscience over the matter, but he was obliged to agree with Catesby. Many good men would die in the explosion, but just as many were hazarding their lives in this holy cause. Patrick did not know all the names of his fellow conspirators nor did he want to, in case anything went wrong and he found himself arrested. He wanted to believe he was the stuff of martyrs, but he also knew men far stronger than he had broken under the torture of the rack.

Patrick caressed the locket, only vaguely aware that the other three men had moved on to discuss all that needed to be done after the assassination of the king, but he had nothing to contribute. He could not seem to think past the explosion, as though the conflagration that would be the culmination of all his years of purpose and planning would burn away his anger and grief, reducing him to a pile of ashes as well.

Catesby's voice seemed to come from a great distance as he reminded them of where all the conspirators would rendezvous after the explosion to incite rebellion and seize control of the government. Fawkes was to set sail for Europe and seek audience with all the Catholic monarchs, enlist support by convincing them of the justice of their cause.

"Justice! At least be honest with yourself and acknowledge your plot for what it is . . . revenge."

Armagil's troubling words echoed through Patrick's mind, but his hand clamped down tight upon the locket. If revenge was what was in his heart, then so be it. He'd confess his sin, do his penance, and trust to God's forgiveness.

Fawkes replaced the logs, carefully concealing the crate of gunpowder as they prepared to take their leave. Thomas

Percy was the first to do so, disappearing into the night. Patrick prepared to follow suit when he was arrested by Catesby's gentle touch upon his arm.

"You are more quiet tonight than usual, Sir Patrick. Not having second thoughts, I trust?"

"No, sir. I assure you there is no possibility of that."

"And you know your part?"

Patrick nodded. "Go hunting with the king, keep him free from any further alarm, and make sure he returns in time."

"I meant your part after the deed is done. You realize something will have to be done about those ungodly women. They may despise James Stuart as much as we do, but we cannot have the success of our holy cause tainted by any association with their petty revenge. Those witches will have to be . . . silenced, including the one that now resides beneath your roof."

Margaret Wolfe, the one to whom Patrick had given his word of honor that she would be safe if she accompanied him to England. He felt a stab of conscience, but that pledge had been given when he had thought Meg to be a good woman, the gentle healer she proclaimed herself to be.

"I understand what needs to be done," he said. "Amelia Rivers was foolish enough to confide in me that she and her sister plan to hold some hellish rite of celebration on the night before the explosion. I know where they intend to meet with the rest of their coven. I shall make sure they are all captured. None will escape."

"Good." Catesby smiled. "Although it is a trifle ironic. When King James perishes in the fire, it will seem as though the witch's curse came true. Had you thought of that?"

"Oh, yes," Patrick said softly. "I have thought about that a great deal."

Chapter Fourteen

"TWO O'CLOCK AND THE WEATHER IS FAIR."

The watchman's voice seemed to come from far off as Meg fought to keep awake. The hours after midnight were the loneliest, most treacherous, most dangerous time of day.

As a healer, Meg knew this. She could offer no logical reason for it, but if someone was going to die, how often it happened in the predawn darkness. But coax them to remain until the sun rose and the shadows of death would disperse.

Blackwood's condition had not changed, but Meg lay with her head pressed to his heart, one arm sprawled across him as though by her physical presence and sheer will, she could prevent his soul from stealing away from her.

She needed to keep him alive until the light broke and then all would be well. An irrational hope, but it was all she had. She just needed to remain vigilant, stay awake.

But she was so exhausted. Her eyes grew heavy in spite of

her best efforts. They closed, but not to ease her into a place of restful darkness; instead, she entered a world of troubled dreams.

Nightmares of her mother stitching Blackwood up in a winding sheet, Cassandra mocking Meg with her laughter. Nightmares of Blackwood's coffin being lowered into the earth while faceless members of the coven whirled around it in a mad dance, tossing handfuls of dirt into his grave.

And nightmares that once again pulled her back to that square where coarse men piled up the faggots of wood around the terrified girl while others restrained the frantic boy.

"Maidred!"

The boy's sobs tore at Meg. She wanted to go to him, but the girl needed her more. The pyre had been lit, the flames licking upward while Maidred Brody screamed.

"For the love of God, help!"

But as Meg found her way forward, Maidred shook her head. "No, it's too late for me. Help him. Save my brother. Stop him from—"

She writhed in pain as the fire engulfed her.

"Save Robbie. Promise me."

"I promise. I promise," Meg muttered over and over until the sound of her own voice jarred her awake. She was disoriented for a moment, not knowing where she was or what was happening.

Memory of recent events returned to her in a rush and she groped for Blackwood, only to find the bed beside her empty.

She bolted upright, her heart thudding in panic. She swept her hair from her face, her gaze darting about the room. The fire had gone out and so had the candles, but the gray light of early morning spilled through the open shutters.

Blackwood stood silhouetted in the window, peering out

22

562256 SUSAN CARROLL

while he wolfed down a slab of bread. And he was stark naked.

Meg's indrawn breath squeaked out of her. Blackwood turned around and wiped a dribble of honey off his chin.

"Did I wake you? I was trying to be quiet, but I needed to piss so bad, I thought my gut would burst and then I was starving."

He was starving? Meg struggled up onto her elbows, staring at him in disbelief. He was starving. He was eating bread and honey. He was . . . not dead.

Her gaze traveled from his mop of disheveled hair, to the coarser hairs shadowing his broad chest, to his lean pale hips, down the length of his sinewy legs and then back up, riveting on his erection.

Definitely not dead.

She should have averted her eyes, but she couldn't seem to stop staring. Her chest tightened with a relief so sharp, it was painful.

Blackwood shoved the last hunk of bread into his mouth. "Sorry for that," he mumbled, gesturing toward his engorged cock. "It's just something that happens in the morning. I have no control over it."

It was his grin that overset Meg, transformed her relief into red-hot fury.

"Damn you!"

She flailed about for something to throw at him and found only the pillows. She fired them one after the other. He dodged them easily, but at least her assault wiped the grin from his face.

He regarded her with an expression of aggrieved innocence. "What have I done now? I thought you would be glad to see me recovered."

"Glad?" she shrieked. "Why would I be glad? I only spent all of last night in hell, fighting to keep you alive, having n-nightmares about you in your grave. Only now you are all right and instead of waking me up to tell me, you j-just get up and relieve yourself and—and break your fast. And you're naked!"

Armagil looked about him until he found his shirt. He struggled into it, the bottom of the linen skimming his thighs. Meg's throat clogged, her fury spent. Hot tears cascaded down her cheeks.

"Nay, sweetheart, don't be doing that." The rope springs of the bed creaked as he clambered on the mattress beside her.

Meg scrambled to the opposite side of the bed, but there was no escaping him. He pulled her gently but firmly into his arms. Meg tried to fend him off, but she had neither the strength nor the will to resist him.

She collapsed, sobbing against his chest. "The—the d-devil take you, Armagil Blackwood."

"Aye, very likely he will, but not for a while longer, thanks to you. Now hush." He rocked her in his arms, pressing kisses against the top of her head. "I am sorry I did not think to wake you, but you looked so exhausted and it was a shock to me, to find myself so well recovered. I needed a few moments to take it all in."

He eased her away from him, scrubbing her tears away with his fingertips. "I never thought I could rejoice so much in such simple things as the raw morning air stinging my bare skin, good coarse bread rough upon my tongue, the sweet taste of honey. I didn't expect to be alive this morning, Margaret. Or to care so much that I was."

"Why must you do that—regard your life as though it is some trifle, easily discarded?"

"Because I am a very trifling fellow who has never been of use to anyone."

"I think there are many people who would disagree with you." Meg brushed her lips against his and whispered, "Especially me."

He stared deep into her eyes for a long moment, then his mouth covered hers in a more demanding kiss. Meg's lips parted before the onslaught, eagerly accepting the thrust of his tongue. His mouth tasted of heat and honey and the subtle tang of desire.

Blackwood's lips caressed her face, kissing the damp tracks of her tears. Meg responded in kind, kissing his brow, his eyelids, his cheeks until her lips found his again.

She touched him, her hands roving over his chest, she rejoiced in the vitality coursing through him. But after all the cold, the terror, the darkness of last night, it wasn't enough.

She needed to feel the warmth of his skin, the rush of his pulse, the steady beat of his heart. Her lips locked with his, she tugged at his shirt, trying to peel it off.

Blackwood's hand encircled her wrist to stop her. Half-panting, half-laughing, he said, "God's blood. First you complain of my nakedness. Now you seek to strip me. Will you never be satisfied, woman?"

"I could be. If you would oblige me."

"Nay, Margaret. A miscreant who came so near death as I did ought to give some thought to reforming his wicked ways. Your reason has been unsettled by your fight to save my miserable life. You are tired and overwrought and I would be a villain to take advantage—"

"Then be a villain. Begin your reform tomorrow."

She silenced him with another kiss. Before he could argue with her any further, she scrambled upright, stripping off her chemise and tossing it aside. Shaking back her hair, she knelt over him on the bed.

Blackwood stared, as though he would devour her naked body. His lips parted, but no sound came for a moment.

"This is not fair, Margaret. First you restore me to health and now you would steal my breath away."

"Aye, your breath, your very reason, and—"

Your heart.

She didn't know where that thought came from and did her best to quell it. She reminded herself that this longing that pulsed through her had nothing to do with love, only desire and a celebration of triumph over death.

Meg straddled herself over his legs. Grabbing the ends of his shirt, she pushed it above his hips. She touched the exposed length of his shaft. Blackwood groaned and closed his eyes.

She caressed him more boldly, marveling at her own recklessness. Perhaps it was partly born of the fear that her reason would return. She had spent far too much of her life being careful, overthinking everything. For once she just wanted to set free the passionate side of her nature she had so long repressed.

Aching with desire, she prepared to settle on top of him, take him inside of her. His eyes shot open.

"No!"

With a suddenness that startled her, he flipped her off of him and onto her back. He hovered over her, the dark expression in his eyes making her feel uncertain.

"N-no?" The heat of desire in her cheeks mingled with the burn of humiliation as she faltered, "Y-you truly don't want me."

He gave a choked laugh. "God's blood, woman, I think it

is damned obvious how much I want you. But not hard and fast, like taking a doxy against an alehouse wall. That is not how I have dreamed of having you."

"You . . . have dreamed of being with me?"

"Ever since I first laid eyes upon you. Even last night in the throes of my fever. Why else do you think I woke up so hard?"

"You said it was a natural thing, something that just happened."

"So it is with you always in my head, enchanting me." He brushed a kiss against her forehead. "In my thoughts, seducing me." He kissed her cheek. "In my dreams, bewitching me."

Enchanting? Seductive? Bewitching? Meg stared deep into his eyes. Those were not words she or anyone else would use to describe Margaret Wolfe. But he meant them.

Blackwood's mouth hovered just above hers.

"Show me," she pleaded. "Show me what you dreamed."

He proceeded to do so, kissing and touching her with caresses that lingered and left her aching for more. Even when she would have kissed him fiercely, seeking to hasten their coupling, he refused to allow it.

Seizing both wrists, he pinned them over her head with one hand, while with the other he continued to explore her as though he meant to learn every inch of her. Meg panted and writhed beneath his touch, feeling as though Blackwood now knew her body better than she did herself, every sensitive curve and hollow, every intimate spot, knew just how to arouse her to the brink of madness with his fingers, his lips.

When he released her to strip off his own shirt, Meg was already slick with need of him. He could tell just what he'd done, a slight hint of masculine triumph playing about his mouth as he dipped to kiss her again.

It was time to give him a taste of her own power. Meg had always been quick to learn and she demonstrated all he had just taught her, of caresses that teased, kisses that burned. When he finally entered her, Meg's cry was a mingling of elation and relief. As they began to move as one, she lost herself in his gaze and discovered it was possible for one's heart to race and be scarce able to breathe at the same time. As heat built between them, Meg closed her eyes at last, giving herself over to pure sensation, desire coiling to an intensity that was almost painful, culminating in a climax that throbbed through her whole body.

She felt Blackwood shudder and sensed the moment when he found his relief as well, and they collapsed, spent, into each other's arms.

MEG DOZED, SPOONED AGAINST BLACKWOOD'S HARD BODY, his arm draped possessively across her waist. The sun teased against her eyelids, warning her that the day was advancing, but she rolled away from it, burrowing her face against Blackwood's chest.

Exhausted from their lovemaking, he was in the same state of delicious torpor as she was, drifting in and out of sleep.

Meg knew she ought to rouse herself. It was not her way to loll abed after the sun had risen, especially when there were still so many problems looming, her desperate need to find the witches' coven and stop them before they caused any more harm, the alarming possibility that her mother was still alive and behind it all, her fears concerning Sir Patrick and his true identity.

But cradled in Blackwood's arms, such troubles all seemed so far away, nothing that could not be dealt with later. She could not remember the last time she had felt so much at peace and so safe. She wanted to cling to this sense of contentment as long as possible.

Reason would rear its ugly head soon enough to chide her for reckless behavior. How often she had dispensed stern advice to the young girls on the island about giving themselves to a man too cheaply, the risks of being left scorned and heartbroken, the dangers of getting with child or even a case of the pox.

"You must take care not to let yourself be overcome with desire. There is no passion so strong, that reason and prudence should not be able to conquer it."

Meg cringed. How pompous she must have sounded. Small wonder that many of those girls had paid no heed to her, likely guessing that Meg had never known true passion herself.

Even when she had taken Felipe for her lover, she had planned her surrender so carefully, seeking the experience as more of a rite of passage than out of any strong desire. He had been a kind and considerate man, but he had never seemed to mind or even notice her lukewarm response to his lovemaking.

She doubted that Blackwood would ever be satisfied with such tepid reactions to his prowess in bed. The thought caused Meg's lips to curve into a smile. At times Armagil could seem so callous and coarse and yet he had been unexpectedly tender and so determined her pleasure should equal his own.

The man had such beautiful, deft, large hands and such a skilled mouth. As Meg recalled the way he had teased and caressed her to the brink of sanity, her skin tingled and she emitted a languorous sigh.

"Mmmm." She nestled her head into the lee of his shoulder and felt him stir out of his half-slumber.

He brushed a kiss against her hair and mumbled, "Did you just purr?"

"No . . . well, perhaps."

She glanced up to find him regarding her with a sleepy grin, his eyes half open in an expression that was seductive and unbearably smug.

"I gather I must have performed entirely to milady's satisfaction."

"Perhaps," she repeated coyly, entwining her fingers in the dark hair that matted his chest. "I might describe for you exactly how well you performed, but I fear it might make your head entirely too big with vanity."

She felt his chest rumble as he chuckled. "No, my dear. I don't think my head would be the part of my body in danger of swelling."

"Seraphine told me you would be a good lover and she was right, which should please her, because there is nothing she likes better than being ri . . ." Meg trailed off, the thought of her friend striking her like a basin of cold water.

Blackwood smirked. "The countess is obviously a woman of great discernment."

"And a fierce temper." Meg pulled out of his embrace and bolted upright with a groan. "Oh, God, I just disappeared yesterday and left no word of where I was going. 'Phine must be nigh frantic searching for me. When she finds me, she'll kill me."

"Well, don't expect me to protect you, love. That woman frightens me to death."

She scooted toward the edge of the bed, but Blackwood sat up and restrained her.

"Nay, stay. The damage is done. I am sure young Tom will arrive later to check on me. We can send him off with a message for her."

"You would hardly wish for the boy to find a woman naked in your bed." Meg bit her lip as the unwelcome thought occurred to her. "Unless he is accustomed to it."

"He would have to knock first. This is London, not your sheltered little island. I never leave my door unlocked at night." Blackwood pressed her back down against the pillows and smiled at her. "So no, the boy is not accustomed to catching me abed with a woman, but for a far more important reason than that I have a stout bar on my door. I am not a saint where the fairer sex is concerned, Margaret. I have never pretended otherwise. But I satisfy my lusts elsewhere. This chamber, such as it is, is my home, my castle. I have never allowed any woman to breach these walls. Until now."

He brushed her hair back and caressed her cheek. "But you are not a mere woman, are you? You are the legendary Lady of Faire Isle, an enchantress of unsurpassing—"

"Oh, stop. Don't talk nonsense. You know right well I am no mystical being. The title has never suited me."

"So I am not to call you your highness?" he teased. "Most august and magnificent one?"

"Just Margaret will do."

"Very well, then, *my* Margaret."

His Margaret. On Blackwood's lips, her name became a caress, a tender endearment, and she liked the sound of it far too much. He tumbled her back down upon the pillow and she caught his hand, entwining her fingers with his. She frowned when she noticed the black spot on his thumb, as though his flesh had been seared.

She touched the wound lightly. "Does this still hurt?"

"No, it feels numb as though the area had gone dead. But better a bit of skin than me." He grinned. "Who would ever imagine that such a pretty little flower would be capable of inflicting such damage?"

"I think that mark will be permanent. I am not sure. I have never known anyone to survive the poison before."

"Which I did, thanks to you. Allow me to demonstrate my gratitude once more."

His mouth claimed hers in a kiss that sent a rush of warmth through her, but not enough to assuage her guilt. She held him back, peering up at him gravely. "It was also my fault you nearly died. That rose was never meant for you."

"Who was it meant for? You?" Blackwood's amorous expression faded to be replaced by concern. "You believe someone is trying to kill you? Who?"

"I think the rose was left for me by one of those same witches who are threatening the king, but I don't believe I was meant to die. She would know that I would recognize the danger. She must have meant the rose to be a sign or a warning."

"*She?*"

"My mother."

"The same mother you watched drown when you were a little girl?"

"She could still be alive. That is the reason I risked coming to England. I had to know."

"Margaret," he began slowly. His voice was kind, but his incredulity was written across his face. "I do not know how you came by such a notion, but you should not get your hopes raised."

"My hopes or my deepest dread? My mother is the figure of nightmares. You of all people should understand that."

"What do you mean?"

Meg hesitated and then admitted, "Tom told me about your past."

"*What!*"

"Gilly Black, the executioner. He is your father, is he not?"

Blackwood relaxed a trifle, but he grumbled, "Damn that rattle of a boy. You should take no heed of anything the lad says."

"Please don't be angry at Tom. He admires you and cares about you deeply."

As do I, she nearly added, checking herself just in time.

"I am glad Tom told me. You have nothing to be ashamed of regarding your past."

"Don't I?" Blackwood's mouth twisted in a bitter expression.

"Not compared to me. Your father may be an executioner, but my mother was a witch and she expected me to . . ." Meg faltered, suddenly remembering Seraphine's caution.

"You need to take another lover, but next time keep your heart and your secrets to yourself."

"Expected you to what?" Blackwood asked when she hesitated.

She was spared the decision of what to tell him when the chamber door suddenly burst open. Blackwood swore and cocked one eyebrow at her. "*Someone* forgot to bar the door last night."

"I am sorry. I was a trifle preoccupied." Meg could already feel the heat of embarrassment flood her cheeks at the thought of facing Tom's wide, innocent eyes.

Blackwood rolled away from her, positioning his body to shield her from view.

"Tom, lad, you need to wait—oh, bloody hell!"

Blackwood's broad back went rigid. Meg risked a peek around him and gasped in dismay. It wasn't the boy who had bounded into the room. That would have been bad enough, but not nearly as daunting as the sight of Sir Patrick Graham, the man's face a mask of shock and rage.

Chapter Fifteen

SIR PATRICK STOOD FROZEN ON THE THRESHOLD, THE COLOR drained from his cheeks. Meg experienced an urge to hide herself beneath the coverlet, but it was far too late for such a childish and futile gesture. Sir Patrick's eyes blazed in her direction and then he looked quickly away as though he could not stomach the sight of her.

All Meg could do was to draw the sheet up to her neck and strive for such dignity as was possible in such an embarrassing situation. Only Armagil was able to retain some semblance of his customary nonchalance.

He swung his legs over the side of the bed, stretching his arms and feigning a yawn. "Graham. This is a surprise. Not that I wish to appear inhospitable, but this is not a convenient moment for me to receive morning callers. You may return, say, in an hour from now, and next time, use one of those admirable fists of yours to knock before bursting in upon me."

Sir Patrick glanced down at his clenched hands and slowly uncurled them. A hint of color returned to his face, but he made no move to leave.

"I burst in upon you because I was in fear for your life. When I returned home this morning, I was regaled with some garbled tale about you summoning Mistress Wolfe because you were dying."

"And so I was."

"You appear to have made a remarkable recovery."

"With all due thanks to Margaret."

Sir Patrick raked her with a glance of scathing contempt. "Aye, I can see exactly what sort of medicine she has been administering."

"Mind your tone, Graham," Blackwood said softly. "And take care what you say."

"I am sure it is understandable that Sir Patrick should be concerned," Meg began, but she was cut off by both men.

" 'Tis no concern of his," Blackwood snapped.

"I need no understanding from you, madam. Indeed I hardly know what to say to you."

"Farewell will suffice." Blackwood jerked on his breeches. Meg found her shift at the foot of the bed, but saw no modest way of donning it with Sir Patrick present.

"Get out, Graham, and let the lady get dressed," Blackwood said as he shrugged into his shirt.

"If you please, sir?" Meg hoped her gentler request would be more persuasive than Blackwood's blunt demand. But Sir Patrick merely turned his back on her.

"Proceed, madam. I would be only too pleased if you would cover your shame."

His words stung, but Meg refused to allow Sir Patrick to

turn what she had shared with Blackwood into something common and sordid.

Scrambling into her shift, she said, "I do not believe that a woman who finds pleasure in the loving embrace of a man has anything more to be ashamed of than he does."

Blackwood snorted. "That will hardly serve as a reproof for Graham, my dear. I am sure he expects me to don a hair shirt and do penance as well."

"It scarce matters what I expect," Sir Patrick said. "You have little respect for my opinion."

Blackwood started to retort, but Meg stayed him with a shake of her head. This situation was uncomfortable enough without the two men quarreling.

She hastened to don the rest of her clothing, her fingers fumbling with the lacings of her gown. Blackwood hurried to her rescue. She should have discouraged him. Helping her to dress was such an intimate, loverlike gesture. It could only further provoke Sir Patrick, and Meg feared that was exactly what Blackwood had in mind. But as he deftly worked her lacings, he smiled down at her with such warmth and reassurance it was as though Sir Patrick was no longer even there.

Sir Patrick turned around in time to witness the tender moment between them and it did nothing to mollify his temper.

"So what did you do, Gil?" he demanded. "Feign some false illness to lure Mistress Wolfe to your bed the moment I was out of the way? Or was the excuse for this tryst concocted between you?"

Blackwood smoothed his hands down Meg's arms. "I was not aware that either of us is obliged to make excuses to you. While we might be friends, Graham, I never gave you leave to dictate what company I keep. I never promised you—"

"No, you didn't, but much good it would have done if you had. You are not the sort of man to ever keep your vows, are you?"

Blackwood flinched at the gibe. But Sir Patrick didn't appear to notice as he went on. "For once I hoped that for the sake of our friendship, my wishes might have been of more import to you than the pursuit of some strumpet."

"Damn you!" Blackwood started toward Sir Patrick, but Meg managed to get in between them.

"Stop it, both of you."

"You call her by such a name again and I swear—"

"Armagil. I said, stop! You both need to calm down and allow me to explain to Sir Patrick what happened."

Blackwood glowered at Sir Patrick, but he backed away. Sir Patrick likewise subsided, but his jaw set in a stubborn line.

He appeared so different from the man she had met in Pernod. Had his gentlemanly demeanor merely been a mask for his true nature, a man hardened by bitterness and hatred? Or were such strong emotions too long suppressed causing Sir Patrick to unravel? His clothing looked disheveled, the lines of his face haggard as though he had not slept at all last night.

When Meg approached him, he averted his gaze as though he could not bear to look at her. Or was it more that he did not want her looking at him, fearing she might see all the pain and bitterness of a boy named Robert Brody?

"Sir Patrick—" When she tried to rest her hand on his sleeve, he shrank from her touch. Meg let her arm fall back to her side. "Armagil did not deceive you or me. He truly was deathly ill. He had been poisoned."

"*Poisoned?*" Graham appeared in no humor to heed anything she had to say, but the word gave him pause. "How is that possible?"

"By means of this." She hurried to fetch the handkerchief in which she had carefully enfolded the remains of the lethal rose. Some of the petals had fallen away, but the flower, which should have been brown and shriveled by now, bore the appearance of fresh bloom, unnaturally preserved.

Sir Patrick's breath hitched at the sight of it. "Silver," he murmured. "The petals are silver like the ones that were strewn to frighten the king."

"The petals in themselves are harmless. It is the thorn that carries the deadly venom. When Armagil found the rose in your garden, he pricked his thumb."

Sir Patrick cast a stricken look toward his friend. "You truly were poisoned?"

Armagil glared at him. "I said so, didn't I?"

"And now you are miraculously recovered?"

"Only because Margaret knew the antidote."

Meg covered up the rose as Sir Patrick frowned, struggling to absorb this information.

"How did that rose come to be in my garden? Where did it come from?"

"Where do you think?" Blackwood asked. "It had to be put there by those same witches who have been terrorizing King James."

"Why would they do that?"

"I don't know. Perhaps to alarm Margaret or maybe they were even seeking to poison you."

"No. *She* wouldn't—I mean they wouldn't—" Sir Patrick broke off, looking discomfited as though he realized he had betrayed himself.

It was as Meg had feared; there was some connection between Sir Patrick and the witches, if only he could be induced to admit it.

Blackwood studied his friend through narrowed eyes. "You know, I find it strange, Graham. I was the one who was poisoned, yet you are the one who looks like you have been wrestling with the devil. It would please me to believe that you unbent enough to enjoy yourself for a change, carousing at the alehouse, but alas, I know better. So what were you doing that kept you out all night?"

"You have no right to be questioning me, especially in front of *her*." Sir Patrick gestured toward Meg. "By God, Armagil, it is as though all the time I have known you counts for nothing. We have been friends for so long. I know you to be a good man, but it has pained me to watch how you have wasted your life. You are like a man who has been sleepwalking through all these years, numbing yourself to all feeling.

"When you are finally aroused enough to care, it is because of her. And you don't even know who she is."

"I know enough."

"Does he, Mistress Wolfe?" Sir Patrick rounded on her. "I doubt that, or instead of asking me about those witches, he would be asking what you know."

"Not enough," Meg replied. "Or I would have tried to stop them ere now."

"Would you? That silver rose that you have stowed away so carefully in your bag—it is the emblem of Megaera."

Meg steeled herself not to react to the name, but her hands clenched involuntarily in the folds of her skirt.

"I am sure you have heard of Megaera, have you not, Gil?" Sir Patrick stared at his friend steadily. "You do remember we discussed the sorceress who was worshipped by Tamsin Rivers?"

"Vaguely. I was probably drunk at the time."

"Do you even wonder how Mistress Wolfe knows so much about these poisoned roses?"

"I merely consider myself fortunate that she did."

"Or how she was so easily able to lift the curse that Tamsin Rivers placed upon the king?"

"Did she?" Blackwood cast a surprised look at Meg.

"Did you not ask her how her audience with the king went?"

"I was a trifle preoccupied with dying in agony. The matter slipped my mind."

"And she did not tell you? How modest of her. Would you like to explain how you cured the king, Mistress Wolfe? Or shall I?"

"I appealed to his reason," Meg said.

"Appealed or claimed power over it?" Sir Patrick turned earnestly to Blackwood. "She knows unholy magic, Armagil, a trick that she learned from other cunning women, something she calls the reading of the eyes. She admitted as much to the king and then she demonstrated her ability to divine thoughts, unravel his memories. She also has the power to bewitch, to seize possession of a man's mind."

"What utter rot," Blackwood said.

"How else do you explain the hold she has gained over you? She is as much of a witch as those women threatening the king. Very likely, she also is a worshipper of this Megaera—"

"Enough." Blackwood cut him off before Meg had a chance to defend herself. "Graham, it is high time you were elsewhere."

Sir Patrick shook his head, but then vented a sigh of pure frustration. "I may as well be for all the good I am accomplishing here. You are far too much under this witch's spell to heed me. And I have a hanging to attend.

"I am sure it is nothing to you, but a good man is about to die today for no sin but being true to his faith."

Blackwood's jaw was set at a hard angle, but as Sir Patrick started for the door, he relented enough to try to prevent him. "Don't be a fool, Graham. You cannot do that priest any good by being there and I am sure Salisbury will have his spies present, taking down names, noting the presence of other suspected Catholics."

"The earl is well aware of my faith. Even if he wasn't, it would be a risk I must take. I am tired of being a shadow Catholic, weary to my soul of the need for secrecy. The least that I can do for Father Gregoire is be there to pray for him, that he will be granted a swift and merciful end."

"He won't be," Blackwood said grimly. "Gilly Black is very skilled at his trade."

"Well, you would know that better than anyone else, wouldn't you?"

With this last bitter retort, Sir Patrick stormed out the door and slammed it behind him. As Blackwood frowned, staring after his friend, Meg tried to read his emotions. Anger? Concern? Guilt over the part his father, Gilly Black, would play in the brutal execution of the priest? But as ever Blackwood was a mystery to her, his expression unreadable. He strode over and placed the bar across the door.

"A trifle late for that, don't you think?" Meg attempted to jest to ease the tension Sir Patrick left in his wake.

Blackwood responded with a taut smile. "I suppose we could not have expected to keep the world shut out forever. But it would have been good to have had a little more time."

"Yes," Meg agreed softly.

He regarded her intently and for a moment Meg hoped he meant to take her back in his arms, but he brushed past her and began donning the rest of his clothes.

"I am sorry about Graham," he said. "I warned you he could be a bit . . . strong in his opinions. Perhaps when he has had time for calm reflection—"

"He will no longer consider me a witch and a strumpet and a threat to your soul?"

Blackwood sighed. "No, I fear that is not going to happen. I think it would be best if you and the countess left his house immediately."

"I had already reached the same conclusion."

"You should find somewhere else to dwell, preferably an island, far, far from here."

Meg struggled to conceal the hurt she felt that Blackwood could part from her so easily. She tried to tell herself his suggestion was made out of concern for her safety.

"I cannot return to Faire Isle yet," she said.

Blackwood splashed water from the basin over his face. "Why not? You have cured the king. You have accomplished all you came here for."

"Not all."

"Oh, yes, I forgot your quest to find your dead mother. Margaret, you cannot truly think—"

"I know not what to think. My mother may not be behind these attacks on the king, but someone is. Some witch who is obviously familiar with the coven of the Silver Rose."

"Yes . . ." His gaze rested upon her for a moment and then he sank down upon the edge of the bed to draw on his boots. He had defended her against all of Sir Patrick's accusations, but surely there must have been some vestige of doubt planted in Blackwood's mind.

"Are you never going to ask me?" she prodded.

"About what?"

"Why I know so much about Megaera's coven, the poison in the silver roses."

He paused, looking a trifle uneasy, then returned to dragging on his boot. "I just assumed it was because you are the Lady of Faire Isle and thus familiar with all this lore and tales of witches like Megaera."

He was offering her an excuse. So why could she not just seize upon it? She could almost hear Seraphine warning her. *There is no need to be so honest, even with a lover.*

Meg moistened her lips. "Yes, I am familiar with Megaera's story because . . ."

Keep your secrets to yourself, Meg.

But when he looked up and her eyes met his, she blurted out, "I am Megaera."

The boot he had been holding plunked to the floor. "What!" His expression mingled shock with disbelief.

"Or at least I was. I—I had better explain."

He stared at her. "Yes, I think you had better."

Meg hugged her arms about herself and in halting sentences told him about the dark days of her childhood when she had been the Silver Rose, the obsession of a deranged mother and the object of worship to a coven of equally mad women.

"They all believed I was destined to become this powerful sorceress who would conquer the world. I—I did possess some unusual gifts," she admitted. "As young as I was, I was good at deciphering ancient codes and languages. I was one of the few who could translate the *Book of Shadows,* a compilation of black arts that had long been lost.

"That is where I learned about how to make the silver roses and the syringes, although my mother never used them for any healing purpose. The coven called them witch blades and employed them as another means to deliver the poison.

"I never wanted to place such lethal weapons in the coven's hands, but Cassandra had means—painful means of enforcing my obedience." Meg swallowed. "But it is also true that Cassandra was my mother and—and I wanted to please her. I wanted her to love me."

She hesitated, looking for any small sign of understanding from Blackwood. But he was hunched over, working on his other boot.

Meg paced the room as she continued, "I know not what dark path Maman might have led me down, but I was fortunate to have a father who rescued me. It was he who placed me in the care of Ariane Deauville. She taught me what it truly meant to be a wise woman, a healer, and that is how I came to be the Lady of Faire Isle."

"So you simply forgot that you were ever this Megaera? No doubt that is why you failed to mention the fact to me."

Was that anger she heard in his voice? Revulsion? If only he would look at her.

"I do not speak of my past easily, Armagil, because yes, I have tried very hard to forget. But it is never possible." Tears stung Meg's eyes.

She drew closer and attempted to place her hand on his shoulder, but he leaped and strode to the hearth, putting the distance of the room between them. Meg cupped her hand and drew it back to her bosom as though that could somehow protect her heart from the ache of his rejection. Her tears threatened to spill over, but she blinked them back, striving for dignity and control.

His back to her, Armagil said, "You speak of strange gifts. So then Graham was right. You can bewitch men, read their thoughts."

"No! I have never bewitched anyone. But I can read eyes to a certain degree and—and—"

"And what?" His voice was like the crack of a whip, making her jump.

"And dreams. I have these dreams." Meg drew in a breath, and in a rush, tried to explain to him about the prophetic dreams that had plagued her childhood, the ones that had tormented her recently involving the death of Maidred Brody.

"I have never had dreams about the past before, so I could not understand what this was trying to tell me, but I finally realized. Sir Patrick is the boy in my nightmares, Maidred's brother. He vowed vengeance upon the king and now he has come back to get it."

"What?" Armagil rounded on her.

"Sir Patrick is Robert Brody. He—"

"The devil he is." Armagil had been pale, but his face suffused red with fury. "This is utter madness and you will speak no more of it, do you hear me? Christ's blood, woman, if this is all the better you can read minds, your powers are quite faulty."

Beneath his rage, Meg caught a thread of fear because he knew Graham well. He had to know that Meg was speaking the truth, but Armagil would do anything to protect his friend. Meg well understood. She would have felt the same about Seraphine. She realized she had made a grave error in confiding her suspicions to him and sought to temporize.

"Perhaps I am mistaken. I admit my skill is not what it once was."

"Can you read my mind?"

"No, I don't think—"

"Try it." His words were a challenge, like flinging a gauntlet in her face.

"I—I would rather not."

But he stormed toward her. Backing her against the wall, he pinioned her with one hand braced on either side of her head.

"Do it, Margaret. Read my eyes."

Meg reluctantly raised her gaze to his and found his eyes as dark and forbidding as the night she had first met him. She made a halfhearted attempt to probe their depths, but it was like trying to embark upon a black storm-ridden sea that threatened to engulf her.

She averted her face and whispered, "I can't."

"Why not?"

"Because you will not let me in, not even when you held me in your arms and we were intimate."

Armagil levered himself away from her. "We coupled our bodies, my dear. There is nothing intimate about that."

"No, that is not true. I felt something deeper and I am sure that you did—"

"I didn't, which is why I tried to warn you that we should not lay together." He strode back to the hearth and vigorously applied the poker, but there were no embers to stir. The fire had turned to ash. "I feared it would be a mistake and I was right."

"Because now you believe I am a witch?"

"I know not what you are, except for one fact. You are not formed for casual tumbles in a man's bed. I should have guessed you would imagine it meant more than it did."

His voice was so harsh, but it softened a little as he added,

"I grant you it was most pleasurable and no matter what Graham said, I would not have you feel ashamed of anything we did."

"Sir Patrick did not make me feel ashamed. You are the one who has accomplished that." With the fire out, Meg suddenly realized how cold the chamber was. She wrapped her arms about herself.

Armagil replaced the poker. His hand gripped the edge of the mantel and he half-turned toward her when another knock sounded at the door.

He swore. "Now who the devil?"

When he flung the door open, Tom burst into the room. The boy let out a glad cry to see Armagil recovered. He flung his arms about Armagil's waist, rushed to hug Meg and back to Armagil again.

The boy's joy was so boisterous, there was no opportunity for any more words between Meg and Armagil, but that was likely just as well, Meg thought bleakly. There was nothing more to be said.

MEG WAS GLAD TO BE LEAVING SIR PATRICK'S HOUSE. SHE AND Seraphine did not have many belongings, but at least the packing and preparations for finding a new lodging gave her something to do other than think about Armagil.

Seraphine, of course, was furious with Meg for vanishing overnight and giving her such a fright. Consequently the countess had haughtily announced that she was no longer speaking to Meg. Which meant that Seraphine had spent the last half-hour alternating between scolding and demanding explanations.

Meg told her all the details of her audience with the king, including the subtle threat made by Lord Salisbury and Meg's suspicions about Sir Patrick's true identity. She was more hesitant when it came to relating all that had happened at Armagil's lodging.

But either Seraphine was far too shrewd or Meg's blush betrayed her. When Seraphine continued to pelt her with questions, Meg gave in. If Armagil could treat their encounter so cavalierly, then why couldn't she?

"In the morning, we celebrated Armagil's recovery by— by—I made love to the man."

When Seraphine whooped and applauded, Meg tried to smile, but ended up biting down upon her lip instead.

"Oh 'Phine, I shouldn't have. It was behavior unworthy of the Lady of Faire Isle, far beneath my dignity."

"Oh, be damned to your dignity. Did you enjoy it? Did the man pleasure you?"

"It is hardly appropriate to discuss . . . yes, it was wonderful, wild, passionate, just as you predicted Armagil would be." Meg attempted a careless toss of her head, but couldn't quite manage it. She added wistfully. "He was also surprisingly tender."

Seraphine's grin faded. "Oh, no! I told you to take a lover, not fall in love."

"I have not." But her words lacked conviction even to her own ears.

"I warned you, Meg. Keep your heart out of it, keep your secrets to yourself. I hope you at least paid heed to the last part of my advice."

Meg refolded a petticoat, steadily avoiding Seraphine's gaze, but she could feel her friend's eyes boring into her.

"Margaret Wolfe, never tell me that you felt obliged to

pour your heart out to the man about your entire past, your lunatic mother, your childhood as the Silver Rose."

"All right. I won't tell you."

Seraphine groaned. "Oh, Meg, whatever is to be done with you?"

"I am sorry, 'Phine. I cannot sort myself like a woman dividing up her clothing into trunks, my mind in this one, my body in that one, my heart locked away over here. I am not fashioned that way, and for all you pretend to be so hard, neither are you. Have you ever taken any other lover beside your husband?"

"It is the way among the nobility, once one has provided one's husband an heir, one is free to—"

"I do not care what one does—what about you?"

Seraphine started to shrug, but faltered beneath Meg's steady gaze. "No," she admitted softly, "there has never been any man but Gerard."

"And there never will be. My heart is searching for the same thing you had with your husband, one man to love, to be true to forever."

"You believe you may have found that with Blackwood?"

"No. He reacted as any sane man would to the revelations about my past, angry, alarmed, and revolted. I cannot blame him, although somehow I thought Armagil might have been different." She sighed. "Perhaps I am not meant to find love."

"Oh, Meg." Seraphine hugged her fiercely, but Meg wriggled out of her embrace.

"We need to finish our packing," Meg said dully.

The servant that Seraphine had engaged arrived to move their trunks downstairs. All of Sir Patrick's household had made themselves scarce, no doubt as fearful of having such a witch in their midst as their master.

But Meg refused to leave without seeing Sir Patrick. She tracked him down to his study and entered the room unbidden, catching him by surprise.

He was examining a lock of hair, his face naked with grief. But upon Meg's entrance, he shoved the hair back inside a locket, concealing both the memento and any emotion. He faced Meg, his features schooled into a mask of stony politeness.

"We are leaving," she said. "But it is customary to thank one's host for his hospitality."

He dismissed her words with a curt wave of his hand. "No thanks are necessary. You performed a vital service and it is I who am in your debt."

"I helped Armagil for his own sake and mine. You owe me nothing."

"I was not referring to Armagil, although if you did indeed save his life, I am grateful. I meant what you did for the king."

"Again, I did not do that for you." Meg regarded him steadily. "I do not even believe you truly wanted him spared the terror of being cursed. If you did, I fear it is because you have plans of your own regarding the king's fate."

He averted his face, the color rising in his cheeks. "So you admit it. You have used your witch's tricks on me. You are privy to my thoughts."

"Only enough to perceive that you are a man in a great deal of pain. But this vengeance you are pursuing will bring you no peace or comfort."

His mouth twisted bitterly. "Won't it?"

"No, it will only end up costing you your life and perhaps even your soul."

"There are some causes worth forfeiting everything for."

Meg reached out to touch his locket. "Do you think she would agree? Is that what she would want for you?"

"Don't speak of her to me. Don't you even dare breathe her name. You know nothing about— Just stay out of my head, witch!"

He wrenched the locket away from her, trembling with anger. He strode away to the windows, his chest rising and falling rapidly. He did not face her again until he had regained control.

"You obliged me by coming to London and attending to the king. I am grateful for that. I did promise you safe conduct and I will make arrangements to send you back to Faire Isle."

"That is kind of you, but I am not going back, at least not until I have found what I came looking for."

"And what might that be?"

"The truth, Sir Patrick."

Chapter Sixteen

"STOP THIEF!"

The angry bellow sounded in Amy's ears. Heart thudding, she shoved her way past a drayman and a lanky shopkeeper closing up a storefront. At this late hour of afternoon, there was no longer much of a crowd for her to lose herself among.

Her only advantage was that she knew this part of the city well and her pursuer was a fat merchant who should have been easy prey if she had not been so clumsy when cutting his purse.

He huffed after her. She could have eluded him easily if he had not roused others to his pursuit, a pair of bored young apprentices who were clearly enjoying the diversion of the chase.

Feeling like a terrified hare with a pack of excited hounds nipping at her heels, she darted around a wagon that was unloading merchandise at a tavern. She knocked over a few of the crates. That slowed her pursuers a little, but not enough.

She'd be taken soon if she did not find someplace to hide. Amy forced herself to run faster even though her lungs felt close to bursting. Her gaze flicking from side to side, she spotted the opening to a narrow alley and shot down it.

Pain blossomed in her side and her footsteps faltered. She could not keep up this pace any longer. In sheer desperation, she crouched down behind a rain barrel and shoved her fist in her mouth to stifle her labored breathing.

She felt the hard knock of her heart against her rib cage and feared it might be loud enough to betray her. She listened, straining to catch the sound of her pursuers. She thought she heard footsteps hesitate at the mouth of the alley.

Amy tensed, trying so hard to hold herself still that she trembled. She caught snippets of her pursuers' conversation.

"*. . . thought she came this way . . . maybe doubled back and dashed into that tavern . . . no, sure she headed into the alley.*"

Amy suppressed a whimper of fear and panic. The moment seemed to stretch into hours before the voices faded away along with the footsteps. Perhaps the apprentices found the prospect of searching for her in the tavern far more enticing or decided the pursuit was not worth it, not if it led them down this foul alley stinking of urine and emptied slop basins.

Whatever the reason for her salvation, Amy gulped with relief and gratitude. She waited for another ten minutes to pass before she dared remove her hand from her mouth and resume her normal breathing. Her hands still shook as she examined her prize. The velvet purse had looked promising enough dangling from the obese merchant's belt. But when she undid the drawstring and emptied the contents into a palm, she blinked with outrage and disappointment.

Pence! Just a few miserable pence. This was all she had risked her neck for?

"That fat miserly bastard!" she hissed. She was so disgusted, she nearly hurled the coins down the alley. But she was in no position to scorn even this pittance. She returned the coins to the purse and slumped down with a mewl of despair.

The devil only knew what sort of filth she was sitting in, staining her cloak. Amy was far too dispirited to care. Nothing had gone right for her since yesterday morning when Blackwood had ruined their test by making off with the silver rose.

She had taken some consolation from the thought of the wretched doctor dying in agony, but even the satisfaction of that had worn off with Bea carping at Amy for her failure and incompetence. Her sister had complained relentlessly about what an idiot Amy was and how they were going to have to brew the poison all over again and the ingredients were so expensive and how they were running out of coin and time.

Amy had hoped the coin from the merchant would solve that problem and the purse itself she had planned to stuff into Bea's mouth and put an end to her cruel taunts. But it seemed she had blundered again, hazarding her life for nothing and leaving herself open to more of her sister's mockery.

Amy leaned her head back against the wall of the tenement building and sighed. She should have known better than to try to steal anything when her mind was in such a state of turmoil. Hadn't her grandmother always warned her about that?

"Never try to pick a pocket or cast a spell when you are distressed or angry, Amy, my pet. It can only lead to failure."

Perhaps that is why the curse that Granddam had inflicted upon James Stuart had never come to pass. Granddam had certainly not been in a calm frame of mind when she had cursed the king, not with the flames licking at her legs, blackening her skin and all.

Years had passed since that dreadful day when Amy had watched her grandmother being burned alive. Yet she still remembered it, still missed Granddam with a terrible ache as though it had happened but yesterday.

Tears filled Amy's eyes and she blinked them back. "Never mind, Granddam," she whispered. "You shall be avenged. Bea and I shall see to it, and then every dream, every wish you ever had for our coven shall come true, I promise you."

The thought heartened Amy and she struggled to her feet. She crept down the alley and stole a cautious look around before emerging. There was no sign of the merchant or those nasty apprentices. The street was even emptier than before, the shop fronts closed up, most everyone having scampered off home to their suppers.

Amy knew she should make haste, too, with the light fading. The watch would be out soon to enforce the curfew. But the prospect of returning to her lodging held little appeal for her, not with Bea awaiting there in her foul mood.

But if she lingered for a bit, Bea would go out soon, heading down to the wharves to earn some coin by spreading her legs for some of the sailors and dockworkers. Of course Amy would have to endure listening to Bea gloat about how much better she was at whoring than Amy was at being a thief. But that was tomorrow. At least Amy might enjoy some of her evening in peace.

She wandered aimlessly until she found herself in the environs of Sir Patrick Graham's house and realized she had flitted there like a moth drawn to the light.

The place was no palace, but with its small tidy garden and smoke curling from the chimneys, it represented all that was snug, safe, and comfortable to Amy. The air had turned much colder with the sun setting. Amy shivered and pulled her cloak tighter as she crept into the garden.

She was relieved to find it empty. If one of Sir Patrick's servants caught her prowling about, she would be hard-pressed to explain what she was doing here. She hardly knew herself; hoping for a glimpse of Megaera perhaps.

Bea might go on and on about the need to make certain the Lady of Faire Isle and Megaera were one and the same before approaching her, but Amy was convinced that she was. Whenever Amy gazed upon Margaret Wolfe, she just *sensed* it.

That was because Amy was a fool who stubbornly believed whatever she wanted to believe, Bea would say. No doubt Amy was still credulous enough to go hunting for faeries beneath the bushes, she'd sneer. But that would have been quite stupid.

No faery would choose to dwell anywhere in this hard, cold, crowded city. They would live in the wilds of the country where there were thick copses of trees and rugged hills where one could clamber to the top and feel free and breathe.

Amy meant to live there herself one day if their plans succeeded. That is—*when* their plans succeeded and the ritual was complete and Megaera fulfilled all their dreams as Granddam had always sworn the great sorceress could.

Amy would live on the grandest estate, wear the most beautiful silken clothes and bedazzling jewels. She would be quite the lady of the manor and maybe she would have a lord . . .

Amy tipped back her head, gazing toward the upper story windows. No candles had been lit as yet, so she could detect no movement.

She inched her way closer hoping for a sight of— She was honest enough to admit to herself it was not Megaera she hoped to espy but *him.*

What if Sir Patrick was in his bedchamber, preparing to change his garb or stripping down for a bath? It would be so lovely to see him naked. Amy licked her lips and felt a squirming of sensation between her legs.

She was sure he would be quite beautiful, all smooth white skin, all lean hard muscles, and with such an impressively large cock, Bea would bitterly envy Amy her possession of him.

She had declared to Bea that she meant to have him for her pet, but Amy hungered for so much more than that. Even if she had to keep him in chains, she wanted Sir Patrick to adore her. So much so that even if she offered to set him free, he would beg her not to do so.

"My beauteous Amelia, do you not understand that I will die if you send—"

"What do you think you are doing here?"

The angry demand startled Amy out of her dreams. She spun about with a hiss, her fingers raised like a cat's claws, preparing to defend herself against one of the household servants.

But it was not the gardener or even that horrid valet Alexander with his thick Scots tongue. It was *him,* Sir Patrick himself. The rays of the setting sun picked out the highlights of his hair, turning it to a burnished gold. Even his eyes appeared to blaze a fiercer blue in the dying light.

Amy's hands fell limp to her sides. "Oh," she sighed.

"Answer me," he snapped.

She couldn't. Couldn't speak, couldn't think, could hardly breathe.

"What are you doing lurking in my garden? How dare you come here!"

Never had she heard his soft, genteel voice sound so harsh. He glanced about him almost as though he were ashamed to be seen with her.

No, not ashamed, she assured herself. Afraid. They shared so many secrets, no doubt he feared discovery.

"Don't worry. I was most discreet. No one saw me. No one knows that I am here."

"What do you want?"

Amy summoned her most beguiling smile. "Why, I only wanted to see—"

She raked him with her eyes, imagined stripping away his doublet, his shirt, and his trunk hose. He shuddered beneath her gaze. From desire? She could certainly feel the heat. Suddenly the oncoming night no longer seemed so cold.

Except for his eyes. They had grown hard as shards of ice.

"You were wanting to see Mistress Wolfe? You are too late. She is gone."

Amy stared up at him, wondering if she dared to trace her finger over the stern line of his mouth. She half-raised her hand when the sense of his words penetrated the warm haze enveloping her.

"Gone? W-what do you mean, *gone*? Where did she go?"

"I care not so long as she does not reside beneath my roof. So there is no reason for you to come here again."

"B-but you just allowed her to leave? To disappear? And after you promised—"

"You would speak to me of promises, witch? After you pledged your word that you would cease tormenting the king if I fetched the Lady of Faire Isle to England?"

"And we have!"

"So it was someone else who nailed that dead cat to the palace wall and left a threatening message in blood?"

"Oh," Amy said in a small voice. "That."

"Yes, *that*."

She hated the sneer that marred his features. It made his handsome face look almost ugly.

"The cat was my sister's idea." Amy spread her hands in a placating gesture. "You know what Beatrice is like, so impatient to have our revenge upon the king."

"And dropping deadly silver roses into my garden? Was that also part of her schemes?"

Guilt flooded her cheeks. Amy gave him a nervous smile. "Roses? What roses? They are usually white or red, are they not? I have never heard tell of such a one as you described. Silver, did you say?"

"Aye, exactly like the one that poisoned my friend Armagil." Sir Patrick stepped closer, and for the first time, Amy noted the shadows that pooled beneath his eyes. He must have scarce slept at all last night, poor lamb, no doubt fretting over the ailing Blackwood.

Armagil Blackwood was a spineless, useless excuse for a

man who deserved whatever evil befell him, but she had forgotten that he was Sir Patrick's friend, even though Blackwood was far from worthy of that honor.

"I am so sorry if Dr. Blackwood is dying, but . . ."

"He's not. Mistress Wolfe cured him."

". . . I am sure that—" Amy blinked. "She what? No, she couldn't. That's impossible unless—"

Margaret Wolfe truly was Megaera.

I knew it, Amy thought, barely able to restrain her dance of joy. Just wait until she told Bea. But Amy's surge of triumph was brief as Sir Patrick stalked closer and she realized how she had just betrayed herself. His eyes blazed with anger and accusation.

"I don't know what hellish game you witches are playing at or why you wanted Margaret Wolfe fetched from her island. But whatever your foul plans are, they end now, do you understand?"

His voice was hard, threatening. Amy didn't like it. One of the things that she loved best about Sir Patrick was his gentle courtesy. She stumbled away from him, but she raised her chin in defiance.

"You needn't act so superior. You have foul plans of your own. You didn't fetch the Lady of Faire Isle because we demanded it. You brought her here for sniveling James so he would not go into hiding and cancel your precious parliament. You needed Mistress Wolfe because you thought she could end his fear of the curse."

"Which she has done."

Amy's mouth fell open. Megaera had cured Dr. Blackwood? She had lifted the curse from the king? No, this could not be right. These were not at all the actions of the dark sorceress Granddam had taught Amy to revere.

"Margaret Wolfe has played her part," Sir Patrick continued. "I have no more use for her and I never had any for you or your sister. If you possess any wisdom at all, you will disappear and never let me see or hear of you again."

Never see him again? The thought was unbearable to Amy.

"But we both want the same thing," she pleaded. "The destruction of James Stuart. Your plot to blow him up is very clever, but his death will come so fast. Bea and I just wanted him to suffer more, to know why he must die. But we'll stop tormenting him from now on, I swear it." Amy rested her hand upon his sleeve with a coaxing smile. "There is no need for such enmity between us. We are allies."

"Allies?" He shook her off savagely. "Do you think that I have ever wanted my holy cause tainted by your filthy witchcraft? You should perish in the same way your wretched grandmother did. But I am offering you a gift of mercy you don't deserve. Leave here now. If you are not out of my sight in the next minute, I'll summon a constable."

Amy's lip quivered with a mingling of hurt and outrage. "You just try it and . . . and I'll tell. Everything I know about you and your friends and your nasty—"

She gasped as he shoved her up against the oak tree, one hand closing about her neck. He did not squeeze hard enough to cut off her air, just enough to bruise her throat. Amy's pulse thudded, torn between fear and the dark thrill of having goaded him into touching her.

"If you ever breathe so much as a word, I'll snap your neck."

"Go ahead. Do it," she rasped. "How holy will you be then? Just remember I have a sister, many sisters to avenge me. So you dare not hurt me. It is a hollow threat."

"As hollow as yours to reveal our plot. Do you actually

think anyone would believe the word of a nothing like you?" he ground out between clenched teeth.

"Mayhap not, but they'd investigate and your plan would come to nothing. You'd die a traitor's death, your guts ripped out, your head stuck up on a pike."

"Not before I accused you of witchery and you end up like your evil grandmother, the flames licking the flesh from your bones."

"And then we'd all be dead and King James could do a merry jig on our graves."

Her taunt appeared to penetrate the haze of his anger. He kept her pinned up against the tree, although his hand eased away from her throat.

"You see, we do still have need of each other," Amy whispered. "I have power, more than you can imagine, just like my granddam. I can curse and cast spells, even love spells." She wriggled suggestively against him.

He sprang back, his revulsion unmistakable. "It would take far more than magic to make a man ever want to touch something as loathsome as you."

He glared at her, his contempt like a cold hard mirror that reflected not the comely seductive lass of her imagination, but a scrawny woman with matted hair, her tawdry dress and cloak stinking of the filth of the streets.

Sir Patrick shuffled his heel as though scraping dung from his boots. He turned and strode toward the house without looking back. Amy rubbed her neck, furious tears spilling down her cheeks.

Oh, he was cruel. He was horrid. She could have loved him forever, but now she hated him. Groping beneath her cloak, she clenched the hilt of her knife.

THE CANDLE BURNED LOW, ITS FEEBLE LIGHT FLICKERING OVER the red-stained water in the basin. Amy huddled in the corner of her lodging, staring at her hands through the flood of her tears. She had managed to cleanse them, but her knife was still encrusted. The bright shiny blade looked as if it was turning to rust.

She needed to finish washing up, but she could not seem to rouse herself, her entire body trembling. Oh, what had she done? What had she done?

"C-couldn't help it. All h-his fault. He made me do it." Amy rocked herself back and forth. She froze at the sound of the door opening.

She heard Beatrice stumble inside and curse. "Amy! God curse you. You have tumbled your clothes all about the room again. You nearly made me slip and break my neck. When are you ever going to learn to stop being such a slattern?"

Amy drew her knees in tight to her chest, but she was unable to muffle a sob.

"Amy?" Beatrice picked up the candle and raised it aloft so that the light spilled over the corner where Amy crouched. "Oh, lord, what the devil is wrong with you now?"

Her sister never had any patience with tears and Amy realized how pathetic she must look, her eyes swollen from crying, snot dribbling from her nose. But she had already borne enough for one day. She could not endure any more of Bea's scorn.

Amy wiped her nose on her sleeve. "N-nothing's wrong. Leeb me 'lone."

Beatrice set the candle back down on the table. She must

have noticed the red-stained water for she muttered another oath. "What's happened? Are you hurt?"

Her throat clogged with tears, Amy shook her head.

"Your knife is all bloody. Did you do for someone? Who'd you stab?"

Amy gulped and managed to get out, "H-his fault. All his fault."

"I daresay it was, whoever *he* might be. Was it just some varlet accosting you in the street or did you know him?"

Amy responded by burying her face against her knees and giving way to another storm of weeping. Her misery must have appeared great enough to melt even her sister's hard heart.

Beatrice surprised her by plunking down beside Amy in her corner. She gathered Amy in her arms, pulling her close. "There, there, Amy, love. Tell me what happened. If some bastard has hurt my little sister, he'd best be dead or I vow I will gut him myself."

Beatrice reeked of strong spirits and the musky scent of whatever men she had lain with tonight. No doubt she had earned a great deal of coin and was mellowed with drink, which accounted for this rare display of compassion, but Amy hungered for whatever comfort she could find.

She burrowed her face against her sister's shoulder. "Oh, B-bea. I have had the most t-terrible day, the w-worst of my life."

For once Beatrice did not scold her for being melodramatic as she was wont to do. "Shh, stop your caterwauling and tell me all about it. Your Bea will make everything all better."

Between hiccups and sobs, Amy struggled to get out her story. Her head throbbed from crying, leaving her thoughts as scattered as her words and somehow she jumbled it all together, her near capture for thieving the purse, Sir Patrick's harsh rejection of her, the confusing behavior of Margaret Wolfe.

"Oh, he was so cruel to me, Bea."

"There, there." Bea patted Amy's shoulder. "So Margaret Wolfe cured Dr. Blackwood?"

"Aye, that is what Sir Patrick said before he seized me by the throat and all but spat on me."

"That means Mistress Wolfe knew the antidote for the poison."

"Did I tell you Sir Patrick called me loathsome?"

"And she was able to lift the curse from the king."

Amy lifted her head from Bea's shoulder and squinted reproachfully at her sister. "I declare you seem far more concerned with the doings of Mistress Wolfe than you are about the way Sir Patrick wounded and humiliated me."

"Oh, the devil take your precious Sir Patrick. Of course, I am more interested in Mistress Wolfe. Don't you see what this means, you little fool? We need test no further. Margaret Wolfe is Megaera."

Clearly Bea's compassion had reached its end. Amy wrenched away from her. "Of course she is Megaera. Haven't I said so all along?"

"And she is obviously possessed of great knowledge and power, just as Granddam always said."

"Much good it does us." Amy sniffed and wiped her eyes. "So far all she has accomplished with her power is to undo everything we did."

"Because we have not yet revealed ourselves to her. The Silver Rose does not know she still has devoted followers."

"I don't think that will matter a jot," Amy said. Usually

she tried to be the optimistic one, but never had she felt so low, so completely without faith. "I don't think Mistress Wolfe cares about being the Silver Rose. Nor will she ever help us with our ritual."

"Oh, yes she will. Trust me for that," Bea began, only to break off. Amy realized the moment when her sister spied her handiwork, for Beatrice's jaw dropped. She scrambled to her feet. Snatching up the candle, she strode across the room to examine the pentagram Amy had painted on the wall. The blood glistened, some of it still appearing wet.

Beatrice spun around to stare at her. "What in hellfire, Amy!"

Amy shrank from her sister's accusing gaze. "It—it was necessary. I had to do it—to ward off any avenging spirit."

Bea's gaze dropped to the floor. Now she had to be noticing the pile of bloodied rags that had not been enough to scrub away the stains leading to the large wardrobe chest.

Amy rose trembling to her feet as Bea followed the trail. She flung back the lid to the trunk, the coppery scent of the blood becoming stronger. Candlelight flickered over the body of the wizened old woman crammed inside. Her gray head was bent to an odd angle, making her look most uncomfortable, but it had been the only way Amy had been able to get the elderly tavern owner to fit.

Mistress Keating stared up at Beatrice with protuberant glassy eyes. Bea was so startled she nearly dropped the candle.

But she made a quick recovery, steadying the taper as she glowered at Amy. Amy shook back her hair, trying for defiance, but she feared that all she sounded was guilty as she wailed.

"I told you this was the worst day. But you were so entranced with the mighty Megaera, you never gave me a chance to tell you the rest of it."

"I am listening," Bea said through gritted teeth.

"After Sir Patrick had been so horrid—"

"Forget that damned Sir Patrick. Tell me how Mistress Keating ended up in our wardrobe trunk."

"Not easily, I can tell you. I have no idea how I managed it. For such a skinny old woman, she was horribly heavy."

"Dead bodies usually are. I am less concerned with how she got in there than I am with why."

"Well—" Amy's lip quivered.

"And if you start crying again, I swear I will slap you."

Amy regarded her sister resentfully, but she blinked hard, managing to stem her tears. "Well, by the time I returned to our lodging, I was already that distressed, wasn't I? And then Mistress Keating pounced upon me. She barged in here, shrieking at me about her missing cat, which makes all this partly your fault, Bea."

When her sister only regarded her stonily, Amy gulped and continued. "The woman just kept squawking about her beloved Grimalkin and saying she knew we had done some-thing to him and how she should never have rented a room to a pair of witches like us and—and she said she'd have the law on us and—and—"

Amy clapped her hands to her head. "I just needed her to be quiet, to stop all her nasty screeching and threats."

"So you knifed her to death. Here in our own lodging?"

"I—I wasn't thinking clearly. It was Sir Patrick's fault. He had me so angry and upset."

"Sir Patrick! Sir Patrick! If I hear you say his name one more time, I really will hit you. If you were so furious with the man, why didn't you stab him?"

"Oh!" Amy huffed. "You think that would have been so much better?"

"Aye, if no one had seen you do it. But as usual, I am the one inconvenienced, having to clean up another mess that you have made."

Amy's lower lip jutted out. "It is not as though you liked Mistress Keating either."

"That is not the point. Don't you realize what this means, you great lackwit?" Bea slammed down the lid to the trunk.

"You murdered our landlady, Amelia. Now we are going to have to move."

Chapter Seventeen

THE SARACEN'S HEAD HAD BEEN A REFUGE FOR ARMAGIL Blackwood ever since he had come to London, as good a place as any for a man to lose himself amidst savory meat pies, tankards of ale, boisterous masculine camaraderie, and willing doxies.

The doctor was known to be congenial company and generous with his purse unless he was too deep in his cups. Then, wary of his temper and his large fists, most men had the wit to keep their distance.

The dark expression on Blackwood's face this evening warned the denizens of the Saracen's Head that the doctor was already far gone in drink. Most of them had the good sense to leave him alone on his bench where he sat slumped back against the wall, his fingers crooked around the stem of his tankard.

A buxom wench who had been eyeing him ever since he

had entered the tavern was the only one who made bold to approach. But a glare from Blackwood and a growl to get away sent her scurrying in the opposite direction.

He had no appetite for the sort of distraction the doxy offered, a few moments of grunting and groping in a chamber upstairs. He wondered if he would be able to find that kind of release for his pent-up tension ever again.

He feared not and all because of *her*. Images kept flashing through his mind of Meg so warm in his arms, her lips so soft as she whispered kisses against his skin, the kind of caresses that could make a man forget himself for more than a few fleeting moments, perhaps for a lifetime.

Blackwood ground his fingertips against his eyes. Christ's blood. He still could not believe it. He had slept with Megaera, the infamous witch who inspired other women to run mad, abandoning their babes, their families, to take part in unholy rituals, poisonings, and curses that led to their own destruction.

The Silver Rose, by her own admission, had possessed unnatural power even as a child. As unthinkable as it was, maybe Graham was right. Perhaps Meg did have him bewitched. Blackwood had never credited such nonsense before, but if she truly was this evil sorceress—

No. No matter what Graham said, Armagil could not reconcile the notion of evil with Margaret. Not with her healing hands, quiet wisdom, gentle compassion, and understanding that seemed to have its roots in some great pain of her own.

Now he knew what that pain was, the full depth of her mother's insanity, the nightmare that had been Meg's childhood. Even telling him about it, she had looked so young and lost, every bit as much of a victim as all those other desperate young women who had been lured by Cassandra Lascelles's madness. He ought to have gathered up Meg into his arms and reassured her instead of rejecting her.

But he was honest enough to admit he had not thrust her away merely because of the shock of learning she was Megaera. Meg might not have cast any spell, but she had certainly done something to him, making him feel too much, remember too much. When she looked up at him, the soft light in her eyes alarmed him. She was falling in love with him and that could only lead to disastrous hopes and expectations. He was not the sort of man any woman could ever rely upon. He had hurt Meg, but truly he had done her a great favor by driving her away.

"How insufferably noble of me," he muttered, lifting his tankard in a silent toast to himself.

Here's to you, Armagil Blackwood, the only man in London who can make a virtue out of being a coldhearted bastard.

He drained his tankard and called for another, seeking to numb himself, to drown out the voices in his head. It even seemed preferable to listen to chatter around him, until he started to catch snatches of the conversation and realized most of it revolved around the execution of the priest.

"Never saw so much blood, not even at a bearbaiting."

"So the traitor was still alive when they cut him down?"

"Oh, aye, although the priest was so purple in the face, I thought he was gone. But old Gilly Black revived him. You should have heard the traitor scream when Black gutted him and shook his entrails in his face."

Armagil's fingers tightened around his mug as he sought to block out the voices and the unwelcome memories that came with them.

Of shivering in the early dawn near Tyburn, the morning

air as raw as Armagil had been in his youth before he had perfected the art of going numb. Of watching Gilly Black check the noose one last time.

"Pay careful heed to how I have reinforced the knot, lad. It is important, although many hangmen make the mistake of thinking the secret to a proper hanging is all in the rope. But it is a much more precise art than that. You have to calculate with care the weight of the prisoner along with the length of the drop. It makes all the difference between a slow death and a quick one, which is all right for your ordinary thief or murderer. But when the charge is treason, the villain must survive the noose so the rest of his just sentence can be carried out."

The old man had actually grinned as he had displayed to Armagil his sharpened boning knife. As soon as he had heard the creak of the cart wheels conveying the condemned traitor to his grim fate, Armagil had ducked behind the tree, retching up his breakfast, much to the old man's disgust.

But then he had been only a boy, he reminded himself as he swallowed his ale. Still too fierce in his emotions the way Patrick Graham was now.

Blackwood flinched when he thought of Graham attending the priest's execution that morning, Graham, whose heart was already overburdened with anger and grief. If Armagil had been any kind of friend, he would have made more of an effort to prevent Graham from witnessing the gruesome spectacle.

Just as he should never have let Meg slip away from him with that hurt expression on her face. If he had just cared enough—

Damn it! He didn't want to care.

"Evening, Doctor," a cheerful voice piped up.

Armagil looked up from his tankard to glare at the cursed fool who dared to approach him. Albert Dunwiddy beamed down at him, appearing quite oblivious to Blackwood's foul humor.

Dunwiddy was a tinker who made his living selling odd bits, many of which Armagil suspected were stolen. He was notorious for cadging drinks in exchange for a bit of gossip or some fantastic tale.

The last thing Armagil needed was any of Dunwiddy's prattle about how some fisherman had found gold in the stomach of a sturgeon or the two-headed goose that was being displayed in the poulterer's shop in Cheapside.

Armagil fished some coin out of his purse and slapped it on the table. "Take it and go."

Dunwiddy's lower lip jutted out in a wounded expression. "Here, now. I should hope I might greet a friend without being suspected of coming to beg."

Armagil lifted his brows. When he shrugged and reached to reclaim the money, Dunwiddy was swifter. He scooped up the coin with an ingratiating smile.

"'Course, never let it be said that Albert Dunwiddy would insult any man by refusing his generosity. I thank you—"

"Spare me your thanks." Armagil waved him off. But Dunwiddy was far too dense to take the hint. When he purchased his drink, he pulled up a seat to join Blackwood.

"I am fair parched," he declared.

"Then it would be prudent to give your tongue a rest."

"But I am bursting with news—"

"Which you should keep to yourself."

"I attended the hanging of that priest this morning."

"I am not interested."

As Dunwiddy proceeded to regale him with all the details, Blackwood gritted his teeth.

"Exactly what will it take to shut you up? Breaking my tankard over your head? If that will work, I can reconcile myself to the loss of a mug full of good ale."

Dunwiddy regarded Armagil with injured surprise. "But I thought you would like to know how well your father did. He has lost none of his skills despite his advancing years."

"Gilly Black is not my father!" Armagil roared, causing more than one head to turn in his direction. The tavern keeper paused in wiping down the bar, ever on the alert for trouble. Armagil strove to rein in his temper while Dunwiddy raised his hand in a placating gesture.

"Of course, of course. Sorry, I forgot that you and he are a bit—estranged. You'll not hear another word from me on the subject."

Dunwiddy took a swallow of ale. "Although if I had a father who had risen to the height of his trade, I'd be that proud to call him—"

"Enough!" Armagil slammed both fists on the table, causing the tankards to rattle.

Dunwiddy grabbed for his, spluttering, "Have a care. You nearly toppled my drink."

"Three seconds," Blackwood growled.

"Three seconds?"

"That is how long you have to remove your carcass from that bench and take yourself elsewhere. Or there will be more than your ale in danger."

Dunwiddy sniffed. "Very well. If you were in no humor for company this evening, you should have just said so. But it is too bad, because I had an even better story to tell you. Even though there's plenty of thieving and killing here in the city, it has been a while since we've had anyone tried as a witch."

Armagil felt his heart stop. "What!"

"Ah, so now you are interested." Dunwiddy gave him a smug grin and reached for his drink. He cried out when Armagil dashed the tankard from his hand.

"What witch? What is her name? Damn you!"

"I don't rightly know. Look what you've done, spilled ale all over my best breeches."

Armagil leaped up. Dunwiddy gasped out a protest when Armagil seized him by his jerkin and hauled the man from his bench.

"You had better know and right quick. Who are you talking about? Someone has been arrested?"

"N-no, not yet. But I am sure it will only be a matter of time before those evil women are hunted down."

"There was more than one of these witches?"

"Aye, a whole pack of them or so I have heard."

"And what have they done? What are they accused of?"

"*Murder.*" Despite his fear of Blackwood's temper, Dunwiddy licked his lips, clearly relishing the information he had to impart. "They killed some woman, used her blood to paint devil symbols on the walls. The poor wench must have been a mite of a thing because they were able to stuff her body inside a trunk."

A mite of a thing? Blackwood's mind leapt to Meg, who barely came up to his shoulder, whose frame seemed so slight and delicate, he'd half feared he would crush her himself when they'd made love so fiercely.

The air left his lungs.

"Her name?" He could barely rasp out the words. "What was the name of the woman killed?"

"I can't rightly remember."

"Curse you! You had better." He gave Dunwiddy such a savage shake, the man's head snapped back.

"Easy now, Dr. Blackwood." Armagil felt a heavy restraining hand descend upon his shoulder. He tried to shrug it off, but the owner of the Saracen's Head only tightened his grip.

"I realize our good neighbor Dunwiddy here can be a bit aggravating." Minton's smile was both placating and carried a hint of warning. "But I allow no brawling in my establishment. You know that, sir."

"I was aggravating no one," Dunwiddy squeaked. "I was just telling him about the terrible murder those witches has done."

"A dreadful affair," Minton agreed. "Poor old woman."

"Old?" Blackwood echoed.

"Aye, an elderly woman who kept an alehouse and lodgings."

"She was the victim?" Blackwood felt able to breathe again. He released Dunwiddy, but Minton still kept a firm grip on Armagil's shoulder.

Dunwiddy smoothed his hands over his jerkin. "Aye, that's what I was telling you before you pounced on me like some mad jack let loose from Bedlam, demanding names, which I tell you I don't know."

"Nor do I know anything more." Minton peered at Armagil curiously. "Why is it of such import?"

"No reason. I—I just—"

"Have had a drop too much?" Minton eased his hold on Armagil and patted his shoulder. "You know I value your custom, Doctor, but I think it is time you headed home to your bed."

"Yes, I—I am sorry." Armagil realized that every eye in the place was trained upon him. He also realized he was trembling. Muttering his apologies, he staggered out of the alehouse and into the street.

Doubling over, he dragged great gulps of air into his lungs. Minton and everyone else in that tavern had supposed Armagil had had too much to drink. But the real problem was that he had not had enough.

He had been far too sober to weather a shock like that. Those few moments when he had feared that Meg might be the murdered woman they were talking about had been among the blackest moments of Armagil's life and that was truly saying something.

Damnation! What had Margaret done to him? He did not know what he had come to feel for her, or if he did, he was unwilling to admit it. He only knew that if anything happened to her, he truly would run mad.

She was so stubbornly determined to track down those witches, and if they were the same ones who had brutally murdered that tavern keeper and reveled in painting with her blood, they had escalated in their insanity. Strewing poisoned roses about and nailing dead cats to the wall seemed tame by comparison.

If Meg did corner those witches and attempt to put a stop to their evil, what might they do to her, even if she was the object of their mad adoration, the Silver Rose? And if she tried to turn them in to the authorities, she risked exposing the secret of her own past. She might well end up in the dock alongside those demented creatures.

So how in the world could he keep her safe? There was

only one way: He had to find the witches first and deal with them himself. But where should he even begin?

He dragged his hands down his face, wishing that his head was clearer. He thought of returning to the Saracen's Head and seeing if he could wring any more information out of Dunwiddy. But he doubted that the tinker knew anything more, and such an action would likely result in Armagil finding himself tossed back into the street and none too gently. Minton truly had no appreciation for a good brawl.

So who else would know more of this murder? Well, the Earl of Salisbury had his army of spies who kept him well apprised of what went on in the city. Armagil actually grinned at the idea of himself trying to force his way in to see the little beagle. He'd have better fortune gaining an audience with James himself, as if that would avail him anything.

Armagil's amusement faded at the thought of the king, the only man in England he considered more useless than himself. There was someone else he might approach, though, another man who had an uncanny knack for keeping his ear to the ground and acquiring information about the darker side of London. The mere notion of seeking him out affected Armagil like an ice bath, rendering him far too sober.

ARMAGIL COULD HEAR THE LAP OF THE WHERRYMAN'S OARS AS he guided his boat away from the shore. Armagil wished he could have persuaded the man to wait for him, but he didn't have enough coin to offer by way of compensation, not when there were still so many other lucrative fares to be had.

The sun was slowly setting, turning the waters of the Thames into a rippling flow of ink. Littledean was a small village set just outside the gates of London. Across the river, Armagil could see the forbidding stone walls of the Great Tower.

The final blaze of the sun glinting off the stonework had the curious effect of making a portion of the battlements appear washed in blood, a reminder of the many prisoners who had come to a grisly end upon the Tower Green.

It was not a prospect that many men would relish, living in the shadow of that ominous tower. But Gilly Black had always boasted of his view.

Armagil trudged along a worn path that led up to a dwelling set back from the river. His breath coming out in clouds of steam, he felt chilled by the sight of the place he had once called home.

Little had changed about the modest house, but even in the fading light, Armagil noted the signs of neglect, bare places in the roof where the thatching had rotted away, the thickness of the weeds that had overrun the garden.

The weeding had once been his task.

"About the only thing you'll ever be good for," the old man had been wont to sneer.

The bitter memory caused Armagil to hesitate. Then he strode up to the door and hammered his fist against it before he changed his mind.

He could see the flicker of candlelight behind the thick diamond grid of the windowpanes. Armagil stamped his feet in an effort to keep warm. He was on the verge of knocking again when the door swung open. Armagil stiffened. He had not been quite prepared to have the old man answer the door himself.

He had clearly interrupted Black at his supper. The old man was still holding a half-eaten chicken leg, a hint of grease smeared on his chin. His jaw fell open at the sight of Armagil and for a long moment they stared at each other.

He and Gilly Black were much of a height, with the same breadth of shoulder and rawboned appearance. Armagil noted that he had finally gained an inch or two over the old man. Or perhaps it was just that Black was starting to stoop with age.

His hair had turned a snowy white, matching his thick brows and giving him an oddly benign appearance. Few would have guessed the hand clutching the chicken leg was the same one that had gutted a priest only that morning.

The old man was the first to speak. Clamping his mouth closed, his lips twisted into the familiar bitter sneer.

"Well, this is quite the surprise. The prodigal son returns."

"Don't ever call me that. I am not your son—" Armagil snarled and then stopped, realizing this was not an auspicious beginning.

"Oh, you made that more than clear when you stormed out of here years ago. So what could possibly cause the high-and-mighty doctor to honor me with his presence now?"

Armagil bit the inside of his cheek, struggling to keep his temper in check. "I need your help with something. I only came here seeking information."

The old man snorted a laugh. "Oh, that's rich, that is. You must be either drunk or mad."

"Actually I am a little of both. So you'd be wise to step aside and let me in."

Gilly's face flushed a mottled red. "I thought I made it real clear the night you left you'd never be welcome beneath my roof again. You never were anything but an arrogant, ungrateful wretch and now you have the sauce to come here a-begging for my help. Pah!"

The old man started to slam the door in his face, but Armagil's hand shot out to prevent him.

"You misunderstand me," he said, keeping his voice cool and level. "I am not begging. I am not even asking."

Ignoring the old man's spluttered protest, Armagil forced him back and muscled his way inside.

Chapter Eighteen

*I*T WAS DIFFICULT FOR MEG TO BELIEVE THAT THE CITY OF LON-don was not much more than a mile wide. She had walked far greater distances than that on Faire Isle. But her island was a place of wide-open spaces where a woman could breathe— windswept cliffs, cool, shaded forests, and uninhabited stretches of shore.

By contrast, the city overwhelmed her with its maze of narrow streets slippery with refuse. Too many people, too many carts, too much noise with the clatter of hooves, the shouts of traders, the curses of brawling apprentices. The jut-ting upper stories of houses and shops cast a shadow over the streets, black-and-white timber frames that had been erected too quickly and appeared likely to tumble down just as fast. There was little aura of permanence here in the heart of the city, just a rush of humanity scurrying to survive.

She felt chilled to the bone and footsore as she trailed

Seraphine along the congested thoroughfare. She had still not recovered from all of the emotional upheaval of yesterday and she never had possessed Seraphine's stamina.

But Seraphine had begun to lag as well, her graceful shoulders bowed down beneath the hopelessness of their mission. They had set out at first light, making cautious inquiries of anyone who might have knowledge of women still practicing the old ways.

Meg could not help reflecting how much easier this investigation would have been back on her island. If any wise woman had strayed into the realm of the dark arts, word of it would surely be carried to the Lady of Faire Isle, just as Meg had been alerted to the supposed bewitchment of Bridget Tillet.

But here in London, all Meg had to rely on was her memories of daughters of the earth who had once attended the councils among the monoliths on Faire Isle. Finding any trace of those women was nigh impossible in this teeming city.

Any questions Meg asked were met with blank looks, wary eyes, and doors slammed in her face. Londoners were noted for being suspicious of foreigners and downright hostile to the French. Seraphine with her beauty and regal presence could exert an influence at least on men. She could be charming if she wished, but her charm was wearing thin after receiving yet another dismissal from a surly midwife.

Nay, she had never heard of any woman calling herself a daughter of the earth, the wood, the sky, or any such nonsense. She was a respectable Christian midwife, thank you very much, who had naught to do with anything hinting of paganism.

Meg had barely time to spring back before the door closed on her foot.

"Stupid cow!" Seraphine flung up her hands in frustration. "This is ridiculous, Meg. We are getting nowhere. Maybe the problem is that we are being too subtle. We should just come right out and ask, 'Have you noticed any demented witches running amok with dead cats and peculiar silver flowers?'"

"Oh hush!" Meg said.

"Why? There is not much likelihood of being overheard amidst all this clatter. I can barely hear myself speak, which is a source of great vexation. I am rather fond of the sound of my own voice."

Seraphine grinned, clearly expecting to provoke some retort from Meg. But Meg gripped Seraphine's wrist and cast an anxious look over her shoulder.

Seraphine's smile faded. "What is it, Meggie?"

"Nothing. Just that for some time now, I have felt as though we are being followed."

Seraphine halted and risked a quick look back. But there was nothing to be seen beyond some porters toting bolts of cloth from a mercer's shop to a waiting cart and a woman haggling with a merchant over the cost of thread.

"I haven't noticed anyone," Seraphine said.

Meg shrugged, trying to dismiss the eerie feeling of eyes boring into her back. Seraphine took another quick look before they set out again.

"If we are being followed, who do you suspect it might be?" she asked.

"It could be one of Lord Cecil's spies or one of the women we are seeking or even . . ." Meg felt the color rise in her cheeks and she ducked her head. "Or—or no one. I daresay I am just being foolish."

But as ever, Seraphine divined her thoughts all too well.

"If you were hoping it might be Blackwood coming in search of you, your giant of a doctor does not exactly blend into a crowd."

"No, he doesn't and I doubt he'd try. I do not expect he will ever seek me out again."

"The more fool him. Seducing you and then casting you off just because you had a bit of—of an unusual childhood. The man is an idiot if he cannot see what an amazing woman you have become. A pox on him, I say."

"Armagil is very wise to be daunted by my past, the strange gifts I possess. I cannot blame him for that."

"Maybe you cannot, but *I* can, so it is just as well he keeps his distance. I hear tell that when a man is turned into a eunuch, he becomes larger and Blackwood is already enough of an oaf."

Meg tried to smile at Seraphine's growled threat, but she could not. What had happened with Blackwood was still too raw a wound for her to treat it lightly. Perhaps she never would be able to. Strange that she could feel such a deep connection to a man she had known so briefly, with whom she had shared only one night. She would always vividly recall those fleeting moments she had spent in his arms, her body one with his. Despite the pain, perhaps such a memory was worth the price, far more than many other women experienced.

Seraphine would have continued to vent her anger toward Blackwood, but Meg silenced her with a press of her hand and a plea. "Please, 'Phine. I would rather not talk about Armagil. We have far more important matters to occupy us."

Seraphine scowled, but subsided. "That is true, but what are we going to do next? This aimless wandering is doing nothing for my feet or my patience."

"I know." Meg bit her lip before admitting, "There is a certain apothecary shop that I know of where we may likely find another daughter of the earth."

Seraphine shot her an exasperated look. "Well, by all the crying saints, Meg! Why didn't we go there to begin with?"

"Because I hoped to avoid it if at all possible. This woman has great cause to resent me, perhaps even to despise me."

"How could anyone hate you? Unless it has something to do with your mother?"

"It does. Everything. The woman I intend to seek out is—is Mary Waters."

"Oh." The mere sound of the name gave Seraphine pause. "But surely she cannot blame you?"

"For what my mother did? Why not? There are a great many wise women who do and Mary Waters has more cause than most. Even if she does not hate me, meeting me can only stir up grievous memories. And she may not have any information that can help us."

"And she very well may! I understand your scruples, Meg, and even though seeking out Mary Waters may be grasping at a straw, we have little choice. While we are dithering our time away, roaming the city, who knows what further mayhem those witches are about?"

Meg nodded in unhappy agreement. "Then we need to head toward the area near St. Paul's Cathedral. That is where most of the apothecary shops are located."

As she prepared to dart across the street, Seraphine stopped her. She drew Meg out of the press of traffic, toward the relative shelter of an alley opening.

"Meg, have you given any thought as to what you are going to do if we do manage to hunt down these witches?"

"No, I confess I have not thought that far ahead."

"Will you turn them over to the authorities?"

Meg considered the fate of women accused of witchcraft, the harsh imprisonment, the tortures, and the inevitable verdict of death by hanging or, worse still, by fire.

She shuddered. "I hope if I make myself known to them, that I can persuade them to stop their attempts to revive the coven. Beside the attack on Armagil, and I believe that was inadvertent, and their efforts to frighten the king, no lasting harm has been done. No one has been killed."

"That you know of."

"If they are like so many of the others, they are merely desperate women looking for hope. I pray I can reason with them."

"How unfortunate then that you obliged me to leave my reasoning implement back at our lodgings."

Seraphine could not stride through London in her masculine garb with her sword strapped to her side. But if Meg knew her friend, Seraphine would have a weapon hidden about her person somewhere.

"What if you find out—as mad as it seems—that your mother is behind this?"

"I will deal with that when the time comes. I must find the witches first."

"I still think Graham would have been our best lead."

"He would die first. He has only one purpose, to avenge himself on James. He would give his life for it." Meg added, "I dreamed of her again."

"Your mother?"

"No, Maidred Brody. She pleaded with me again to save her brother. I know you don't believe me. Armagil accused me of being mad."

"I don't know what to think. I have seen too much proof

of your powers to doubt you. But I think you have pledged enough of your life to undoing the evil of your mother. You don't need to go about making promises to dream ghosts. Sir Patrick or Robert Brody, whoever he might be, can shift for himself."

Meg said nothing. Perhaps Seraphine was right, but Meg could not so easily forget the tormented eyes of Maidred Brody. The girl had been led astray like so many other innocents, lured by the promised magic of the Silver Rose. But Meg did not see how she could give ease to Maidred's troubled spirit. How could she possibly deter Robert Brody from his destructive path? The man despised and mistrusted her. The only one who could possibly have any influence over Sir Patrick was Armagil.

But she had not even been able to get Armagil to concede that Sir Patrick and Robert Brody were one and the same, so how could she ever persuade Armagil to intervene? Even if Armagil did not despise her as Sir Patrick did, he certainly mistrusted her now that he knew who she really was. Save Robert Brody? It would be all that she could do to contain the threat posed by the witch coven. The entire situation felt overwhelming and hopeless.

Absorbed by her unhappy thoughts, Meg trudged beside Seraphine in silence until she espied three gilded pills painted on the wooden sign, the familiar symbol that denoted an apothecary shop. The establishment boasted shelves well stocked with bottles and vials of intriguing concoctions. The aroma of dried herbs perfumed the air, reminding Meg poignantly of her own stillroom on Faire Isle. She would have found the scent soothing had she not been so tired and anxious about the reception she would receive from the shop's owner.

But the visit to the first apothecary produced nothing but more blank looks in response to her inquiries. And the second shop. And the third.

As they entered the fourth, Meg began to fear she was pursuing another futile quest. But as soon as she clapped eyes upon the woman behind the counter, Meg tensed. She had no need to even ask for a name this time. Although the woman could not have been much more than twenty, her soft round features bore a striking resemblance to an older face Meg remembered well, along with a gentle voice and loving arms. Patience Waters had offered Meg her only refuge during the chaotic days of her early childhood.

Meg pressed Seraphine's arm to let her know they had found the right shop.

"Please, let me handle this," Meg whispered as the woman emerged from behind the counter, wiping her hands on her apron.

She approached them with a warm smile that reminded Meg so much of Patience, it brought a lump to her throat. The woman's gaze skimmed over Meg and alighted hopefully on Seraphine, which didn't surprise Meg. Seraphine's exquisitely cut cloak and haughty carriage loudly proclaimed the prospect of an important and wealthy customer.

Beaming, the woman dipped into a curtsy. "Good afternoon, milady. And how may I serve you?"

"Well, I—" Meg began, trying to inch forward, but she was cut off by Seraphine demanding bluntly, "Are you Mary Waters?"

The woman blinked, her smile wavering a little. "Why, yes, that is, I was afore I married my Ned. Now I am Mistress Robards."

"But your grandmother was Patience Waters."

"My grandmother was Prudence. Patience was my great-aunt." Mary Robards's expression became more guarded as she added, "But she died a long time ago and—and under very distressing circumstances."

Meg sighed. She had hoped to ease into this more gently, but Seraphine's brusque questions left Meg no choice but to plunge in.

"I know. Patience Waters was my nurse. My name is Margaret Wolfe."

The woman trained her gaze on Meg for the first time, looking her up and down. Mary paled and she actually recoiled from Meg.

"You are not welcome here. You get out of my shop right now or I will fetch my husband or—or a constable."

Mary prepared to bolt, but Seraphine grabbed her arm. "You'll do nothing of the kind."

"Release me at once or I—I will scream."

"'Phine, let her go." Meg hastened to reassure the woman. "Mary, we mean you no harm. I just need to ask you a few questions."

"No! I want nothing to do with you or your coven."

"I don't have a coven."

"Truly? Tell that to those witch friends of yours coming around here to purchase herbs."

Witch friends? Meg's pulse quickened with the hope she might be on the right trail at last. Seraphine released the woman and Mary backed away, rubbing her arm.

"Please, leave me be," Mary directed her plea to Meg. "Isn't it enough that you got my Aunt Patience killed?"

"Meg did no such thing," Seraphine snapped. "She was only a child, for mercy's sake."

"Nay, 'Phine, I do feel responsible for Patience Waters's death." Meg turned sadly to Mary. "Your aunt was a most kind and wise woman, a true daughter of the earth. She acted as my nurse for the first five years of my life. She nurtured me and tried to protect me from my mother's madness. When she learned of my mother's insane plans for me, Patience confronted her. She threatened to take me away from Cassandra, spirit me off to the refuge of Faire Isle.

"I—I overheard their quarrel. It was so loud and violent, I was frightened and started to cry. Patience came to soothe me. She told me not to fret, all would be well. She sang to me, rocked me to sleep in her arms and when I awoke the next morning—" Meg swallowed. "Patience was gone. I never saw her after that night. My mother said she had dismissed my nurse and she had returned to her own family."

"She didn't!" Mary cried. "She never came back to us. She simply disappeared."

Meg nodded unhappily. "I was but a child, but even then I sensed my mother was lying to me. I always feared that Cassandra had—well, I know how ruthlessly my mother dealt with anyone who opposed her. Please believe me when I say I loved your Aunt Patience dearly. I would have given anything if I could have . . ."

Meg's voice thickened and she could not go on. Seraphine draped her arm around Meg's shoulder and gave her a bracing squeeze. When Meg had regained command of herself, she said softly, "I am so sorry, Mary."

Some of the hostility had faded from Mary's eyes, but she retreated behind the counter. "If you are truly sorry as you claim, then you will leave me alone and order your minions to do the same."

"I have no minions. In fact, I wish to find those witches you spoke of. I fear they might be trying to revive the old coven. I want to stop them."

"Then I wish you good fortune with that. Those two harpies seem as determined as they are terrifying."

"There are two of them?" Seraphine asked. "Do you know their names?"

Mary cast a nervous look over her shoulder as though fearing she might be overheard and draw a curse down upon her head for telling. She leaned forward and all but whispered, "They are sisters, I believe. Their names are Beatrice and Amy Rivers."

Rivers? The same last name as the old woman who had cursed the king? Meg and Seraphine exchanged a significant glance, their suspicions confirmed. These were definitely the witches they were seeking.

"And what did they want from you?" Meg asked.

"At first, they but came to buy herbs. But they began hinting at other things, that there was some great day coming that would change everything for daughters of the earth, a new power that would arise and end the reign of men. They spoke of *you*."

Mary darted a half-wary, half-resentful glance at Meg. "How you would be their deliverance and their avenger. The Silver Rose."

Meg shook her head. "I am not this Silver Rose, Mary. I never was, except in my mother's mad imagination."

"Aye, mad is the word for it," Mary agreed. "I might have been able to shrug off all of these witches' wild talk, if they had not been so terrifying serious and so determined that I join them in rebuilding the coven. They said if I didn't, I would be very sorry.

"I was too scared to ask what they meant by that. When I ordered them out of the shop, they went. I have not seen them for several days." Mary shivered. "And I pray I never do again."

Meg moistened her lips. There was another question that she had to ask, even though she dreaded the answer.

"Were these two sisters always alone? Were they ever accompanied by an older woman, very thin, very pale, and blind?"

"No, I don't recall ever seeing anyone like that."

If Cassandra Lascelles had been with these two women, Mary would have noticed. Meg's mother had always had an unforgettable presence. The fact that Cassandra had not been seen with the Rivers sisters did not entirely rule out the possibility that she was still alive and behind all this. But Meg still breathed a little easier.

"So do you have any idea where we can find these Rivers women?" Seraphine asked.

"Yes," Mary said, but she directed her reply to Meg. "You swear that you truly are not one of them. That you mean to stop them and—and you will keep them from ever returning to torment me again."

"I will do my best," Meg said quietly. "I swear upon my honor as the Lady of Faire Isle and a true daughter of the earth."

Mary studied her for a long moment before saying, "They have lodgings at an inn near Westminster. The Two Crowns. That is where I was ordered to go whenever I stopped being foolish and decided to join them."

"Thank you. How can I repay you for your help?"

"By staying far away from me and my family. I want naught to do with any of the old lore, even the white magic my grandmother and Aunt Patience practiced. It is much safer that way."

Mary Waters was not the only woman to feel that way. The numbers of the daughters of the earth were dwindling. Meg understood the fears of those who wished to abandon the ancient knowledge, but it saddened her all the same.

Mary returned to her mortar and pestle, vigorously grinding marjoram into a fine powder. She did not even look up as Meg and Seraphine turned to leave.

They were almost at the door when Mary called out, "Mistress Wolfe, wait."

She and Seraphine both paused to look back.

"There is something more about those two sisters. The older one, Beatrice, is so cold and cruel. I vow she could flay a puppy alive and laugh while she did it. But the younger one, Amelia . . ." Mary shivered. "For all she can sound so pleasant, she's got a great emptiness in her eyes. Then all of a sudden she'll look at you like the devil just lit a fire inside of her. She's the dangerous one. If you do confront her, you had best take great care."

Chapter Nineteen

THE TWO CROWNS BORE THE LOOK OF A LESS THAN REPUTABLE establishment, weeds overrunning the yard, the building itself showing signs of neglect. Paint had flecked off the inn sign, making one of the crowns look broken in half. Rather than a symbol of regal splendor, it more resembled the jaws of a trap.

You had best take great care.

Mary's warning echoed through Meg's head. But she felt less fear than she did an oppressive weight settling over her heart. It was too late for taking care, too late for any hope of a peaceful resolution if the gossip she had heard was true.

Everyone from an ostler idling against the fence to a pair of urchins begging for coin: All were too eager to impart the terrible tale of how the innkeeper's wife had been brutally murdered two nights ago.

"I heared they cut old Mistress Keating up into a hunnerd

pieces," one of the boys told Meg. He looked far too young to be taking so much relish in such a gruesome tale. He grinned, displaying missing front teeth, until his older friend elbowed him in the stomach.

"Tell you all about it for ha'penny, mistress," the older one said, sticking out his grubby hand. But the younger boy would not be repressed.

"It was witches done it. They cut her up and fed her to the devil's hound. Then they leapt on their brooms and vanished and no one can find them."

"I hope they swoop back and grab you, you prating doltard. You shoulda kept quiet 'til they paid us."

The two boys might have come to blows, but Seraphine intervened, offering them both a coin. She plied them with questions they were unable to answer, but Meg had heard enough.

She approached the inn door, her stomach knotted with dread. She heard Seraphine calling out for her to wait, but she steeled herself and plunged inside.

The taproom was no more appealing than the inn's exterior, the floor strewn with soiled rushes, the aroma of sour spirits fouling the air. Meg espied the portly innkeeper at once, serving up tankards of ale, laughing and jesting with his customers.

Keating looked so little like a man suffering from the shock and grief of a murdered wife that Meg entertained a fleeting hope that the gossip from the inn yard would prove unfounded. When Seraphine joined her, the eyes of every man present turned in their direction. Meg doubted that respectable women ever crossed the threshold of such a rough den, especially not one as beautiful as Seraphine.

Seraphine appeared impervious to the stir she was creating, but Meg's cheeks burned from all the leers and ogling stares. As the innkeeper ambled toward them, Meg sought for words to frame her inquiry after the Rivers sisters without arousing the man's suspicion.

But Keating forestalled her with a grin. "Ah, I know what you ladies be after."

"You—you do?" Meg asked.

"That'll be a penny apiece."

"A penny? For what?" Seraphine demanded.

"That's what I'm charging for visiting the chamber where the terrible slaughter of my poor Lizzie took place."

Meg's jaw dropped open and Seraphine gasped.

"You are *charging* people to see the room where your wife was murdered? What manner of ghoul are you?"

Keating shrugged his beefy shoulders. "A practical one. My Lizzie was a hardfisted woman who knew how to rake in a coin. She would have been the first to applaud my enterprise. And if it comes to calling someone a ghoul, my fine lady, I am not the one traipsing all over town to have a gander at a blood-spattered room."

When Seraphine drew in a furious breath, the innkeeper raised his hands placatingly. "Not that I blame you. I enjoy a good thrill myself. But it is only fair I should be compensated for providing it."

"My friend and I are not thrill-seekers, you fat, impudent rogue. All we desire is inform—"

"Pay him, Seraphine," Meg said quietly.

"What! Meg, you surely cannot wish to view this—this room of horrors?"

"Pay him."

Seraphine frowned. But she must have seen the resolve in Meg's face. Although she grumbled under her breath, she fished two coins out of her purse and slapped them into Keating's outstretched palm.

The man smirked and directed them to the chamber above the outer stairs. He gave Seraphine a broad wink. Meg could tell she was torn between wanting to box the man's ears and intercepting Meg. But Meg was too quick for her, darting out of the taproom.

She was halfway up the stairs before Seraphine caught up to her and grabbed hold of her elbow.

"Meg, wait. There is nothing to be gained from your viewing a room that can only add to your nightmares. We are too late, surely you must see that. Those Rivers sisters have gone too far. They have committed murder and will have to answer for it. You may as well let the magistrates deal with them. You cannot save them now."

"I know that. But I am not convinced the authorities will be able to find them. They have not been able to do so thus far. And you heard what Mary Waters said. Those women are determined to revive the coven of the Silver Rose. I can no longer help the Rivers sisters, but I must stop this madness from spreading and I still need to know if my mother is somehow behind all of this."

"So you think to do what—find some clue in that room that the officers overlooked?"

"Perhaps. It is not my strongest gift, but you know that sometimes I am extraordinarily sensitive to the atmosphere of a place where violence has been done."

"I know that, my dearest friend, which is why I would not have you enter that chamber for any price. But if you insist upon doing so, let me go in first."

Meg shook her head. "The witches are long gone, and unlike James Stuart, I have no fear of ghosts. There is no longer anything or anyone in that room who could hurt me."

But as soon as she entered the chamber, she realized she was wrong. The room was so small that the man's large presence seemed to fill it.

He stood with his back to her, studying something on the wall. Meg's pulse skipped a beat, the breadth of those shoulders, the tilt of the head, the unruly mass of hair so familiar to her, she recognized Armagil before he turned to face her.

He looked as startled to see her as she was him. Until she had set foot in this room, she had resigned herself to never seeing him again. Her heart hammered with an unbearable mixture of joy and pain. Other than his initial surprise, it was impossible to tell what Armagil might be feeling.

"You!" Seraphine cried in a voice thick with loathing. Her hand groped to where her sword should have been and Meg was mighty glad it wasn't there.

"What the devil are you doing here?"

Unperturbed by Seraphine's angry greeting, Armagil replied, "I imagine the same thing you are. I heard the gossip about the murder and came to see for myself."

"What, there was no bearbaiting or hanging today to afford you better entertainment?"

"I'm not seeking to be entertained, only informed as to the whereabouts of the women who committed this crime. I believe they may be the same ones who tried to poison me."

"And what a pity they didn't succeed."

"A pity indeed," Armagil drawled. "Because my landlord is a fine fellow and then he could have been the one to profit handsomely by exhibiting my lodgings."

Seraphine had to bite back an urge to smile and that appeared to make her angrier than ever. Meg could tell that her friend ached to give Armagil a tongue-lashing he'd not soon forget.

Meg hastily pulled her aside and in urgent whispers convinced Seraphine to desist. Perhaps in other circumstances, she would not have succeeded, but as much as Seraphine burned to avenge the wrong she perceived had been done to Meg, she could not do so without revealing to Armagil how badly hurt Meg had been. And if there was one emotion Seraphine fully understood, it was pride.

She was less compliant when Meg urged her to retreat belowstairs and question Keating and the kitchen girl more thoroughly about the Rivers sisters. Meg knew that despite Seraphine's best efforts, she would not be able to contain herself if she remained in Armagil's proximity too long.

After an intense whispered exchange, Seraphine conceded to her wishes, but not without a fierce warning glare at Armagil.

When the door closed behind her, an awkward silence fell. Armagil attempted to smile. "I appear to have fallen from the countess's good graces. Not that her opinion of me ever was very high."

"She is merely overprotective of me, always fearing I am some fragile creature easily hurt."

And have I hurt you? Armagil's eyes asked the question even if he did not. Meg found it easier to avoid looking at him and focus on the room instead. She had feared she would be assailed by a powerful aura of terror and rage. But Armagil's presence was so overwhelming, it blocked every other sensation except for awareness of him.

All she had were her eyes to rely upon and there was little to be seen except evidence that the occupants of this chamber had abandoned it in some haste—the rumpled bed, a few stray belongings left behind. Chief of these was an empty wardrobe chest stained with what appeared to be blood.

Meg could not bring herself to inspect it more closely. Instead, she bent and picked up a stray piece of ribbon and rubbed it between her fingers. Silky, a soft shade of blue, it spoke to her of innocence and girlish dreams, completely at odds with the violence done in this room.

She touched it to her cheek and was filled with an inexplicable sense of sadness and disappointed hopes. Conscious of Armagil's eyes upon her, she lowered her hand.

"There is little here to be seen," she said.

"No. I would be inclined to demand that Keating return my penny. Except for *this*." He stepped aside to reveal what the breadth of his shoulders had concealed, the symbol painted on the wall.

Meg's stomach clenched, the sight of the pentagram smeared in blood far more disturbing than the stained trunk. She felt the first icy whisper of the room's aura and the ribbon dropped unnoticed from her hand.

She forced herself to approach the wall. She was loath to admit it, but she was grateful for Armagil's solid presence at her side as she inspected the symbol.

"It is a pentagram, is it not?" he asked. "The mark of the devil."

Her throat had closed. She cleared it and struggled to respond in a dispassionate tone. "Not necessarily. In a proper pentagram, the top of the star represents the spirit. The other four points are the elements, earth, air, fire, and water. It is usually considered to be a good sign, a protection against evil."

"When it is not painted in blood," Armagil said dryly.

"Y-yes. And whoever fashioned this inverted the star, so that it is pointing upside down."

"That is significant?"

"It shows that her spirit has become enslaved by her carnal desires. She needs to face the darkness within her before it rises up to take complete control of her."

Except that it already had. Meg rested her fingers near the tip of the star. She was assailed by a maelstrom of rage, pain, and hatred. She snatched her hand back, her senses reeling.

She swayed and might have fallen if Armagil had not caught her.

"Meg?"

Seized by an uncontrollable shivering, she could not answer him. He drew her into his arms and held her hard against him. She burrowed against his chest, grateful for his strength. He stroked her hair, murmuring something she could not understand, but it didn't matter, the tone was so soothing and gentle. His tenderness and warmth gradually drove back the darkness.

She could have clung to him forever, but as she regained her senses, she felt confused by his behavior. When she risked a glance up at him, he smiled.

"Better?"

She nodded.

"What happened?"

"I—I don't know. Sometimes I just sense things I wish I didn't. When I touched the wall, it was as though I could feel the witch's darkness."

She expected him to recoil, but he didn't.

"Is that another of your—er—gifts?"

"Yes."

He sounded more curious than wary, more like the man

she believed she had known, the Armagil who had made love to her so passionately, not the one who had turned cold and all but ejected her from his bedchamber. Her heart ached with such hope it was painful, but she could not bring herself to trust the emotion or him.

As she drew away from him, he seemed reluctant to let her go. Meg stepped back and tried to read his eyes, but he averted his gaze.

"Why did you really come here, Armagil?"

"I already told you. My reason is the same as yours. I am on a witch hunt."

"Does that include me?"

"I do not regard you in that light."

"That was not the impression you gave me when we parted."

"That is because I am an oafish clod. I admit I was shocked by what you told me. When you confessed to being Megaera, it left me overwhelmed. I was not sure what to think or feel."

"And now?"

He risked meeting her gaze and for the first time gave her one glimpse behind the barrier.

He loved her.

Meg's breath caught in her throat. Armagil had experienced the same powerful emotion that she had when they had lain together. But it frightened him and not because of her strange heritage. So what was it? Something in his own past perhaps? Some terrible event that left him estranged from his family to the point of denying his own father? For one moment, she could see the shadow of the tenderhearted boy he had once been. But Armagil lowered his lashes, shutting her out.

Something had turned him into the hardened man he had

become, afraid to risk his heart. But Armagil loved her in spite of himself. That thought brought a tremulous smile to her lips, but she suppressed it. It would be unwise to push him any further, force him into avowals that he was not ready to make.

"You are determined to track down these witches and yet I find it hard to believe that it is because they poisoned you," she said. "You have so little regard for your own life."

"I lost all my coin dicing at the tavern last night. I could afford no other amusement."

"And how did you even find this place?"

Her question clearly caused him unease. "I heard gossip about the murder and I am familiar with a man who has an uncanny knack for knowing about crimes that take place in the city."

"What man?"

Armagil replied grudgingly. "Gilly Black."

"Your fath—" Meg started to gasp, but checked herself at the sight of Armagil's scowl. She amended, "Mr. Black. You reconciled with him?"

"I would hardly call it a reconciliation. I went to him for information, nothing more."

"That must have been very hard for you, to go to him and ask for such a favor."

Armagil shrugged.

"Why would you do such a thing?"

He shot her an exasperated look. "You are extraordinary in so many ways, Margaret Wolfe, but in one respect, you are like every other woman in the world. You ask too many damned questions."

He turned away from her as though he could outpace her gentle probing. But in this small chamber, there was nowhere to go. Just as she feared he might fling open the door and bolt from the room, he spun around and snapped at her.

"It is all because of you, you little fool. You will persist in putting yourself in danger. The only way for me to protect you is to find those witches myself. If anything were to happen to you, I couldn't bear it." His voice dropped to a hoarse whisper. "I think I would go mad."

Meg's heart swelled. She longed to fling her arms around his neck, but instead she held out her hand as she would to reassure a beast she found wounded in the woods.

Armagil stared at her hand and then placed his palm against hers, entwining her fingers with his.

"So you do care about me," she said. "What happened in your chamber was not some careless tumble."

"No, I am sorry I said that. I just needed—I wanted to—"

"Push me away because I alarm you."

"You do. And it has naught to do with thinking you are a witch. It is those eyes of yours. They are always searching my heart for something I am afraid to give. I am a weak man, Margaret. And a coward."

She pressed his hand. "I do not believe that."

"Oh, I would have no difficulty shielding you if someone came at you with a naked length of steel. My life is worth nothing. But when it comes to opening myself to the pain of great loss, I am as craven as a milksop boy."

"So you would rather close yourself to the prospect of love and great joy as well?"

"My only experience of joy is that it is fleeting, leaving one hollow when it is gone." He heaved a deep sigh. "But whatever fears you rouse in me, it is too late now. All I can do is keep you safe as best I can."

Meg was warmed by his words, by the tenderness in his

eyes. She should not press him for anything more, but a thought had occurred to her, one she hardly dared mention.

"I am grateful you wish to protect me, Armagil, but there is something far more important you could do."

He brought her hand to his lips. "Tell me. I would do anything for you."

"Protect Robert Brody instead."

He swore and dropped her hand as though it had become a live coal.

"But even now Sir Patrick could be—"

"Nay, Margaret, I implore you. Do not start that nonsense again about Graham being Robert Brody. I have already told you that it is not possible."

"I am convinced that it is. I dreamed again about Maidred."

"Stop," he said. "I can reconcile myself to your other strange gifts, but these dreams of yours are too unsettling. I don't want to hear anything more about them."

He held up his hands to silence her. Then he groaned and lowered them. As though he could not help himself, he demanded, "Fine, damn it. Tell me what you dreamed."

"The same thing as before, Maidred begging me to save her brother. Her pleas have become more desperate and I can do nothing. You may be the only one who can help."

"Save a man I don't even know? Someone who is merely the figment of your nightmares?"

"You do know him. And I am convinced you are the only one who can stop Sir Patrick."

"Stop him from what?" Armagil demanded.

"You know perfectly well what. Sir Patrick, or should I say Robert Brody, is bent upon getting his revenge upon James Stuart."

"If the king killed someone he loved, perhaps Brody is entitled to it."

"No, it will only mean your friend's destruction. Even if Sir Patrick could destroy James and somehow get away with it, don't you know what it will do to him? That kind of blood-lust leaves a stain on a man's soul that cannot be washed away. I know. I came too near embracing that kind of dark-ness myself."

"Even if what you say is true, what do you think I can do about it?"

"You are his closest friend."

"*Was.* We have not even spoken since the day we quar-reled over—" He stopped, looking uncomfortable.

"Over me," Meg finished softly. "You will never know how much I regret being the cause of such a rift between you, but that does not change one thing. You know Sir Patrick better than anyone. You must have some idea what he is plan-ning."

"I never meddle in anyone else's affairs. That would re-quire too much effort on my part. I don't know what Graham might be plotting except . . ." Armagil frowned and then ad-mitted, "I fear he is not acting alone."

"You think he is in league with the witches?"

"No. I cannot fathom how they figure into all this, but Graham would never willingly consort—well, I am sure he made it painfully clear to you how he feels about sorcery. But I have been aware for some time that Graham has been at-tending secret meetings. I suspect other men who are Catho-lic zealots."

"Then they can have but one aim, the assassination of the king, which would further Sir Patrick's own desire for ven-geance. Even now he is gone off with the king on that hunting expedition. It would be the perfect opportunity to strike against James."

"Then it is likely already too late."

"No. If it was, I don't think I would still be dreaming about Maidred."

"So you would have me do what? Abandon you and go haring after Graham?"

"I will be safe enough until you return." When he cast her a skeptical look, she insisted, "Truly. Those witches have gone deep into hiding and I have no idea where to find them."

"But you won't stop looking."

"I will until you return. I give you my word on that. Please, Armagil. You are the only one Sir Patrick will listen to. You are the only one who can give peace to Maidred's spirit by saving her brother."

"Me?" Armagil gave a harsh laugh. "You have no idea how amusing that is. Sending me after Graham is like sending a jackal to stop a wolf. I have no love for James Stuart either. He is a miserable excuse for both a man and a king."

"But you would not see him dead."

"Wouldn't I?" he challenged, his jaw set at a hard angle.

"If you had wanted to become an executioner you could have done so years ago. You chose to become a physician instead."

"Considering how skilled I am at that, the two professions are often one and the same." His bitter expression faded. He sighed. "Very well. Perhaps I have stood by idle for far too long. I shall go after Graham, although I cannot guarantee you will be pleased with the results."

"I have every confidence and trust in you."

"As I said before, you are a little fool." But he softened his words by kissing her. And then he was gone.

AMY STOOD BENEATH THE OVERHANG OF THE HOUSE THAT JUT-ted two stories above her. Clutching her cane, she leaned back against the wall. To any passersby, she would look like some tired old beggar woman huddled beneath her shawl, seeking a respite from the chilling wind. As long as no one paused to study her too closely. To her relief, no one did.

She was taking a grave risk by venturing so near the area of London where the hue and cry after her was bound to be the most intense. From her vantage point, she could see the sign of the Two Crowns swaying in the breeze, keep watch over the door where Margaret Wolfe had vanished inside what seemed ages ago.

If Amy were caught—that did not bear thinking about. It caused the hand clutching the cane to tremble. Unlike her sister, she got no thrill from the prospect of danger. The shiver of excitement that raced beneath her fear came from an entirely different source—Megaera.

By now, the Silver Rose must be studying the symbol Amy had painted on the wall. Would she understand its meaning? Would she be impressed by what Amy had done? Would she comprehend that in Amelia Rivers, the Silver Rose had a true follower indeed?

A hand clamped down on Amy's shoulder. She squeaked in fright and twisted around, lifting the cane to defend herself against the lad who had seized hold of her.

Bea's eyes mocked her from beneath the brim of the feathered toque. Amy lowered the cane with a tremulous sigh, her pulse still thudding.

"Damn you, Bea! You nearly caused my heart to stop. I thought you were a constable."

"Which I well could have been for all the more heed you were paying, staring off again with that mooncalf look in your eyes."

"I am keeping sharp watch for the Silver Rose," Amy hissed back.

"And doing a poor job of it. What is taking so long? She probably slipped past you and is long gone."

"She did not! And if you feel you could do so much better, you should have been on the watch yourself, you who claim to love danger so much."

"I enjoy taking risks, but not stupid ones. Your disguise is so much better than mine. You make a far better old woman than I do a boy."

Amy gritted her teeth at the gibe. Her hands clamped down on the cane as she resisted the urge to crack it over her sister's head. Bea had been more spiteful than usual since they had had to flee their lodgings at the Two Crowns. But she did not think that that was the true source of Bea's displeasure. No, her sister was simply jealous because Amy had done something that Bea had never dared to do, for all of her bravado.

Amy had actually killed someone. After her initial shock at what she had done had passed, Amy had felt fierce and brave, much more so than Bea. She had boasted of her deed to her sister every chance she got.

She would have done so now, but her attention was caught by someone emerging from the inn. She and Bea both tensed with anticipation. To Amy's surprise, it was Armagil Blackwood.

"What is *he* doing here?" Bea muttered.

"I don't know." Disappointed, Amy sagged back against the wall. "Probably drinking himself into a stupor as usual."

Except Blackwood did not look drunk. He strode away from the inn with more purpose in his step than Amy had ever remarked before.

"I don't like this, Amy," Bea grumbled in her ear. "What reason could Blackwood have had for coming to the Two Crowns? Could he be looking for us?"

"Oh, why would he?"

"Maybe your precious Sir Patrick sent him. He did threaten to turn us over to the law."

"He wouldn't dare. And he is not *my* Sir Patrick," Amy sniffed, her cheeks stinging with the remembered pain and humiliation of his rejection. "He is just a stupid useless man, as unworthy as his ass of a friend. Neither he nor Blackwood are of any concern to us."

"But—"

"No! I don't want to speak of *him* anymore." Amy banged her cane against the ground. "We shall make both of them pay when we have come to power."

She waited for Bea to echo her agreement. But her sister frowned instead. "About that. I am thinking that we should forget all of this, leave London, and make a new start elsewhere."

"What!"

"I have no desire to be hanged. Or burned alive as our grandmother was."

"Aye, our grandmother. How good of you to remember her. She must be avenged."

"Sir Patrick and his friends will see to that."

Amy could hardly believe she was hearing this. Entirely forgetting her guise of a hunched-over old woman, she straightened, spluttering in her indignation.

"You would completely abandon everything, all Granddam's teachings, everything she promised us, the cause that she died for. Why don't you just spit upon her grave? Fie upon you, Bea. Fie."

Bea ducked her head, for once having the grace to look a little ashamed.

"Very well. If you want to turn craven and flee, go ahead," Amy continued. "Spend the rest of your life getting poked by some man in a dark alley for a few coins. Keep at it until you are so old and poxed, no one will want you. Then you can beg for scraps until—"

"All right. All right," Beatrice muttered. " 'Tis just that I am wearied of waiting, all these games we have been playing with the king and Sir Patrick. When is all this to end, Amy?"

"You know when, the night of—" Amy broke off. Across the busy street, Margaret Wolfe emerged from the inn, accompanied by her friend, the French countess. She was the sort of woman Amy had always detested, graceful and arrogant in her beauty and grand title. But she was of little consequence set next to the grave, dark-haired woman at her side.

Amy studied Megaera, her heart swelling with adoration. "Our Silver Rose looks so tired. She has expended a great deal of effort searching for us."

"Then don't you think it is about time that she found us?" Bea demanded.

"Soon." Amy's lips curved in a feline smile. "Very soon, my dear sister."

Chapter Twenty

THE LIGHT OF DAY HAD BEGUN TO FADE ACROSS THE FROST-hardened fields. Most of the courtiers who rode after the king showed signs of fatigue. Cold, tired, and hungry, they longed to return to the castle and the comforts of a roaring fire and good meal, Sir Patrick Graham among them.

Only the king appeared indefatigable. James Stuart astride the saddle was a different man from the one who shambled through the corridors of Whitehall with his halting gait. A skilled horseman, he never showed the least sign of exhaustion even after a hard day's ride.

If his shoulders looked stiff as the sun dipped lower over the horizon, it was owing to anxiety as the beaters tramped through hedges and bushes, searching for some trace of the missing dog. All of the hounds had returned from the chase save one.

"Jowler! Jowler, here boy!" the master of the hounds called, the cries accompanied by shrill whistles.

The king straightened in the saddle and bellowed out the dog's name, then sat back waiting for a response that never came.

"Damn that fool dog. Where could he have got to?" the king demanded of Sir Patrick. James's vexed laugh did little to disguise his mounting fear.

"I am sure he will turn up, Your Grace," Patrick said, although he had difficulty concealing his own dread. Though neither of them voiced the thought aloud, Patrick was certain the same worry preyed upon them both, the image of a dead cat nailed to the palace wall.

Patrick tried to dismiss the notion, but he could not help reflecting. If anyone wished to wound or alarm the king, Jowler would be the perfect point of attack. James loved that dog as if it were his own child.

Patrick's mind flashed back, remembering Amelia Rivers's sly face and hate-filled eyes, and he silently cursed the woman. He should have throttled the witch when he'd had the chance. Or else swallowed his anger and feigned a smile to maintain her delusion that they were partners in the enterprise to destroy James Stuart.

He had had the stomach to do neither and this could well result in his failure. If out of spite those witches had harmed that dog, the only thing greater than the king's grief would be his terror. Whatever magic Margaret Wolfe had invoked to ease James's fears would all be undone. He would snatch up his family, retreat into seclusion, and the parliament would be canceled again.

All the planning, the amassing of all that gunpowder would have been in vain. Catesby, Fawkes, and the rest of his fellow conspirators would have to patiently await the next opportunity. Sir Patrick should be obliged to do so as well. Returning the true faith to England was all that mattered, far more important than Patrick's own private vengeance.

But the locket hidden beneath his shirt containing the sacred strands of *her* hair had begun to feel heavier of late, a weight pressing against his heart like a silent reproach. He had bided his time far too long already, playing the part of faithful courtier, tolerating the king's disgusting displays of affection while concealing his loathing.

Patrick could no longer endure it. If that dog turned up dead, he would not wait for James to react and go to ground like a terrified hare. Patrick would strike now, even if it meant the forfeit of his life—nay, his immortal soul.

A shout came from a distant stand of trees, one of the beaters bawling out, "Found him."

Patrick observed the king tense with anticipation. The initial outcry was followed by an ominous silence. Patrick expected at any moment to see a stricken servant emerge from those woods bearing the bloodied remains of that hound.

His mouth dry, Patrick edged his mount closer to the king's. His hand dropped to the hunting knife attached to his belt. He began to inch the blade out of the sheath when a blurry brown creature shot out of the woods.

Jowler streaked across the field, racing toward his master. The king let out a whoop of joyous relief, echoed by the other courtiers. Sir Patrick released a deep breath, his hand falling away from his knife. A tremor coursed through him, partly the product of his own relief and a curious sense of deflation.

He struggled to regain command of himself. Fortunately, all eyes were upon the king as James dismounted. He hunkered down to greet his dog, scolding Jowler in a jovial tone.

"You old rascal. Where the devil have you been?" James ruffled the fur around the dog's neck, laughing as Jowler tried to lick his beard. "Nae, sirrah, your apologies are not accepted. Do you think to—eh? What's this?"

James's laughter stilled as he removed something that had been attached to the hound's collar. Patrick craned his neck to see what it was; a small roll of parchment. The king straightened. As the king unfurled it, Patrick's heart sank, fearing the witches had struck again after all, threatening James with the curse.

Ignoring the way Jowler nudged at his hand in a bid for more attention, James perused the note. The king was well out of Patrick's reach. All he could do was study the king's face as he read, expecting to see James blanch with horror. Instead the king's mouth pursed with a strange expression, what appeared to be a mixture of amusement and irritation.

Curiosity was mirrored in the faces of the other courtiers, but no one said a word. Patrick, unable to tolerate the suspense any longer demanded, "What is it, Your Grace? What does it say?"

James shrugged and walked over to Sir Patrick. Handing the note up to him, the king bade him read it aloud.

Patrick accepted it and then read in a hesitant tone.

"Good Master Jowler, the king pays more heed to you than he does to his own people, so perhaps you would be so good as to convey this message to him. Instead of racing across the countryside, ruining fields and destroying crops in pursuit of his sport, the king should know that his time would be better spent back in London, attending to matters of state and his royal duties."

Patrick blinked and then added, "It is signed, 'A concerned friend.'"

Silence fell, the other men present uncertain how to react, everyone waiting to take their cue from the king. James scowled for a moment, then let out a huge guffaw. The other courtiers were quick to join him. Only Sir Patrick felt unable to join in the mirth.

Despite the insolent nature of the message, James had decided to treat it as a foolish jest. Bending down to scratch Jowler's ear, he said, "You are a good messenger, but I doubt the rogue who had you fetch this thought to pay your fee. I suppose I shall be obliged to do so in the form of a juicy marrowbone."

Sighs of relief could be heard all round as the king returned to his horse and gave the signal to return to the castle. As the entire hunting party moved off the field, only Sir Patrick hung back. He glanced about him, half expecting to see the author of the message emerge from hiding.

Patrick peered down at the note again, not able to credit his eyes. He recognized the bold hand that had penned those words all too well. There was no mistaking the distinctive flourish of the loop that formed the capital letter *A*.

Patrick crumpled the note in his gloved fist, rage coursing through him.

Armagil.

THE CASTLE AT NEWMARKET WAS MODEST COMPARED TO MOST of the royal residences. The king used it only when hunting, the palace too small to house the train of servants, courtiers, and ministers who followed in his wake. Many were obliged to seek lodgings elsewhere in the village.

Sir Patrick considered himself fortunate to have found

accommodations at the local inn even if he had to share his chamber with two other courtiers. He had promised Catesby he would remain close to the king, keep a watchful eye over him. But his hatred and resentment of James seethed too near the surface these days. Any time away from the king was a welcome respite.

As he strode through the inn door, he found the taproom thronged with men. Most of those were of low rank, the sort who trailed after James in the hopes of presenting a petition or obtaining some mark of the royal favor. The sound of raucous laughter and loud voices assailed Sir Patrick. He was greeted by several of the men, urging him to come join them, but Patrick had ever despised such boisterous company. He declined curtly, heading up the stairs.

He had not gone more than a few steps when he espied a familiar figure ensconced in a far corner. Armagil had somehow managed to commandeer a stool. He leaned back against the wall, cradling a tankard of ale to his chest. No doubt he was already far gone in drink.

Sir Patrick's lips thinned. Fueled by his anger, he lost all sense of cold and exhaustion. Descending the stairs, he elbowed his way through the throng until he loomed over Armagil.

His friend looked up and said, "Ah, here you are at last."

"Here *I* am?" Patrick all but choked. "No, more to the point, here *you* are and I can think of no good reason why. What the devil are you doing here, Armagil?"

"Sampling some indifferent ale and waiting for you to return from the hunt." Armagil's lips twitched with the hint of a smile. "Did the king find good sport today?"

Patrick sucked in his breath. Any doubts he might have

had about the authorship of that note were dispelled by the unholy twinkle in Armagil's eyes.

"Damn you!" he snapped. Armagil's brows arched at his angry tone. It was all Patrick could do not to dash the tankard from his hand. Instead he withdrew the crumpled note from beneath his jerkin and flung it at him.

Armagil caught it one-handed while balancing his mug without spilling a drop, an adroit feat for a man who was half drunk. He glanced down at the note with a wry smile, but made no move to inspect it closer.

"Well? Do you not wish to read it?" Patrick demanded.

"I don't have to. I know what it says."

The coolness of Armagil's admission only added to Patrick's rage. His hands balled into fists. "Curse you, Armagil. I could—could—"

"I can well imagine, but smashing in my face will only draw attention that neither of us desires. It was only a trifling jest, man. Stop looking daggers at me and sit down, have a drink."

Patrick glowered at him, but realized Armagil was right. The tension between them was drawing a few curious stares. Patrick managed to locate a stool and pulled it near Armagil. There was little risk of being overheard amongst this din, but he leaned closer as he ground out, "Only a jest? You lay in wait for the king's dog—"

"I did nothing of the kind," Armagil interrupted. "I was ambling along the lane when I came across Jowler. The dog must have remembered me from the time I treated his paw. He came bounding up to greet me and it was then I was struck by the notion of attaching the note to his collar. It was a mad impulse, nothing more."

"An impulse? And you just happened to have parchment, ink, and quill tucked in your purse."

"No, there was a modest farm nearby and the daughter of the house was more than willing to supply my needs."

"Oh, I'll wager she was." Patrick sneered.

"I am talking about my need for pen and ink."

"And why was this girl so terribly obliging to a complete stranger?"

"Her father's lands have more than once borne the brunt of the king's pursuit of his sport. When she realized what I meant to do, I had her full approval."

"Stupid and heedless, the pair of you," Patrick muttered. "Most especially you. You could have brought down the king's wrath on that girl and her family."

"If I had been caught, I would have taken the full blame. But I gather that I have escaped detection. Did the king even read my note?"

"He did. He was vexed at first, then he passed it off as a foolish prank."

"A pity."

"A relief. You could well have alarmed James enough to flee back to London."

"I sense that would not have suited you, perhaps because you do not intend for him to ever return."

Armagil's soft-spoken suggestion jarred Patrick back to the moment on the hunting field when he had come so close to unsheathing his knife. He suppressed a guilty flinch.

"Don't be absurd. I desire nothing better than for the king to return safely to London. It is of vital importance that he attend the opening of parliament."

"Of importance to him or you?" Although Armagil's eyes were lowered, he appeared to be studying Patrick intently.

Patrick was struck by the suspicion that his friend was not as drunk as he had supposed. Evading the question, he said, "You still have not explained what you are doing here. Why are you not back in London abed with your witch?"

He thought he saw a spark of anger in Armagil's eyes, but if so, Armagil quelled it. "I have scarcely seen Margaret since the day she saved my life."

"Is the spell she cast over you wearing thin? I pray it may be so."

Armagil traced his finger around the rim of his mug. "Whatever happened that day in my chambers, I am the one to blame. Margaret is not a sorceress, Graham." A smile touched his lips. "At least not an evil one."

"Whatever she is, the woman unnerves me. You realize she accused me of being Robert Brody. Now where would she get a notion like that?" Patrick stared hard at Armagil.

"You know damned well she didn't get it from me. I have told her it is impossible, but she is not convinced. She suspects you mean to destroy the king and she fears you will lose your soul in the process."

"It is mine to lose, is it not? Is that why you are here? Did *she* send you to stop me?"

"Margaret did ask me to seek you out, reason with you," Armagil admitted. "But I came of my own accord. I am concerned about you."

Patrick laughed bitterly. "Since when?"

Armagil flushed. "I am your friend and always have been, albeit a poor excuse for one."

Patrick softened in spite of himself. "No, you have ever been loyal from the time we were boys, keeping my secrets as I have kept yours. I believe you are a man of abilities with a great capacity for—for devotion. That is why it has nigh bro-

ken my heart to watch you waste your talents in such idleness
and dishonor, wrapping yourself in your indifference. I—"
Patrick checked himself. "Forgive me. You hate it when I lecture you, but—"

"No, you are right. I have made a poor use of my life and
it shames me. I feel as though I have been asleep for a long
time and have been jarred awake." Armagil set down his mug
and Patrick saw that it had scarce been tasted. Far from being
drunk, Armagil was stone-cold sober.

"You ask why I am here? To do something that I should
have a long time ago." Armagil leaned forward, his eyes more
intent and clear than Patrick had ever seen them.

"You want revenge upon James Stuart? I have come to
help you."

Chapter Twenty-one

THE COLD AIR SEEPED THROUGH THE WINDOWPANES. DESPITE the fire that crackled on the hearth, Meg could not seem to get warm. November had arrived on a chilling wind that spoke of the coming of winter. A gray pall had hung over the city most of the day, the light fading early.

Meg wrapped herself in her shawl as she lit the candle to examine the note that Tom had delivered to her from Armagil. He had been gone for over a week with no word from him. Her fingers trembled with eagerness as she scanned the lines that had obviously been penned in some haste.

Margaret,
The king has returned safely to London. I have talked at length with Graham and we have reached an understanding, but I must remain by his side so I cannot come to you. All is well for the nonce, but

continue being cautious and remain close to your
dwelling. No matter what transpires in the days
ahead, there is something you must know, something
I should have told you, but there is no time at present.
   Graham is waiting for me. I must go. Forgive me.
A.

Meg read the letter several more times, biting her lip in
frustration. She had waited on edge for days to hear from
Armagil. How like the aggravating man to send such an
abrupt message that conveyed so little.

She already knew that the king had returned to London
unharmed. The entire city was aware that James was back in
residence and preparing for the opening of parliament tomorrow. What did Armagil mean about reaching an understanding with Graham? Had he prevailed upon Sir Patrick to
abandon his plans for revenge? Obviously not enough to
trust him entirely or Armagil would not feel obliged to remain so close to his side.

And what was it that Armagil needed to tell her but had
been unable to do so? That he loved her? Was that so difficult
for him that he could not have taken another moment to pen
a few words more? His note raised far more questions than it
answered.

Meg shook her head in vexation, but folded up the note
and tucked it inside her bodice as though it had indeed been
a love letter. Doubtless it was the closest to one she would
ever receive from Armagil.

She smiled wryly, trying to take some comfort from the
fact that Armagil was back in London and for the moment
the king appeared to be safe, at least from the vengeance of
Robert Brody. But what of the Rivers sisters? Nothing more

had been heard of the two women since the night of the murder. Seraphine speculated that they might have fled from London and she could well be right. It would certainly have been the wise thing to have done, but *wise* was not a word Meg would have applied to either Beatrice or Amelia Rivers.

She shuddered, remembering all the dark emotions she had sensed when she had touched that pentagram. Pain, rage, and torment that ran too deep for reason. No, those madwomen might have been forced to go to ground for a while, but Meg doubted they would so easily abandon their desire to be avenged upon James Stuart or their plans to revive the coven of the Silver Rose.

But how much longer could she and Seraphine remain in England to search for the witches? Meg had already neglected her duties as Lady of Faire Isle for too long and their funds had begun to dwindle. Seraphine was loath to draw upon more credit from her husband's agents, so she had gone out to sell one of her brooches.

Meg had hated to have her friend do so, but Seraphine had merely shrugged and said she had never found the ruby becoming. Meg had strongly suspected that Seraphine was merely tired of being mewed up in the house. Her restless friend felt the need to be doing something, an emotion Meg well understood. She was restive herself.

Meg paced to the window and pushed open the murky diamond-paned casement. A chilling blast of air knifed through her woolen gown. She drew her shawl more closely about her and leaned forward to peer out.

The lodgings Seraphine had found were situated in the environs of Westminster and Meg could just make out the towers of the old palace in the distance, the ancient stone walls conveying a sense of order and serenity. Tomorrow morning all that calm would be shattered by the bustle and fanfare of the king arriving to address his parliament, the quiet halls thronged with the most important men in the realm.

Despite the bitter cold, the evening sky had cleared and the morrow promised to be a fair day. Then why did Meg have this unsettled feeling of a mighty storm a-brewing? She frowned, directing her gaze to the deserted street below.

Likely her disquiet sprang from the fact that it was nearly dark and Seraphine had yet to return. It was not uncommon in London for women to venture to the shops alone. But Seraphine was not familiar enough with the city.

"I should have accompanied her," Meg fretted, feeling all the more guilty because of the reason she had not. She had not wanted to be gone from the house in case Armagil had come seeking her.

At the very least she should have insisted that Seraphine take along the maid whose service they had engaged, but Seraphine had protested, "Eliza is a fat, idle creature who walks at the pace of a snail. I could complete my errand thrice over in the time it will take me to drag her along.

"Don't worry about me, Meggie." Seraphine had flashed her most dazzling smile. "I shall be back before you've had time to miss me."

That had been what—nearly three hours ago? Reveling in her freedom, Seraphine was likely in no hurry to return, lingering as she explored the shops and purchased some provisions with the coin she had acquired from selling the brooch. But what if she had gotten lost? Or her hasty temper had caused her to run afoul of one of the merchants? Or what if—

"Stop it," Meg adjured herself. Seraphine could be brash

at times, but Meg knew of no woman better able to look out for herself.

Drawing back from the window before all warmth escaped the chamber, Meg closed the casement. She ought to go belowstairs to see how Eliza was progressing with the preparations for the evening meal. The maid could not be trusted to stay on task. But that would mean listening to Eliza's barrage of complaints about her endless aches and pains, most of which Meg suspected were imaginary.

If Eliza burned the meal again, Meg could always slice up some bread and cheese. Propping up some pillows, Meg clambered atop the bed to await Seraphine's return. She tucked her shawl about her shoulders and yawned. Lord, she was tired. With so much on her mind, she had not been sleeping well.

At least she had not been haunted by any more nightmares of Maidred Brody. If Armagil had succeeded in dissuading Sir Patrick from his scheme of revenge, perhaps the girl was finally at peace. Meg prayed that it was so.

She stared into the flames crackling on the hearth and felt her eyelids growing heavier. Despite all of her best efforts, Meg nodded off.

And promptly began to dream.

Meg stumbled as she raced along the twisting corridors of the tunnel, chasing after the cloaked figure. She could not see his face, but she knew who it was.

"Robert Brody! Stop," she cried. "Robbie, where are you going?"

The boy ignored her, disappearing around the next bend. Meg plunged after him, emerging into a large cavern. For a moment, she could not see where Robert had gone. Then a torch flared as he struggled to light the end of a rope.

Why it should be so important to him to fire that rope, Meg could not fathom. But she felt an equally compelling urge to stop him. She rushed forward, but she was too late.

The rope had turned into a fiery snake, twisting and hissing and shooting off sparks. It coiled its way toward a mountain of barrels, its tongue flicking out deadly flames.

Suddenly the entire cave exploded in a blinding flash of light and heat that lifted Meg off her feet and hurled her through space.

She was lying sprawled on the floor of hell, the entire city of London quaking and caving in around her, buildings falling in a hail of stones, the night lit up by flame and rent by the screams of the dying.

Meg staggered to her feet, but she was hemmed in by gyrating bodies. Witches capered around her in a mad joyous dance led by Tamsin Rivers, her long gray hair streaming like a banner in the wind.

"Death to ye, James Stuart and all your kin. May ye all perish in the flames." The old woman cackled and pointed to the blazing palace.

Beyond the burning beams, Meg saw the king clutching his young son, desperately trying to lead his family to safety.

Meg tried to run to his aid, but she was dragged back, held fast by a pair of strong arms. "No, Robbie, let me go!"

She twisted in his grasp, fighting to break free, only to dislodge his hood. The fabric fell back to reveal not Robert Brody's youthful features, but those of a grown man, regarding her through sad, weary eyes.

Meg ceased her struggles, staring up at him. "A-Armagil?"

He looked at down her, his beard-roughened face streaked with tears. "Forgive me, Margaret."

She pulled away from him. "Forgive you for what? Arma-gil, what have you done?"

She could not hear his reply as the witches enveloped her again, chanting her name. "Megaera! Megaera!"

She tried to get away from them, but they surrounded her, propelling her toward a witch who stood apart from the oth-ers, cloaked and hooded in black.

"Megaera." Her mother called to her, Cassandra beckon-ing with a dead white hand.

No! Meg sat up in bed, her heart racing. She tried to blot out the nightmare, but she could still hear that persistent voice, still see the phantom woman in black gesturing to her.

She knuckled her eyes, but the phantom remained. It hovered by the foot of her bed, whispering her name.

"Megaera."

She wasn't dreaming. Meg froze, so petrified with shock, she was unable to speak or move.

"Ah, you have awakened, my Silver Rose," the specter rasped.

Awakened? This—this *thing* had been lurking in her room, watching her sleep?

"W-what—" Meg's mouth had gone so dry, she could barely form the words. "W-who are you?"

"Surely you must already know."

Maman? No, it was impossible. As much as Meg feared her mother might still be alive, this person who had invaded her bedchamber could not be Cassandra Lascelles. She was not tall enough.

Recovering from her initial shock, Meg noted other things as well. The woman's hood was drawn too far forward for Meg to discern her features, but the hand that she had stretched out to Meg was slight, nothing like Cassandra's long elegant fingers. The woman's other hand toyed with something beneath the flap of her cloak—the hilt of a knife.

Fear sent a rush of warmth through her frozen limbs, enabling Meg to move. She scrambled off the bed, staggering a little as she gained her feet, heading for the door. But the intruder was quicker. In a whirl of black, she leapt ahead of Meg, barring her exit.

"No, milady. Wait! There is nothing for you to fear."

"Who are you?" Meg demanded again in a stronger voice. "How did you get in here?"

"Why, Eliza was obliging enough to let me in."

Something in the sly way these words were intoned filled Meg with dread.

"You forced your way past my maid to gain admittance? Did you hurt her?"

"No, why would I hurt Eliza? She is one of us."

"One of us?"

"Another witch, part of your new coven, milady. She is waiting for you below with the others."

Eliza, a witch? That placid, idle creature who would not bestir herself to add another log to the fire even if she was freezing? Meg pressed her hand to her temple, feeling as though she was still caught up in some kind of mad dream.

She stiffened as the full import of the cloaked woman's words struck her. "Others? There are others? How many?"

"Enough," came the vague reply. "And all of them your devoted followers, but none more so than I."

She pushed back her hood, revealing a round face well past the first blush of youth, creases bracketing her mouth, her chin starting to sag. Her unkempt hair was streaked with tinges of gray. Only her eyes remained youthful, wide with a dream-ridden quality.

"Mistress Rivers?" Meg hazarded.

"You know who I am?"

The woman beamed with delight until Meg added, "Beatrice?"

Her lips puckered into a childish pout. "No, that is my sister. I am Amelia Rivers, but my granddam always called me Amy."

"Of course, Amy. I should have known," Meg murmured, all the while Mary Waters's warning echoed through her head.

"Amelia . . . She's the dangerous one. If you do confront her, you had best take great care."

Meg retreated. Her heart leapt in alarm when Amy's hand shot out to grab hers. Her fingers were icy, sending the same chill through Meg she had experienced in the room at the Two Crowns. She had little doubt that this was the hand that had dripped blood while painting that pentagram.

Meg quelled a panicked urge to jerk free, run to the window, fling open the casement, and scream for help. Amy was calm at the moment, but Meg sensed it would take little to send her into the sort of frenzy that had driven her to kill Mistress Keating.

Desperately, she attempted to probe Amy's eyes, but it was hopeless. Reading the eyes of a madwoman was like trying to piece together images in a shattered mirror.

"I have waited so long for this moment when I would stand before you and pledge my love and loyalty to the Silver Rose."

Meg tried not to cringe as Amy carried Meg's hand to her lips and pressed a fervent kiss upon her knuckles. The woman's eyes glowed with an unholy devotion.

"My granddam always promised me you would come one

glorious day to reward all of your true followers. She was the one who kept your legend alive long after the evil witch-hunters destroyed your coven in France. Granddam was one of the few who managed to escape, but she carried away all the secrets she had learned. She knew how to make those incredible silver roses and she taught me and Bea. Granddam was a great friend of your mother's. Tamsin Rivers, surely you must remember her."

Meg nodded weakly, although she had no recollection of any such person. She had been so young at the time, but she remembered quite clearly that Cassandra Lascelles had had no friends. There had been a few trusted members of the coven that Cassandra had allowed into her inner sanctum and taught the art of brewing the deadly poison, but Meg was certain Tamsin Rivers had not been one of them. If Tamsin had acquired the secret of making the lethal roses, then she had done so by spying upon Cassandra, a dangerous pastime. Tamsin Rivers would have had to have been a clever and brazen woman indeed.

"My mama and papa died when Bea and I were very little. My granddam was all the family we had," Amy said. "After we had to flee France, we moved from place to place, Granddam always afraid the witch-hunters might find us. We finally settled in Edinburgh, where Granddam earned our keep by selling potions and telling fortunes. But she never forgot about her devotion to Megaera, even after she was arrested and condemned to burn."

Amy's eyes filled with tears. "Granddam was so fierce and brave, but when the flames rose up and began to scorch her skin, she screamed and screamed. I can never forget it. Sh-she died so horribly."

"I know," Meg said gently. No matter what Tamsin Rivers

might have done, being burned alive was a fate too cruel for anyone. She pitied the old woman, but even more she pitied the granddaughter who had been forced to witness such a dreadful spectacle.

"I am sorry."

"Sorry?" Amy's face flushed with anger. "She died for *you*. And how did you repay her? You removed her curse from James Stuart."

Amy's grip tightened so painfully that Meg gasped. "I didn't. I merely made him believe that I did." That was true enough as far as it went.

Amy glared at her. "You mean that you tricked him?"

"Y-yes."

Amy blinked at her. "Oh." Her face cleared like the sky after a sudden cloudburst. Her grip on Meg's hand slackened, allowing Meg to draw away from her.

"That was very clever of you. I daresay you wished to lull him into a sense of false safety. I *told* Bea there must have been some reasonable explanation for what you had done. My sister and I would have preferred that the villain remain tormented and afraid, but it doesn't matter. By this time to-morrow, James Stuart will be roasting in hell."

Meg rubbed her throbbing hand. "Tomorrow? What is going to happen tomorrow?"

Amy ignored her alarmed question. "It is what is going to happen tonight that is important. The coven of the Silver Rose will be reborn. All that is required is your presence, milady. Come with me now. We must make haste."

Amy opened the bedchamber door, indicating that Meg should precede her. But Meg hung back.

"Where would you have me go?"

"All of your followers have gathered, waiting to proclaim

you our queen. Tonight you will fulfill your destiny and assume your place as the most powerful sorceress in the world."

A chill swept through Meg. It could well have been her mother talking, that same fanatical light in Amy Rivers's eyes. Meg would as soon have marched straight into hell before accompanying her anywhere. But what choice did she have? In her impatience, Amy brandished her knife, gesturing Meg toward the door.

Meg hung back, trying to stall for time. Surely Seraphine would return at any moment. But the brief flicker of hope that thought aroused quickly turned to dread. Yes, Seraphine would return, but with no idea of the danger that awaited her.

The redoubtable countess would be more than a match for the likes of Eliza, but Amy had spoken of others. Meg had no idea how many more of these deluded women might be gathered below and Seraphine would be taken completely unaware.

The best course would be for Meg to go with them, get them all away from the house as quickly as possible. She would be safe enough as long as Amy and the rest of the coven regarded her as Megaera. And was this not the reason she had come to London, to uncover the truth, to stop any attempt to revive her mother's coven? This gathering tonight might prove her best and only chance to do so. She could finally put an end to the madness that had stalked her ever since her childhood. All she need do was find the courage to play the part of the Silver Rose one last time.

❦❦❦

THE NIGHT WAS BITTER COLD, BUT CLEAR, THE CRESCENT OF moon suspended like a scimitar over the city. Meg's eyes had adjusted to the darkness, but she still stumbled as she followed Amy down a narrow alley, the rest of the group close at Meg's heels. They consisted of Eliza and two other women, hardly the force that Meg had anticipated with such dread.

They were all cloaked in similar fashion to Amy, crude rose emblems stitched into the black fabric. Meg had been unable to make out little of their features beneath the hoods, only noting that they both seemed young. She could sense their nervous excitement, but beneath that she detected a threading of fear. It gave Meg hope that she might be able to gain control of them and perhaps Eliza as well. The maid had been far too abashed to look Meg in the eye, even going so far as apologizing for her deception, mumbling, "Sorry, mistress."

"*That is milady,*" Amy had reprimanded her sharply, then bade her hold her tongue unless spoken to, a command Eliza had done her best to obey.

As they hurried along the streets, Meg could hear Eliza behind her, panting for breath, despite Amy hissing for her to be quiet. Eliza moved much faster than Meg would have imagined the heavy woman capable of, but it was necessary in order to keep pace with Amy.

Undaunted by the darkness, Amy skittered through the maze of streets and alleys with all the stealth of a rat. Meg had half hoped they might be caught by one of the king's officers charged to keep the peace, but Amy was adroit at avoiding the watch. No doubt she had had a great deal of practice.

It was just as well they were not stopped, Meg thought. She would not fare any better than the others if she were hauled up before a magistrate. Her tale of being kidnapped by a quartet of witches would sound most unlikely. Besides, if the coven were to be stopped, Meg needed to see her mission through to the end.

She wondered if Seraphine had returned to the house by now. When the countess found both Eliza and Meg gone, she would doubtless be alarmed. Seraphine would know that Meg would never have been imprudent enough to leave the house after dark, certainly not with the fires unbanked and lit candles still burning. Only the direst of circumstances would have impelled Meg to do so. Seraphine would be nigh frantic with fear and would set out in search of her.

But Meg despaired of Seraphine being able to track her. Meg was not sure herself where she was, except somewhere in the environs of Westminster. When they emerged from the alley, Meg saw the distant outline of the majestic abbey.

Amy held up one hand, bringing them all to an abrupt halt. She scanned up and down the inky expanse of the street ahead before nodding with satisfaction.

"It's clear. We are almost there. Come on."

Amy led the way across the street, Meg and the others stumbling to keep up with her. Meg had formed no clear idea of where this gathering of witches was to take place. Perhaps in a graveyard, or an abandoned building, or some dark cellar.

When she realized where Amy was heading, Meg's jaw dropped at the sheer audacity of the woman. Amy ran to the arched door of a small church, its stone walls covered in ivy. With a nervous glance around her, she scratched at the door, calling out softly.

A muted response came back and the door creaked open. Amy gestured to Meg and the others to precede her, whispering, "Hurry!"

Meg hesitated on the threshold, her courage faltering as she was overwhelmed by memories from her childhood, all the horror her mother's coven had inspired in her. She still had occasional nightmares about being surrounded by desperate women staring at her with hungry eyes, plucking at her skirts with greedy hands, their voices shrieking out all their impossible demands.

Megaera! Megaera! Make me young again. Make me beautiful. Curse the husband who beat me. Cure my sister of her deafness. Raise up my child from the dead.

She closed her eyes for a moment to remind herself that she was no longer that beleaguered little girl subject to her mother's mad ambitions. Even nightmares had to come to an end.

Behind her, Amy made an impatient sound and shoved Meg into the church. She heard the others crowding in behind her and the door being pulled closed.

All the candles had been extinguished, giving Meg the sensation of plunging into the cold depths of a cavern. The nave that stretched before her was enveloped in darkness and she struggled to take stock of her surroundings. The church had to be ancient, perhaps as old as Norman times, the windows high and narrow, the air perfumed with ages of incense steeped into the walls.

A faint light flickered as a group approached from the front of the church. The tallest of them carried a lantern and growled at Amy, "About time you returned. What took you so long?"

"I had to be careful not to run afoul of the watch, didn't I? Don't you be snipping at me, Bea. This is our great and glorious night, the one we have waited for ever since Granddam died."

"So have you brought *her* then?"

"Most certainly." Amy gave Meg another nudge forward.

The lantern was raised aloft, momentarily blinding Meg as the light shone directly into her eyes. She blinked, focusing on the woman before her.

Unlike the others, Beatrice Rivers had made no effort to conceal her face, her hood flung back. Her resemblance to Amy was marked, although her features were gaunter and her eyes more close set. Her expression was hard, a hint of cruelty playing about the set of her lips. Her gaze spoke more of skepticism than Amy's fervid adoration.

"Behold our Silver Rose," Bea intoned, mockery in her voice.

Her announcement was received with disappointed murmurs from the two other women who had been waiting with Bea in the church.

"That's the Silver Rose?"

"She doesn't look so powerful to me."

"I thought she'd be taller."

"Silence!" Amy shrieked. "How dare you be so disrespectful. Of course this is Megaera. Do you think my sister and I would not have made sure of that before risking this gathering? Tell them, Bea."

"Aye, she is Megaera, but whether she is as powerful as all the legends claim . . ." Beatrice shrugged, a challenge in the thin smile she directed at Meg.

"Most certainly she is!" Amy turned to Meg. "Show them."

"Yes! Show us! Show us!" The chorus was taken up by other eager voices. Meg shrank back in dismay, but there was nowhere to retreat. She was surrounded by a crowd of expectant figures, although not as many as she had feared. Including the two Rivers sisters, there were only seven of them.

Meg moistened her lips and tried to infuse a note of command into her voice. "First, draw back your hoods and show me your faces. I must see who dares to proclaim herself one of my coven."

There was hesitation, then one by one, hoods were pushed back. Meg dreaded to discover that one of them might be Mary Waters, the poor woman they had tried to coerce into joining the group. She was relieved to discover that Mary was absent.

Most of them looked ill-kempt and ill-fed, their faces bearing the marks of a hard life, making it difficult to guess ages. The only exceptions were Eliza and a slender girl who could have been no more than fifteen.

When Meg approached her, the girl shrank back. But when Meg cupped her chin, she stilled, only the quickening of her breath betraying her apprehension. Meg's skill at reading eyes was not as sharp as it had once been, but this child was all too easy, her eyes as wide and wary as a newborn fawn.

"The young man whom you loved betrayed you. As soon as he won you to his bed, he abandoned you for another. Now your heart is broken."

"Ohh!" The girl quavered. "'Tis true. H-how did you know?"

"It is written there in your eyes for anyone with the ability to read them." Meg brushed a strand of hair back from the girl's face. "But you are young and strong. Your heart will mend and you will be the wiser for your pain. You will find a truer love one day."

The girl's eyes filled with tears. "Th-thank you, milady."

Meg heard whispers of astonishment from the rest of the group. *She knew. The Lady just looked into Dorcas's eyes and she was able to read her heart.*

Amy crowed, "See. I told all of you."

"An easy enough feat to read the mind of a foolish chit of a girl like Dorcas," Bea scoffed. "What of my eyes?"

Bea thrust the lantern into Eliza's hands and posed before Meg, her hands thrust on her hips, her sharp chin jutted out in defiance.

The last thing Meg wanted to do was probe the murky darkness she suspected lay behind Beatrice Rivers's belligerent façade. But she forced herself to peer deep into the woman's eyes. They were hard and cold, but surprisingly brittle, like a thin layer of ice. It was easier than she had expected and she plunged into a mind as full of bitterness and anger as Amy's. But Beatrice frequently found a release for her pain in cruelty.

Meg flinched as she caught flashes of Bea wielding her knife against birds, mice, puppies, cats, her victims always creatures weaker than herself. Until today . . .

More recent images forced themselves upon Meg, images she did not want to see or believe.

"No," she whispered, breaking the contact with Bea's eyes. Steeling herself, she flung back the flap of the woman's cloak and recoiled from the sight of the bright jewel pinned to Beatrice's gown.

"That belonged to my friend," Meg said hoarsely. "Where did you get it?"

Bea looked startled, but swiftly recovered, tugging the ends of her cloak closed. "Found it, I expect."

"You didn't. You stole it! You attacked Seraphine. You came at her from behind and you—" Meg choked, unable to continue.

There were gasps from the rest of the group, but only of more amazement at Meg's uncanny perception. As Meg scanned their faces, most of them looked away from her, cheeks flushing with guilt. They all knew what Beatrice had done. Only Amy appeared untroubled.

"Where is Seraphine now? What have you done with her?" Meg cried.

Amy placed her hand on Meg's arm in a soothing gesture. "You need no longer concern yourself about *her*. The countess is resting quite comfortably."

Meg shook her off and whirled back toward Beatrice.

"Where—is—she?" Meg grated, trying to delve into the woman's cold eyes.

Bea's smile mocked her, but her gaze flicked toward the darkness pooling behind them. Before anyone could stop her, Meg snatched the lantern from Eliza and rushed to the front of the church. Her footsteps faltered as she made out the shape of something stretched out on top of the altar where the candles should have been.

Not something, but someone. The body of a woman lay atop the marble slab, her golden hair spilling over the edge of the altar.

"Seraphine!"

Chapter Twenty-two

THE LANTERN SWAYED IN MEG'S HAND, SENDING WILD ARCS OF light over the woman laid out upon the altar like some pagan sacrifice. Meg set the lantern down and bent over Seraphine, searching for the pulse at the base of her throat. Seraphine was deathly pale, her skin cool and clammy, but her life force throbbed beneath Meg's fingertips. Meg emitted a shaky breath of relief as the worst of her fears subsided.

But the images Meg had read in Bea's eyes played through her mind, visions of the heavy cudgel slamming down upon Seraphine's head. Meg raised Seraphine's head, probing gingerly. No blood, thank God, and the skull was not cracked, but she felt the swelling of a huge lump. Pray heaven it would not prove too serious, but she needed to get Seraphine away from here and tend to her.

Meg had seen what results blows to the head could produce. She'd treated people who had never awakened, others who had roused only to have their wits permanently impaired. The longer someone remained unconscious, the less likely they were to recover.

Meg massaged Seraphine's temples, and patted her cheek. "'Phine. 'Phine, you must wake up."

Meg was heartened when Seraphine stirred and emitted a low groan, her eyelids fluttering.

"Seraphine!"

"Oh, leave her be. She'll be all right. For now," Beatrice said.

Meg looked up to see that the coven had trailed her to the altar, Bea standing belligerently in the front. All of her fear forgotten, Meg was seized with a blazing anger.

"How dare you! You obviously knew this woman is my friend. How dare you attack her!"

The others shrank back from her rage, looking confused and guilty. But Bea sneered. "It is her ladyship's own fault. London is a dangerous place and she was snared by one of the oldest tricks there is. Our sweet and innocent little Dorcas there wept and cried for help while Amy pretended to beat her and drag her into the alley. When her high-and-mighty ladyship followed, I—"

"I know what happened. You struck her from behind." Meg glared at Dorcas. "My friend is a kind and courageous woman who would never stand idly by while she thought a helpless girl was in trouble. You all played upon her nobility, cowards that you are."

Dorcas hung her head and started to cry. "I—I—am sorry, milady. But Amy and Beatrice—they s-said I had to—"

"Shut your mouth," Amy ordered.

Meg directed her anger back at Beatrice. "Dorcas might have lured Seraphine, but you were the one who struck her from behind like any sniveling thief. It is the only way you could have subdued someone as formidable as Seraphine. If you had confronted her directly, you would not have fared well, I promise you that."

Beatrice flushed, her face contorting in an ugly expression. She reached beneath her robe, drawing out her knife. Dorcas squeaked with fright, her alarm echoed by some of the other women.

But Meg was far too angry to care. "What? Now you think you have the stomach to threaten me? I am no helpless bird or kitten."

Bea started menacingly toward Meg, but when Meg refused to be cowed, Bea hesitated, a tremor passing through the hand that gripped her knife. Amy dragged her back.

"Stop it, Bea!" she shrilled. She whirled toward Meg, holding out her hands in a placating gesture. "I am sorry if we have distressed you, milady. But we thought it was necessary."

"Necessary to attack my friend. Why?"

"For assurance. We were not certain you would be willing to join us tonight."

"I have proved that I am. I came with you willingly, did I not? So cut the countess loose that I may attend to her."

Amy looked uncertain, but Bea said, "I think it best the countess remains where she is. I am by no means convinced of your loyalty to our cause. Thus far you have not behaved much like the sorceress our grandmother promised. You even tried to remove the curse she placed upon the king."

"Oh, that was all a trick, Bea," Amy said. "She explained it to my satisfaction."

"She will never explain it to mine."

Meg started to retort, but she was distracted by a sound

from Seraphine. She realized that Seraphine had opened her eyes.

Meg leaned closer, anxiously peering into her eyes. She saw a great deal of pain, but a hint of clarity as Seraphine struggled to focus.

"'Phine. Can you hear me? Do you know who I am?"

Seraphine moistened her lips. "'Course I do. Don't have to shout."

Meg gently stroked her brow. "Everything is going to be all right. I am here."

Seraphine tried to shake her head and flinched. "Shouldn't be. Damned fool to let them lure—" She trailed off and Meg was uncertain whether Seraphine was berating Meg or herself. But her lucidity was a good sign.

"Don't worry. I am going to get you out of here."

Seraphine's lips moved and Meg had to bend closer to hear her.

"Forget about me. Get out now. Run."

"No! I am not going anywhere without you."

Meg straightened and glowered at the assembled women. "One of you give me your knife."

"I don't have one, milady," Dorcas said.

"None of us do 'cept Amelia and Beatrice," Eliza added.

Beatrice stared at Meg with a look of sullen defiance while Amy began, "Milady, we only need you to—"

"I don't give a damn what you need. I want my friend released immediately. Give me your knife so I may free her."

Amy hid her knife behind her back, pouting like a child concealing a forbidden toy. The others shifted uneasily, watching the confrontation with wide eyes as Meg stalked closer to Amy.

"Give it to me!"

"Or you'll what?" Beatrice jeered. "Turn her into a toad? Are you really possessed of any dark powers?"

"If you persist in defying me, you all will find out exactly what power I possess," Meg snarled. "When I was a mere child, I alone was able to read from the *Book of Shadows*. I committed to memory enough black spells to destroy this entire city, let alone the likes of you."

"So do it then," Bea challenged, but Meg could hear the thread of unease in her voice. The other women shrank back, only Amy daring to stand her ground.

She eyed Meg reproachfully. "There is no need for you to be so—so hostile. We are all your devoted followers, prepared to do your bidding. But first you must help us with our ritual and deliver on all of your promises."

"I never promised you anything!" Meg shouted. Some rational part of her brain urged her to remain calm. It was unwise to challenge a madwoman, but Meg had endured far too many years of coping with this dark legacy of her mother's, the legend of the Silver Rose. Something had snapped inside of her, the same as it had that day upon the riverbank when she had defied her mother, refusing to do Cassandra's insane bidding any longer.

She stalked into the circle of women. "You deluded fools, risking your lives, your very souls to participate in this lunacy." Meg jabbed her finger in Amy's direction. "What kind of nonsense did that woman fill your heads with?"

The women skittered back, Eliza stammering a reply, "She—she told us all about the coven of the Silver Rose that started in France. Strong, fierce women led by you to acquire powerful magic that would topple kingdoms, strike terror in the world of men—"

"Oh, they struck terror all right, by murdering helpless

infants, poisoning innocent people. And did Mistress Rivers tell you what happened to all these fierce women? They were hunted down by witch-hunters, tortured, hanged. A few managed to escape like *her* grandmother—but when Tamsin Rivers tried to revive the coven of the Silver Rose in Scotland, she was tied to a stake and burned alive."

"B-burned?" Dorcas quavered, her horror reflected in the faces of the other women.

"Don't listen to her," Amy cried.

"So it is not true?" Eliza asked.

"Y-yes, but my granddam will be avenged and nothing like that will happen to us." Amy glared at Meg. "Because she will use her power to protect us."

"If you don't allow me to take care of my friend, I will not lift one finger. You are all already at grave risk, holding this brazen gathering here in a church, for mercy's sake. What were you thinking?"

"She is right," Dorcas quavered. "I never thought we'd be safe here."

"Bah!" Amy said. "The priest of this parish is too busy rutting with his mistress and his sexton is likely dead drunk."

"And what of the watch? The king's officers? Do you think this meeting will go unnoticed by James Stuart? Any more than it did all those years ago in Edinburgh?"

Amy's lips curved in a smug smile. "We have nothing to fear from the king this time. He will be dead soon, perished in flames just as my granddam predicted."

"Tamsin Rivers's curse? If she'd had any real power, the king would have been struck down a long time ago."

"She did have power! She still does."

"Your grandmother is dead, Amy."

Amy flinched from Meg's blunt words. "No, she reached

beyond the grave to take possession of the minds of weak-willed men. They will do her bidding and fulfill her curse."

"If you are depending upon Sir Patrick Graham, you will be disappointed. He has been dissuaded from attacking the king."

Amy shook her head furiously. "Sir Patrick may be a cruel knave, but he wants revenge upon James Stuart as much as me and my sister. Nothing this side of hell could deter him."

"And yet someone has, his friend Dr. Blackwood."

Amy had been waxing as angry as Meg. But to Meg's astonishment, the woman burst into a fit of giggles, the sound almost obscene as it echoed off the rafters.

"B-blackwood? That drunken sot? Why would he interfere?"

"Because Sir Patrick is his friend and Blackwood does not wish to see him hung for treason. Armagil promised—"

"He promised?" Amy's laughter abruptly ceased, her mirth replaced by a look of icy scorn. "If you knew anything at all about the man, you'd realize he never keeps his oaths. He never bestirs himself except to look for his next cup of sack. He'll do nothing to prevent what is to happen tomorrow."

That was the second time Amelia Rivers had referred to some mysterious event she anticipated.

"What do you mean?" Meg demanded. "What do you expect to happen tomorrow?"

Amy clamped her lips together. Meg thought she meant to evade the question again. But a triumphant light sparked in Amy's eyes, and as though she could not resist boasting, the words came tumbling out.

"Gunpowder," she cried gleefully. "Stacks and stacks of it are piled in the cellars beneath the old palace of Westminster, just waiting for the parliament to gather in the chamber above. As soon as the king begins his speech, the fuse will be lit and then *wham*!"

Amy made a dramatic gesture, her hands whooshing upward. "They will all be blown to hell and there will be total chaos. The government will collapse and the men will destroy each other, fighting to seize power. But the power will be ours.

"Don't you see, Megaera? This is the perfect time for you to fulfill your destiny. Teach our coven your darkest magic. We women will be the conquerors of England and you shall be our queen."

Meg stared into Amy's glassy eyes and saw not a hint of reason remaining. The woman was insane and this gunpowder plot she had described was equally mad. Meg would have dismissed it as more of Amy's ravings if she had not had that disturbing dream.

The powder kegs stacked in the cellar just as Amy had described, the explosion, the falling buildings, the king trapped behind the wall of fire.

But Armagil had written to Meg, assuring her that all would be well, except that the note had been so vague, explaining nothing of where he had been or what he had been doing this past week.

Now Meg remembered something that Armagil had said on the day they had parted, how reluctant he had been to intercede with Sir Patrick.

"Sending me after Graham is like sending a jackal to stop a wolf. I have no love for James Stuart either. He is a miserable excuse for both a man and a king."

What if instead of dissuading Graham, Armagil had been persuaded to join him? No. Armagil might despise the king, but he was not a Catholic. Nor did he have any motive to seek revenge as Robert Brody did. Even if he had, Armagil would never consent to take part in a plot that would result in so much destruction, the loss of so many innocent lives.

Meg did not care what anyone said about Armagil. She might be ignorant of much of his past, what had caused the breach with his father. But in her heart, she *knew* Armagil Blackwood. At his inmost core, the man was like her, a healer, not a destroyer.

And yet she could not shake off the haunting image from her nightmare, Armagil drawing back his cowl to reveal himself as the sky had rained fire around them.

"Forgive me," he'd whispered.

Meg pressed her hand to her temple, her mind reeling. She felt an urgent need to go and find him, but her first priority was to rescue Seraphine, get her away from this cluster of would-be witches.

Meg thought of the coven her mother had founded. Many had been cast off by their families, persecuted, desperate for any scrap of hope for a better life. But many more had been like Cassandra herself, dangerous, formidable, and criminally insane.

These women that the Rivers sisters had assembled were pathetic by comparison. Most of them were now looking more scared than excited. The only true fanatics in the group were Amelia and her sister Bea—

Meg tensed as she looked about her. Where was Beatrice? She whirled around, dismayed to discover that while she'd been arguing with Amy, Bea had stolen up to the altar.

She stood poised over Seraphine, fingering her knife.

"What are you doing? Get away from her," Meg cried.

"Bea is only standing guard over the countess until you agree to lead our coven and perform the ritual," Amy said.

"Coven?" The unexpected sound of Seraphine's voice, as weak as it was, startled them all. She was coming more fully awake, struggling against her bonds. "Miserable excuse for a coven . . . need to be thirteen of you."

"There are more of us. They will come soon," Amy insisted.

"If anyone else was coming, they would have been here by now," Bea retorted.

"It doesn't matter. We have more than enough for the ritual. There are seven of us."

"Only be six when I get my hands on the stupid witch who gave me this headache," Seraphine muttered.

Beatrice hissed. Before Meg could prevent it, her knife flashed, slicing open Seraphine's cheek. Seraphine cried out in shock and pain.

Meg started to launch herself at Beatrice, but the tip of Bea's knife pressed against Seraphine's throat.

"Come a step closer and she's dead," Beatrice warned.

"If you don't put down that knife, you'll be the one who is dead and in a way more horrible than you can imagine." But the tremor in Meg's voice made the threat sound hollow.

"Ease off, Bea." Amy scowled at her sister as she took hold of Meg's arm. "The countess won't be harmed, I swear it. Not as long as you perform the ritual."

Meg shook her off. "Ritual? What is this ritual you keep harping about? What the devil do you want from me?"

"The ritual of the dead. I want you to part the veil to the afterlife and summon my grandmother."

"What!"

"Don't do it, Meggie," Seraphine rasped.

Don't do it? Meg didn't even believe that she could.

"I possess no skill in the arts of necromancy," she protested to Amy.

"Yes, you do. Don't lie to me. My granddam saw the spell performed many times at your house in Paris."

"By my mother, not me!"

"You have to know how as well. Cassandra intended you to be the most powerful sorceress in the world. She would have taught you."

"Necromancy is one of the blackest arts there is and I was terrified of it. I may have been forced to watch my mother perform the ritual, but I refused to learn."

Amy's mouth trembled, her eyes darkening. "So you won't resurrect my granddam?"

"You aren't listening to me. I can't!"

"You had better try or—or—" Amy advanced on Meg, brandishing her own knife.

"Maybe Megaera would be inspired if she had to search for her friend the countess among the realms of the dead," Beatrice taunted. "Should I slit her throat or just cut her apart a piece at a time?"

Bea shifted her knife so the tip was now inserted inside Seraphine's nostril. She did not so much as whimper, but her eyes dilated with fear. Seraphine could have braved death with defiance, but she had a horror of disfigurement.

Meg had made the mistake of believing Bea to be the weaker of the two Rivers sisters, only able to vent her cruelty upon defenseless animals.

But Seraphine was as helpless as a kitten, still dazed from the blow, her hands and feet trussed. Meg could tell that the sight of the blood streaming from the gash in Seraphine's cheek excited Beatrice, emboldened her. Amy might have been the one to commit murder, but Bea was thirsting to do likewise, if only to prove herself Amy's equal.

How did I let this situation get so far out of control? Meg berated herself. She could try to wrestle the knife from Beatrice, but even if she could somehow overpower the stronger woman, there was Amy to deal with as well.

Meg could expect no aid from the rest of the coven. All they did was huddle together and watch like a flock of trembling sheep.

The last thing in the world Meg had ever wanted was to emulate Cassandra Lascelles's practice of the dark arts, but as her gaze met Seraphine's, her friend's terror mirrored her own. Meg realized she had no choice.

"Very well," Meg said thickly. "I will try to do it—raise the spirit of Tamsin Rivers."

AMY CHALKED THE OUTLINE OF THE PENTAGRAM ON THE STONE floor in the center of the church. The coven gathered around Meg in a circle, each of them holding a lit candle. They had drawn their hoods forward again, perhaps to hide their fear and guilt. Or perhaps in the hope that the thin covering of cloth would somehow shield them if this dark magic they expected to witness somehow went wrong.

Meg had hoped that Bea would join the rest of the group, but she maintained her vigil by the altar, her menacing blade never more than a hairbreadth from Seraphine's face.

Meg had to block out her fear for her friend so that she could remain calm and think. Her gaze darted desperately toward the door, praying this gathering would be stumbled upon by someone, anyone, a minister of the church or even a member of the city's watch. Meg thought she'd rather risk being arrested for a witch than contend with the madness of the Rivers women.

But all remained silent outside these thick stone walls, as though a spell of obscurity had settled over the church, isolating them from the rest of the world.

Amy set a copper basin filled with water in the center of the pentagram. She lit a thick black candle and positioned it so that its light flickered across the surface of the water. Tamsin Rivers had obviously fully described the details of the ritual to her granddaughter, leaving Meg little room for fakery or evasion.

When Amy motioned her to begin, Meg protested. "Is that all you have brought, only the basin and the candle? There is a potion required to enable the conjurer to reach the necessary state of trance."

"Your mother never needed one. Granddam always said that Cassandra had a natural affinity for raising the dead."

I am not my mother, Meg started to snap, but it was something she had been declaring for too much of her life. She was suddenly weary of protesting it.

As she stepped into the center of the pentagram, Meg made one last effort to reason with Amy. "There is a reason necromancy is an art shunned by most wise women. Not only is it wrong to disturb the realms of the dead, but by opening the portal, you risk some malcontented spirit crossing over."

"That is exactly what I want," Amy said. "I want my granddam back again. She should be here with us to share in our triumph tomorrow."

"But it might not be your grandmother who emerges. It is just as possible that I may let loose something else, something dark and dangerous—"

"Stop trying to frighten me and get on with it or—" Amy did not need to complete her threat. All she had to do was gesture toward the altar where Seraphine lay helpless, Bea's blade resting against her throat.

Meg knelt down beside the copper basin. She had spied upon her mother more than once when Cassandra had performed this terrifying rite. Meg had watched the water in the basin roil and steam, had heard the sepulchral voices that cursed Cassandra for disturbing their peace. But her mother had never made any effort to teach Meg the arts of necromancy. Cassandra had not believed she had the gift.

As Meg peered into the water, she saw her reflection dance in the flickering candlelight. The soft brown hair, the green eyes were her father's, but the pallor of her skin, the intensity of her expression belonged to Cassandra Lascelles.

Meg feared that her mother was right. She did not have the gift for summoning the dead. But as she noted the traces of Cassandra mirrored back in her own features, Meg was even more afraid that she did.

She did not want the ritual to succeed, but she had to produce enough of an effect to save Seraphine's life and very likely her own. As she knelt over the basin, she noted that she was not the only one who trembled with apprehension. The candlelight wavered because most of the women who surrounded her, clutching their candles, shook with fear.

It would not take much of a supernatural display to alarm these pitiful creatures, send them shrieking from the church in terror. With luck, that might draw the attention of the watch or bring one of the church wardens to come and investigate. Or if Meg created enough chaos, perhaps she could manage to free Seraphine and spirit her out of there. It was a slim hope, but the only one she had.

She sent up a silent prayer to the heavens and the good mother earth for forgiveness of the profanity she was about to attempt. Then Meg closed her eyes, delving deep down into her soul for that whisper of her mother's darkness that she'd always feared lurked within her, and had done her best to suppress.

As she intoned the words of an incantation in an ancient tongue long forgotten, Meg stared into the basin, allowing the gleam of the copper, the candlelight shimmering in the water to mesmerize her.

Meg waved her hands over the basin and swayed. The incantation might have been her mother's, but she knew she owed her performing skills to her father. Among the motley assortment of professions he had pursued, Martin Wolfe had once been an actor upon the London stage.

Meg tossed her head and moaned, summoning every bit of drama she could into her movements, her voice echoing eerily off the church rafters. She had no intention of rousing anyone from the dead, but she had to find some way to convince Amelia Rivers that she had, that the shade of her grandmother was present.

Meg repeated the incantation again, allowing her voice to reach a feverish pitch as she cried, "Tamsin Rivers! I charge you to reach out to us from the realms of the dead. Your beloved granddaughters Amelia and Beatrice are waiting."

A hiss escaped from one of the women, or so Meg thought until she realized the sound came from the basin. The water began to roil, vapor rising until the surface of the bowl was shrouded in mist.

Meg's heart beat wildly in her chest. Her hands froze in midair and she was unable to make another sound until Amy prodded her sharply in the back.

"It's working," Amy said excitedly. "Don't stop. Go on."

Meg moistened her lips, forcing herself to continue. "Tamsin Rivers. C-come to us. Part the veil between our worlds and speak to us. I, Megaera, summon you. Obey me."

The mist swirled and to Meg's horror, a shape began to emerge, like that of a woman groping her way through a fog.

"Megaera." The ghostly voice was no more than a whisper and yet it seemed to fill the entire church.

Someone shrieked and dropped her candle to flee. Meg thought perhaps it was young Dorcas. The others leapt back from the pentagram. Meg's breath escaped in a terrified rush. She needed to stop this *now,* break the spell before it was too late, but she was not certain she could. She could not even avert her eyes as the emerging figure called to her again in a voice that was chillingly familiar.

"Megaera."

The mist swirled and parted. The face that shimmered beneath the water was not that of an old beldame like Tamsin Rivers, but that of a much younger woman. Ebony hair framed porcelain skin and high cheekbones, a countenance cruel in its beauty.

"M-maman?"

Cassandra Lascelles stared back at Meg, her eyes no longer opaque with blindness as they had been in life. Her gaze was piercingly clear as though she was truly seeing her daughter for the first time.

"Meg, what madness is this? Why do you risk the dark magic to seek me here?"

Meg? Her mother had never called her that before, deploring any such gentle nickname as weakness. Neither had Meg ever seen Cassandra's face shadowed with such a look of sorrow and regret.

"Maman, is that really you?" she whispered.

Before the specter could reply, Amy crowded up close beside Meg. "That is not my granddam. What trickery is this? You banish this creature at once and bring forth my granddam."

Quivering with the anger of her disappointment, Amy nudged the basin. The water sloshed, the image of Cassandra wavered and nearly vanished.

"No! Amy, please," Meg said. "It is my mother."

As much as she had feared Cassandra and deplored her insanity, something stirred inside of Meg, that innate longing of a child for a mother's love. Even knowing this was wrong, the dangers of what she'd conjured, for the first time Meg understood the lure of necromancy.

"Just give me one moment more," Meg begged of Amy.

"No, get rid of her now!"

Ignoring her, Meg reached out to Cassandra, wanting so badly to touch, but fearful of disturbing the fragile link her spell had wrought.

"Maman, please speak to me again. Tell me what it is like where you are. Are you at peace? And can you ever forgive me for what happened that day on the riverbank?"

"It is not my place to offer forgiveness, but rather yours for all that I did—"

"No!" Amy yanked Meg back, thrusting her knife beneath

Meg's chin. "You stop this and do what you promised. I want my granddam!"

In her agitation, she nicked Meg's skin, a droplet of her blood splashing into the basin. Cassandra's eyes flashed, and the water transformed, becoming a pool of red.

The vision of Cassandra disappeared beneath the bloody tide, but her voice boomed like a clap of thunder. "Miscreant! You dare to harm my daughter."

The water boiled and hissed, a vapor rising from the basin in a black mist. Meg reared back and gasped as the dark haze passed through her like an icy blade, freezing her lungs. She heard Amy shriek. She released Meg, her knife falling from her hand.

Other voices were screaming, but the sound was muted as though someone had stuffed cotton in Meg's ears. The stone walls, the candles, the pentagram—all spun before Meg's eyes. She was dimly aware that something strange and terrible was happening to Amy Rivers. The woman collapsed on the floor. She foamed at the mouth, her body jerking spasmodically.

Meg felt herself tumbling forward and tried to catch herself before a great blackness blotted out everything. The dark was strangely cool and peaceful and rousing from it seemed far too difficult a feat. But a voice intruded upon her peace, nagging at her.

"Margaret! Margaret, sweetheart, open your eyes."

Someone's large, warm hand chafed her wrist and then patted her cheek with increasing insistence.

Meg tried to avert her head. "Maman, stop. Let me rest for one minute more."

"Margaret! Damn it, woman, wake up."

The next tap was more urgent, more forceful, almost a smack. Meg opened her eyes to peer reproachfully at the man bending over her, his hair a wild tangle, his eyes almost as wild, dark with alarm and concern.

"Thank God, she's coming round," he remarked, but she had no idea whom he was addressing. Mayhap the fool talked to himself.

Meg blinked, bringing him into clearer focus. "Armagil?"

"Praise heaven. You know who I am?"

"C-certainly, although it's a wonder I had not forgotten. You stayed away so long," she said reprovingly. "But I am glad you are here now. I was having the most terrifying dream."

She struggled to sit up in bed, but her hand didn't come down upon the downy softness of her mattress. As she braced herself, her palm flattened against a cold stone floor and it was wet.

Leaning against Armagil, her gaze tracked in bewilderment from her wet palm to the overturned copper basin, the black candle toppled over into a puddle of water, its wick extinguished.

She wasn't in bed. Nor had she been dreaming. "Easy now," Armagil crooned, wrapping his arm about her, helping her into a sitting position. "Are you all right?"

Was she? Meg did not know how to answer that. She gazed wildly about her for the coven, but in the meager light left by the remaining candles, she saw no one. She would have thought herself alone with Armagil, but for the keening.

The sound was nigh inhuman in the wildness of its terrible grief and Meg longed to bury her face against Armagil's shoulder to blot it out. But she forced herself to search for the source of it.

Her gaze alighted upon Beatrice Rivers. Hunkered down upon the floor, Bea sobbed, clutching her sister's inert body in her arms. Amy's head lolled back, her neck as limp as a cloth doll, her eyes glassy and unseeing, her mouth frozen in an expression of horror.

"What—what happened?" Meg faltered.

"Damned if I know. We'll sort it out later. We've got to get out of here before the king's soldiers arrive. Can you stand?" Without giving her a chance to reply, Armagil hauled her to her feet.

She was a little shaky at first, until she gained her balance. "But—but—" Meg dragged her eyes from the awful specter that was Amy Rivers to search for Seraphine. The altar was empty.

" 'Phine?"

"I'm here, Meggie," she replied. Seraphine had been leaning against a pillar, pressing a handkerchief to her bloodied cheek. She approached Meg on unsteady legs.

"But what . . . how?" Meg faltered.

"No time for questions. There is a side door behind the altar. We'll have to go out that way." Seizing Seraphine by the arm with one hand and Meg with the other, Armagil propelled them ruthlessly forward.

Meg hung back, her gaze drawn back to the pitiful spectacle of Beatrice wailing over her sister. "But we can't just leave—"

"Yes, we can!" Armagil and Seraphine said in the same breath.

Armagil added, "There's nothing you can do, Margaret. That wretched woman is dead and we may well be too if we are caught in here. Now move!"

He hauled her into the darkness of the side transept,

where a plain door was located. The next thing Meg knew, she found herself thrust out into the night. The chill blast of wind caused her to shiver, but revived her like a bath of cold water.

She caught the distant sound of shouts, as though a large force of men were descending upon the church. Taking a step forward, she stumbled over something hard and realized that it was a gravestone. The side door had led them out into the churchyard. Seraphine was still far too unsteady on her feet. Armagil swooped her up to carry her, urging Meg to follow him.

She did so in a daze, trailing after him through the cemetery, plunging into a maze of streets and alleys. She followed Armagil blindly, with no idea of where they were going. Her mind struggled to make sense of what had happened back at the church. What had she done? Had she really summoned up the spirit of her mother? What had struck down Amy Rivers in such a deadly fit? And how had Armagil come upon them so suddenly? None of it seemed real. It was like being caught up in one of her nightmares.

The only thing that reassured her she was awake was the solid presence of the man guiding her to safety. That and the sound of Seraphine hissing curses at him.

"Damn you! Put me down, you great oaf. I can walk."

Armagil must have judged that they had put enough distance between themselves and the church. Winded from carrying Seraphine, he plunked her on her feet none too gracefully. They crouched in the shadows of a shop, pausing to catch their breath.

Meg was startled to realize that it was one of the buildings adjoining the vast rambling palace of Westminster. The night that had seemed so quiet when Amy Rivers had led her to the church was now astir with the ringing of horses' hooves, the tramp of booted feet.

"Have all these men been called out to hunt witches?" Meg asked Armagil in a fearful whisper.

"Not just witches," Armagil replied tersely. "I must get you and the countess to safety and then there is something I have to do. I have to warn—" He broke off, tensing. "Damnation, I am too late."

When Meg started to ask what he meant, he clamped his hand over her mouth to silence her. Torches flared at the end of the street. She, Armagil, and Seraphine flattened themselves against the side of the building as a group of soldiers marched past, dragging someone to where another troop awaited with horses.

For a moment Meg feared their prisoner might be one of those poor deluded women who had been at the church, perhaps even the foolish little Dorcas. But then she saw that it was a tall man. Despite the fact that his hands were bound, he struggled against his captors. The torchlight briefly illuminated a face that stirred Meg's memory.

But it was Seraphine who whispered, "It's that Mr. Johnston who crossed with us from France."

"No," Armagil corrected grimly. "That's Guido Fawkes. And if they force him to talk, there's going to be the devil to pay."

DAWN SPILLED ITS SOFT WHITE LIGHT OVER THE BEDCHAMBER as Meg drew the coverlet over Seraphine. The swelling from the blow had gone down and Meg had brewed a posset to ease her headache.

She had finally adjudged it safe to allow her friend to sleep, which was just as well. Meg doubted she could have kept Seraphine awake much longer. She was exhausted, as was Meg. But with the events of last night tumbling through her mind, Meg's nerves were far too jangled for repose.

She tucked the coverlet snugly about Seraphine's shoulders. Her golden hair spilled across the pillow as she hugged it to her as though seeking comfort in the arms of a lover. The pose made the formidable countess appear unusually vulnerable, the sight bringing an odd lump to Meg's throat.

Meg tenderly stroked back a tendril of Seraphine's hair, being careful to avoid the neat line of stitching that closed the gash on her cheek. Seraphine had endured the pain stoically as Meg had sewn her up. But Meg had seen the fear in her eyes even though Seraphine had tried to jest.

"I suppose I shall have a frightful scar, which will be good. No miserable witch will ever dare trifle with me again."

"I am so sorry, 'Phine," Meg had replied.

"Why? It was my own stupid fault. Letting myself be tricked so easily."

"No, it is mine for ever allowing you to come with me to England upon this mad venture in the first place."

"And how exactly would you have prevented me? What black magic do you possess that would—" Seraphine had checked herself, looking uncomfortable. Last night Meg had displayed a dark power neither of them had ever suspected she had and Meg sensed they were both unnerved by it. Meg did not even feel up to discussing it, so she had been relieved when Seraphine had drifted off to sleep.

Meg would have to keep careful watch over her. There was always the danger of infection and fever setting in from any wound, but for now she felt it safe to leave Seraphine to sleep.

Meg tiptoed out of the room and into the hall beyond. She still had little idea of the place that Armagil had brought them to in the dark hours of the morning. She had been too exhausted, too concerned about Seraphine to do other than note that it was some manner of alehouse.

She expected to hear sounds from belowstairs, the bustle of a business opening for the day's custom. But all was quiet except for Armagil's footfall as he approached from the opposite end of the hall. She rather expected that he had been waiting for her to emerge from the room.

As he drew apace with her, he looked as haggard as she felt, shadows pooling beneath his eyes.

"How fares the countess?" he asked quietly.

"Well enough, all things considered. She's asleep."

"And you?"

"I—I am fine."

Armagil tipped up her face and traced the bruises that lack of sleep had formed beneath her eyes. He offered her a tired smile. "Little liar. You look as though you just clambered back from the brink of hell. Why didn't you heed me, Margaret? I told you to remain close within doors last night."

"You did, but you offered me no explanation."

"And you could not simply trust me? Whatever possessed you to go to that church last night?"

Meg leaned wearily against the wall as she explained how Amy Rivers had managed to invade her lodging, the treachery of the maid, Eliza, how the coven had captured Seraphine and used her to compel Meg to enact the ritual of the dead. She trembled as she described what had happened, how her mother's image had appeared, how Cassandra's voice had thundered with all the rage of an avenging spirit, how the black mist had risen to envelop Amy in a dark embrace.

"That must have been quite a performance," Armagil said. "How did you ever produce such a terrifying effect? No wonder Rivers collapsed in a fit."

Was that what Armagil believed had happened? Meg was loath to disillusion him, but she could not be otherwise than truthful.

"It was no trick, Armagil. I—I really did raise my mother's spirit from the dead."

"Margaret—" He shook his head in denial, but Meg reached out to clutch his arm.

"It is true, Armagil. It *was* my mother, although she was somehow gentler to me than she had ever been when she was alive. She called me Meg and—and she truly looked at me, as though she was really seeing me in a way she never had before."

Armagil placed his hand gently over hers. "You whipped yourself into some kind of trance. You only saw what you longed to see."

"Then how do you explain what happened to Amelia Rivers?"

Armagil shrugged. "You gave her a good fright as you did all those foolish women. Only Amelia's wits were more disordered. She obviously suffered from some sort of apoplexy."

Armagil's explanation sounded so rational, so sane, but Meg could not accept it. She knew what she'd seen, what she'd felt. Cassandra Lascelles had lashed out from beyond the grave to protect Meg, striking Amy Rivers dead. Her mother had loved Meg, after her own intense and ferocious fashion.

Armagil drew her into his arms. Straining her close, he

stroked her hair. "Whatever happened last night, it doesn't matter now. The coven is at an end and you know your mother was not behind any of this. She is dead, Meg. You can let her go. You are safe now."

"Yes," Meg murmured. She desired nothing more than to lean against him, sink deep into his strength and warmth, but there were still too many troubling questions left unanswered.

She drew away from him and demanded, "Am I safe, Armagil? Are any of us? I don't even know where we are."

"The White Bull tavern. The proprietor is a friend of mine. I did him a service once, cured his son of a bout of the brain fever. The lad's recovery owed more to his own stamina than my skill, but Mr. Armbruster feels himself in my debt. And he is also like Graham, a secret Catholic. So to answer your question, my dear, yes, we are safe. Armbruster would never betray us."

"Betray us to whom?"

"To whomever might come looking."

"Armagil!" Meg cast him a look of frustration with his continued evasions. "What were you doing abroad so late last night? How did you know where to find me and Seraphine?"

"Graham told me. He has long known about Amy Rivers's plans to hold some sort of witches' Sabbath in the church upon the night of November fourth. I gather that woman was rather besotted with Graham at one time and confided much in him. Of course when I went there, I never expected to find you and Seraphine amongst them."

"Then why did you go?"

"I wanted to see the Rivers sisters arrested, but I also wanted to make sure that there was no one present who was innocent, no foolish child who had just come looking for excitement, no young girl like—like—"

"Maidred Brody?" Meg filled in softly.

"Yes, precisely. If there was, I hoped to warn her to escape in time."

"That was not the only person you intended to warn, was it?"

"I don't know what you mean."

"You also meant to alert that Fawkes person that he was about to be arrested, did you not? I know all about the powder plot, Armagil. The terrible thing that Sir Patrick and his friends were planning. Amy Rivers told me."

"Then you must realize it would have been better if Fawkes had been able to escape. They'll take him to the Tower and put him on the rack." Unable to contain his agitation at the thought, Armagil took to pacing the hall. "Fawkes is a tough, stubborn man, a martyr when it comes to his faith, but no one can withstand that kind of torture. He'll give them the names of his fellow conspirators."

"And—and will yours be among them?"

Startled, Armagil halted in midstep "Mine? No, of course not. Why would you think that? What are you accusing me of?"

"I am not sure. It is just that you disappeared for a fortnight with barely a word and you have been so secretive since your return." She regarded him steadily as she admitted, "I had begun to fear that Sir Patrick had persuaded you to join him."

A stain of red spread across Armagil's cheeks. "No," he said bitterly. "I was far too busy betraying Graham. If you could have but seen the look in his eyes when he realized I was working against him—" Armagil checked himself, unable to continue.

"Where is Sir Patrick now?"

"He is here. I have him trussed up below in the cellars."

"You are holding him prisoner?"

"It was the only way I could stop the bloody idiot. Even knowing the cause is lost, he is burning to go after the king himself even if it means throwing his own life away." Armagil's voice was rife with anger and reproach, but Meg sensed it was mostly directed at himself.

"You did the right thing, Armagil. You have saved your friend." She attempted to take his hand, but he pulled away from her.

"By saving him, I have also lost him. Graham will curse me for this betrayal until the day he dies." Armagil ground his fingertips wearily against his eyes. "I should go to him now, give him the satisfaction of damning me."

"I will go with you, help you to explain why you acted as you did."

"That would be most unwise, my dear. There are no words adequate to excuse my actions."

Turning away from her, he descended the stairs, his broad shoulders bowed as though laden with all the guilt of the world. Meg experienced a stab of guilt herself. She had been so consumed by her dreams of Maidred Brody, of heeding the girl's plea that her brother be saved, Meg had not thought twice about enlisting Armagil's aid. She had not considered what it would cost him to betray Graham's trust.

She had been the one to convince Armagil to interfere with Robert Brody's vengeance. No matter what Armagil said, she could not allow him to face Sir Patrick's wrath alone.

Creeping quietly after him, she watched from a discreet distance as Armagil vanished through a door that led to the cellars. After a moment, she followed. Pausing halfway down the stairs, she hesitated, letting her eyes adjust to the dimness of the room.

A lantern had been left burning to chase away the darkness. The small chamber was a storehouse of stacked crates, bottles of wine, and hogsheads of ale. Sir Patrick sat on the floor, his legs bound, his hands tied behind him. He looked nothing like the quiet and tidy gentleman Meg had first met. His hair was disheveled, his clothing torn, a bruise darkening one cheek.

Armagil must have had to fight to subdue Sir Patrick, even been obliged to hit him. Meg's heart quailed at the thought of the pain that blow must have cost Armagil as well as Sir Patrick.

Sir Patrick leaned back against one of the barrels, his entire posture that of defeat and despair. But as Armagil approached him, Sir Patrick stiffened. His eyes blazed with hatred and contempt.

"What the devil do you want?"

"I would like to be able to free you," Armagil replied. "If you would but give me your word of honor that you will not—"

"Who are you to talk to me of honor, you treacherous bastard? Go to hell."

Armagil sighed. He poured out a cup of wine and, hunkering down beside Sir Patrick, offered him a drink. Sir Patrick averted his face.

"Graham, please. You have taken nothing since yesterday. It will avail no one if you starve yourself or die of thirst."

Sir Patrick compressed his lips stubbornly for a moment. He finally consented to take a swallow from the cup Armagil pressed to his lips, but he looked like he wanted to spit the wine back in Armagil's face.

"So tell me what is happening out there in the city," Sir Patrick said. "You owe me at least that much."

"As I already told you, Fawkes is lodged in the Tower. There is a great deal of unease in London. The streets this morning are rife with rumors, but from what I have heard, most of your friends have managed to flee."

"Catesby means to rouse the Catholics in the Midlands to rise up and join us. There is still hope that something of our plan may be salvaged. For the love of God, release me and let me join them."

"You'd never make it out of the city. The gates are all closed, as are the ports on the river. It's over, Graham," Armagil said gently. "This rebellion of yours was finished before it ever began. I heard that someone sent an anonymous letter to one of the peers, Lord Monteagle, days ago, warning him to stay away from the opening of parliament, that something dire was going to happen. His lordship was asked to tell no one, but he took the letter straight to Robert Cecil."

Graham refused to drink any more of the wine, his mouth twisting bitterly. "Ah, if there is one thing you are good at, it is composing anonymous letters."

"I never sent that note."

"Do you expect that I will ever believe that?"

"No, I don't think you ever will." Armagil set down the wine cup and straightened to his feet with a tired sigh. "You will not wish to hear it, but here is what I believe. Robert Cecil has always had his network of spies at work. I think he has known about this gunpowder plot for a long time and allowed you, Fawkes, Catesby, and the rest to proceed, giving you just enough rope to hang yourselves. He may even have written that letter to Monteagle himself, so that he could feign that he'd learned of the plot and dramatically swoop in to stop Fawkes at the eleventh hour, Cecil thereby earning the eternal gratitude of the king."

"A fascinating conjecture," Graham sneered. "Even if this far-fetched tale were true, it does not excuse you."

"I am not looking for excuses. I would have gone to Cecil and betrayed the plot myself if it had been necessary."

"And that is what I don't understand," Graham cried. "My God, Armagil, I trusted you. I told you everything because you convinced me you had finally recovered some sense of honor, but I should have known better. Year after year, I have watched the disintegration of your character. Even as you became more and more dissolute, more indifferent to all moral obligations, I persisted in believing you still retained a spark of nobility. Instead you proved yourself a very Judas, the most despicable wretch to crawl upon the face of the earth. What kind of villain have you become?"

"I could well ask you the same thing," Armagil retorted. "How could you embrace something as cowardly and reprehensible as this gunpowder plot? Your urge to kill James, that I could understand. But to destroy his wife and his son, and countless other innocent men, many of them Catholics such as yourself . . . it's madness."

"Such sacrifice was necessary for—for the one true faith. This is a holy war."

"Oh, don't spout that cant to me," Armagil snapped. "For you, this was about revenge on the king and you didn't care who else was destroyed in the process."

"A vengeance you should have wanted as well!" Graham shouted back. "But there is no loyalty, no truth in you, nothing that you hold sacred, not friendship, nor your promises, not even what you owe to your own blood."

Armagil said nothing, but he flinched, each of Sir Patrick's harsh words seeming to strike at him with the force of a blow. Meg could not bear to listen in silence any longer.

She rushed the rest of the way down the stairs, crying out to Sir Patrick, "Stop this at once. Can you not tell how this is tearing Armagil apart? Do you not know why he has done this?"

Sir Patrick shot her a venomous look. "Now I see all too clearly. He is still in thrall to his witch. I might have guessed."

"Meg, go back upstairs," Armagil said tersely.

"No, I will not allow him to abuse you any further. You must let me speak to him."

"I refuse to listen to anything from your vile lips, strumpet."

"You will heed me whether you wish to or not," Meg said. "It is nigh killing Armagil to act against you. He has only done so out of the greatest love one friend can bear another. Even if this mad plan of yours had succeeded, it would have destroyed you. Can you not comprehend that, you stupid man? Armagil only wanted to preserve your life and your soul. He did what he did for you and the memory of your sister as well. Maidred would not have wished for you to have such blood on your hands. I know she would not."

"You *know*." Sir Patrick mocked her with a harsh laugh. "You know nothing. I never had any sister." He twisted his head to glare at Armagil.

"Because I am not Robert Brody. He is!"

Chapter Twenty-three

THE TAPROOM WAS SILENT AND EMPTY, THE SHUTTERS DRAWN closed. Armbruster had put it about that his wife was ill of highly contagious fever, possibly the pox. The tavern would be closed until further notice. A clever ruse that would keep even the most curious away.

Meg rubbed her arm, bruised from how hard Armagil had gripped when he had hauled her up from the cellar and away from Patrick Graham's acid mockery.

His angry taunts had followed them up the stairs.

"So the great sorceress never guessed the truth and Armagil never told you, even when he took you to his bed. But why would you? He's forgotten himself who he is. Just like he forgot the sister he watched burn to death, all his promises to avenge her—"

Armagil had slammed the cellar door closed, mercifully

shutting out the sound of Graham's bitter voice. He stalked behind the counter and helped himself to a large cup of sack. Meg noted the way his hand trembled as he poured. He curtly offered her one as well, but she shook her head, sinking into the nearest chair she could find.

Still stunned by Sir Patrick's accusations, Meg studied Armagil's countenance for any sign that it could really be true. How could she have been that blind, never suspecting that he was Robert Brody?

Armagil tossed down the cup of wine and regarded her, almost belligerently. "Well, have you nothing to say?"

"I am still trying to make sense of this." She pressed her hand to one temple. "What Sir Patrick said about you being Robert Brody—it does not seem possible."

"You find it easier to believe that Sir Patrick Graham, the scion of an old English family, could be Brody rather than a miscreant like me? I suppose there's some logic in that. He seems a far more likely candidate for the soul-wounded heroic avenger than I."

"I believed what you led me to believe, Armagil."

"Nae, I'm fair sure I told ye more than once, lass, that Sir Patrick Graham was nae Robert Brody, but ye refused to ken a word."

Armagil's lapse into a Scottish brogue as thick as King James's was so startling as to be cruel. When Meg stared at him reproachfully, he looked a trifle ashamed. Refilling his wine cup, he sank down in the seat opposite her.

"I should have told you the truth," he said.

"Why didn't you?"

He shrugged. "Because to me Robert Brody is dead and gone a long time ago. I buried the poor lad alongside what remained of his sister on the shores of Edinburgh. Haven't you realized by now that it is easier to forget the past if you never speak of it?"

"Silence does not make it all go away, Armagil."

"No, nor does burying it in the bottom of a wine cup, although I have certainly given it a good effort for many years." He started to take another swallow, then sighed and pushed the cup away from him. "So I suppose you are wondering how a callow boy from Scotland ended up as Armagil Blackwood, a far from respectable English doctor."

"You appear to have convinced all of London that is who you are. Everyone thinks you are the son of Gilly Black."

Armagil grimaced. "I know. No matter how many times I have said that man is not my father. I guess that is what happens when you are a habitual liar. When you do tell the truth, no one believes you. But Armagil Black did sire me in so far that I borrowed his name when I required a new one.

"At least I took part of his name. I altered it to Blackwood because—well—that is how wood looks when it has been charred just before everything is consumed to ash. Do you know that unlike most men I take no pleasure from a fire blazing on the hearth? I'd almost rather freeze to death." His gaze turned inward and for the first time Meg saw it in his eyes, all the despair and torment of the boy who had been Robert Brody.

She reached across the table and laid her hand upon his. He didn't appear to notice she had done so as he stared back across the years at the darkest day of his life.

Then he gave himself a shake. Curling his fingers around hers, he offered her a sad smile. "I will share my history with you, Margaret, but if you don't mind, I'd prefer not to speak of the day my sister died. If your dreams are to be believed, you have seen the horror of it for yourself."

"I did," she acknowledged quietly. "More than Maidred's pain, I saw and felt her brother's grief. How Robert Brody—I mean you—vowed to avenge her death."

"Aye, a very romantic tale that, don't you think? The distraught and noble brother plotting and scheming for years to take his vengeance upon the king. A story worthy of the London stage." Armagil's mouth twisted ruefully. "Unfortunately, that is not my story. Graham is the sort of a man who possesses that kind of calculation and patience.

"I was far too hot-blooded for that, especially in those first raw days after my sister died. I had two other sisters, you know, Brenna and Annie, who were dependent upon me. But I was too lost in grief and rage to have any care of them. I started spending too much time in the tavern, drinking and foolishly venting my spleen against the king. How one day that witch's curse was going to come true. I would make it so.

"I would have said anything in the first savage thrust of my grief." He regarded Meg earnestly. "But I was never so far gone in my bitterness that I would have raised my hand against the king's innocent bride or his babes. You must believe that, Margaret."

"I do. You are not like Sir Patrick."

"Don't judge Graham too harshly. He has demons of his own, but I will get to that part of my tale anon. But back to that autumn that Maidred died, I vowed the king would not live to celebrate another Christmastide and so I watched for my first opportunity.

"Even then James was an avid hunter. It was far too easy to lie in wait for him in the rugged hills around Edinburgh. I had some skill with a longbow and I practiced and practiced until I felt ready. I crouched behind some trees until James came into view. I actually had him in my sights. It would have been such an easy shot."

"What happened?" Meg prompted when he fell silent.

"What happened? I was too weak to follow through. I tried to think of May, the horrible way she had died, how James could have spared her. He loomed like a devil in my mind. Perhaps I could have done it, if he had not dismounted. Off of his horse, he looked somehow more vulnerable.

"He dismounted because he was concerned one of his hounds had been injured. There he was kneeling in the meadow, not a monster, not even a tyrant king, just an ordinary man, fretting over his dog. I nocked the arrow and pulled back the bowstring, but suddenly my vision blurred and my hand shook. I loosed the shot, but it went far wide of the mark and I had to flee before I was caught.

"I managed to escape the field, but I was seen running away. I dared not go home to my sisters. I feared it would only be a matter of time before I was caught. Part of me didn't really care. I had failed to protect Maidred, failed to avenge her. I deserved to die."

"Oh, Armagil." Meg longed to comfort him, but he abruptly released her and reached for his wine cup. He took a deep swallow. Peering into his mug, he continued his story.

"Sometimes when you are at the lowest ebb of your life, help can come from the most unexpected places, whether you deserve it or not. My good angel was the turnkey, Master Galbraith, who had been in charge of the gaol where my sister was imprisoned.

"He was a most compassionate man and he had been deeply moved by what had happened to my sister. He and his wife took charge of my younger sisters and he helped me to escape from Edinburgh, gave me enough coin to make my way to London. His wife was English and she had a brother who worked in a similar trade to her husband."

"Gilly Black."

Armagil nodded. "I have spoken harshly of Gilly, but indeed I have no right. He was very generous to take me in, and as much as I deplore it, Gilly is very skilled at his trade. I imagine there were people condemned to die who were grateful for his abilities to provide them with a swift end.

"Gilly had no son and he took a great liking to me. He offered to adopt me so I changed my name to his, worked to bleed Scotland out of my voice and my memory and become what he wished me to be. The executioner's boy, his apprentice. But try as I might, his work repulsed me.

"I was unable to execute the one man I thought deserving of death, so how was I ever going to slaughter complete strangers? Gilly was furious with my weakness. He had taken me in and he found my unwillingness to embrace his trade ungrateful. Perhaps I was, for I could not remain silent beneath his abuse. I made my disgust with his profession all too plain.

"I would have been put out on the streets and left to fend for myself. But by then I had already met Patrick Graham.

"His mother was imprisoned in Newgate, where my father frequently worked. She was an ardent Catholic. You may not realize it, but it is the great ladies who do much to keep the faith alive, hiding priests in their homes, arranging for secret masses. Miranda Graham was one of those women, but she was caught doing so and a warrant for her arrest was issued. She fled to Scotland and took her young son with her, seeking the protection of the king. Her late husband was reputed to be some distant relation of James, and Lady Graham depended upon that connection to carry weight with His Majesty. But James was far more concerned with currying favor with Elizabeth, who was still on the throne of England. He hoped to be named as her heir, so he denied the Grahams asylum and turned them over to the English.

"Because of his youth, Patrick was pardoned and made a ward of the court. But his mother was locked away in Newgate for two years, until she died of gaol fever."

"Then that lock of hair he carries—"

"Belongs to his mother. She was a very forceful woman, and imbued him with a passion for their religion. He regards his mother as a martyr and a saint. His part in the gunpowder plot was partly inspired by his zeal for his faith, but the rest was all his desire to avenge what he regards as James's betrayal of his mother."

"So you and Sir Patrick became friends when he visited his mother at the prison. Not at Oxford?"

"Oxford came later. Graham did not have much by way of fortune, but he helped me to gain an education there. I had failed to care for my sisters, not just Maidred, but Brenna and Annie as well. I thought perhaps I might find atonement by becoming a doctor. I could at least learn to be of use to someone. But you have seen how well that has turned out. Graham is right about me. I am a complete wastrel, loyal to no one."

"That is not true, Armagil." Meg smiled ruefully. "I might be a little taken aback by some of your methods, but I know you have helped a good many people. Even when it is hopeless, you always try."

"Just like I tried to protect Maidred. I failed in that, failed to save her. I couldn't even keep my promise to destroy the man I hold responsible for her death." Armagil shook his head bleakly and returned to his wine cup, but Meg placed her hand over the brim to stop him.

"Don't you see, Armagil, that is exactly what you have been doing all these years? Punishing the one you hold most responsible, *yourself*. I did not fully understand my dreams about Maidred until this moment, when she kept pleading with me to save her brother. I thought she was talking about Sir Patrick, but she meant you."

"And so now what, because you made a promise in a dream, you are going to commence some sort of campaign to be my salvation?"

Meg leaned across the table and lightly touched his cheek. "I wish I could, but I fear only you can do that. For fourteen years you have been tormented because you could not prevent Maidred's death. It is time for you to forgive yourself."

☙❧

TIME PASSED IN A SUCCESSION OF ENDLESS GRAY DAYS AND anxious waiting. Celebrations had been held and thanksgivings offered for the preservation of the king and parliament. In the midst of all the ringing of bells, the bursting of fireworks, no one heard the screams of the man being tortured in the Tower.

As Armagil had feared, even a hardened soldier like Guido Fawkes broke under the pain of being racked and offered up the names of his confederates. Arrest warrants were issued, including one in the name of Sir Patrick Graham.

Every time Armagil slipped away from the tavern to gather more information, Meg awaited his return in an agony

of suspense. She feared that Armagil, known as a close friend
of Sir Patrick's, might be seized and hauled off to the Tower
for questioning himself.

She breathed a sigh of relief when he returned unharmed,
although the tidings he brought were generally grim. Fear
and suspicion ran rampant through the city, hatred of Catholics stirred up to a fever pitch. Homes of known recusants
were broken into and looted, and anyone suspected of Catholic leanings was subject to arrest. Even the Spanish Embassy
was assaulted by an angry mob. Disaster was only averted by
the wily ambassador tossing handfuls of coins into the crowd
and crying out, "God save and preserve King James."

In the middle of all of this unrest, the trial of one Beatrice
Rivers for the crime of witchcraft merited little notice, except
by Meg. When Armagil brought word to her that Bea had
been condemned and summarily hanged, Meg could not help
feeling a stab of pity, despite everything the woman had done.

Amy and Beatrice Rivers had been tainted by the legend
of the Silver Rose from the hour of their birth just as Meg had
been. But Meg had been fortunate to have her father and Ariane Deauville to rescue her from the coven's madness. Amy
and Beatrice had had no one but their grandmother. Armagil
was not the only one whose life had been altered irrevocably
by the witch burnings in Scotland.

Meg thought it a testament to Armagil's true character
that he had not set out on a course of destruction and vengeance like the Rivers sisters or Sir Patrick Graham. The only
one Armagil had been set on punishing was Armagil. Meg
wondered if he had paid any heed to her when she had urged
him to forgive himself. Ever since that afternoon he had confessed to being Robert Brody, Armagil had made it plain he
had no wish to discuss the matter any further.

His withdrawal left Meg in a lonely place, for she did not have Seraphine to converse with either. The redoubtable countess had not been herself ever since that night in the church.

Seraphine kept mostly to her room, making no effort to join in any discussions of plans for their escape from London. At first, Meg attributed her friend's lethargy to Seraphine recovering from the assault, but her wounds had healed, even the stitches on her face had been removed.

Although she tried to pretend it was nothing, Meg frequently caught Seraphine peering into the mirror, examining the scar, a bleak look in her eyes. For all of her intelligence, courage, and charm, the countess had always set too much store by her appearance. Seraphine had often jested that the only value she held for any man was her beauty. The sad thing was that Seraphine truly believed it.

Meg wished she could comfort her friend, reassure her, but Seraphine was even better than Armagil at avoiding topics she did not wish to discuss. Meg hoped that once they were able to set sail to Faire Isle, her friend's spirits would be restored.

They were all going a bit mad, shut up within the walls of this tavern, fearing that any unexpected rap on the door might signal a troop of the king's soldiers. This particular afternoon was made worse by the icy pelting of sleet against the windowpanes.

Armagil had risked going out again, to see if there was any hope of the ports opening soon and to find a captain who would be willing to sail them downriver with few questions asked.

The chief difficulty was going to be slipping Sir Patrick on board, especially when he would likely resist with all the fury of a man being impressed into the Royal Navy. Armagil might even have to render him unconscious. During the ensuing days, Sir Patrick's resentment had not abated one jot. Armagil was still obliged to hold his friend prisoner to keep Sir Patrick from rushing out and stupidly throwing his life away. Meg feared the continued incarceration was wearing far more on Armagil than Sir Patrick.

She was sitting in the taproom, trying to mend a tear in Seraphine's gown, when the kitchen boy trudged up from the cellar, bearing a laden tray. Meg saw that Sir Patrick had refused to eat again.

Perhaps it was too many days spent shut up in this building, her nerves on edge, but suddenly she lost all patience with Sir Patrick. Ignoring the kitchen boy's protests, Meg took the tray from him, unlocked the door to the cellar, and stomped down the stairs.

She had not been near Sir Patrick since that first day, but she saw that Armagil had taken great pains to see to his friend's comfort. A makeshift pallet had been prepared, books and candles provided. Sir Patrick was no longer fettered. Stretched out on the pallet, his head propped against the pillow, he was absorbed in perusing some religious tract. He appeared more pale and gaunt, but presented a calmer appearance than when Meg had last encountered him.

He glanced up at her entrance, and when he realized it was only Meg, she noted that a gleam of calculation came into his eye.

"Don't even try it," she warned. "Even if you did get past me, Mr. Armbruster, his son, and the kitchen boy are all just upstairs. You'd not get far."

Sir Patrick scowled and returned his attention to his

book. "Take that tray back upstairs. I already told that oaf of a boy I was not hungry."

Meg plunked the tray down on top of a hogshead. "You will oblige me by eating anyway. You are not going to be allowed to starve yourself to death."

He cast her a contemptuous look over the top of his book. "I had no idea you were so concerned for my welfare."

"I don't give a damn about you. But I am very much concerned for Armagil. He has risked a great deal to keep you safe and I won't have you plaguing him further."

"You should be more worried about yourself, witch. As I understand from Blackwood, the cellar beneath Westminster was not the only place stormed on the night of the fourth. The king's officers raided a certain church as well."

"Amelia and Beatrice Rivers are both dead, if that is what you are referring to."

"Good." Sir Patrick moistened his fingertip and turned a page. "The apprehension of one witch usually sets off a hunt for many others. You should have a care to your own neck, Mistress Wolfe."

"No one is searching for witches, Sir Patrick. They are too busy hunting down Catholics."

A muscle in Sir Patrick's cheek twitched, but he replied calmly, "I am sure Richard Catesby and the others are far from London, rallying our supporters in the Midlands. Our cause is far from being defeated."

Meg stared at him. A great deal had happened during the past week, and obviously Armagil had not told Sir Patrick. Concerned for the state of his friend's health and mind, Armagil must have sought to spare him further distress. Meg had no such qualms.

"There will be no rallying, no support from the Midlands or anywhere else. Most English Catholics remain loyal to their king. They have too much sense to wish to instigate a civil war against their own countrymen, one that can only result in tragedy, innocent blood spilled on both sides. And as for Robert Catesby—" Meg hesitated.

Graham lowered his book to glare at her. "What of Catesby? What have you heard?"

"He and the rest of your fellow conspirators were cornered in a farmhouse by the king's troops. They have all been taken."

"No, you lie!" Sir Patrick flung his book aside, his face flushing with rage. "I do not believe you."

"You have only to ask the kitchen boy or Mr. Armbruster. The event was so strange, it is being much talked of and wondered about."

"What is so strange about good honest men being set upon by the king's dogs?"

"It was the gunpowder. The conspirators got theirs wet riding through the rain to the farmhouse. As they prepared to withstand the siege, they tried to dry out the gunpowder by the fire and it exploded, just as they meant to do to the king. Some were maimed or blinded. They had to flee from the fire and the king's troops were outside waiting. Robert Catesby was killed outright. But he was likely one of the fortunate ones. Those who survived have been dragged back to London to suffer a traitor's death and you well know what that means."

The book dropped from Graham's hands and he sagged back against the pillow, murmuring, "Hanged, drawn and quartered. A death I should be sharing."

"Mayhap you should," Meg agreed, only to immediately repent. "No, I don't mean that, Sir Patrick. No one should have to endure such a savage fate. There is nothing your death can accomplish except to deeply grieve Armagil."

"Nothing to be accomplished? Catesby, Fawkes, and the others will be hailed as martyrs. They will have died for the good of our faith."

"They are more apt to be cursed and reviled. Do you still not see what you all have done? Even though most of the conspirators have been captured, the search and the arrests continue. They are raiding houses, dragging Jesuit priests from hiding."

Sir Patrick looked stunned. Clearly this was a consequence of his actions that he had never anticipated.

"Our priests?" he asked in a stricken tone. "But none of those good holy men were involved in our plot."

"It doesn't matter. This terrible plot of yours has only given Robert Cecil the excuse he needs to persecute Catholics further, to completely erase your religion from England."

"My mother died to protect our priests, to ensure our faith continued, while I—I—" A tear streaked down Sir Patrick's cheek.

Meg had been exasperated with the man, but he was so devastated, she regretted some of her harsh words.

"I am sorry, Sir Patrick. I only wanted to make you understand that your death will not help—"

"Just leave me alone," he said, flinging his arm across his face. He rolled away from Meg, presenting his back to her, leaving her no choice but to retreat.

She returned upstairs. Locking the cellar door, she leaned against it. When Armagil returned, he was going to be mightily vexed with her. She'd only meant to persuade Sir Patrick to eat, to behave more reasonably, but now she feared she had made everything worse.

But she did not have long to dwell upon her mistake, as she heard the sound she'd been dreading these past few days. Someone was hammering at the tavern door, clamoring for admittance despite the notice warning of contagious illness.

Mr. Armbruster rushed into the taproom, his pistol primed and ready. With a jerk of his head, he indicated that Meg should hurry upstairs to barricade herself with Seraphine in her bedchamber. Heart hammering, she moved to obey, although if it was indeed the king's officers outside with a warrant, hiding would do no good.

Meg paused halfway up the stairs, listening anxiously. She could hear Armbruster roundly cursing whoever was outside. "We are closed. Can you not read the warning, you damned fool? Do you wish to be exposed to the pox?"

The reply from beyond the door was muffled, but enough to make Meg blink, something in the person's accent familiar.

Meg rushed back down the stairs just as the tavern keeper was bolting the door closed. "Mr. Armbruster, wait. I believe I know who it is."

Over Armbruster's protest, Meg unlocked the door and cracked it open. The figure standing impatiently upon the threshold was the last man in the world she would have expected to see. Meg gaped at him with a mingling of joy and astonishment. Gerard Beaufoy stared solemnly back at her. The Comte de Castelnau had finally come in search of his wife.

❧❧❧

MEG STOOD OUTSIDE THE BEDCHAMBER DOOR AND KNOCKED softly. She had all she could do to persuade Gerard to wait until she apprised Seraphine that her husband had arrived.

Meg might be delighted to see him, but there was no telling how Seraphine was going to react.

Meg inched the door open and peeked inside. " 'Phine?"

She was dismayed to see that Seraphine was still in her shift. She sat on a stool near the hearth, desultorily running a comb through her hair.

"Seraphine, you are not even dressed."

Seraphine shrugged. "What is the point? I am hardly expecting any visitors."

Meg glanced nervously over her shoulder. "Well, in fact, you do have one. A visitor, I mean."

"Who? Oh, it doesn't matter." Seraphine waved her off. "Tell whoever it is that Madame la Comtesse is not receiving any callers this afternoon. Not unless it is someone looking for a terrible fright."

"You know I have never alarmed that easily, ma chère. You always complained it showed a lack of imagination on my part," Gerard called out.

Seraphine froze at the sound of her husband's voice. Unable to wait any longer, the count shouldered his way past Meg into the room.

Seraphine shrieked and leapt up from the stool, clapping her hand to her cheek. "Gerard! What the blazes are you doing here?"

"I had hoped for a slightly warmer reception, my lady. As to what I am doing here, that should be obvious. I have come looking for my wife."

"Why now, all of a sudden?"

"It is not just now. I have been searching for you for months, first on the Faire Isle and then along the coast of France and now here in this miserable city."

"Well—you—you picked a very foolish time to come to

London. Have you not heard what has happened? This is not the best time for Catholic foreigners to be wandering about the city."

"I am here under the aegis of the French ambassador. That is safety enough, I think. The only folly I committed was in not coming after you sooner."

As Gerard stalked closer, Seraphine backed away from him. Still covering her scar, she glared at him. "Well, what do you want?"

"What do you think I want? You. Please do not shrink from me, Seraphine. You cannot know how I have missed you. Each day without you has been a torment unto madness."

"You must be running mad to say things like that. You were wont to say I drove you to distraction."

He smiled. "I would rather be mad with you than without you, ma belle."

"Ah, that is the problem. I am not your *belle* any longer. You do not know what has happened."

"Yes, I do. Margaret has told me."

"Has she?" Seraphine scowled at Meg where she still hovered uncertainly in the doorway. "But you have not yet seen this."

Seraphine whipped her hand away. Tilting her cheek forward, she exposed her scar. Meg could see the level of dread Seraphine sought to conceal beneath her show of defiance.

"What? That trifle?" Gerard leaned forward to brush his lips across her cheek. "My foolish comtesse. You should know I would always find you beautiful should you have a dozen such scars."

"Humph! That is because you have always been dreadfully nearsighted," Seraphine said, but her lip trembled.

"What I need to know is what you did to the woman who gave you this. Do I need to find a solicitor to defend you against murder or am I merely obliged to help you bury the body?"

"N-no, I did nothing to her."

"Mon Dieu, then you have mellowed a great deal since I saw you last. Have you mellowed enough yet to come home to me?"

"I can't imagine why you would want me. I have always been a most dreadful wife to you and we no longer have a son. Our little boy is—is—" Seraphine's breath hitched, her eyes welling.

"I know, ma chère. I know." Gerard eased his fingers through her hair. A sob escaped Seraphine, the tears and grief she had suppressed for so long spilling forth.

As Meg stole quietly from the room, her last sight was of Seraphine melting against the comte, finally seeking comfort in her husband's arms.

Meg started back down the stairs only to encounter Armagil bounding up them. His face was flushed with excitement.

"Good news. The ports have been opened again and I have found us a ship. With any luck, we will be able to set sail by next evening's tide."

Chapter Twenty-four

MEG STOOD AT THE DECK RAIL WATCHING THE COAST OF France drawing ever closer. And from there she would find passage back to Faire Isle. Her heart quickened at the thought. The island had ever been her refuge, and with the ghost of Cassandra Lascelles finally laid to rest, Meg thought she would truly find peace there.

The only disquiet that remained in her mind centered upon the man striding toward her across the deck. Or was it more accurately a disquiet of the heart?

She was reminded of that first voyage they had taken together when she could barely tolerate Armagil Blackwood. He was still just as untidy, just as rough in his appearance, but never had any features been more dear to her. She wanted to drink in her fill of the sight of him because she did not know how much longer she had.

He had embarked with them to make certain Patrick Graham did not succumb to an urge to return to London and play the martyr. Armagil had not made clear what he planned to do once he had seen Sir Patrick safely on French soil. Meg had been reluctant to ask, fearing she might not like the answer.

He joined her at the rail, smiling down at her. After a mumbled greeting, they both fell silent. They had been through so much together, as adversaries, lovers, friends, it was strange she should suddenly feel so awkward, uncertain of even what to call him. Armagil? Robbie? She sensed that Armagil felt just as uncomfortable, after having bared his soul to her, all the secrets of his past.

He finally remarked, "It's been a smooth crossing."

"Yes," Meg agreed softly.

"I daresay the countess has been glad of that, although I notice that she and Monsieur le Comte have scarce left their cabin."

"I don't think that has anything to do with Seraphine being ill," Meg began and then blushed.

Armagil chuckled. "I doubt that it does either. So does this mean that the wayward lady has decided to return to her lord?"

"Seraphine and Gerard have had a rather stormy marriage; the painful loss of their son all but tore them apart. They are so very different, the comte so serious and quiet. And Seraphine is, well—" Meg smiled wryly. "Seraphine. But they love each other very much, and I always believed that if they could find their way back into each other's arms, all would be well. I am very happy for her." Meg could not quite prevent a note of wistfulness from creeping into her voice.

Armagil eyed her shrewdly. "You will miss her."

"Very much," Meg admitted with a sad smile. "Oh, there

have been times she has vexed me to the point of wanting to strangle her. But my island will be a much quieter place without her. Yet I am content, knowing she will be where she belongs.

"And what of your friend? I noticed that Sir Patrick is speaking to you again. Has he forgiven you for interfering with his vengeance?"

"I believe so. If he has not entirely, I hope he will in time. He intends to journey on to Douai. There is a seminary there for Jesuit priests. He means to take holy orders."

"And then return to England?"

"I fear so. Not to stir up more rebellion, but there will be difficult days ahead for English Catholics and he hopes to at least bring them the comfort of the mass and their holy rites."

"It will be very dangerous for him."

"It will, and yet since he has arrived at this decision, Graham seems more at peace than I have ever known him."

"And what of you?"

"I am well. Why, has my sister been haunting your dreams, telling you otherwise?"

"No, I have not dreamed of her again. I believe Maidred is no longer afraid for you. Her spirit is at rest."

"That is good. I still wish I could have—I will always wish—" He swallowed.

"I know." Meg laid her hand over his atop the rail. Armagil gave it a grateful squeeze.

Meg summoned up her courage to ask. "So what will you do now?"

"I intend to return to Scotland."

"Oh." Her heart plummeted. She drew her hand away from his, struggling to maintain a cheerful demeanor. "That—

that will be wonderful for you to go home after all these years, but is it safe for you to do so?"

"I think enough time has passed. I no longer bear much resemblance to that callow boy named Robert Brody. I have to take the risk, Meg. It is a journey long overdue. I have to find my other two sisters and ask their forgiveness for abandoning them. Hopefully they will not spit in my eye and walk away, although it is certainly what I deserve."

"I am sure they will be overjoyed at your return, Arma—" She checked herself with a wry laugh. "I hardly know what to call you now. Armagil? Robbie?"

"I prefer Armagil. You are not the only one who has been finally able to lay the past to rest."

"So you will still be Dr. Blackwood. Will you try to establish a practice in Edinburgh?"

"It is not my intention to remain in Scotland, Margaret."

"You will return to London?"

"No, I thought I might set sail on a voyage of exploration. You see, there is this mysterious island I have heard of, a place mostly inhabited by women—which would suit me very well. I hear it is governed by a beautiful sorceress."

Although her heart beat faster with a mixture of hope and joy, Meg strove to match his light tone. "A foolish rumor. There is no sorceress—at least not a beautiful one."

"Beautiful," Armagil insisted, tipping her face up to meet his. "As beautiful as she is wise. So tell me. Do you have any idea how I should go about applying to this dazzling lady for permission to dwell on her island?"

"Don't be absurd. You require no permission. Faire Isle is a place of refuge. Anyone is welcome and I am sure Hortense will be delighted to see you."

"Bah, she has likely taken up with some bandy-legged sailor and forgotten all about me by now. I am more concerned to know if you will be glad to see me."

"Yes, very."

"There is so much you can teach me, Margaret. I want to learn all of your ancient magic to become a better doctor, a true healer."

"I will be happy to share what knowledge I have." She gazed up at him, searching his eyes. "Is that your only reason for coming?"

"No, I believe I have a few things I can teach you as well."

"Such as?"

His mouth crooked into a wicked smile. He drew her into his arms and kissed her until she was breathless. When he finally drew back, the teasing glint in his eyes softened to something more tender.

"I do love you, Margaret. I thought I should tell you that in case you are still having trouble reading my eyes."

She placed her hand along his cheek, smiling mistily up at him. "I fear you will always be a difficult man to read. So I am very pleased to hear you say you love me. You should mention it more often."

"Every day, milady. You may depend upon it."

About the Author

SUSAN CARROLL is an award-winning romance novel-
ist. Some of her most recent titles include *Twilight of
a Queen, The Huntress, The Silver Rose, The Courtesan,* and *The Dark Queen.* She lives in Rock Island,
Illinois.